I0587646

JUMP POINT

AJ Kilgore

"To invent, you need a good imagination and a pile of junk."

THOMAS EDISON

CONTENTS

CHAPTER 1

Busted

I t started with a beam of light. The shaft pierced the gray, midday sky over Golden, Colorado, shot straight across Highway 6, onto the School of Mines campus, through the open window in room 103, and right into Mitch Campbell's drooping eyes.

He could have blinked and played it off but like a dork, he jerked awake and yelped. His hand spasmed as he pulled himself back from the chasm of sleep-deprived dreams into the harsh, bright reality of class. He fumbled his tablet, and it clanged to the floor right as Dr. Bische walked past his bench. Bische, mid-lecture, didn't pause, but he cocked an eye down and frowned. Busted.

The particle potential well that Mitch had plotted just prior to passing out stared up at Bische, plain as day, obviously meant for Quantum Physics and not at all relevant to *this* class, Electromagnetics. Mitch couldn't pretend he'd been listening—again. Couldn't hide that he was studying for his *next* class—again. And, despite being warned weeks ago to study other classes on his *own* time, was taking advantage of his and Bische's relationship—again.

Hastily, Mitch tapped the tablet's home button with his shoe, closing the image, but Bische's raised eyebrow declared that the damage was done. He foresaw an uncomfortable conversation in the near future: about time management, program expectations, and whether your faculty advisor could still be your friend. For now, chastened, Mitch picked up his tablet and, opening his ears to listen, panicked.

"...summing up the point of this whole semester. Based upon these fundamental principles, you should see the next logical step."

Crap! Which principles? What point? The whole semester? Dang! Why'd I fall asleep?

He glanced up at Bische's smartboard, hoping for a clue, but all it showed was the lab exercise they had just completed. Then he felt a sharp poke in his arm and looking around, spotted a tablet at his elbow. Speckled kittens, button-eyed and adorable, pranced across the screen, chasing a pine cone. With a wink, Maggie Heinz, his benchmate, tapped the screen's corner revealing page 200 of the laboratory text. "Thank you!" Mitch mouthed, scrolling forward through his tablet to the same page. He pricked up his ears as Bische continued.

"...which is why you all are now prepared to take the leap, shut down your bench simulators, and build your own device."

Phew! Mitch relaxed. He hadn't missed a thing. Just more device building, more recipe following, more doing what he was good at and, gloriously, no new thinking. Gods, what a relief to have at least one class where his hands could do all the work while his brain took a break. No formulas to memorize or deep concepts to grasp or massive tomes to read. Just an oscilloscope, a box of parts, and the thrill of making something real. He'd lost track these past months of what he had expected college to be like, but he was sure it hadn't included so much friggin' theory. Maybe he imagined it being more like his summers working for Bische. Just the four of them— him, Bische, Wayne, and Dean—locked in the doc's tool room with parts and ideas, building amazing machines through trial and error, needing few, if any, books. Reality was proving to be craptastic at best and he had to admit he was struggling to keep up. *So, yes, Doc, give me a build project for finals. I need at least one easy 'A'.*

He visualized what the contents of page 200 would be as he tapped the scrollbar in the corner of his tablet. "Attach the blue sensor here. Clip the black wire there. Yada, yada..." Perfectly simple. I got this, Mitch thought to himself, feeling a surge of confidence. When page 200 finally scrolled into view, there was only one objective; "Power a machine by any means." Jackpot! This'll be easy. There was a brief note about taking a stab at something "original", but Mitch skipped to the end of that for the list of "Related Labs" looking for the quickest thing to rebuild. Then Bische's voice cut in...

"Now some of you may be thinking 'This will be easy!' Just pull up, say, the chapter on mechanical waves, make a loudspeaker and boom! You're done." He paused. "No."

Mitch stopped. His blood froze. He'd just opened the chapter on waves, then looked up from the text and winced. Bische was staring right at him, with that awful, knowing, half-smile. Dammit! Bische always did that, always caught him taking a shortcut, like he had a fine-tuned "Mitch-dar" that told him exactly when Mitch was about to mess up. It was annoying as hell. He stared back, exasperated, the silent question obvious in his eyes. Why do you do that? How do you always know? Bische looked away, but kept smiling.

"Good engineers can do the bare minimum" he continued, slowly pacing the space between the benches lining each side of the lab. "But we are not training you to be good. We want you to be great. You started the semester here, at the surface." He slid his hand along the top of one bench to illustrate. "Each week we've examined a new tool to help you crack into it." He emphasized "crack" with a tap of his knuckle. "Now you need to use those tools to dig deeper."

This was Bische's standard speech. Mitch had heard him deliver it, with slight variations, before each class assignment. Bische would go on about how engineers aren't artists, but still need to think creatively to come up with innovations that solved the world's problems. Then he'd wrap up by explaining that a motor is a motor, and no matter how you slice it...

"...it will always be a motor. The trick is in figuring out what the motor will do. That is the creative part. Creative thinking took us from loudspeakers to microphones; from simple oscillators to electric generators. In each case, someone took that common motor and saw an uncommon way to apply it. This is what you need to do."

Bische's pacing had landed him in the center of the lab, and there he paused. His eyes circled the room, locking briefly and intensely with each student until they landed on Mitch, slicing through his confidence like a hot knife through wax. "This is not an assignment. This is a dare. Make your device. Be uncommon. You have four weeks."

The lab timer in the corner beeped, Bische's way of signaling the end of class. Bische stood near the door as everyone filed out. Dean, whose bench was on the other side of the room, craned his head over toward Mitch and called "Lunch?"

Mitch shushed him with a gesture, then drifted to the center of the group, hoping to sneak out masked by the crowd. He ducked his head down, trying to avoid Bische's piercing, judgmental eyes. Halfway to the door, he chanced one furtive glance up. Bische was gone. *Score!* he thought to himself. *Guess I'm getting out of here alive.*

"Campbell. A word, please."

The command came from somewhere near his back. Bische had skirted the edges of the classroom and snuck up on him. *Crud puppet!* Mitch cursed under his breath. *Here it comes.* Maggie waved at him sympathetically. He watched, forlorn, as the last of his classmates left. Bische closed the door, turned to Mitch, and said "Caught you skating again, didn't I?"

Mitch blushed and looked away, but noted the good humor in Bische's tone. Finding his courage, he defiantly met Bische's knife-like eyes, and said, "Why can't we just reuse a lab in the book? What's it there for if we can't use it?"

"The book is a guide to thinking. Not a substitute for it. Or does using your head take too long? You know that this is about more than the assignment."

"I know. You're right," Mitch conceded. "I'm sorry for working on the other class while you talked, but, Doc... come on. Quantum P and Metallurgy are killing me. I need the extra time. You know I know all *your* stuff."

"Oh? How? Because you've memorized the table of contents? Because you follow the steps of each exercise? So what? You've been doing that since you were 10."

"So, building power cells and ICs for you last summer doesn't count for anything?"

"Not today! Building on *those* skills counts. Resting on your laurels doesn't."

"Okay, maybe—"

"You've spent the entire semester blowing off quizzes, racing through labs, and working on other classes. Not one original thought has passed your lips. Not one thing you've built has deviated from the expected. I've taught you better than that."

"Yeah. But..."

"The Innovators Program deserves better than that."

"Right, but..."

"You haven't analyzed or theorized or extrapolated. You've just completed."

"Isn't that—?"

"No. Completing is not learning. Anyone can check a square and hand it in. But does it show insight? Not at all." Bische paused and leaned in. "You are *meeting* expectations, son. With your brain, you have the ability to exceed them."

"Look, I—"

"As of now, you will get a 'C' or worse if you can't show me real work."

"What?! My scholarship!"

"It's not my job to pad your GPA. You said you could do the work, but you *have* to prove it. I didn't fight Hubert Wilkins to admit you to this program only to have you give me your warmed-over, high-school-freshman-level work. "

Mitch's mouth moved, but no other sounds came out. He couldn't believe Bische had pulled the scholarship card. If anyone knew he needed the scholarship, it would be Bische. *Why'd he throw that in my face?*

"Ditch the text. Don't regurgitate. Show me that you can use your head. You've got four weeks, Campbell. Scoot." Bische gestured toward the door. Mitch, glowering at Bische, stomped out of the lab.

His boots banged out a steady rhythm in the hall. One word repeated over and over in his head.

"Jerk, jerk, jerk..."

Regurgitating? Bullshit! How could Bische even say that? He'd more than proven himself to Bische time and time again.

"Screw him!" Mitch growled. He had ten minutes before Quantum Physics—just enough time to grab a sandwich in the Student Center. "I'll show Bische who skates," he mumbled to himself. "And I sure as hell don't need four weeks."

CHAPTER 2

Disaster

Three weeks and six days later, Mitch found himself wishing he had more time. Bische's lab hummed with activity. It was First Check-In, the day that students with completed projects could present them and call it a semester. It was also the day for struggling students to solicit help. As Mitch's maker reputation spread over the course of the semester, more often than not his classmates called on him. Today was no different. He floated from one bench to another, soldering a piece here, rebuilding a breadboard there, thoroughly enjoying solving real problems, but completely losing track of time. Three hours later, a host of completed projects flitted, whirred, and glowed on benches thanks to Mitch's ministrations, but not one device belonged to him.

It's not like he hadn't had any ideas these past weeks. In fact, he'd had at least one idea a day. The problem was that his ideas seemed to be the same as everyone else's. As soon as he'd start building something, someone else would appear with the exact same creation. He couldn't bring himself to submit a device that someone else had already built. He needed to do something original. He couldn't prove Bische right!

But now that it was zero hour, Mitch had to admit that maybe he already had. He returned to his own bench and his latest attempt: a wireless charging station. It was only half done, which was just another way of saying not done at all. Worse, from what he saw surveying the room, it was not completely unique—it was one of three chargers in fact. He had built it quickly, a win at this point, but it was simple as hell and trite at best. The only interesting thing about it was its independence. The other two chargers were tethered to wall sockets. His charger gathered passive energy from three different sources—heat, light, and radio waves, depending on which was more abundant. A bit of inventive heterodyning had made it super-fast as well, maxing the charge in five minutes or less.

"At least it works" Mitch muttered to himself as he tightened a last screw on the case. Three fuel sources plus heterodyning—none of that was in the textbook and no one else had done it. Bische *had* to be impressed. At the very least, he would have to admit that Mitch had applied himself. Stepping back an hour later to admire his handiwork, Mitch felt a glimmer of hope. Now that it was finished, his little charge box looked pretty cool.

"What's soup, Campbell?" Maggie breezed in, all snap and sass, her smile ahead of her by seconds.

"Playin' ketchup, Heinz," Mitch replied, gamely adding on to her word play. She chuckled and, cruising to her side of the bench, cheerily deposited her completed project, a shoe box-sized affair with collection ports on one end and inverter panels on the other. Mitch blinked. He couldn't believe it.

"That's a self-powered charging station, isn't it?" he asked, moving to her side to give it a closer look.

"Good guess, Campbell. Hey! You built one, too?" She sidled over and picked up his box, inspecting it from all sides. "Nice work. Great minds think alike, eh?" She paused over the power collectors. "Three sources?" she asked, a note of awe in her voice. He nodded absently. "Wow. I barely got two and that took a whole week. The moisture converter alone only started working last night. I can't imagine connecting *three*. And you did it in one night? You rock, Campbell!"

Mitch, examining her box, was starting to not think so. In addition to the moisture converter, Maggie's charger included a discovery beacon. Any device needing power could find it easily and hook into it over the ether. As if on cue, the box "pinged", having already found a needy tablet battery in the room. Two benches down, the tablet owner accepted the charge and was rewarded with a holo banner declaring "Have a pack of Heinz." The owner shot Maggie a thumbs up. The device chimed, and Maggie raised her arms victoriously over her head. "It works!"

Mitch sighed deeply. Not only had Maggie done essentially the same thing as he, she'd done it better, with humor and pizzazz. *Can't compete with that.* His box, which had seemed so cool five minutes ago, might as well go in the trash.

"Campbell! Incoming!"

Phoomp!

A hot, sweet-smelling wad of goo zinged passed Mitch's head and embedded itself on the wall behind his work bench.

"Whoohoo!" came the triumphant cheer from across the room. "Five down. Six to go."

The whooper, Dean Chambers, pointed what looked like a bazooka at Maggie's bench.

Phoomp!

Another goo wad landed just inches from her charger. "Whoohoo!"

"Chambers!" Maggie feigned irritation, but couldn't quite smother her normal bubbles and giggle. She smooshed a bit of sweet goo into her mouth, and then, in her best Bische voice said, "As it happens, we're working."

"Just passing out snacks," crowed Dean. "Six down. Five to go."

The bazooka was Dean's answer to Bische's challenge. "I call it The Corn Capper," he'd explained to Mitch the night that he'd finished it. "'Ol' Cornie for short. Or 'The OC'. 'TCC', 'Cornball', what have you. You get the point."

The Corn Capper combined Dean's two loves: junk food and cartoon violence.

"Just toss in some corn kernels, a handful of Skittles, pull the trigger and—" *Phoomp!* "—rainbow popcorn balls! How about 'Big Ballie?' 'The Phoompster?' Oh, wait—how about 'Chamber's Flaming Fire'!" Mitch remembered staring at him blankly, semi-comatose from studying for the Metallurgy final. Dean, taking his silence as affirmation, had said, "Okay, 'Flaming Fire' it is." He'd cackled maniacally and pointed the beast at the elevator down the hall. *Phoomp!* "Ha ha!"

Obnoxious as it was, it dispensed free sweets, so Ol' Cornie was a big hit in the dorm—who doesn't like free sweets? And Mitch had to admit, it was a genius design. Dean slapped a power pack and mini-amp onto an old music player to make an engine that functioned purely on sound waves. As soon as "Hot Goulash" by Tower of Cows started up, everyone within two feet of their room knew it was treat time.

That had all happened over three weeks ago, just one day after Bische had announced the assignment. Despite being Dean's best friend, after dodging hot candy balls for close to a month, even Mitch was feeling a bit annoyed.

"You'd think he'd get tired of shooting that thing."

Wayne Hirano had walked over to Mitch's bench, having wisely deserted his own. "I'm nine of eleven on Dean's list. Not that I'm worried."

Dean's enthusiastic embrace of his new toy had inspired Wayne's own entry for the challenge. He'd built a dual field emitter that projected alternating electric and magnetic fields, each one perpendicular to the other, then coerced into a lattice. That made it a great blocker. It effectively nullified the Corn Capper, disintegrating Dean's sizzling glops of goo into sweet-scented wisps of gas. It was simple and elegant and Wayne had completed it—from spare parts in his room, no less—the same night the Corn Capper came to life. Mitch shook his head, thinking back on it. Though he, Wayne, and Dean had been pals since forever, it never ceased to amaze him just how freaking brilliant they both were.

Not to mention competitive. An arms race of sorts had developed between Dean and Wayne over the past three weeks, each of them tweaking their respective devices to thwart the other. *Good thing we're friends*, Mitch mused.

"You know," he said, turning to Wayne. "Dean's latest addition is a field disruptor. He thinks it'll, and I quote, 'crumble Wayne's shield like sugar glass.' You gonna let that pass?" Disconsolate as he was, Mitch couldn't help but stir the pot a little.

"Yeah, heard that," said Wayne, stifling a yawn. "Spent some quality time last night adding a smart oscillator. Any disruption re-triggers the field and the oscillator moves it in time with the disrupter. Dean should be nicely thwarted." Wayne grinned. "Let's watch, shall we?"

Dean had arrived at Wayne's bench. Posturing dramatically, he flipped the switch on Ol' Cornie, and shouted,

"Eat Skittle, Little Man!"

The gooey blob sprang from Dean's device, sizzled briefly in mid-air, and then flew backwards, landing squarely in the center of Dean's jeans. "Owwwwwww!"
Their labmates roared with laughter. "Ow, Wayne! Who told you?!" yelped Dean. He hopped gingerly from one foot to the other, swatting burnt, acrid popcorn from

his crotch.

"Seriously, Chambers," Wayne called. "You're so predictable. I saw that coming a mile away."

"Yikes, that burns," Dean hobbled to Mitch's bench, fanning his crotch the whole way. Their labmates laughed louder. Everyone knew it was just for show. The candy cooled quickly, and nothing had stuck to his pants. Now he shook a finger at Wayne. "You got me, Hirano, but I've got plans for you. We get back to the dorm, you better—hey. What's wrong with you?" Dean said to Mitch.

Staring solemnly at Maggie's device, Mitch had sighed, loudly, and flopped his back against his bench. "It's no good, guys. I'm doomed."

"Nonsense," said Wayne, scanning the bench. "What happened to your charging station? What'd you call it? The 'lame-o-doohickey'?" Dean punched him in the arm. Wayne shrugged and mouthed, "What?" Mitch gestured unhappily toward the trash.

Dean peered into the receptacle. "Now what'd you go and do that for?" He retrieved the discarded device and examined it. "Looks pretty good to me."

Mitch sighed again. "Maggie beat me to it."

"Duuude..." Dean rolled his eyes. "You're *thinkin'* too hard. You're psychin' yourself out. Honestly, Bische won't care if you make the same thing as somebody else. How many different 'motors' are there, anyway, for cryin' out loud? Just hand it in."

"That's easy for you to say. You're done. Both of you." A bitterness gripped Mitch that he had not expected. He turned away, not able to face his friends. "And not just done, mind you, but totally inventive, Nobel Prize, first-couple-of-days done. I should be, too!" His impatience with himself, always simmering below the surface, welled up suddenly, erupting as an angry growl. "I don't know what's wrong with me! I should have aced this. Now I'm stuck." Mitch punched his bench top. The timer in the corner went off, signaling the end of the period.

Bische came out of his office. "Good work, everyone. The official Project Day turn in is tomorrow. Anyone needing extra time," his eyes fell deliberately on Mitch, "can stay late tonight. You all know where the key is. Just be sure to lock up before you leave."

Wayne and Dean went back to their benches. Mitch looked around. Everyone was packing up to go. So... it would just be him.

Bische headed out with everyone else. He turned to Mitch as he reached the door and help up one finger. "Tomorrow, Campbell." Then he spun on his heel and left.

Dean thumbed his nose at Bische's back, then said to Mitch, "Seriously, just give him the lame-o-doohickey. It's game night, I'm getting pizza, and I got a plan for beating Wayne. I need you, dude."

Mitch shook his head sadly. "Bische said original and he meant it. If I'm honest, it's my own fault for doing shit work and expecting an 'A'."

Dean thought a moment, then reached across to his own bench and pulled a car battery out of the bottom drawer. "Take it," he said, plopping the battery onto Mitch's bench.

"What am I supposed to do with that?"

"Duuude." Dean tapped him on the forehead. "Inspiration, maybe? Tape a wire and a fridge magnet on it. Tell Bische it's a cooler."

"Hilarious, Einstein."

Wayne returned with a couple of steel coils and tossed them onto the bench next to the battery.

Despite his misery, Mitch smiled a little. "More inspiration?"

"Just doing my part to help." Wayne tapped his contribution. "These are high-tension magna-coils from one of my Metallurgy labs. They emit a strong magnetic field. The more you twist them, the stronger they get. Watch."

Wayne cranked the pin on one coil until it was down to half its original size, then he held it next to the battery case. Like an attacking cobra, the coil leapt from his hand and onto the battery's side.

"Neat trick," said Mitch.

"Such is my specialty," Wayne said with a bow. "In case you care, I agree with Dean. You are thinking way too hard about this. The best stuff you've built always started out as jokes. So here's two of my jokes. Play around a little. Something good might happen."

"Not getting my hopes up," said Mitch. He couldn't look at his friends. He appreciated their help, but it was still... what? Embarrassing? He shook his head.

"Neither are we, buddy, but you never know," said Dean.

They left, and Mitch was alone. He pulled his "lame-o doohickey" from the trash, set it down next to the car battery and the coils, and had no idea of what to do next.

CHAPTER 3

Discovery

Thirty immobile minutes passed, with Mitch just staring out the window and sighing. The maintenance crew showed up in the corridor, noisily emptying trash barrels and flushing the toilets in the lobby bathroom. The whine of the floor buffer knocked Mitch out of his inaction. Hard as it was to not be depressed, he knew he had to snap out of it and do something. He turned back to his bench and thought, *What if I just surround these pieces with whatever junk I can find? If I throw enough stuff onto the bench, something might come to me.*

He rustled through Bische's recyclables drawer and all of the open parts bins for anything remotely useful. There wasn't much. The best was a mini-satellite dish, complete with transmitter, that he'd found wedged under Bische's smartboard. He perched it on top of the car battery, just to have a place for it, but seeing that it looked good there, he attached the leads to each terminal and soldered the base in place. He then double wound the magna-coils, latching one to each side of the battery, so that they poked out like oversized headphones.

He grabbed the fan case, inverter panels, and a circuit board from his charger and attached them all to the dish and battery with a couple of copper-tungsten wires filched from Wayne's bin. He flipped the switch on the dish, but nothing good happened. It made an ugly noise, overheated, and burned off a lead. *Yikes!* He had to use a pencil eraser to flick the switch off before the whole caboodle melted down.

He thought some more, rummaging idly through Maggie's bin. His fingers came across a trimpot, and he wondered what would happen if he added that to the mix. He unhooked everything, soldered on a new lead, and redid the connections on the circuit board to include the trimpot. Then he loosened the nuts on the battery terminals and attempted to twist the fan wires around each pole. At that moment, one of Dean's popcorn slags decided to drop from the wall behind his bench and onto the dish's switch. An electric arc flared out from the center of the dish, like the flick of a serpent's tongue, and zapped the back of Mitch's hand.

"Gah!" Mitch jerked away from the spark, only to jam the fan wire deep into his thumb. "Ow!" He shoved his thumb into his mouth and sucked hard, but that did little to ease his pain—and even less to quell the swell of frustration and anger he felt for his plight. He closed his eyes, trying to calm down, but instead saw the faces of his friends, happy and confident about their devices, secure in the knowledge that they weren't a few points away from failing what should be their easiest class. *Everyone else is partying right now,* he thought. Partying or relaxing back at the dorm. Everyone else was having fun, slamming beer and snacks and living it up. Because they were done. They were original. Their scholarships weren't on the line.

But here he was—trapped in the lab. Bleeding and almost electrocuted by this miserable, bad joke of a thing. "I should be eating nachos!" he yelled at his creation. He lost it. He reared back and threw the wrench hard at his bench and the lame, lame, lame device.

He'd expected the wrench to bounce off of the dish and clatter back down to the floor. It would have been loud and violent and satisfying. But instead of smacking the device and making a glorious, frantic racket, the wrench curved up and floated to the center of the dish. It hung suspended for a moment, and then, as if an invisible finger had flicked it, slowly, clockwise, it began to spin.

As he watched, dumbfounded, the wrench spun faster, and the whole contraption began to whine. Around the wrench, the dish whistled and popped, then like a flare of lightning, a blue beam shot out. It anchored itself to the center of the dish, but spread up until it formed a cornucopia-like cone that reached halfway across the room and almost as high as the ceiling.

Mitch dove to the side away from the beam as it erupted from the contraption. Now he stood beside it, frozen, his eyes wide, his injured thumb, surprisingly, still in his mouth. His first coherent thought was, *What just happened?* That was swiftly followed by, *Holy fucking shit!*

Not five minutes ago, all that filled the lab was his rage and frustration. Now, from the center of his asinine device, pulsed a Beluga-sized megaphone. Mitch didn't know whether to congratulate himself or faint. Tentatively, he reached out with one hand and tapped the cone with his fingertips. It wasn't solid at all, but kind of staticky and bouncy, like the aura around the edge of a light socket. He put both hands against it, measuring and shaping it like a mime as he walked along the cone's side. When he got to the front of it, he peered inside. His cheek muscles twitched, and warm sweat trickled down his armpits. What he saw was both beautiful and wrong.

Stars. Stars and the evening sky. But he knew it couldn't be that. He looked away, shook his head, and then peered inside the cone again. On second glance, it seemed more like a painting of the evening sky, the starlight not moving and twinkling as it should. For a moment, his analytical mind took over. No, what it really looked like was points of light—maybe a hundred. Maybe more.

"No way. No... freakin'... way." He scanned the ceiling, hoping to see a hole to prove that these indeed were stars and that the deep blue was in fact the outside sky. But no, the ceiling was intact. The effect came entirely from the cone. These were lights, not stars. And there was noise, definitely noise.

Not just the whine from the whirring wrench, but the familiar sound of people talking, glasses clinking, and the occasional swell of live, raucous music. On top of all that, he could swear he smelled burgers—burgers, fries, and, oh yes, beer. It was his favorite scent—the fragrance of leisure, entertainment, comradery, and fun times. *Had the doohickey conjured a sports bar?* He had to see.

Forgetting his fear, Mitch stepped into the cone, listening and sniffing his way through the darkness. From the outside, the points of light pocking the cone's roof and sides had looked flat as dust, just flecks of paint against a midnight sky. Now, up close, they appeared more like pearls, shimmering in a mesh of azure blue. Mitch paused by each, ears pricked and nostrils flared, straining to find the restaurant jewel.

After just five steps, he located the music and burgers, as well as the glorious aroma of jalapenos and cheese. Nachos! His stomach rumbled, reminding him that he'd missed dinner. He had a sudden impulse to pluck the pearl, hold it close and inhale deeply, maybe even give it a lick. He reached for it, and as his hand got close, the circle of light became disk-like and expanded. He jerked his hand back, and the circle of light shrank. On a whim, he reached into his pocket, pulled out a quarter, and tossed it toward the light. The circle widened ever so slightly. The quarter quivered, suspended in the light beam for a second, and then was gone.

Had the quarter stuck to the light or bounced back from it, Mitch would have felt better. But his stomach dropped when the coin disappeared. Either it had fallen through the light hole or... the light was a death ray that disintegrated it completely.

"Stop freaking out," he chided himself aloud. How could a death ray smell like nachos and beer? The light, he reasoned, had to be a passageway of sorts, and all that happened to the quarter was that it fell straight in. He held a finger to his mouth as he talked through the logic. "If the quarter fell in, that means the bar is real. And if the bar is real, that means—" Mitch paused as he wondered if the light hole could expand wide enough to fit a hungry human, desperately in need of a cold drink and fried food. "Couldn't hurt to try it out," he said.

He squatted low and shifted his shoulders to edge into the hole, but as he leaned forward, a dark something blotted out the light. He dodged instinctively. *Whiz!* The dark thing flew past him and landed heavily on the floor of the cone. He got up to look and let out a triumphant whoop.

It was a dart. Mitch pumped his fists above his head in delight. "I'm right. It *is* a bar." He picked up the dart and chucked it impulsively back at the light hole. Cheers erupted, followed by applause, and a faint, less-than-sober voice proclaimed, "Now that's what I call a trick shot!"

Mitch bent again to peer through the hole, hoping to catch sight of his handiwork, only to be greeted instead with a furious argument, growing angrier and louder by the second. A female voice shouted, "You womanizing jerk!" And then— *Splash!* Cold, foamy liquid flooded out of the light, landing squarely in Mitch's face, soaking through his t-shirt and jacket. A burn like none he'd ever felt before penetrated his eyes. "Gaaah!"

Had Mitch been a normal patron, sitting beside the couple in the bar, he would have seen this for what it was: an angry woman tossing beer at her date. He would have laughed and fumbled around for a napkin or the edge of Dean's shirt to wipe his face. But tonight was not normal. The more his eyes stung, the faster the fear he'd squelched moments before rose back to the surface. For the second time tonight, he lost it.

Screaming and flailing, Mitch clawed his face, certain that some unearthly, intelligent ectoplasm had attacked. Deceptive, it lured victims to its bright white lair with yummy smells and happy sounds of drunken camaraderie, then *bam*! It latched onto their unlucky faces to drag them back into its cruel, extra-dimensional hellscape. The fun times he'd heard were just echoes of other fools who, like him, had been sucked unwittingly into this alien's nth-level vortex. To Mitch in this moment, the brackish fluid was pure plasma, and his eyes were being liquefied in their sockets.

This last thought—blue plasma liquefying his eyes—increased his panic. He tumbled backward, landing hard on his butt, and skidded along the floor into the opposite wall of the cone. He slapped at his face and felt his fingers sliding too easily over his cheeks. "Gaaah! Face melt! Gaaah!" He needed a sink, fast.

He scrambled to his feet. Prying one eye open barely enough to see the cone's opening, Mitch staggered out into the general direction of the emergency eye-wash station. Diving at the steel basin, he punched the handle, then sighed with relief as the lukewarm water washed the burning, acid foam from his face and eyes.

As the burning receded, Mitch gradually calmed down and immediately noticed a very familiar smell: rich and malty, slightly sweet, kinda hoppy. Able to open his eyes again, he looked down at his shirt, sniffed hard, and laughed. It was Guinness, his favorite beer. *What a dork!* he thought to himself. Then he noticed something else on his shirt—a square bar napkin, no doubt tossed along with the beer. Peeling the napkin back, Mitch read, "Sutter's Pub. 415 W. Pike St, Seattle, WA. Where fishmongers come to play."

Seattle? He looked back at the blue cone, a canopy really, and its embossed stars, one of which was a portal to a bar four states away. He wondered where the other lights led, trapped as they were, like flies in blue amber. Would they all be from Seattle? Could he go through the light like the dart and the quarter and sample the delights of Sutter's Pub? Many questions bubbled up, but one thing was sure in Mitch's mind—he was most definitely getting an 'A' on this project.

Sidling back to the dish, he reached into its heart and dislodged the wrench. Like a light switch, the canopy blinked off. "Wait'll the guys see this," he said, storing the wrench carefully in the top drawer of his bench. Feeling happier than he had in three weeks and six days, Mitch sprinted all the way back to the dorm.

CHAPTER 4

Breathless

"Dean!" Mitch burst through the door of his and Dean's dorm room, breathless and excited.

"Heya, buddy!" Dean called over his shoulder. "You done? Congrats! Grab some pizza!"

Dean had wasted no time shedding the semester. His backpack lay heaped near the trash can, like a crumpled piece of paper. The lights were out and the game machine on—loud. Metal music and laser blasts blared from the thrift-shop speakers tacked across the walls. Hyper-muscular avatars gamboled across his computer screen, bombing, burning, and crushing the landscapes of Warrior Ops XIV: Duty Bound. A pizza box from Stinky Keith's lay open and annihilated on Mitch's desk.

Dean sat splayed inside his bean bag on the floor, surrounded by greasy paper towels, pizza crusts, and crushed Monster beverage cans. An oversized headset covered his right ear. His fingers danced confidently across his game controller, vaporizing mercenaries and aliens with deadly precision. Between the music's shreds and snarls, he called out commands to his virtual platoonmates, like a general sounding the clarion for war.

They'd just cornered Wayne, who for weeks now had been terrorizing players with a hacked power shield that stole their energy and reset their progress. Now Dean and crew had him trapped in a gully, away from his shield, his body armor leaking energy. All they needed was five more minutes and Wayne would be back at square one, but boy was Mitch excited. He kept rambling on and on about something Dean could barely hear, much less understand. At the back of his mind, he was kind of curious to know why Mitch was worked up, but he was *so* close to making Wayne eat dirt, the next five minutes had dibs on his attention. If only Mitch would shut up!

"Hey, didja hear me?" Mitch spoke into his exposed ear.

"Yeah, great," he lied. "Grab a controller, willya? Wayne's going doooown."

"You didn't hear me!" Mitch said, getting excited all over again. He reached over Dean and turned the speaker volume down.

"Now listen. I created this... thing." He paused, clearly believing he'd said something lucid.

"Well, glad you cleared *that* up," Dean replied. *Pew! Boom!* There went Wayne's thrusters.

"Seriously, dude, it's—I don't know. It's like a—portal. It's full of lights!"

"Riiiight." As he focused more on Mitch, he sniffed and caught a whiff of... what? *Was that beer?*

"...and I leaned into one and this couple was fighting and *that's* why I smell!"

"Riiiight. You magnetized my battery and got transported to a bar. Totally believable." He decided to focus back on the game. *Pew! Smash! Take* that, *Wayne!*

"No. I mean, yes. I mean, right. It was the magna-coils. From Wayne. And a mini-satellite dish. It's hard to explain, but it works!"

"Suuuure. You electrified Wayne's mattress springs and a space-time portal magically appeared." *Donk! Wayne's avatar fell over, his progress bar down to thirty percent. Yes! Just a little more...*

"Dude, it's real. Come see. It ate quarters. A dart came out!"

"Mitch, that's a vending machine. Bwah-ha-ha-ha!" Dean quacked at his own joke, then sniffed the air dramatically. "*And* you're drunk. Just admit it, boy-o. You were at a bar, boozin' instead of doing your project. Now you're hopped up on Guinness and freakin' out cuz it's due tomorrow and you know you're toast."

"Asshole!" Mitch grabbed the controller out of Dean's hand and slammed it down onto his desk. "Look at me!" he demanded. On the screen, Dean's avatar froze. Immediately, Wayne retaliated, shooting an arm missile at the rest of the platoon before jogging up the hill to retrieve his shield.

"Not cool, Mitch. Wayne, don't kill me!" Dean yelled, flopping out of the bean bag and dashing across the hall to plead mercy. Wayne smiled coolly at Dean, finger poised above the button that would send him back to zero. The cool smile turned to sincere surprise as he looked passed Dean and into the hallway. "Mitch? Are you covered in plasma?"

Dean looked back and yelped. Mitch's arms, jeans, shoes, and the doorknob to their room were smeared in an iridescent blue goo.

"Geez!" Dean rasped, his voice a hoarse whisper. He stumbled backward, deeper into Wayne's room. "What'd you do to yourself, buddy?" he asked, his irritation with Mitch replaced with genuine concern.

Mitch looked confused, but as he raised his arms to examine the blue goo smeared across his sleeves, a smile slowly spread across his face. "Something abso-freakin' awesome. You gotta come see."

Wayne logged out and stowed his controller. "That's all I need to hear." He picked up his jacket and joined Mitch in the hallway.

Passing Dean, Wayne tapped him on the chest. "You got lucky, pal."

CHAPTER 5

Exploring

W ell, Mitch," said Wayne, examining the device, "you won't get points for design. This thing is mo'fugly."

"Blame yourselves. They're your parts. I just made 'em work."

Wayne could see no possible way for the junk pile on Mitch's bench to do anything more than catch fire. Had it not been humming, he would have doubted it did anything at all. He and Dean exchanged dubious glances.

"Yeah, it looks messier than it is," said Mitch as he reached into the top drawer of his bench. "That's just the engine, though. This here's the linchpin." He held the wrench out to Wayne. "Take it."

"A wrench," Wayne said, with the kind of evenness one reserves for close friends, family, and the insane. "And what does it do?"

"You'll see," Mitch said brightly. "Stand here." He pressed the wrench into Wayne's hand and positioned him in front of the device. "Now toss it at the dish. Aim for the center."

Dean snorted. Okay, Mitch was covered in blue goo—that was interesting. All the babble about some portal to Seattle—that was intriguing. But now, this ugly, hodge-podge of throwaways? Dean shook his head. It had to be a joke. He leaned close to Wayne's ear. "No way this thing works."

Wayne was less certain. Whether the machine worked or not hinged upon one, undeniable fact: Mitch was not an idiot. In three weeks, he had built and dismantled no less than twenty different machines, the only problem with each being that someone else had beat him to it—or seemed to. Wayne suspected that half of those "other" machines had actually been copied from Mitch's bench after he'd run off to Quantum Mechanics each day. Despite what Mitch thought of himself, he was a genius. If anyone could make a stargate out of chicken wire and chewing gum, it'd be Mitch.

"Only one way to find out," he whispered back at Dean. Squaring himself in front of the device, Wayne tossed the wrench at the dish and—amazingly, just as Mitch had described—the wrench hung in the center, bobbed for a few seconds, and then began to spin. The hairs on the back of Wayne's neck stood straight up as tendrils of light pulsed out of the edges of the dish.

"Look out!" Mitch yelled, pulling his friends to the side just as the funnel erupted, bisecting the room with a dark, shimmering, whale-sized, iridescent blue canopy.

"Q.E.D," said Wayne, brushing himself off as he got to his feet. He walked around the edges of the canopy, examining it from top to bottom, fascinated. "Mitch, my friend, you do not disappoint. At least now we know the source of the goo."

Mitch blushed. "I got, um, startled, and fell down pretty hard. It only sticks to you if you smack into it. Just walking around on top is like walking on rubber. See?" Mitch entered the canopy and bounced up and down on his toes for effect.

"Hmmm..." said Wayne. "Not so much rubber, I think, as repulsion." Arms outstretched, he moved along the edges of the cone, poking the "wall" and "floor" occasionally, as if testing its ripeness. "It's more like a residue or a bleed over. A byproduct of the different field interactions. And those dots... what are those? Lights?"

"Right! I thought at first they were stars, which was crazy. Then I thought they were holes in the canopy thing, and that the lights were behind the holes, but see? Nothing shines out." Mitch waved his hand in front of a dot, but nothing shone back on his hand. "And there's no shadow, either. Look at the wall over there." Mitch shaped his hand into a shadow puppet of a dog. Nothing appeared on the wall across from the dot. "And then I thought, man, they're clearly lights, but what if they aren't shining so much as stopped? Like whatever electromagnetic field combination that's in the cone somehow grabs photons like flies and traps them."

"Whoa, that's wild," said Wayne. "Hey, Dean, gimme your keys. I want to try something with your pin light."

Dean still lay on the floor where Mitch had pulled him, wide-eyed, ashen, and swallowing hard. "Wayne, can't you hear it sizzling every time you touch it? It's plasma, dude. We could be dying here!"

"Will you calm down? It's safe as houses." He touched it again and this time heard a small snap. It didn't hurt, so he continued, "Just get over here."

Dean rose slowly and edged cautiously toward the canopy, holding his keys out from his body at arms' length. Wayne grabbed the keychain and began pointing its pin light at various sections of the canopy. "Mitch, what happened after you invoked... this?"

Mitch regaled them with the story of Sutter's Pub, the dart game, the cheating boyfriend, the angry girlfriend, him slipping in the girlfriend's tossed beer, and then sliding into the wall.

"*That's* why you reek of Guinness," said Dean, looking at Mitch with renewed respect. "And you kept it together? Geez. If brown ooze from a hole leaped out at me, I'd think some alien was trying to melt my face."

He blushed again and said, "Yeah, well, uh, the beer smell was a dead giveaway."

"Oh, right," said Dean. Wayne caught Mitch's eye, clearly not fooled. They both chuckled.

"So, Mitch, no one saw you?" Wayne asked.

"Don't think so. I mean, nobody went, 'Hey, there's a guy's face in the wall.' "

"Curiouser and curiouser." Wayne stretched out his arms, seemingly to measure the length from the light of Sutter's Pub back to the wall. He swiveled slightly from side to side, muttering "North... due west... about a thousand miles..." His right arm assumed the position of a clock, in that he began moving rigidly at various angles. "...45. 90. 180? No, 90. Definitely—"

"Dammit, Wayne!" Dean snapped. "Quit being enigmatic. If you know how this got here, tell us."

"I don't *know* for sure what's going on, Dean. I just have a theory about what *might* be going on." Wayne continued his air measurements.

"Well, spill it, Einstein." Dean was beside himself with exasperation.

"I want to examine one of the lights first. Mitch, what happens when you walk into the light?"

"Don't know yet. But I'm game to find out!"

"That works. One sec..." Wayne left the canopy, rummaged around in what sounded like Bische's random equipment drawer, and returned holding a long bungee cord, a couple of carabiners, and four coffee stirrers.

"Okay, someone's gotta go in. One of us can volunteer, or we can draw straws."

Dean protested immediately. "Wayne, no. This always happens. You grab straws or sticks or something, then we draw and I wind up with the short stick. You'll volunteer to make yourself look good, but I end up the schmuck on the short end."

"Well, you could just volunteer right out and save us the trouble," said Wayne.

"Look, guys," Dean paused, his fist clenching increasing. "I know I've been hiding it pretty well, but really." He took a deep breath. "Okay... this blue funnel thing... it's freaking me out."

Wayne choked back a snort. Mitch covered his mouth and looked away, but then both of them started laughing uncontrollably. "Hiding it pretty well? Good one, Dean."

"What? You could tell?" This set off another uproarious round of laughter. Mitch wiped his eyes and said, "Dude, it couldn't have been plainer if you'd scrawled 'Scared!' on your forehead."

"Alright. K. I'll get a grip." Dean sighed and raked his hand through his hair. "Let's pick straws. Mitch holds, though. Wayne, close your eyes."

Mitch palmed the coffee stirrers and rolled them vigorously between his hands to mix them up. He held them out toward his friends and said, "Choose."

"You've got to be kidding me!" Dean blinked at the stirrer in his hand. It was, of course, the short one. "Wayne!"

"I did nothing. Luck of the straw, man." Wayne double looped the bungee cord around one of the carabiners, and then hooked it to the back of Dean's belt.

"Now, don't worry. I've thought it through. You should be fine, just like the dart and the beer. Jump in. Jump out. Piece of cake. Ready?"

"No. I—"

"Good. 3, 2, 1, go!" Mitch and Wayne gave Dean a shove toward the light of Sutter's Pub. Panicked, falling backwards, Dean grabbed a big fistful of Mitch's shirt and Wayne's sleeve. Off balance, they all toppled toward the dot of light.

"Whaaaaaaaaah!"

The point enlarged into a Wayne, Mitch, and Dean-sized oval. They popped through it and hung briefly in air, like trophies on the wall, then fell in a heap to the beer-sticky, peanut-shell-covered floor. The dart board had acquired more drunken players—Seattle University students it looked like, from the sweatshirts and hoodies. The boys expected shouts of fright or surprise, and instead were greeted with cheers. "Nice parkour, dudes," said one guy, pointing to Dean.

"It's the bungee cord," whispered Wayne. "Go with it." They jumped up and struck their best Cirque Du Soleil poses. More cheers, laughter, and clapping.

Out of nowhere, it seemed, came steins of beer and plates of nachos and the easy bon ami of the sodden, appreciative crowd. The boys scarfed it all down happily. Dean drained his beer, no trace of his earlier fear, and announced to the room in general, "This is awesome!"

"I told you!" Mitch shouted back.

More cheers as Wayne landed a dart in the bullseye. "Guys," he yelled, coming back to the table. "Seattle can't be the only place we can get to." They looked at each other, and then all three said simultaneously, "Las Vegas!"

The band chose to start playing loudly and frantically at that moment. The drunken crowd stumbled over to the tiny stage to egg them on. Perfect timing for a getaway. The jump point was clearly visible as a diamond-blue pin of light against the brick bar wall. They leapt toward it, landed back in the canopy, and began the serious business of searching for the light of Las Vegas.

They found every place but. A mall in Vancouver, Laclede's Landing in St. Louis, Jai Alai in Miami. "Geez, we're getting farther away," said Dean.

"Let's split up," suggested Mitch. "We can cover more ground that way. First one to find Caesars Palace calls the others to come join him."

They each chose a new dot of light at random and jumped. Mitch landed with a thud at the base of the Golden Gate Bridge. "Dang. Overshot it." He jumped back and tried the next light dot over and landed with a harder thud beside a papier-mâché russet potato. A sign above it read, "The Potato Museum." *Idaho?* thought Mitch. *Now this is just getting silly.*

He wondered if there was a light dot between San Francisco and Idaho. If the dots were arranged directionally, then a dot between these last two places had as good a shot as any of being Vegas. He leapt back through his entry point, but someone slammed into him mid-leap. It was Wayne. They both rolled together, falling uncontrollably for about thirty seconds, and then landed with a softer thud onto a mat in a dark, cold room. As his eyes adjusted, Mitch noticed the outlines of cabinets and huge blocky boxes that reminded him of early computer consoles he'd seen once in a museum. In the far corner stood a seriously-old-looking beast, with a bank of flashing light bulbs on one side and a CRT monitor embedded on the other. Mitch spotted an old-fashioned VT100 terminal in the opposite corner. Tape to tape reels lined the rest of the walls.

"Hello, 1985."

"You ain't kiddin'," said Wayne. He let out a low whistle. "It's like we jumped back in time."

"Total old school," Mitch continued. "Look at that box. Is that a refrigerator or a mainframe?"

"Mainframe. That's just one computer, man. Today, we could easily fit *ten* RAID in a box that size."

Mitch inspected the mainframe. Pulling open its cabinet door, he poked his head in and said, "Aslan, you in there?"

Wayne laughed. Immediately a large, angry klaxon blared from a speaker in the mainframe's cabinet door. "Yikes!" yelped Mitch. Quickly, they scrambled back into the light hole, reaching the Canopy side just as Mitch heard the faint jingle of keys.

"Phew, that was close. We almost got caught," he said.

"Yeah, but by what?" Wayne shook his head. "Look, we need to do this more controlled like."

"You're right. Maybe we should—"

Dean popped back in, eating a slice of pizza. "Found another break room, but this one had food. Wait a minute." Excitedly, he leaned his ear close to the hole directly across from the one he'd just left. "I think I hear a casino in this one!" He crammed the last piece of pizza crust into his mouth and dove head-first into the light hole.

"Wait!" Mitch and Wayne called after him, but too late. He'd already fallen in. Mitch pressed his face up to the light hole and saw Dean standing in a trench, a faint yellow glow behind him.

"Must have picked the wrong one," Dean smiled sheepishly up at Mitch.

"Obviously," Mitch grinned back. "Come on, knucklehead. Climb out of there. Wayne thinks we need a plan for these jumps."

Dean scanned the wall. "There's nothing to grab onto. Man, where am I?"

"Can't tell. It's super dim."

"And kinda dank, frankly. It sorta reminds me of a—".

Dean paused as a faint clacking sound arose in the distance. The ground rumbled. They both realized what it was and said simultaneously, "Subway!"

Mitch reached through the hole. "Quick, throw me the bungee!" Incredibly, it was still wrapped around Dean's waist. Dean tossed the free end of the bungee toward Mitch's outstretched hand. "Wayne, help!" yelled Mitch as he just barely grabbed the still-attached carabiner. The sound was unmistakable now, growing louder by the second. Dean took a running leap. Wayne and Mitch yanked hard. Dean practically flew back through the light hole just as the cars of the subway roared passed.

They lay panting in a heap on the floor of the canopy. "Isn't the floor where we started?" asked Wayne.

Mitch pushed up on one elbow and said to Dean, "New York, maybe?"

Dean flopped onto his back and nodded weakly. "A plan's looking pretty good right now."

"Let's plan tomorrow," said Wayne wearily. "Right now, I could use something cold to drink."

They popped back to Sutter's Pub. Soon, iced mugs and burgers filled the table and they reveled in the food whilst reliving their jumping adventures. Then Wayne raised his drink to Mitch and said, "To Genius!"

Dean lifted his mug to match him. "To Guinness!"

Mitch completed the toast and said, "To good friends!"

*****

About a hundred miles away from Bische's lab, in a cold facility beneath Cheyenne Mountain, keys jingled in the lock of a control room that had almost been forgotten. It would have stayed that way had it not been for the alarm blaring just inside the door and the text sent to the key-bearer just after the alarm went off.

He walked over to the ancient bank of monitoring stations and flipped the switch next to the blinking red "Proximity Alert" light. This quieted the alarm, but didn't explain why it had gone off in the first place. No one was in the room, but him. No one passed him in the corridor leading to the room. There were no cubbies, closets, stairwells, or other rooms along the corridor for someone to hide in, so he was pretty certain no one else had tried to break into the room. And yet the "Proximity Alert" was screaming bloody murder.

He scratched his dry, balding head, puzzled, and then chuckled to himself. On a whim, he walked over to the large cabinet at the far end of the room, opened it, and switched on the PDP console. Data he had expected over thirty years ago, but had never seen until that moment, sat there clear as day on the console's sole monitor. Strength left his knees. He sat down heavily in the workstation chair next to the cabinet. Recovering, he looked around the room for the phone, picked up the receiver, and punched in the number for the one functioning extension in this part of the facility.

"It's Scott. Get down here pronto. There's something you ought to see."

*****

About 6000 miles away from Cheyenne Mountain, in another old, poorly lit, forgotten room, a much younger man sat reading a book. He leaned first backward, then sideways in his chair, straining toward a dim light bulb, hoping to brighten the yellow page. His round face glistened. His uniform jacket—adorned with the name tag "Chung Ae"—lay draped over the back of an adjacent chair. His hat sat on top of the closest monitor. A thin line of sweat had just begun forming near each armpit seam of his neat, military, short-sleeve shirt.

The room was a relic, a converted bunker in a squalid sub-basement of a much larger facility known to all in Pyongyang as The Bureau. The buzzing of the low-watt, '50s-era light fixtures barely drowned out the humming of too many '90s and early '00s computers, daisy-chained together into a powerful espionage network, which twenty years ago had been the pride of The Bureau, but today, though nearly useless, was too risky to turn off. Better, more modern and relevant facilities had been built above the sub-basement, but Chung Ae, the lowest-ranked Monitor Tech, had no access to them. He was the sole assignee to this room, more because someone had to do it, rather than for any special skill he possessed. At times, he thought that somehow he'd drawn the short straw, but in all honesty he was no different from anyone else in his unit. They all worked on useless tasks within forgotten programs, victims of their or their family's poor politics or, worse, Dear Leader's arbitrary wrath.

With the monitors and computers and overall lack of ventilation in the room, it was a bit warm. The cup of tea Chung usually got at the start of his shift never had to be reheated. In fact, he welcomed sipping the tepid drink over the long hours of his watch. If he put the drink close to the back of one of the computers, the fan would cool it off even more, and after a time, he'd have a kind of "iced tea."

At any rate, he was reading to kill the boredom. He was supposed to be noting

34

strange internet activity and blocking any illegal access, but as far as he could tell none ever happened. The only network chatter consisted of academics from the local university squawking at each other, and occasionally a foreign IP snooping for a minute and then leaving, presumably just as bored as Chung.

Chung knew that nothing important existed here, and for all of Dear Leader's machinations nothing likely ever would. So he sat each shift making token notes about activity, but mostly reading technical journals and maintenance manuals he'd pick up at the markets over the weekend. This particular shift, he had dived into a worn text with the cover "Xitan Alpha Mainframe Maintenance". The insides, however, read suspiciously like a bootleg of the thriller novel "The Eiger Sanction." He told Kyung Ru, the unit's Black Market contact and his main supplier of "misnamed technical texts", that reading such books helped improved his English. Truth be told, he just liked the action. Way better than "Keyless Entry Systems."

The Frenchman had just been pummeled by rocks on the icy north face of the mountain, when a message began flashing on the monitor under his hat. This was not new. At least once per shift, some unintelligible gibberish flashed on the screen. This time, as always, the message disappeared after a few seconds, just a flux of phantom data on an otherwise dead network. He dutifully scribbled the time and port into the log without thinking about what it meant and got back to poor Montaigne's demise.

Thirty seconds later, the message flashed again and kept on flashing for a full minute despite Chung's efforts to ignore it. With a sigh, he closed his book, keeping his place with one finger, and leaned over to look more closely at the screen. The pattern at the start of the gibberish resembled a data breach, but in an American network, not theirs. He really didn't know what to do about it. He hit the Enter key on the keyboard to see if that would make the message go away. Instead, a long thread of binary data spooled out across the screen.

Huh. Another first. He'd never seen anything like that happen before. In fact, he had to admit that this might be categorized as "strange," and thus require him to call his superior, Hyun Shik, for the first time. Ever. A few seconds later, the "Acknowledge and Send" popup appeared on his screen, confirming the need to report the weird data. The thought made him groan aloud, as he knew that Hyun Shik rewarded silent monitors, but severely punished "reporters" who made him work.

Chung had two options: 1) hit the Escape key to ignore it, making the

"Acknowledge" disappear, or 2) click the "Send" button to route it over to Hyun. "Escape" let him get back to his book, but it would only work thrice. The third "Escape" would escalate the data packet to the real monitor room, which didn't play around. A serious Monitor Tech might show it to a general or, worse, Dear Leader himself, drawing the kind of scrutiny that often led to unpredictable, if not deadly consequences. "Send" meant donning his jacket and hat and sweating even more up ten flights of stairs to Hyun's office to be yelled at and publicly abused. Option 2 was not pleasant, but it trumped Dear Leader's life-altering cruelty. He knew what he had to do.

Chung sighed as he stood and re-dressed himself for official duty, sad that he wouldn't be getting back to his book tonight. He printed a copy of the odd data stream and started the long slog upstairs. He did not know it yet, but he would not be getting back to his book for some time.

CHAPTER 6

Models and Money

Mitch was riding on a river of light, flowing peacefully through a blue corridor. Famous landmarks flew by along the photon stream's bank, like floats in a travel parade. Friends and family leaned out of bright windows, waving and cheering and calling his name. Movie stars and moguls ran along the bank, stretching out over the river to shake his hand. The light river bent around a curve and suddenly it was quiet and the bank was bare. Then Bische appeared, a looming giant, stepping out toward the river from his laboratory door. Cupping his hands around his mouth he called, "But how does it work?"

To Mitch's horror, he realized he didn't know. He tried to think of an answer, but his mind went blank. He opened his mouth to speak, but his throat felt clogged. His lips moved, but no sound came out. Bische shook his head sadly and closed the door, pausing first to rip Mitch's scholarship to pieces. The river transformed into a hot, beery plasma, its bubbles rising up to erode the deserted shore. Just as his shoes burned away, he heard the familiar jangle of keys. *We're gonna get caught!* he thought, in a panic. He leaped toward the bank, desperate to reach Bische's door, but missed and fell into the plasma, screaming.

He bolted upright in bed.

"Mornin', buddy."

It was Dean returning to the room, coffee carafe in hand, keys dangling from a clip on his jeans.

"Morning," Mitch said thickly, strangely groggy again despite the adrenaline rush of his dream. He ruffled his curly locks to knock out the cobwebs, then glanced at the clock. It struck him how little time had passed between the most momentous thing to ever happen in his life and this very moment. Had it only really been six hours since they'd stumbled back, victorious, from Sutter's Pub? Wayne and Dean had crashed immediately, but Mitch had been too elated to sleep. He'd logged into the student portal and completed his lab report, writing it in a happy, almost manic flurry. He signed up to do his demo in the very last slot late morning and only succumbed to the softness of his pillow after clicking "Submit."

Now that he was truly awake, the excitement welled up in him again. He couldn't wait to start the day! He jumped out of bed and dressed. "What's for breakfast?"

"Wayne's got eggs and fruit" said Dean as he carefully carved three thick slices out of a chunk of parmesan cheese. "If you've got Pop-Tarts, we can have cheesy tarts."

Mitch grabbed the box out from under his bed. "Score! Three packs left. Blueberry good?"

"Perfect." Minutes later they pulled the treats out of the toaster oven and carefully carried them and three mugs of hot coffee into Wayne's room. Wayne had already set up the card table, adorning it with three hard-boiled eggs and a can of their favorite Dollar Store pineapple—Harmony Gold.

"Mmmm..." said Wayne, hovering above the plate of pastry and inhaling deeply, "Cheesy tarts... breakfast of champions."

"Never a truer word was spoken, my friend," said Mitch. "We *are* the champions. We're the new kings of travel!" They clinked their coffee mugs in a toast.

Dean couldn't contain himself. He paced the length of Wayne's room, wolfing down his cheesy tart and gesturing wildly with his coffee mug, blurting out plans.

"Guys. We need to chart the ports. We need to figure out which light hole goes where. We've got a travel *gold* mine, guys. We could call ourselves 'Golden

Lightways.' People would be *all over* it. We'd be travel *gods*, like... Richard Branson!"

"Wow. Last night you were nearly catatonic with fear and now you're all 'Let's sell tickets and become millionaires.'" Mitch chuckled between spoonfuls of pineapple.

"Hey, it's a new day, Mitch. And, come on, you gotta admit, this is, like, freakin' awesome. It is the most awesome discovery in the history of awesome, Mitch. We gotta jump *on* it. We gotta *run* with it!"

"You just want to go wakeboarding with naked models on your back," said Wayne, rolling his eyes.

"Exactly! And not just me, boy-o. A hundred, nay, a thousand guys just like me. We all wanna ride a light beam to the Bahamas, pick up a hot babe on the beach, strap 'er on and ride, ride the wild surf. King of the world!"

"King of the jail more like it. You'll get cuffed by the cops two seconds after 'strapping 'er on.' Either that or she'll scratch your eyes out."

"Dude, if I'm like Richard Branson, she'll be begging me to hit the waves, then leap on some photons. 'Oh, take *me* to Japan, Mr. Chambers—no, *me*. Let's go to Cabo San Lucas, Mr. Chambers. Let's—' Ooof! Hey!"

A rubber Koosh ball hit Dean squarely in the face. Mitch laughed and ducked for cover behind Wayne's Barcalounger, two more Kooshes at the ready for the ensuing battle.

Zing! Dean fired the Koosh back over Mitch's head. "Big mistake, Campbell." He launched a second Koosh at Mitch's bare foot, exposed on the side of the lounger, and ducked behind Wayne's desk for cover. *Thwack!* Another Koosh hit the side of the desk just as Dean crouched down.

"No hot babes for you, buddy. Ow!" He'd made the mistake of peeking out for his taunt, and Mitch had nailed him in the neck. They were both laughing hard now, happily flinging Kooshes back and forth like snowballs—the Barcalounger and desk their respective forts.

What goofs, Wayne thought, smiling as he watched his slap-happy friends. The long night showed in Mitch and Dean's easy silliness. Wayne, meanwhile, was thoughtful. It wasn't lost on him that what they did—what Mitch's patch-work machine made possible—should, in fact, be impossible. He'd allowed himself to be carried along by the sheer fun of popping about the country via conveniently imprisoned points of light. But upon waking up, it occurred to Wayne that the process should have made more sense than it did.

There had to be a reason why the transitions from one side of a light hole to the other came so easily. Why had they not gotten lost between points? Why was the light trapped at all? Maybe it had something to do with where they popped to more so than where they popped from? He hummed absently to himself, studying the map on his wall.

"Wayne, what are you doing?" asked Mitch, still laughing and just barely ducking away from another poorly timed huck by Dean.

Wayne thought a moment, then answered with his own question. "Where did we go last night, Mitch?"

"Let's see." *Zing!* "We started in Seattle." *Wham!* "Then you went to Frisco." *Bonk!* "Dean popped into Vegas. We all grabbed brats in Chicago." *Thunk!* "Then Dean fell into New York, and we ended where we started, Seattle." *Whack!*

Wayne nodded and walked slowly over to his map. "And do you see a pattern with all of those places?"

Dean bounced up and finally landed one solidly in Mitch's back. "Dude, who cares! It's just plain awesome. Let's put it in a bag and sell it already." He tossed two more Kooshes across the room at Mitch's head.

"We've got to understand it before we can sell it, Rockefeller," Wayne continued patiently. "There's a deeper connection between those places. Particularly in *where* we each landed. Don't you see it?"

"Alright, time out," Mitch called and crawled out from behind the Barcalounger. "Wayne, just spit it out, please."

Wayne cupped his hand over his mouth and deepening his voice intoned, "I find your lack of curiosity disturbing." A flock of Kooshes flew at him, which he'd expected and easily dodged. Mitch and Dean rarely tolerated his Darth Vader impression.

"Okay, okay," he said raising both hands placatingly. "Back to business." He turned to face the map.

"Now, you, Mitch, landed in Seattle right here—downtown at 5th and Pike. Not only is there a bar right there, but across the street from the bar is a satellite facility for Seattle's main data center."

Wayne paused to see if this nugget held enough info for Mitch and Dean to infer the rest. His friends stared attentively, though blankly, back at him. He decided to try again.

"Alright, then I popped out in San Francisco, here, at the intersection of Market and the Embarcadero. What happens to be right there? Another data center, about the same size as the one in Seattle. The same thing happens in St. Louis, Chicago, and New York. In each place, we either landed on top of or next door to a big data center. Somehow the points of light—maybe the whole canopy even—they're all tied to the data network."

Suddenly, comprehension dawned in Mitch and Dean's eyes.

"Do you have the list of all the data centers?" Mitch asked excitedly.

"All the non-classified ones. There's no way any normal person can get the full list."

"Then this means we *can* map the canopy!" exclaimed Dean.

"We can match the points of light to specific facilities in the network," said Mitch.

"Right! You've got it!" Wayne beamed at his friends. They'd finally figured it out.

"Let's get started right away." Mitch glanced over his shoulder as he hurried to the door. "Print the list, Wayne. I'll get my gear and a compass and—oh, French biscuits!"

Mitch's eyes went wide as he noticed the bouncing clock which was Wayne's screen saver. "The time! Guys, we'll be late!"

It was time to unveil their projects. Mitch and Dean dashed across the hall and began shoveling their tablets and other random paraphernalia into their backpacks. Wayne was already set, having packed up last night. He locked his room and waited calmly as Mitch and Dean scrambled about. It occurred to him that once they got to the lab and Mitch demonstrated his device, it wouldn't matter that they were late. His, Dean's, and all of the other submitted projects wouldn't matter either, compared to Mitch's device. All that would matter would be the canopy and its trapped points of light. They jumped down the stairs, sprinting toward their destiny.

CHAPTER 7

Spite

D
r. Hubert Wilkins felt the buzzing in his suit pocket and knew who was calling him before the ringtone, intentionally quiet and generic, melodically confirmed it. The phone rang twice, stopped, and then began again, ringing three more times before ending, just as they had agreed. *Drat!* he thought as he fished out his phone and verified the caller ID. *I don't have time for this.*

Just five minutes before, he'd left his office, virtually sprinting to the stairwell and down the three flights to the first-floor labs, hurrying to not miss his chance for gold, real gold. This was the morning he'd lobbied a full year for—heaping flattery, gifts, and avaricious promises on carefully selected board trustees until a vote in his favor was inevitable. The final tally, rendered late last night, had been confirmed by President Hayman this morning. He'd won! And with this victory came a new title—Director of Commercial Development, a vast improvement over his current post, Dean of Physics. As the DCD, he now had power over every grad student, undergrad, and professor in the school and the pleasure of sampling the pies of all of their research.

Of course, whatever he vetted would be co-opted by the university and enveloped into its revenue stream. The terms of his appointment ensured that he'd be compensated with 1% of the profits from each viable project, which was not insubstantial finder's fee, but also not where the real money lay. The true ingots came from "farm deals"—side ventures on the Dark Market for virgin technologies. Furious shadow bidding by corporations, private buyers, and the occasional foreign government made such ventures as lucrative as they were secret.

Hubert had but a glimpse of this subculture while Dean of Physics. Most of the projects he'd stolen from students were rejected by the keepers of the Dark Market. "Too cerebral." "Impractical." "Not deadly," they said. They were right. The doctoral dolts allocated to him lacked imagination. Only one professor consistently rated the best students, and that was Hayman's golden boy, that know it all, Gabriel Bische. Hayman favored him and his Innovation Program, to the detriment of other departments, in Hubert's estimation. All the brilliant students got funneled to him. All the quirky projects were Bische's for the picking. Hayman claimed that the school's special arrangement with Bische existed solely to raise CSM's prestige, but Hubert couldn't believe that was the whole of it. These projects were too ingenious to not be making one or both of them a lot of money. If they weren't taking advantage of it, that was money on the Dark Market table, and if they didn't want it, he would gladly wipe the table clean. As the DCD now, he had the power to do it.

But only if he made it to Room 103 on time. Damn it all, why were doctoral reviews scheduled together with Project Day? The pitiful laggards assigned to him had nothing of interest to discuss. It was all just theoretical research. Not a tangible moneymaker in the bunch. Now most of the morning was gone, and he'd missed a sizable chunk of the project demos. His only recourse was to get the agenda, so that at least he had descriptions of the projects he would officially lay claim to. Even descriptions were worth something within the speculative Dark Market, but Bische guarded the agenda fiercely, only distributing it during the demos. Once he locked the door near the end of the morning, you had to beg him to get one, and he'd be damned if Bische forced him to beg.

Any claim Hubert made to said projects—in the name of the university of course— would be all the weaker if he was not there to witness their demonstration and officially note their potential commercial worth. Hubert checked his watch. He had nine minutes, at the most. That might be enough time to deal with the nuisance caller. Ducking under the first-floor stairwell, Hubert spoke the decryption code into his phone and dialed.

A crisp, heavily accented voice, answered. "Dr. Wilkins."

"Yes, hello. What is it? It's not a good time. I'm very busy." Hubert spoke brusquely, hoping his terseness would convey the need to end the call quickly.

"Such directness. Refreshing," said the voice, cold with sarcasm. Hubert bit his tongue. Despite his irritation at having to deal with this now, it would not do to alienate the caller, his current link to the Dark Market. Once word spread of his new position, he was sure he'd cultivate other, more palatable allies. For now, he needed to play nice.

"I am sure you are aware of what you promised us," the voice continued.

"Yes, I'm working on it. Just this morning I received good news. I should have something for you soon."

"Soon? My employer has been waiting. Patiently. 'Soon' was two months ago. 'Late' is approaching. You do not want to be 'late,' do you, Dr. Wilkins?"

The implied threat was not lost on Hubert. A small worm of anxiety inched into his stomach, slowly twisting into a knot. "I... I..." he stammered.

"I know your assistant is not looking forward to it." In the background, Hubert heard scuffling, and then a muffled cry. It was his lab tech, Christian. *Oh my, they must be upstairs*, Hubert realized, horrified. He knew Christian would not talk. He was as liable as Hubert. He had no recourse with the authorities. Bad luck for him, but it couldn't be helped. He listened, cringing as Christian begged, glad that it was his assistant being tortured and not him. "No... No! Nooo!" Christian cried out again. Then there was a terrible crunching sound, interrupted only by more wailing. *Must have been his hand*, Hubert thought. He could call security, but then what would he tell them? How could he explain this man without giving himself away? He gulped and said as evenly as possible, hoping to calm the caller, "Please. Stop. This isn't necessary."

"Oh, Dr. Wilkins, I think it is. So that you understand. You do not want to be 'late.' Understand? If I do not hear from you in two days, I will not call."

"What about Christian? You can't just leave him there. Someone will find him and report it." As terrified as Hubert was of this man, he could not afford anyone happening upon Christian in whatever state it was he was in. It would lead to questions and formal inquiries and ruin. He was so close. This couldn't happen now.

"Hubert. I do you favor. I take him to hospital—leave him outside to walk in alone. To show you I can be kind."

"Thank you. I will not fail you."

"No, Dr. Wilkins. You will not. One way or other. We will get what you promised." The line went dead.

Hubert gulped and checked the time. Only three minutes left! He sprinted down the hall toward Room 103, no longer just the source of riches. Without a doubt, Hubert knew, he could not be 'late.'

CHAPTER 8

The Reveal

Hubert! To what do I owe the pleasure?"

Hubert, trembling and out of breath, arrived at Room 103 to find Bische guarding the door, a stack of agendas in hand. He sidled quickly past the towering professor, glancing anxiously at the clock on the far wall. Two minutes before the top of the hour. He'd made it!

Despite being rattled by the phone call, Hubert couldn't resist the urge to gloat. With a sneering smile, he looked up at Bische and said, "I have a note."

"From whom? Your mother?"

Maggie Heinz muffled a titter. Hubert's face, already predisposed to redness, tinged crimson. "You'll wish it was my mother," he snapped back.

"Well, she did ask me to say 'Hi' to you when I left this morning."

Hubert clenched his teeth. The indignity! But he knew he'd have the last laugh. He forced an even wider smile and handed Bische the Board's letter. Bische sobered a bit as he read, much to Hubert's satisfaction. *Make light of* that, *Golden Boy*, he thought. Bische handed the letter back.

"Score one for you, Hubert."

"Director Wilkins, if you please."

"Alright, Director. That note doesn't apply to me or my students, of course."

"It will! I have the assurance of the Board."

"The Board didn't hire me. President Hayman did."

"The Board trumps Hayman. You'll see," said Hubert, punctuating his utter contempt for Bische with his best derisive scoff.

Bische chuckled. "What a dastardly laugh, Hubert. Good to see that practice in the mirror paying off."

Hubert snatched an agenda from Bische's stack and huffed off to a table near the front. Conceited ingrate, he thought furiously. *The day of reckoning will be here soon enough, Golden Boy, and when it comes we'll just see whose laugh needs practice.*

He turned his attention to the presentations, scanning the descriptions for potentially lethal or, at least, destructive traits that might appeal to his "friends" upstairs. He flipped through the pages in disgust. *Blast, the kids today, so concerned about the environment and social justice.* Two thirds of the presentations were dolphin-hugging contraptions for scrubbing carbon dioxide, or cleaning the oceans, or generating affordable energy. Not a strategic or aggressive bone in their bodies, from the looks of it. The closest thing to weaponry was some "flaming projectile" device that shot hot candied corn. He looked up the creator—Dean Chambers. That buffoon. The assessment of Chambers this semester was the one time he and the other professors in the department had agreed. Chambers showed real talent, but was often too eager for a laugh. Only he would be silly enough to waste time converting a potato gun into a molten popcorn ball shooter. Hubert wondered if he could use that to his advantage. If Chambers could be persuaded to replace the corn seeds with radioactive pellets—-

A commotion by the door interrupted Hubert's scheming. Bische had just removed the door jam, preparing to close the room and start the class, when a faint voice yelled, "Waaaaaiiit!"

Multiple arms thrust through the slit in the door, wedging it open. Bische pursed his lips, but didn't resist their attempts to enter. Soon, three disheveled bodies stumbled into the lab. Hubert recognized Chambers immediately—tall, beefy, and grinning oafishly. *No surprise he's late.* Behind him was a strange-looking youngster, though familiar. Who was it, Kimoto? No—Hirano, that was it. Hubert brightened. Now there was a true genius. Perfect scores on both entrance exams, pulling a 4.0 with a full course load, and according to Dr. Rebar in Metallurgy, a true innovator due to some kind of super strong magnetic coil he'd made. Excited, Hubert looked up Hirano's device, but was disappointed to see "Shield Generator—Prototype." What nonsense was this? Electromagnetic shields were fantasies. Teams of researchers had tried to create one, to no avail. They either didn't work or were too large to be practical. Brilliant or no, if whole companies couldn't do it, he strongly doubted Hirano's prototype worked. Hubert's frustration mounted. After all his work and planning to get here, could it all be just a wild goose chase?

The third tardy student scrambled over to Bench #22, Chambers and Hirano close behind. He had no idea about this one. Even the device on the bench was a mystery as it was covered with—what? *Was that a tablecloth?* Hubert looked up the bench number and nearly spat with contempt. Oh, Campbell. Bische's pet. Completely unremarkable, this one, just some charity case Bische had pleaded to be let in. The dolt's device didn't even have a description. As distasteful as Hubert found it, he saw no other recourse but to invest in Chamber's flaming projectile launcher. Would that be enough to satisfy the caller? The knot in his stomach twisted more at the thought of leaving today empty handed. That settled it. Chamber's device would have to be enough.

"Thank you all for coming," Bische was saying now. The three latecomers whispered frantically at Campbell's bench. Bische continued with his introductory speech, talking louder, trying to drown out whatever was happening with Campbell, Hirano, and Chambers. Bische's increase in volume seemed only to cue the three to whisper louder amongst themselves. Most eyes had turned toward them, a result Hubert found amusing. Bische, still talking, walked across the lab until he was just behind the three, his shadow looming large against the wall. That got their attention. Abruptly, their argument ended. Mitch spun around to face him.

"Campbell, you seem ready to go."

Campbell's face went white. *The boy's got nothing*, Hubert thought. Then to his surprise, Campbell said, "Alright. If you're sure I should go now."

"Everyone is already watching you, Campbell. Might as well." The class laughed at that. Campbell smiled sheepishly, then wheeled his cart to the front. He coughed nervously a couple of times, then said,

"Okay, first, I know. It looks like crap. Second, I forgot to write a description—I can do that today. Third—yeah, I used your dish, but it was late and there it was and that's that." The boy paused and took another breath. "Okay, now, fourth—"

"Cut the bullshit, son," Bische said cheerfully. "Don't make it worse by rambling. Just show us what you've got."

Taking a final deep breath, Campbell yanked off the table cloth and rather feebly said, "Ta da?"

Hubert couldn't believe it. The boy revealed a random pile of junk. A collective murmur arose around the room, along with more than a few snickers. "What is this?" Hubert demanded.

Bische's eyes had locked with Campbell's. They both ignored him. Bische said quietly, "Looks interesting enough. What should it do?"

Campbell thought a moment, and then answered, "It's an optical conveyor."

"More like a trash compactor," came a voice from the back of the room. The snickers evolved into true laughter, rippling through the crowd like a wave. Campbell glared at his classmates and continued, "It traps photons in a plasma matrix, kinda like flies in a spider web. When you touch them, they latch onto your electromagnetic frequency and pull you through the optical pocket like a kind of... photon car."

"Soo-per Car!" yelled the comedian from the back of the room.

The class erupted. Bische swung around, and in a voice that wasn't so much loud as it was firm and commanding said, "Quiet!" The group settled down. Bische bent over the monstrosity, examining first the ridiculous dish at the top and then the tight wire coils perched like bookends on either side of the main section's box. Straightening, he said, "This can't possibly work as you describe. Magnetic fields don't trap light—ambient or otherwise. And plasma doesn't simply arrange itself into an enclosure. It is not a container—it must be contained. These are things you should know, Mr. Campbell. Given your past history in our department I would say you do know them, and so must either be deluded or making a bad joke. Which should I choose?"

To the boy's credit, he stood his ground, scowling up at Bische deliberately while the professor delivered comments that would make most students wither. Campbell opened his mouth, but then closed it again, as if he decided that talking was a wasted effort. Then he maneuvered Bische to the side of the device, switched it on, and tossed a metal rod into dish's the center. Immediately, a dark blue funnel leapt out from the dish, filling two thirds of the room. The crowd gasped. Hubert was perplexed. *What the devil was this?*

"Behold! The Canopy!" Campbell said dramatically before stepping toward the funnel's opening.

"Campbell, wait—" Bische began, but as he reached out to restrain him, Mitch dodged.

"Sorry, Doc. You won't believe me any other way."

And then the Campbell boy did something truly astonishing. With an impish grin, he waved to Bische and the crowd, stepped inside of the blue funnel—and vanished!

CHAPTER 9

Fried

Campbell!" Bische shouted, rushing toward the Canopy, pulling up just short. His first instinct was to dive in after the boy, but rationality won out. If Mitch disappeared after contact with this thing, what on earth would happen to him?

Behind him, the class let out a collective gasp. "Whoa, he fried himself," said the jokester in the back.

Maggie whirled around, aghast, "Shut up, Billy!"

The ripple of Maggie's worry spread through the room like a burgeoning wave, threatening to burst into panic. Bische knew that if he couldn't immediately go after Mitch, he'd have to at least do something to keep the class from unraveling until he figured out how to save him. Did he need to be saved? He noticed Dean and Wayne, both grinning like idiots as they lapped up the effects of Mitch's shocking exit on the class. *Good*, thought Bische. *If they aren't freaking out, Campbell must be fine, damn the boy.* "Hirano, Chambers, explain," Bische demanded.

"It's okay, Doc," said Dean, laughing.

"Yes, really, he's fine," said Wayne.

"He disintegrated, Hirano. I don't call that 'fine.'" Bische had moved directly in front of them and was speaking quietly. "I need answers, boys. Now. Before this gets out of hand."

Bische gestured toward the murmuring class, and at Hubert in particular, who had edged closer to the Canopy, staring at it quizzically, as if wondering why Mitch was hiding inside. "Wilkins is confused right now—his natural state, granted—but once it registers that Campbell's disappeared, he'll scream 'Lawsuit!' or some such and there will be hell to pay. Talk fast."

Dean and Wayne sobered at this. Dr. Wilkins was well known for flying off the handle, pulling funding from professors, and even kicking people out of programs at the slightest provocation. Neither wanted to get Bische or Mitch into trouble.

Dean started the explanation. "Sorry, Doc. Mitch is alive. He didn't disintegrate. He got transported. He walked into one of those lighted pinholes and now he's someplace else."

"Nonsense. That looks like pure plasma, Chambers. You don't just walk into it and get 'transported.' One touch and you don't exist."

Wayne picked up the thread. "Yes, normally, that's true. But it's not really plasma. It's actually an exudate, a byproduct of—"

"Dr. Bische!"

Damn! It was Wilkins. The light of comprehension shone in Hubert's eyes as he made his way to Bische's side. "The Campbell boy. He's vanished."

"Brilliant, Hubert. You've deduced it perfectly."

"And you've done nothing about it!"

"In the middle of that, actually. If you would just go back to—"

"I won't go back to anywhere. Your pet just destroyed himself. You can't deny it. This has scandal written all over it, and it won't be the school that suffers. It'll be *you*. I'll see to that. The Board will demand you resign!"

"He's not 'destroyed'," said Dean, a bit petulantly.

"Stay out of this, Chambers," Bische quietly warned him.

"Doc, he can't make you resign. Mitch is fine," said Dean, directing his last words defiantly at Hubert.

"Dean's right," chimed in Wayne. "It's safe. We're proof. We did the exact same thing as Mitch last night."

"You what?!" Both Bische and Wilkins spun around to face him. Wayne blanched and took a step back.

"All three of you went gallivanting around in that contraption?!" Hubert sputtered. Wayne and Dean exchanged anxious glances. Hubert waited, but neither of them made any attempt to reply. Finally, he swung toward Bische and declared, "They *all* could have *died*. Then where would the school be? The Board will have your head!"

"Better on the chopping block, than up my own a—" Bische began, but an increase in the hum from the Canopy interrupted him.

"Look out!" Maggie exclaimed. "It's making noise!"

The Canopy fizzled and snapped. After Mitch disappeared, the class had collectively sidled closer to the cone, curiosity trumping their initial fright, but now they scattered as the enclosure crackled. "I betcha it belches out Campbell's skeleton," quipped the jokester.

"Shut *up*, Billy!" Maggie retorted.

At that moment, as if he did it every day, Mitch phased out of the Canopy's inside wall, overly laden with an enormous tray full of nachos, fried cheese sticks, and two pitchers of soda. He had on a new shirt, emblazoned with the slogan "Sutter's Pub: Seattle's Dock for Darts and Bock." With a magician's flourish, he set the tray down on Bische's desk. Then waving an imaginary wand above his head he sang more confidently, "Ta da!"

Wayne and Dean rushed up to greet him, while Hubert, Bische, and the rest of the class stared on in stunned silence.

"Snacks. Smooth," said Dean, high-fiving him before diving into the cheese sticks.

"And soda. Nice touch, brah," said Wayne. Covertly, he pantomimed an angry face, pointing toward Bische and Hubert.

Mitch peered over Wayne's shoulder at the professors, then warily asked Bische, "So, Doc, something wrong?"

"Yeah, you fried yourself, dude," the back-room jokester answered instead.

"Shut up, Billy!" yelled his classmates, en masse.

"Yes, please, Mr. Hoag, stop disrupting this class," said Hubert, who then launched into a diatribe against the general lack of decorum and respect being displayed by the class as a whole.

Bische took advantage of the distraction to slip away from Hubert, shoving a stool between them to further block the easy path to Mitch. Grabbing the boy by the shoulders he said, quietly, "Tell me quick, before Hubert's done. Are you alright?" He seemed to be. Bische could see no burns or injuries or signs of derangement.

Mitch flashed an impish grin and replied, "Depends. Am I getting an 'A'?"

"This is serious, Mitch." He hadn't been stern, but he spoke with an intensity that underscored the gravity of the situation.

Mitch sobered and said, "Of course I am, Doc." He gestured toward the Canopy. "It's as easy as walking through a door."

"Do you understand what you did?"

"Trapped some light beams, obviously." The boy's grin returned, accented by pride in his feat.

"By what means did you trap them? Can you explain how it works?"

"Sure, I just... I mean... It's... uhm..."

Mitch paused, the smile fading, his face morphing from happy to thoughtful to panicked, as if he'd suddenly forgotten the answer. He frowned at the floor, then tried to speak again, but stopped, stymied, the explanation seemingly eluding him.

Wayne stepped up next to Mitch. "You see, Doc—"

He got no further. Bische raised his hand and said curtly, "No, Hirano. Just Mitch."

"Good, lord, the boy has no idea what he's done," spat Hubert, having dodged the stool and finally arrived behind Bische. "It's a wonder he's alive."

Hubert's vitriol snapped Mitch out of his panic spiral. "I know what I did," he protested, and began rifling desperately through his backpack for his tablet. "Just give me a minute. I posted it all to the project site."

"If you can't explain it, son, you don't understand it," said Bische.

"All the more reason for me to confiscate this right now," said Hubert. His tone was indignant, but Bische detected a hint of greed in his eyes. It was just like Hubert to cry foul first, then weasel a way to take the very thing he derided for his own. If Mitch had truly discovered a new means of travel, no way would he let Hubert waltz out with it.

"You can't call dibs on this, Hubert." said Bische.

"Just watch me," Hubert shot back. "I have the support of the Board."

"And as I said earlier. I don't answer to the Board."

"We'll see about that. You think President Hayman will stick by your side after you nearly lost a student and potentially endangered many others?"

"I know for a fact that he will," Bische said confidently.

"Then you're an utter fool. He'll have no choice. The Board will demand that he order you to release all projects. I'll see to it personally."

"Until you do, understand that you'll touch nothing in this lab."

"It's not me, but you who needs to under—"

"Um, hey, Docs?" Billy interrupted. "This argument is fascinating and all, but class is over in ten minutes, Campbell's demo was hella freaky, and this is my last class before Santa Day, and I'm, like, ready to jet."

"Good point, Billy," said Bische, glad for the interruption. Arguing with Hubert was pointless, and he was surprised he'd let himself get sucked into doing it. The sooner he got Hubert and everyone else out of here, the sooner he could sort things out with Campbell and crew. He could also send a heads up to President Hayman. There was absolutely no way he'd allow Hubert to take a potato battery out of this lab much less an instant transport device. Bische addressed the room.

"Today was just a formality, really, more for the department than for any of you. With the exception of Campbell, all of you demonstrated your devices to me at First Check-In, and so will be graded accordingly. Anyone with more to say to me about their project can do so at my scheduled office hours. I'll be here through the end of the week. As for the rest of you, you are released for the semester. Great job, everyone. See you after break."

A cheer went up through the room. Though most, including Billy, packed up their projects and scrammed, several more queued up next to Mitch, Dean, and Wayne, peppering them with questions about the Canopy and whether or not they could get a 'ride' in it.

"Come on, man. Let me use it. I've got $20."

"Yeah, Mitch, it'd save us the drive to Illinois. Joy and me will give you $20 apiece."

"How about New York? If it's near a subway, I can get home from there."

"If the subway doesn't hit you first," said Dean. "The light hole we found dumps you right out on the tracks."

"Crazy! Man, I'd still do it."

"Me, too. I'll have to stay here for break otherwise."

The would-be travelers crowded closer around the boys, waving money and pleading their cases. Mitch threw up his hands and said, "Why not?" He beckoned the crowd to follow him to the blue cone. Bische moved to intercept the throng, but Hubert, surprisingly, beat him to it.

"Stop!" Hubert shouted, flinging out his arms to block the Canopy's entrance. "This is untested equipment, built around non-existent science. You must turn it off at once."

"Untested? That's my fourth trip to Seattle and I'm still alive," argued Mitch.

"You could die from the effects hours from now for all we know," countered Hubert, ", then who would your parent's blame? The school! No more trips, not one of you. Not until I talk to the Board."

Mitch looked to Bische, who shook his head ever so slightly. "As much as it pains me, I must agree with Dr. Wilkins, at least for today. Put your money away, please, all of you."

The students complied, though with a fair amount of unhappy muttering. Hubert settled back into his scheming, confident, smirk. Bische hid his irritation and continued smoothly to Mitch, Dean, and Wayne, "Could you three stay here a moment and help me tidy? The rest of you, I have an appointment and so must insist you leave. You, too, Hubert. I'm sure we'll be talking soon enough."

"I'll be back, you wait. I'll return with the Board's official statement, and Campus Security if need be. Any project I designate will be mine." He spun on his heel and left with the rest of the class. Soon Bische and the boys were alone.

Mitch pointed to the device. "Good enough for scholarship, Doc?"

"Bit of an understatement, Campbell," said Bische dryly, but the pride in his eyes was unmistakable. Mitch breathed a sigh of relief.

"You're still on the hook to provide at least verbal proof of understanding, but that can wait. Right now, so help me, if you want to protect your discovery from Dr. Wilkins, you're going to have to publish your findings, and I mean fast."

"How fast?" asked Wayne.

"End of the week, no later."

"What?!" the three exclaimed.

"That's not enough time," said Mitch. "And who would accept the paper anyways, so close to the holidays?"

"It's not as crazy as it sounds, Campbell. Several journals take submissions year-round, especially the school's in-house imprint, *Technical and Applied Physics Monthly*. And I happen to know the editor, Dana Hughes. If you give me the paper by Thursday, she can rush it through the reviewer process in time for next week's publication."

"What good is that going to do for us, though?" Mitch asked.

"Once you publish, there is a clear trail to you three as creators, and to the school as sponsors. Hubert can't just swoop in after that and take what he wants. He can't do an end-around with the Board to bypass President Hayman, either. He'll be forced to work with both." Bische paused, his eyes boring into Mitch's, then said, "I have just one question for you, Campbell. Do you or do you not know how this monstrosity works?"

Mitch looked at his friends, and with their thumbs up as confirmation said, "Yes. Yes we do."

"Good enough. Now get yourselves out of here and start writing. I'll take this..." he gestured toward the device, at a loss for what to call it.

"Canopy?" Mitch suggested.

"Fine. I'll lock it in the back room until the paper's uploaded and approved. Hopefully, for Hubert, out of sight will be out of mind."

*****

Hubert all but skipped out of Bische's lab, his earlier fear rapidly transforming into excitement, and his ambition swelling in proportion to it. Instantaneous travel! Surely this was a far more attractive prize for his impatient customer than a simple bomb or Chambers' infantile energy gun. A device like this would make borders obsolete, restrictions meaningless; the potential for power—limitless. Upon this last point, Hubert planned to fan the flames of interest with the customer, maybe doubling or tripling his asking price, possibly fulfilling, in one fell swoop, his long-held dreams of avarice.

He couldn't have planned a better outcome to Project Day. Bische's students did not disappoint. If even the dullard Campbell could have such a stroke of genius, imagine what the others could do, once sufficiently prodded. He needed control of that group immediately; Hayman would *have* to allow it. The sooner it happened, the sooner Hubert could lay hands on all of the projects, discredit Campbell, and then unload the boy's device, quietly, to his secret buyer.

He bounded up the stairs and back to his lab, fondling the phone in his pocket, no longer dreading the upcoming call to the customer. He swiftly crossed through the outer room to his office, steadfastly ignoring the mess no doubt caused by the ugliness with Christian —who he firmly hoped was fine, yet mute at whichever emergency room the customer had abandoned him to. He locked the door, and dialed the coded sequence into his phone.

The customer's cold, passionless voice answered, "This is sooner than expected, Dr. Wilkins."

"I know, but I have something for you now."

"Something? There is only one 'thing' that I want, Doctor. What you promised."

"This is better. Extraordinary. Your leader will be more than pleased."

"Shall I come now? Can you show me?"

Hubert hesitated. In his excitement, he'd forgotten that these people were in town. The sound of Christian's bones being snapped bubbled up in his memory, and he shuddered, wondering if he would suffer the same fate—or worse. Calling before he had Campbell's device in hand had indeed been a mistake, he saw that now. How could he recover?

"I—I have some paperwork to do first. To avoid, uh, raising suspicions. I'm taking a big risk, you know." Some of Hubert's natural indignation, never far from the surface, shone through. These people had to know it wouldn't be so easy. Surely they could respect the need to move within channels, make things as legitimate as possible.

There was silence on the other end of the line. It stretched out uncomfortably for several seconds. Had the man not breathed heavily a couple of times, Hubert would have thought he'd hung up. Strangely, that would have been more frightening than what amounted to his continual annoyed sighing. Finally he said, "Dr. Wilkins. Your luck amazes me. I texted this information to my employer, fully expecting him to tell me to cut your intestines out for making him wait. Instead, he says this extraordinary 'thing' must be fantastic for you to risk dying over paperwork. He will wait, then. You caught him on a generous day."

"Thank you!" gulped Hubert, thinking it best to avoid the selling price discussion and just end the call quickly, lest his luck run out. "Good—" he began. The customer interrupted.

"Do understand, however, that this is just for today. I tell you, as a friendly sort, that our leader can change. Often, he changes his mind—"

"Yes, yes of course," Hubert interrupted, "Thank you. Good—"

"—and when he does," the customer continued as if Hubert had not spoken, "I must say, Dr. Wilkins. He can be cruel."

Now Hubert was confused. "Er, uh, what do you...?" he stammered.

"Not always. Sometimes he will ask me to cut off a finger or break an arm, and then just leave it at that, but other times—in special cases—he will demand something more interesting."

Hubert squeaked.

"For example, one time, he had me crush a man. I pinned him to a wall then smashed into him with a truck. And then he had me take pictures, which he laughed at, as he finds such images amusing."

Hubert's insides roiled. He gulped again, suddenly nauseous.

"You understand, Dr. Wilkins?"

All Hubert could get out was "Ulp," followed by a belch.

The customer laughed.

"Good. You understand perfectly. We will talk again soon, Dr. Wilkins."

"Goodbye?" Hubert croaked. The line went dead. He hoped better for himself.

CHAPTER 10

All the Monies

Hyun Shik, Chung Ae's superior officer, was not an intelligence analyst. He understood little about science, even less about engineering, and absolutely nothing about computers, networks, or data. Why he'd been put in charge of Network Information Analysis and Monitoring, Chung did not know, but his meager experience in military politics made him aware that non-combat assignments had little to do with aptitude or skill. They had a lot to do with who you knew, but, more often than not, with who remembered your mistakes. For Hyun, it was the former, his highly decorated uncle, whose dying sister had begged him to find a safe job for her under-skilled son. If Hyun had more imagination, his assignment could have been the start of a great career. Instead, he applied nearly all of his time and effort pursuing the one thing a non-combat soldier lacked—money. Dirty, capitalist, essential money.

Chung reluctantly headed to Hyun's cube, clutching a print out of the inconvenient data surge that protocol dictated he bring to Hyun's attention. In a perfect world, Hyun would accept the print out, praise Chung for his alertness, start slogging through the lengthy acknowledgement process, and Chung would be on his way. But the world was imperfect, and Hyun was lazy and incompetent. Chung predicted a tongue lashing, not praise, for interrupting his superior. Then Hyun, as punishment, would assign him to complete the requisite protocol himself, a task that could take hours. If Chung could be certain that he was the only one who'd noticed the data surge, he would have turned around and tossed the print out in the trash. Unfortunately, the data blip was so large it had triggered the anomaly alarm, so there was no hiding it. Miserably, he trudged forward, knowing that he'd miss the last tram for the day and that his tepid tea would likely be his dinner.

Chung was close enough now to see Hyun hovering impatiently over someone, as they huddled conspiratorially in front of a monitor. Hyun spoke quietly, glancing over his shoulder every couple of seconds, as if wary of eavesdroppers. He poked the screen repeatedly, leaving greasy smudges behind, ashes from his cigarette drifting down like dirty snow onto the desk below.

"It'll never work," the seated soldier growled, pushing Hyun's fingers away from the monitor. Chung recognized the gravelly voice of Kyung Ru, his black market contact and a fellow underling from Radio Monitoring downstairs. The scheme must have been particularly difficult for Hyun to rope in Kyung, one of the few people in their department who, like Chung, actually had computer training. Kyung had even more than Chung—a PhD in engineering from Chŏngjin Technology University—a fact that helped Kyung routinely get away with calling out the ridiculousness of Hyun's schemes. Why Kyung was not the commander of their unit was a subject of some debate within the lower ranks, as he obviously possessed the superior experience. The rumor was that he'd been demoted out of spite, having insulted the intellect of some General one time too many. Normally this would mark him for death, but Kyung's black market ties made him inconvenient to kill. The General no doubt gained more satisfaction by disgracing him, forcing him to fill his days counting random radio blips while reporting to a complete idiot.

Chung could see the monitor now. Instead of a data stream, the screen showed a FlixNet queue. "You are a fool if you think anyone will believe this is a real account," Kyung growled.

Hyun poked the screen again, more emphatically. "It is real. It's Bong Chol's, but he's reassigned to the rocket program. My cousin is the janitor for that program. He says the rocket is just a trash can strapped to dynamite. Dong Chol is as good as dead. This is our chance."

"Idiot, you need more than one pirate account to sell. If a thousand people all use the same account, that will draw attention. You'll be shut down before—"

Chung cleared his throat. "Sorry, Commander Shik, sir. My apologies, but I have to show you this." He handed Hyun the print out and brought up the suspended acknowledgement on another workstation.

Hyun grabbed the print out, glanced once, then tossed it dismissively at Kyung. "This looks like every print out you give me, just longer. So what?"

"Better acknowledge it," said Kyung, inspecting the sheath of papers. "Else my cousin Jek will report you to Dear Leader. You'll be next in line for rocket duty before the end of the day."

"I outrank your weasel cousin," Hyun grunted, but he keyed in his acknowledgement code anyway and, as predicted, made Chung his protocol delegate with a resentful click. Smirking, he turned to Chung and said, "You don't listen. I told you not to bother me. Now you pay the price."

Chung thought to say, *having you for my commander should be price enough*, but as satisfying as it would be to give voice to that insult, he also realized that it would be counterproductive. A different idea came to mind, one that might save him from extra paperwork. "Sir, you said not to bother you unless it was data from the internet or America. I think this is both."

Hyun's eyes widened and Chung pressed his lips together to hide a smile as the seed of interest took root in his commander. If the internet and America were involved, it could mean real money, lots of money, better than FlixNet money. Hyun tried to grab the print out back from Kyung, but Kyung blocked his hand, and rubbing his chin said, "Looks like somebody sent a shitload of data across the Net."

"Didn't I just say that?" snapped Hyun. "It's a lot of squiggles. But what's in it? Movies? Music? Missile plans?" Hyun was nearly salivating, no doubt imagining the lucrative contraband the data might represent.

Kyung traced his finger from one data point to another. "Huh. That can't be right. Let's see the original." He logged out of his workstation and stepped aside to let Chung log in and pull up the monitoring station's ledger. Kyung squinted at the data as it spooled out to the screen. "When did this happen?" he asked.

"About twenty minutes ago," said Chung. Kyung took over scrolling, moving backward through the data until he reached the right timestamp and then slowly perused forward, skipping over some sections, but zooming in on others.

"What is it?!" hissed Hyun impatiently.

"If I was crazy," said Kyung, "I'd say this was biodata. But I'm not crazy."

"Biodata? What does that mean? Is it like a thumb print? An eye scan? This must be very secretive and expensive, yes, this biometric signature? China or Russia would pay big for American secrets!" Hyun pantomimed a growing stack of money.

Kyung rolled his eyes and made a disgusted sound. "I didn't say anything about a 'signature.' I just said biodata."

"Well what's the difference? Speak plainly!"

Kyung beckoned the commander and Chung to look over his shoulder. "See this piece here and here? That is hair protein, I think. And this here, running through all the rest of the data, that is brain waves or a pulse. Not sure which, but it's one of them, I'm sure. I fixed bioimaging machines in grad school. The data always looked like that."

Chung gasped, comprehension dawning suddenly. Hyun furled his brow, however. "So this is x-ray data?" No one would care about medical records. He was so disappointed he almost spat.

Kyung faced them. "It will sound like I have lost my mind, but I think this is a digitized body. Someone digitized themselves."

Hyun stared at him blankly for a moment, and then laughed. "That's ridiculous. Someone emailed their body? Please, be serious. If you don't know, I will call someone else."

"I *am* serious. And see here, that continuous stream and underneath it the huge wave spreading from one end to the next? That means the signal was stable from point A to point B. So not only did they digitize themselves, but they went somewhere. Easily."

It was beginning to sink in. Hyun stopped laughing.

"And look here and here. The streams are different, but the wave type is the same. Someone went many somewheres, multiple times. This guy is joy riding around the internet. Hmmm, I wonder..."

Kyung scratched the stubble on his chin, then said, "I bet we could run this data through the traffic imager. That might prove that I'm right." With a few clicks he opened the imager program and told it to process a slice of the data. Slowly on the screen before them emerged a young, male head covered in thick, bushy curls. They stared at the image, amazed. "Well, what do you know?" said Kyung. "I'm right."

Hyun could not believe his luck. This was bigger than a single payout. If they could figure out what the Americans had done and copy it, they could charge people for the privilege. They would be rolling in the won.

"Guys," said Chung. "It thinks it's happening again." He pointed at the monitor. The same message that had flashed at him earlier flashed once more. He hit **Enter** and the now familiar binary stream spooled out across the monitor.

Hyun grabbed Kyung's shoulder. "Can you replicate this?" he demanded.

"Pfft, you must be joking," scoffed Kyung. "This isn't hacking a video site. This is real science. Real science requires approval, not to mention time and money."

"We've got those!" said Hyun, gesturing toward the monitor and himself.

"Time, yes. Money? Ha!" Kyung guffawed and flicked the ash off his cigarette. "You can't pirate that many FlixNet accounts. And you are deluded if you think your approval matters."

Bah!" spat Hyun, shaking his fists. "You are a coward! You have no vision! You'd rather drink yourself to death than do something real!" He ended his tantrum by kicking Kyung's chair.

"Better the bottle than the firing squad," said Kyung, inhaling his cigarette down to a stub. "Because that is our fate if Dear Leader finds out that we are working on an unsanctioned project."

"I—have—dis—cretion!" said Hyun, pounding his monitoring. "I am your commander. I command you. You, and you!" Chung jumped a little as Hyun rounded on him, surprised that his superior remembered that he was there. Then Hyun marched to his workstation, pulled up the duty roster, jabbed a couple of buttons, turned around, and said, "There! You are both reassigned. We will work downstairs. No one will know or care."

He stood between them, hands on his hips, huffing and wide eyed. Kyung glared, but said nothing. Chung stared at them both, stunned by this development, and cursed himself for being diligent. He considered what lie he could tell Hyun to convince him that Kyung was mistaken, but doubted he'd listen in his current state, so Chung held his tongue, the safest tactic, and waited for Hyun to calm down.

Had the traffic imager been hidden, that might have happened, but Hyun spotted the outline of the bushy-headed American and his eyes glittered anew. He smiled suddenly and said, "This is stupendous!" He clasped his hands around their forearms. "Friends... We must harness this. We must take this from the Americans. We must build a Black Market 'Body Fax.' And when we figure it out, the world will beg us to use it. We'll be rich. We will leave the stinking army. We will own *all* of the monies!"

Chung and Kyung exchanged glances. Overriding other things, Hyun Shik was their commander. He could make life difficult for them should they refuse. His argument was irrational, yet strangely compelling. Chung wondered what it would feel like, having all the monies.

CHAPTER 11

Proof

Hubert strode toward President Hayman's office filled with an odd mixture of confidence and bile. His confidence stemmed from the email print out, safely ensconced in his left breast pocket, from Dr. Reba Rebar, Metallurgy professor. The letter confirmed what he'd suspected from the beginning, but which Gabriel Bische had consistently denied. The idiot boy Campbell's instant travel machine was in fact not created solely with spare parts from Bische's private stores, but included components manufactured in Rebar's lab, by the boy's genius friend Wayne Hirano. That put it firmly, unequivocally, under possession of the University.

Hubert saw no way for Bische to weasel past this discovery, nor for Hayman to deny the University's claim to at least partial ownership. Rebar's confirmation would officially end Bische's delays, leaving Hubert freedom to quietly exploit the device as he wished. Oh, what joy it would be, Hubert imagined, seeing the shock and betrayal play across Bische's face as Christian boxed up the machine and marched it right out of his lab. *Ho, ho, that will be a glorious day.*

The one thing putting a damper on Hubert's victory lay crumpled in his right fist. It was a flyer, festooned with the faces of Idiot Boy and his friends, superimposed in front of the travel machine. Giant black letters above the picture declared, "Big Blue is calling YOU!" Then across the middle, bolded white, it read, "Ride a light beam and see the world—for free! Jump! Go! Simple!"

He couldn't believe it. They were actually soliciting students to test the device, for free no less. It was intolerable. Bad enough so many had already seen the machine in action on Project Day, but after that, they had the temerity to submit a paper about it to the in-house journal, who published it, incredibly enough, without his or the Board's permission. Even so, Hubert had held out hope that he could keep a lid on the situation—until today, when these infernal flyers appeared. Once Campbell and crew's tests began, the cat would truly be out of the bag, and any prospect he had of quietly removing the device, much less profiting from it, would be lost. Discretion would be virtually impossible. The sooner he put a stop to all of this the better.

"Doreen," he said tersely, nodding to the perennially frazzled, high-strung secretary manning the desk in President Hayman's outer office.

"Oh, Dr. Wilkins, you can't go in there," she said, reaching over her desk to block Hubert's progress.

"And why not?" Hubert snapped, side-stepping her outstretched hand. "I have business with the President. It's his open hour."

"Not anymore," Doreen replied anxiously, glancing at the door. "He's in a meeting. He can't be disturbed. I'll schedule another time if you —"

"This can't wait," Hubert said brusquely. With a perfunctory knock, he opened the door.

"Leland, we have to talk about this damned Can—" He stopped, shocked. Seated directly across from President Hayman was Bische, his face turned toward Hubert now, looking slightly amused.

Hubert fumed. "What's *he* doing here?"

"Hello, Hubert. Not to worry. I was just leaving." Bische stood and gracefully strode past Hubert to the door. "Thanks for your time, Leland," he said and was gone.

"Why was he here? What did he say to you?" Hubert demanded. He felt his confidence ebbing.

"Just a friendly chat. But now to you, Director Wilkins. So glad to see you." President Hayman smiled genially. "What 'damned can' brings you here?"

Hubert knew Hayman was changing the subject. He'd have liked to press him further on Bische's visit, but right now he needed Hayman on his side, so let it pass. Brandishing the flyer, he asked, "Have you seen this?"

Hayman perused the paper dispassionately. "Looks like a standard call for research subjects."

"There's nothing standard about that device!" said Hubert, flummoxed by Hayman's passivity. "The Campbell boy's admitted he doesn't fully know how it works. And now they're casting about for guinea pigs to jump into it? Not only is it a gross misuse of what is rightfully University property, it's also a lawsuit waiting to happen!"

"Ah, yes, we were just discussing this, Gabriel and I. We must protect the students, after all. So we ran it by legal and they drafted a release form. As long as the subjects sign it, the school is protected." Hayman smiled again, as if that settled it.

"But... but..." Hubert stammered. He had to think fast. It could all slip away! "This is about more than test subject legalities. This is misappropriation of school materials." *Yes, that's the tactic.* "That Campbell boy stole school property. Dr. Rebar affirms it." He handed President Hayman the printed email, silently praying it would be proof enough.

Hayman perused the email, then looked up at Hubert and said, "Legal was clear on this point as well. We can't prevent Campbell and his friends from testing what they've created, especially since they've published their findings. The Innovation Program charter, as well as Gabriel's arrangement with the University as the program director, stipulates no less."

Hubert seethed, but seeing no other path forward, continued arguing the point. "Dr. Bische's 'special arrangement' does not allow for school resources acquired outside of his lab. And these magna-coils were definitely made for a metallurgy assignment. Not for Project Day. Campbell is in violation. It's as clear as glass."

President Hayman frowned, and Hubert knew he had scored a point. Finally the momentum was shifting his way.

"I see," Hayman said finally. "What do you propose we do about it?"

This is your moment, Hubert thought. He leaned on Hayman's desk and in a near whisper said, "We take it. Take it now, away from these hot-rod kids, and put it into competent hands. My tech, Christian, for example. He's very experienced—my best graduate assistant, by far. We solicit, quietly, one other expert, perhaps, to work with Christian to evaluate the tech. And if it passes, after careful cultivation, we put it to use— for the school. We've got to do it now, Leland." Hubert paused, a bit winded from his plea.

President Hayman studied him a moment, and then said, "I agree."

Hubert rocked back on his heels, stunned that his speech had actually worked. He'd expected more of a fight from Hayman, given his and Bische's relationship. This indeed was the best outcome. *My God*, he thought. *I've won.*

"Thank you, President!"

"Certainly, Director Wilkins. Of course, we do need to follow the proper process, to ensure that whatever claim we lay is airtight. That tends to take about 10-14 days"

"Of course, President." *Damn*, thought Hubert, *another delay*. "But shouldn't we proceed before things," he held up the flyer, "get too far out of hand?"

"Point taken," said Hayman. He spoke into the intercom. "Doreen, step in here please."

Doreen appeared at the door, her eyes darting to either side of the room before landing contritely on the president. "I am so sorry, Dr. Hayman. He just barreled right past me—"

"It's alright, Doreen," President Hayman said kindly. "Could you please prepare commercial transfer documents made out to Dr. Dische, under Dr. Wilkins' jurisdiction, for this item?" He gestured for Hubert to hand over the crumpled flyer about the travel machine. "Should you need more information about it, please talk with either me or Dr. Wilkins. No need to contact Dr. Bische. Is that clear?"

Hubert nodded approvingly. No need to tip their hand and risk Bische doing something foolish like hiding the device. Doreen shot a worried glance at President Hayman, but said, "Yes, sir. I'll start on this right away."

Hayman turned his attention back to Hubert. "Is there anything else, Director?"

"No, I think that's quite enough. I'll contact that expert at once." And with that, Hubert marched out, smirking. *Strike two for the Golden Boy.*

*****

Hayman waited thirty seconds, long enough for Hubert to have cleared the outer office and be on his way. Then clearing his throat, he said, "Did you get all of that?"

The door to his office bathroom opened. A tall, angular, very fit woman exited and said, "Every word. Well done."

Hayman bowed his head modestly. "I'll assemble an appropriate set of 'investors' to accompany you."

"Great. We'll be in touch." With a wink and a graceful turn, she left.

*****

Beneath the first-floor stairwell, Hubert keyed in the secret number on his burner phone, chuckling as he composed the text message for his "expert."

"The device is ours in ten days' time. Prepare to return." He hit send with a flourish and pocketing the device, rubbed his hands in glee. "Take that, Gabriel Bische!"

CHAPTER 12

Lab Central Station

Hold the door!" Mitch called out to the clot of scarves, hoodies, and backpacks who rushed through the frost-caked entrance of the CASE building. The first decent snow of the season had arrived the night before, along with a bitter cold front, leaving the day gray and icy. It was a hard cold, the kind that froze skin to metal, and it slapped Mitch's face like a lash as he dashed, gloveless, across the quad from his Calculus class back to Bische's lab. A girl at the back of the group took pity and left a crack open in the door for him to squeeze through.

"Thanks!" He sighed deeply, reveling in the warmth of the alcove. "My hands are frozen."

"No problem." She turned to head down the hall, but then Mitch shook off his hood, revealing his face, and she said, "Oh! You're that guy!" She held up a flyer and pointed at Mitch's face hovering in front of the travel Canopy, just beneath the word bubble, "Big Blue is Calling YOU!"

Mitch grinned and aped his stance from the flyer, eliciting a giggle. "That's me! You gonna sign up?"

"I'm on my way there. Heard it's wild. Got great buzz. S'all my roommate's talked about since Project Day. I can't believe you're the guy! Can you get me in? I wanna go to Nebraska this weekend."

"No problem," said Mitch magnanimously. "We've got room."

"Not what I heard." She showed Mitch a message stream on her phone. "My roommate's there. She says she's stuck at the back of the line. Can you move her up too?"

Mitch frowned, confused. *What line*, he wondered? When he'd left for Calculus an hour ago, only four guys had shown up for the test trial. "Your friend's joshing you. Really, it's fine." They'd reached the lab. "See? There's hardly anyone h—"

The word "here" died on his lips as Mitch opened the door to the lab. The place was packed. A line stretched from the front of the Canopy all the way to the back of the room, snaking into the supply cupboard and then back out again toward Bische's desk. Techno music blared from a speaker that hadn't been there when he'd left an hour ago. A waitress from Sutter's Pub, decked out with a camera, accelerometer, and other sensors strapped to her vest, wound her way through the line, doling out beers and burgers, making change, and taking more orders. The line-standers danced, ate, and talked loudly, waiting for their turn in the Canopy. Billy "The Joker" Hoag, stood on a stool at the back, scrolling through a song list up on Bische's smartboard, queueing songs called out by the crowd. He turned toward the opened door and yelled, "Mitch!"

Everyone, it seemed, looked over. The lab erupted in applause and smatterings of praise. "You're the dude!" "It's awesome!" "Way to go!" Mitch just stood there, open mouthed and amazed.

His door savior waved frantically to a pretty, petite student across the room. Pointing at Mitch, she shouted, "Debbie! It's the guy! He can move us up in line!"

Mitch heard a happy squeal that filled him with panic. "No, wait. I didn't know—" She ignored him, ran to the back, and dragged her friend to the front. Mitch pushed his way through the crowd to head off the inevitable argument sure to ensue between his savior and whoever was at the front of the line.

Before he could make much progress, he heard Dean shouting his name, amidst the babel. "Mitch, over here!" Reluctantly, Mitch changed direction and waded through the crowd toward the folding table at the right side of the Canopy. Five fishing reels had been clamped to the edge of the table, a bungee cord attached to each, with each bungee pulled taut into the Canopy, disappearing into five different light holes. Wayne sat at the table, staring intently at a split screen of flashing images and scrolling data while Dean peered over his shoulder.

75

"Guys, what's all this? What happened?!" Mitch gestured at the table, the bungee and crowd of expectant travelers.

"PicsterGram post, dude," said Dean, grinning broadly. "Billy uploaded our flyer. Kinda filled up in here, didn't it?"

"*Kinda* filled up? Dude, Bische is gonna kill us!"

"Relax, Mitch," said Wayne. He copied a column of numbers from the scrolling data stream into a spreadsheet. "We've got fantastic data. Field variance. Potential wave bubbles. Maggie found Europe. *Europe*, brah! Bische'll forgive a little mess for excellent data."

"This is more than a 'little mess,' guys. This is supposed to be research. Not a party."

"Why can't it be both? Ah, thanks, Karen." The Sutter's Pub waitress handed Dean a nacho basket and a coke. Dean pointed proudly to her sensor array. "Wayne's idea. She goes back and forth, so we capture repeat light jumps. Killer data, Mitch. The accelerometer numbers are a complete surprise."

Karen pulled off the camera and sensors and handed them to Wayne. "Shift's ending. Gloria's coming on. Want I should send her over?"

Before Wayne could reply, Mitch interjected, "No! I mean, it's fine. That's enough for today."

"K. Thanks for the extra tips." Karen winked and disappeared back through the Sutter's light hole.

Mitch watched her leave, unsure what to think. "Well, more data is good, I guess. But what about, you know, caution? Reels, dude? I thought we agreed. Just one person at a time."

"Uh, it was BORING," said Dean. "...for us and the other guys waiting to go. It was also slow as hell, especially when more people showed up. Found these reels in the supply room—Bische is a pack rat, btw. Then Wayne got harnesses and bungees from the climbing wall in the gym, and voila!" Dean waved his hands over the contraption with a flourish.

"We even have a time limit on each reel. Everybody gets twenty minutes. You want more time, you gotta pay. That was my idea, so's we get petty cash for expenses. When time's up, we just reel 'em in."

A timer velcroed to the Sutter's Pub reel started beeping. "Speaking of which, looks like Stevie's time is up." Dean silenced the timer. Then holding his hand above the reel's retractor switch, he grinned and said, "Watch this." With a flick of his wrist, he engaged the auto-retractor. It spun rapidly, reeling in Stevie like a big mouth bass.

Within seconds, Stevie flew backward out of the canopy, flopping awkwardly to a stop at the edge of the data table.

"Whooooo!" crowed Stevie, staggering. He surveyed the room with a lopsided grin, bleary eyed, belching, and very clearly drunk. Mitch struggled to steady him while Dean unclipped his harness.

"Thanksh, man. You're th'greatesh. Hey?" Stevie swayed, blinking several times as he tried to focus on Mitch's head. "Iz'at Mitch? Dude? You da' maaaan, man! Big Blue's awesome. I'd do it again. It's gr—" Stevie's face went blank, as an evil-sounding gurgle emanated from his gut. Pushing out of Mitch and Dean's grasp, he dove at the eye-wash station and upchucked mightily.

"Well, at least he hit the basin," Wayne noted.

Mitch groaned. "Guys this is seriously out of hand." He looked at his watch. "Geez! Bische is due back from lunch in ten minutes. We gotta clear these folks out and clean up before—"

"Too late."

Bische hadn't raised his voice, but somehow it sliced through the inebriated chatter, dance beats, and Stevie's dry heaving to land squarely in Mitch's ears like a velvety gong. Dean and Wayne, who could see Bische, exchanged guilty glances. Both of them paled and seemed to shrink two inches, telling Mitch that the look on Bische's face must have been fearsome to behold. Too late, indeed. The disappointment and anger in those two words hurt Mitch worse than any amount of cold, lashing wind.

CHAPTER 13

Shut Down

*O*f course, Bische would sneak up behind me at the worst possible moment, Mitch thought. It always happened. Humiliating him seemed to be one of Bische's many talents. Mitch knew that this time, at least, he deserved it, so he might as well suck it up and dive into the pain. He turned toward Bische's quiet fury and suppressing the urge to wince, began, "We can explain—"

"This should be good," Bische said dryly.

"We've got hi-fidelity data—" tried Wayne.

"Certainly. The song list on the board is proof of that."

"—and we plotted some new light holes—" added Dean.

"Mapped by puking Stevie there, no doubt."

Stevie, hearing his name, pushed away from the basin, shot Bische a thumbs up, and weakly called out, "Whooooo!"

"Lovely."

Wayne tried again. "The spectral data's kind of fascinating, actually —"

"What's more fascinating," interrupted Bische, "is that you think I still care."

"K, timeout, guys." Mitch lost patience with their mincing and ultimately himself. A bit more harshly than he intended, he turned to Bische and said, "We get it. You can stop the whole piercing eyes, gazing into our souls, sarcastic thing. We know you're mad."

"From your attitude, I doubt it."

"No, really." Exasperated, Mitch gestured out to the room. "You're right. You should be mad. The lab is trashed. There's too many people here. It's my project, so it's my fault. I'm sorry."

"No, Mitch, it's on us, too," said Dean, chastened.

"Absolutely," added Wayne. "We're sorry. We should have never let it get this crazy."

Bische's face softened. "An apology. Thank you, that's a start." He surveyed the room. "This would be wildly inconvenient if I had classes today, but I don't, so count yourselves lucky." With that, the tension between them lifted. The boys brightened visibly.

"Wayne's right, though, Doc," said Dean. "We've got really good data."

"I look forward to seeing it, but right now—" *Buzz! Buzz!* The sound had come from Bische's jacket pocket. He pulled his phone out and barked a bitter laugh as he read the message. "Wow. It just gets better." Shaking his head, he walked over to the fishing reels, triggered their retractors, and curtly told the boys "Unhitch them." Then he went to the smartboard and stabbed off the music. In the same even, but penetrating tone he'd used to accost Mitch, Bische addressed the room. "Get out. All of you. Now."

Bische's reputation was such that everyone left immediately, without questions, most even taking their Sutter's Pub trash with them. Mitch, Dean, and Wayne had also queued up to leave, but Bische stopped them, locking the door after the last of the other students.

"Shut that down, Campbell." he said indicating the Canopy. "There's something you all need to see."

Mitch removed the wrench from the center of the dish, winking the blue funnel out of existence. Bische pulled up his message account on the smartboard and opened the first item in the list. Beneath the president's letterhead it read...

*****

Gabriel Bische
Professor/Director, Innovation Program
Center for Applied Science and Engineering (CASE) Bldg, Room 103

Dear Dr. Bische:

Please be informed that the university's Board of Governors has submitted a formal claim for the light-based travel device created recently by students in your Innovation Lab. The basis for this claim is to thwart the improper appropriation of the university's intellectual property, specifically the use of a magnetic alloy (dubbed "magna-coils") forged in Dr. Rebar's metallurgy lab to satisfy the requirements of an assignment unrelated to the travel device.

The Board is aware of the university's agreement with you regarding projects completed in your lab, using materials provided by you. This agreement does not extend to university materials external to your lab. Therefore any projects assembled using said materials can be considered proprietary to the school and can be claimed as CSM intellectual property.

To comply with this policy, any assembled, functioning version of the light-based travel device that relies on university materials must be packaged and delivered to the Commercial Development Office by close of business the last day of this academic term. Thank you for your cooperation. Should you have questions, please contact the Office of the President for additional information.

Sincerely,

Leland Hayman
President
Colorado School of Mines

*****

"This is crazy. We can't just let them take all of our work," said Mitch. "This is ours, regardless of their 'claim.'"

"Hayman has a point about the coils," said Bische.

"But the alloy is mine!" said Wayne. "It was my idea, not Dr. Rebar's. I thought it up in class and made it as soon as we got to lab. The coils were just proof you could apply it. If it's my idea, why can't I use it?"

"You likely could under different circumstances. I doubt Rebar is the one making the fuss. And though Hayman signed it, this letter is not his style," said Bische. "He'd have talked to me directly and found a way to make this work for everyone." Bische studied the letter intently. "I'd say Dr. Wilkins had a hand in this decision."

"But you said publishing the paper would keep him off our backs," said Dean.

"Normally, it would have, but somehow he got hold of the fine print on my agreement. Only the legal department knew about the loophole. Leave it to Hubert to weasel it out of them."

"I still don't get why he cares so much," said Mitch. "When he saw the Canopy on Project Day it was like I'd committed a crime."

"Knowing Hubert, I'd guess he just wants to claim the device for himself. The letter says to hand it over to the Commercial Development Office, not the legal department. This is a glory grab if ever there was one."

"This can't be happening," said Mitch, dropping his head into his hands. "Doc, there's gotta be a way out."

Bische paced in front of the smartboard, chin in hand, thinking. Abruptly he said, "There is a possibility. All of you, heads up."

He waited until he had each boy's attention.

"Tell me," he began. "If you could start from scratch, what would you change?"

Mitch chewed his lower lip. He'd actually mulled over that very question last night as they trudged back and forth between the lab and the dorm, ferrying computers and other equipment they needed to conduct the test trials in Bische's lab. If the Canopy weren't so fragile and bulky, they could have carried it to the dorm instead, done all of the testing in the common room or the quad, and avoided trashing Bische's lab. The fact that it wasn't portable was a major liability.

"It's too clunky."
"It's unwieldy."
"You can't move it."

Mitch, Dean, and Wayne had all spoken at once.

Bische chuckled. "Valid criticisms, yes. But how would you fix it?"

"I was thinking last night..." Mitch started, slowly. Then as the idea coalesced in his brain, he continued, gathering momentum as he spoke. "Well... once Wayne figured out the data center link, we worked backwards and got the calculations for how the canopy scales. Why it stays the size it does and why it has the number of trapped points of light it does. What if we focused on trapping just one light point at a time? Wouldn't we be able to scale the components down and make it smaller? Maybe put everything except the magna-coils on a chip?"

"Dude, that's brilliant!" said Dean. "I was thinking, too, that if we could slap a CPU to the thing, I could write a program that maps light points to data centers, so we could pick a location we want and wrap a field around it to trap it. We could do that on a pi board if everything else was on a chip."

"That just leaves the magna-coils," said Bische.

"Yeah, about that. I found this on the net." Wayne opened a browser on the smartboard and searched for Tamblyn Tech. The front page showed a variety of 3D printers. Wayne clicked one and said, "This guy here, the Ursula T2, is a 3D metal printer. The specs say it can print pico-sized wires and includes a supercoiling ratchet. With this, I could smelt the alloy myself, and then twist as tight as we need it to support the right magnetic field. It's sweet. But all this talk..." Wayne paused and sighed.

"Is just talk," finished Dean rather bitterly.

"Bingo," said Wayne, nodding agreement as Dean continued.

"If we have to use only the stuff that Doc here gives us, we're hosed. I know it's kind of messy in here right now, but once we tidy up, I still won't see a clean room for the chip or a 3D printer or this wire doohickey for the coils."

"Who says you have to stay here?" said Bische.

Mitch snapped his fingers. "That's it, guys!" he said excitedly. "We go off campus. And I know just the place, too."

He grinned like a maniac at Dean, who frowned as he realized what Mitch was thinking. "No, Mitch."

"Aw, come on, man. Her house is only, like, five miles away from here, and her garage is huge. She practically begged you to come help her."

"No, dude, we can't ask her. It's one thing to help her out. It's another if I wind up beholden to *her*."

"What's this, then?" asked Wayne.

"Samantha," Mitch replied.

"Oh!" Wayne's eyes widened. "Sorry, Dean, I forgot your sister worked at Tamblyn Tech. Even so, that doesn't mean she can hand us an Ursula T2 or slip into a clean room and build us a microchip."

"Actually, it kinda does," said Dean with a sigh. "She's the R&D director now."

"Serious? No way! When did that happen?"

Mitch took over the smartboard and googled "Samantha Chambers." The first link led to a picture of Samantha, with CC Tamblyn herself, being interviewed at last year's TechCrunch Disrupt conference. The second link led to Samantha's profile on the Tamblyn Tech corporate site. Her smiling face appeared, looking very much like Dean, only slimmer and prettier, and with longer hair. The contact info beneath the image displayed the title, "Director of Research and Development."

"Well, what do you know?" said Wayne. "Not surprising, really. She's a genius."

"Yeah," Dean replied, "Everyone keeps reminding me."

Mitch patted his friend's shoulder. "It might work out. She's not that bad."

"You didn't grow up with her," Dean countered.

"True, but she still reached out, despite growing up with *you*." This made Dean laugh, so Mitch continued. "All we have to do is collect the mail, shovel the walk, and mow the lawn when she's gone, which she will be—a lot. Tamblyn keeps her on the road. It's a sweet deal, really," said Mitch.

Dean shook his head. "You know if I ask her, she's gonna wanna help. I mean, like, directly. She'll poke her nose in and give advice and criticize everything and just not leave us alone."

"She won't be there, dude! And if she is, maybe that's what we need. I mean, look around in here. This isn't just sloppy, this is kind of a mess. Maybe we need someone riding us. It'd force us to be better. It'll make sure we nail this."

"He's got a point, Chambers," said Bische. "Gaining control of your work might be worth eating a little crow."

Dean relented. "Okay. I'll talk to her. But this is temporary, Mitch. After we work out the kinks, we find our own spot. Agreed?"

Mitch and Wayne nodded to each other, and then to Dean, both said, "Agreed!" The three of them gathered in a circle and shook hands to seal the deal.

Bische gave them a moment to celebrate consolidating their plan, then said, "Now that that's settled, let's see if we can meet the minimal requirements outlined in Hayman's letter." He pulled it up on the smartboard once more, deliberately rereading each line. He paused at the last paragraph, a smile slowly spreading across his face. "Very sly, Leland," he said aloud. "Very sly indeed."

"What do you see, Doc?" asked Mitch.

"The last paragraph. Notice that it says 'any assembled, functioning version' of the device. There's your out. Disassemble it, make the new one off-campus, and you should be home free. Mitch you can help me with that. Hirano, you focus on saving the data collected today for use with your new setup off-site. And Chambers?"

"Yeah, Doc?"

"How about you clean this mess up."

They each set off with their respective tasks. Bische and Mitch searched the back room for a container large enough to hold the device. They found one in the dish's original two-handled box. Bische removed the molded, packing foam to make room for the battery and magna-coils. Then Mitch undid the clamps holding the dish in place and folded it down on top of the battery casing. It all just barely fit. Mitch looked a little wistfully at the box as Bische fastened the latches and stored it on a shelf in the supply room. It'd been such a big part of his life for the past month, it felt almost like a betrayal to disassemble and put it away.

"Something bothering you, Campbell?" asked Bische, breaking into Mitch's reverie.

Mitch thought a moment, then said, "I'm glad we have a plan. But... having the plan doesn't mean it'll work."

"True. It's the actual work that makes things work. Now you know why I always demand it," said Bische.

"Right," said Mitch. He picked up a broom and started sweeping up the refuse of the many Sutter's Pub meals still littering the floor. Bische watched him and hoped that the work would be enough.

CHAPTER 14

Lots of Math

C hung stood miserably at a server rack in the back of the tiny sub-basement room, longing for a chair to sit in and wondering for the hundredth time why he hadn't simply ignored the odd data stream he'd seen on his screen a month ago. Had he kept his mouth shut and logged it as normal data, he'd be sitting down right now, reading his black market novels, back to his boring life, which he missed terribly.

Instead, he'd spent the past month standing hours at a time in front of this rack, his feet howling, blindly chasing a unicorn he was sure they would never catch. Briefly, at the start of the month, he had thought that Kyung might save the day. The odd collection of discarded tech he'd procured—data disks, a router, network cables, and a transmitting switch—made a kind of logical sense, as did the sensor harness he built and the monitoring software he used to test it all daily. The LED indicators, data readouts, and coded beeps from the server rack dazzled and impressed Hyun, who visited the sub-basement throughout each day, seeking continual updates.

"Are we close?" he'd ask.

"Closer," Kyung would say.

The more insistent Hyun became, the more inspired Kyung was to add "improvements" to their setup, embellishing their daily reports with intricate diagrams, and welding odd pieces of hardware to the rack. By the third week, for Chung, just a junior engineer, these improvements were all a bit overwhelming,

86

which was when he realized that overwhelming Hyun had been Kyung's plan all along. Stepping back, he saw that all they'd built was a glorified server, on top of which sat flashing lights, useless equipment, and literal bells and whistles. Kyung banked on Hyun's short attention span as the means of their salvation, hoping that the lack of body faxing, but preponderance of dull data, would bore him enough to cancel the project. But Hyun's relentless financial ambition left him excited about every new addition. As the dark, limitless depths of his unyielding greed became obvious, Kyung's attempts to thwart his attention lost focus and imagination. Chung despaired.

Kyung's latest attempt tried to "solve" their problems with a receiving switch. He told Chung to attach it to a rack near the front of the room, along with a steel plate and a mass of sensors wired haphazardly into a breadboard. It was ridiculous, but Chung did it anyway, as the rack was near one of the only two chairs in the room. Then Hyun showed up with a body scanner, which was equally stupid, as if the scanner was the final, miraculous piece to the puzzle of sending one's atoms through the network. But Chung would gladly have wired an egg timer into the rack for more time in the chair, so he hooked the scanner up, too. His respite ended when Hyun succumbed to his management instincts and decided to "supervise" Chung and Kyung to speed up results. Thus began the long series of futile "tests" to send things from the back of the room to the front.

Today's thing was a potato. Chung smothered chuckles as Hyun shouted idiotic commands at him from the front of the room. "Hold the scanner closer." "Check the scanner plug." "Is the switch turned on?" *He will tell me to kick the tires next*, Chung thought to himself, *and the potato will rot into vodka before it flies through the ether across the room.*

He'd been holding the scanner in his cramping hands, at various angles, for the past three hours and couldn't tell which was worse—the boredom or the pain. Settling on boredom, he decided to amuse himself by freeing a wire near the scan button, rigging it to shoot an electrical arc directly at the potato. Now, Hyun's useless commands were rewarded with pops and sparks that Chung pointed out with false excitement and hidden glee. "It's moving!" he yelled, wide-eyed, pointing at the sizzling spud with his free hand while covertly zapping it with his scanner hand. Hyun let out a ragged cheer and bent expectantly over the steel plate, waiting for the potato to appear. Chung laughed at this, but stopped short when Kyung stared shrewdly at his scanner hand and shot him an annoyed glare.

Brrrp, brrrp. Chung's workstation, silent and abandoned these past weeks, chirped. Chung, conditioned over long months by the sound, looked toward his monitor quite involuntarily and saw the same crazy pattern that had started this whole mess spooling out across it. Dropping the scanner and all pretense with the potato, he walked back to his desk. "Guys," he said. "I think it's happening again."

Kyung darted over to the workstation, escaped out of the "Acknowledge," and typed frantically. "What are you doing?" demanded Hyun. "Get back over here!"

"No, you fool! We can trace it," Kyung said, his fingers pounding the keyboard. "If the packet's just starting, we can track it back to its source." He typed a few more commands, and then sat back to watch as a line of numbers and dots appeared parallel to the scrolling data. "Hmmm," he said, staring intently at the screen, the thoughtful sound rising from him like a rumble. "It's crazy."

"What? What do you see?" said Hyun, moving excitedly to his side.

"This is definitely a lot more data than last time. It might even be..." He paused and counted the separate, snaking strings of codes and numbers. "...five. Five people this time, faxing themselves simultaneously."

"That's fantastic!" shouted Hyun. "A whole group? It's like an amusement park ride! Whatever they are doing, it must be working perfectly!"

The flow of the data and tracer both slowed, converging into one line of pulsing dots until finally it stopped all together, displaying only a single address.

"Manse!" *Victory!* Kyung shouted, pumping his arms over his head. "We have the source!"

"Don't stop!" said Hyun, punching Kyung in the back. "Look it up! Where is it from?"

The "Acknowledge" popped up again. Kyung hit "Escape" and typed some more. "Looks like 'physics.mines.edu.' Perfect. It's a school." He pasted the URL into a browser. Images of students wearing protective eye gear, examining petri dishes, and working drill presses appeared. "Even better. It's a science school."

"Why is that better?" asked Hyun.

"No secrets. Science is open. Scientists brag. They *want* to tell you what they're doing. Whoever built the body fax would have written about it. I'd bet on it." Kyung clicked randomly on links and images, his initial triumphant expression transforming into a frown. Finally, grunting in frustration, he pushed up from the workstation. "I can't read a thing on that site."

"Let me try," said Chung, plopping thankfully down into the vacated chair. "My English is pretty good." He immediately noticed a search field in the upper right corner and said, "Tell me a keyword to look for."

"Body fax!" said Hyun excitedly.

"That's our name for it, genius," growled Kyung. "This is science. We need science terms." Kyung paused, thinking. "Try the English word for 'transmit.'"

Chung typed it in. Zero results. They tried others—conveyance, matter transfer, matter channel, data tunnel. Zero results. Then Hyun suggested, "Try 'ride.'" Chung typed it in, expecting the same empty page to return, but was surprised to see exactly one result—"Ride a light beam and see the world." Chung followed the link to a Physics Department article about three friends who built "an amazing travel machine" out of a car battery and a satellite dish. At the top of the article was Mitch's flyer—"Big Blue is calling YOU". At the bottom of the article was a link to the paper published in the school's quarterly journal—"Photon Propagation Cessation Using Complementary Electromagnetic Fields Forms Stable, Matter Transmitting Tunnels." Chung clicked the link and was prompted to save a document.

"Open it! Open it!" hissed Hyun.

Chung, his hand shaking in anticipation, had to try twice before opening the document properly, but once he had opened it and started reading, its treasures were self-evident. There it all was—diagrams, a parts list, and instructions. They'd found the right document! Kyung and Hyun whooped, hugging each other like long-lost cousins. "This is it!" they cried, pounding each other on the back and dancing around the room. Chung paged through the document, his excitement fading into worry. Yes, there was a parts list and instructions, but they were followed by complicated diagrams and lengthy calculations.

"Guys," he said. "It's a lot of math."

Hyun paused, breathless from dancing. "Aren't there pictures? It can't all be numbers."

"There's pictures, yes, but... I don't know." He pointed at a diagram of the battery hooked into the dish and then beneath that a photo of the dish and blue funnel. "I can't see how anyone could travel through that."

Kyung and Hyun crouched down to peer over Chung's shoulder.

"Maybe the bed spring there expands," said Kyung, pointing to a magna-coil highlighted at the edge of the diagram.

Hyun smacked Kyung on the back of the head. "Idiot! Obviously that charges the battery. Chung is right. They must zap you with the dish."

Chung shook his head. "I don't think that is how it happens either."

Kyung sighed. "Okay," he said. "Let's just get the parts and assemble it. We can do math later. Let's just make it and turn it on."

"Alright," Chung agreed, though he still was not completely convinced. "But how will you get the parts?"

"The bed springs we get from Bong-Chol's bunk."

"Aha!" said Hyun. "I told you it was a good thing he'd shipped out."

Kyung continued, "I know a guy in an RV park who can get us a smallish dish."

"What about the battery?" asked Chung.

"Even easier," said Kyung, with a grin. "The car battery we take from Hyun's car."

"Wonderful!" said Hyun and then, "wait... what?"

"Don't worry," said Kyung, clapping Hyun heartily on the back. "Once we get this working, you won't need your car again."

"You're right!" Hyun laughed, grabbing Kyung's hand in a hearty handshake. "Manse, partner!"

"Manse!" yelled Kyung.

They danced. Chung read. And the last "Acknowledge" popup blinked forlornly on the screen. After ten minutes, it expired, opened a funneling port, and shunted the data packet on through.

CHAPTER 15

Thwarted

Hubert, the investment group in tow, strode confidently toward Bische's lab the last day of term, a copy of President Hayman's letter neatly folded in his suit pocket. Any doubts he'd had that Bische would hand over the device were overshadowed by his immense desire to gloat. Hubert was sure he still had the upper hand and that the device was his to do with as he wished, the great Bische be damned. He went over in his mind exactly what he planned to say, the barbs he'd use to twist the knife. Oh, how he would savor the look of defeat and embarrassment in Bische's eyes as he forced the Golden Boy to cough up Campbell's accidental goldmine. Hubert would take what was rightfully his from Bische's impotent, overrated hands and saunter straight into the history books, pausing first at the bank.

"You'll rue the day you ever insulted me," Hubert muttered as he thrust open Bische's lab door.

*****

Bische barely acknowledged Hubert and crew's entrance. He sat in his back office, feet up on the desk, eating a burrito and swiping through the morning news on his tablet. He looked up once, past Hubert, at the group behind him. Returning to the news, he said coolly, "Why the entourage?"

"They are investment partners of the school," said Hubert, stepping into Bische's line of site, belligerent as ever. He continued blathering, but Bische ignored him, choosing to scan the group instead. With the exception of Hubert, they all seemed a bit too fit. His eyes landed on the tall, imposing woman at the back of the group. She was slim, but sturdy looking, alert and watchful, looming over the others. Seeing herself under scrutiny, she graced Bische with a shrewd, amused smile. He immediately got the sense that, had she wanted to, she could easily snap any one of them in half—particularly Hubert. This thought made him chuckle.

"...laugh as you may. You always think you're so clever. You flaunt your relationship with the president, your inventions, your Fisher prize, as if you're the only genius on campus. Well," Hubert retrieved a letter from his pocket and held it in front of him like a talisman, "you're most decidedly not! This letter proves you aren't the hot shot you wish you were. Times have changed, Dr. Bische. It's a new day. And the one lording it over you from now on is going to be me!"

Hubert marched triumphantly out of the office and back to the lab, but stopped short. He rushed to the front table, pulled open drawers, looked back at Mitch's bare bench and ran to it, throwing open the cabinet below it, staring gape-mouthed into the opening, seemingly surprised that it, too, was empty. Bische took a last bite of his burrito, wiped his hands, and left his office. The watchful woman caught Bische's eye and cocked an eyebrow. Bische winked back.

Hubert whirled toward him with frantic eyes. "Where is it? Where's Campbell's device? Where have you taken it?"

Bische busied himself with closing the drawers Hubert had pulled open, pausing at the junk drawer to put back its cables and odd bits of wire. Addressing Hubert he said, "To answer your questions in order: gone, disassembled, and irrelevant."

"I don't believe it," said Hubert. "You've hidden it. Tell me where!"

"There was no need to hide it, Hubert. It had served its purpose and is no longer necessary. The pieces are packed and thoroughly useless to you or anyone. Better things are now in play."

"Speak plainly! What do you mean?"

Bische sighed. "My apologies, Hubert. I should be considerate of your speed, such that it is." The comment drew quiet snickers from the investors. A light shade of red crept up from Hubert's collar into his face. "It means that the device doesn't exist as such anymore. It's back to random pieces, all boxed and locked away. The boys have started over, elsewhere, with their own materials, on their own time. Simple as that."

Bische reached into his breast pocket and produced a black, plastic, oblong case, about half the size and slimness of a cell phone, and with a connector port jutting out one side. Bische held it up for them all to see. "This, Hubert, is the mobile Canopy. The boys are calling it a 'Jump!Go'. Catchy, don't you think?"

"You will hand it over this instant." Wilkins reached for the device, but Bische easily sidestepped.

"I think not."

"That was made with school materials on school property. This letter states it belongs to me—er, the school." Wilkins shook the piece of paper for emphasis.

"That 'letter' can go to hell. Whoever wrote it—you, I imagine—was wholly misinformed and, frankly, a bit of a prick."

"I'll have your job!" Wilkins fumed, his face now beet red. Specks of foamy spittle built up at the corners of his mouth, ejecting forcefully after every other word.

"You will continue to have nothing." From the start of their exchange, Bische had seemed mildly amused, but now his voice was cold. He'd grown tired of Wilkins' bluster and threats. Stepping away from the junk drawer, he faced Hubert directly, allowing his full 6'2" tower over the flustered dean. "If you swallowed your spit and shut your face for five minutes, you would have heard what I just said. All of this work occurred off-campus. They got their own funding, sourced their own parts, and built this nifty piece of hardware—fine craftsmanship, I might add. They will sell it to you for $99, $50 if you are a student. And if you want me to hand it over to an untalented hack such as yourself to take credit for, you will either have to pay me $99 or fight me for it. Which are you game for, Hubert? Me... I'm looking forward to that fight."

Bische smiled, his expression devoid of any mirth or warmth. Hubert shuddered, and the color drained from his face. "Have it your way," he murmured, then spun quickly on his heel and left. The rest of the investment group hurried after him. *Guess that didn't go quite the way Hubert planned*, Bische thought.

He'd returned to tidying the junk drawer when behind him he heard, "$99, you say?"

It was the watchful woman. He wasn't surprised.

"Shouldn't you be chasing after Dr. Wilkins?" said Bische with undisguised disdain.

"Oh, hang Hubert. His interests are his own. I, on the other hand, support the free market. I can help those young men get out of the garage and into real industry."

"Nice story," said Bische. He continued arranging the contents of the drawer.

She worked too hard to adopt a look of innocence. "What do you mean?"

Bische turned to face her. "You are entirely too fit and far too intelligent to be hanging out with Hubert," he said, crossing his arms and leaning back against the lecture table.

"It takes one to know one," she replied wryly, wisely deciding to drop whatever act she been putting on.

Bische was taken aback. *Well, isn't she a sharp tack?* To keep the conversation off himself, he said, "So I take it your presence has little to do with investments."

"Not the traditional kind, Hubert's interests notwithstanding. Here's my card."

" 'Travers and Lake,'" he read. "'Business Intelligence.' With a Kipling address, no less. Next to the Federal Building?"

"Observant," she said.

His fingers traced the card until they detected a raised area on the back. He turned it over. Embossed in the upper right corner, like an Easter egg made for him to find, was the head of a bald eagle, on a white shield, embedded in a blue sphere. Bische's smile grew wider as he realized what it was. "Interesting insignia. You're

Travers, I take it?"

"One and the same."

He knew that name, though he hadn't seen or heard it in years. He studied her while she regarded him, but only got the sense that she was bemused and knew nothing about him beyond what she could see. She did not resemble the person he remembered from long ago, at least not in ways that he would expect. The name must be a coincidence, he decided, but testing the waters, he continued, "I'm familiar with your Agency. We've had some dealings in the past. Any mention in your records?"

"Nothing formal. But there's always talk." Her eyes twinkled, and a secret knowledge seemed to pass between them. They shook hands, her skin smooth and warm at the surface, but underneath, her grip felt as hard as steel. Snap Hubert in half, indeed. "Keep in touch," she said, gathering her purse and notebook. "We'd love to hear back from you or Mitch. Sooner's better than later."

"Come now. Whatever Hubert's doing, it can't be that bad."

"Oh, you'd be surprised what bozos like Wilkins stumble into." She turned to leave, then looked back and winked. "Or maybe *you* wouldn't be."

At that, he laughed. "Thanks for the card. Perhaps Campbell or I will use it."

"Don't wait too long," she said. "Hubert won't." And then she was gone.

Bische tucked her card into a corner of his junk drawer and mulled over her parting words. He couldn't imagine that Hubert would be involved in something insidious enough to damage Mitch's plans, but if it drew the Agency's attention, his lack of imagination was beside the point. *Time to batten the hatches*, he thought. *Hubert can't cause trouble with what he can't get.* The facility manager's office was right next door to his. "Afternoon, Lainie," he said, poking his head through her door. "Can you reset the key card access control list for my lab?"

CHAPTER 16

The Benefactor

Hubert scurried back upstairs toward his office, but had no idea what he'd do once he got there. Campbell, defected; the device, gone. He couldn't deny it—this was all a complete disaster. And to be laughed at by the investment group in front of the hated Bische? That was the ultimate insult. But there was no time to dwell on it. He had to think and think fast.

He called Christian. Maybe they could use Campbell's paper to cobble together a copy of the device. If the Campbell idiot could do it, surely Christian, who was much more capable, could do it too. Christian's line just rang and rang, with no answer by the time Hubert reached his office. Damn the boy. Where was he? That broken arm was no excuse to shirk his duties!

He hung up angrily, fumbled for his keys, and let himself into the office. That's when he noticed the light on in the adjoining lab. *Oh, thank God*, he thought. *Christian must be here.* He threw open the door of his office, barely glancing at the lab's occupants, then immediately started rifling through the top drawer of the cabinet by the door, searching for the file with Campbell's paper. He became vaguely aware of the scent of cigarettes. Odd to smell that, as Christian did not smoke. Must have been one of the students from the last class.

"Good, you're still here," he yelled out into the lab. "You didn't answer your phone. We've got trouble. Campbell's device is locked away. We lost our claim to it. We'll have to build one ourselves to keep those damned Koreans at bay."

"I am sorry to hear that, Doctor." Hubert doubled over, like he'd been punched in the stomach. That wasn't Christian. The voice—cold, sarcastic, and slightly accented—belonged unmistakably to his Korean investor.

Hubert spun around and stammered, "How—? What are you—?" Unconsciously, he sidled to the right of the file cabinet drawer, putting it between himself and the intruder.

"It disappoints me that you do not know me. People say my voice is... distinctive." The man was slight, dressed in a sharp, thin-legged, black suit and a gray, silk, collarless shirt, buttoned all the way to the top. His jet-black hair was shaved on either side, and spiked on top with gel. A pair of black sun glasses adorned his pocket. He leaned, half-sat, against the edge of the lab bench closest to Hubert's office, he legs partially tucked into the space beneath the bench. Another black-suited man stood just a step behind him, taller, wearing a white-collared shirt and gray tie, with sunglasses, his hands clasped in front, at a kind of attention, like he was the first man's bodyguard.

The first man stood up, unfurling with an ease that reminded Hubert of something—not a cat, but some... creature... more graceful, decidedly deadly.

"I'll formally introduce myself," he said, dropping his cigarette to the floor and stubbing it out beneath the toe of a perfectly shined, expensive-looking shoe.

"People call me Geomi, The Spider."

"How did you get in here? What do you want? "Hubert regained his voice, though only slightly. What he hoped would sound commanding and indignant instead sounded hoarse and whiny to his own ears. *Oh, lord, they've come to kill me.*

"We came through the door, Dr. Wilkins. And we want what is ours," he said evenly. "Our employer's celebration is approaching. We had hoped to retrieve the gift you promised. But what did you say? Did I hear that you don't have it?"

"I can explain—" Hubert began, but the man—the assassin?—raised a hand to cut him off.

"It is good that you can. Our benefactor would like to hear you explain."

"What?!" Hubert exclaimed. "Is he here too?" He looked around, even more frightened. Surely someone would have noticed such a group entering the building. Even more so than these two, the man's employer would stand out. Hubert couldn't afford to be seen with any of them, but that went double for this "benefactor."

"It is your good luck that he is not. Our benefactor can be quite physically... imposing. So we must be satisfied with only the phone." The Spider reached across the cabinet drawer and pulled out Hubert's special phone, concealed within an inside pocket of his suit jacket. The action made Hubert's skin crawl as it proved without a doubt that he'd been watched. That was the only way this Spider could know the secret place he kept it.

"We will call him now and you two will speak."

"Absolutely not!" said Hubert. The Spider raised an eyebrow, his bored expression turning unexpectedly hard. To Hubert, it seemed that the man's body coiled inward, his relaxed stance tightened, poised to strike. Reflexively, Hubert stepped back, raising his hands to protect his face. The Spider advanced, slowly, backing Hubert up until his legs brushed the edge of the office chair. The Spider's associate rounded the chair, roughly pushing Hubert down into it.

"I—I mean—someone will find out," Hubert whined. "I'm well known. He—all of you—your cover will be blown if you're seen with me."

"This phone is untraceable, correct?"

"Y-yes," Hubert gulped out.

"You called me many times on it." He paused to gesture around the lab. "No one is here to expose us. One more phone call should be fine."

The Spider typed in the code. *He knew that too! How much did they know?* Hubert wondered, panicking. *Who else have they told?!*

"Before I call, I must say, the benefactor is not happy. Disappointment... angers him, makes him take things away, especially when you don't give him what he wants. "

The Spider's hand flicked out, quick as a serpent's tongue, and Hubert felt a searing pain spread across his crotch.

"He can take small things, like your tiny balls. Or he can take large things..." again, the hand struck, this time the pain burning into Hubert's gut. "...like your intestines. So be careful, Dr. Wilkins. Think before you speak."

The Spider dialed a number, propped the phone up on the light stand at the edge of Hubert's desk, and hit the speaker button. A woman answered.

"Ye, Jin Ae," he said. The Spider and the woman traded rapid Korean, none of which Hubert understood aside from 'American' and his own name. Then the woman said a final thing, which Hubert took to mean "hang on" or "one moment," and a sudden silence permeated the room. After several seconds, a new voice spoke over the speaker, not as accented as The Spider, a little higher, and surprisingly friendly.

"Hello, Dr. Wilkins! So glad to finally meet you."

Hubert, feeling sick and breathless from the gut punch, just stared miserably at the phone. He debated staying silent, on the off chance this call might be recorded, but a slight twitch from The Spider's hand prodded him to speak.

"H-hello?"

"There you are! You promised me something, Doctor. I take promises seriously, I hope you understand. Geomi?"

"Ye, Jidoja." The Spider and his benefactor traded even more rapid Korean. The Spider retrieved his own phone from his pocket and poked and swiped on it throughout their conversation. Eventually he found whatever he'd been looking for.

Holding the phone up to Hubert's face, he said, "The benefactor asked me to show you this."

The image displayed a man's legs, presumably The Spider's, standing over another man—not the missing Christian, thankfully—who stared glassy eyed into the camera. The other man's face was bloodied, and as the Spider scrolled the picture up slowly, Hubert saw the man's stomach cavity exposed, completely disemboweled. Hubert suppressed a retch.

"Do you understand, Dr. Wilkins?" the benefactor asked, as if The Spider had merely shown him a mathematical proof.

"I—I understand," Hubert said, his voice a hoarse whisper.

"Good! I expect great things from you, Doctor. You have more time, but not forever. Do not disappoint me." The line went dead.

"Two weeks, Dr. Wilkins," said The Spider. He nodded once to his associate, and without another word, they both left, and yet the various pains Hubert felt—in his balls, his guts, his psyche—remained. Two weeks. Was that enough time to save his life? His gaze wandered out into the lab, landing on the toolbox. And just like that, he knew what he had to do.

CHAPTER 17

Guard Duty

H is suffering is incomplete," said Dear Leader, one eye peering out at Jin Ae from behind the large easel standing across the room in the North Palace's main study. Jin, Dear Leader's aide and bodyguard, was at that moment straddling an unfortunate actor dressed as a South Korean General, trapping him on his knees in a perfect arm lock and forcing him to kiss a picture of Dear Leader's grandfather, the Supreme Leader. Dear Leader's tone was more analytical than malicious as he looked back and forth between the canvas and Jin, trying to determine why his mind's eye and the scene before him did not entirely match.

The poor actor. Jin knew he hadn't planned on this. He was plump, young, and reminded her of her brother Chung. Somehow, he'd been convinced that his assignment today was to entertain their ruler with heroic selections from Dear Leader's own plays. When he'd arrived, he proudly showed her the slips of passages he had memorized, the voices he could imitate, the many costumes he'd prepared. He'd seemed so idealistic. She listened, not having the heart to tell him that none of it would be required, that Dear Leader merely needed a model to pose for his horrific painting, "Grandfather's Greatest Hour."

She felt guilty now, looking down on his round, miserable face, a sharp contrast to his initial, joyful excitement, only thirty minutes ago.

*****

"What an honor this is!" the young actor exclaimed when Jin opened the front door. "I have never seen the palace!" He swiveled his head to and fro, gawking at Dear Leader's haphazardly assembled treasures, tastelessly strewn throughout the Great Hall, like expensive hoarder trash. He happily chatted away as she led him to the velvet red carpet in the center of Dear Leader's study. She nodded absently at his stories before helping him into the South Korean General's top-coat, the left breast of which was still encrusted with blood. She patiently waited for Dear Leader to enter, and when he did, said quietly to the young man, "You must kneel and kiss that picture while I hurt you."

"Hmmm..." he said, quizzically, sifting through his pages, "I do not see that scene here—Aaaargh!" She swiped his leg, knocked him down, and applied the arm lock, regretting the need for such violence, but bound by duty to continue, despite his pitiful yelps and desperate attempts to break free. "Hold still!" she hissed, putting her mouth close to his ear. "It will hurt more if you struggle."

He managed to prop one knee beneath him, but Jin stomped the back of his leg and tightened the arm lock. "Don't move! Pok will shoot you if you try to get away." She gestured to Pok, the other guard, who promptly walked over and pressed the mouth of his rifle against the back of the man's head. That stopped the wriggling. Her mouth again at the actor's ear, Jin said "Cry loudly now. Do as I say and I will ease up on you." The actor, already whimpering at this point, started blubbering in earnest.

Dear Leader, who had been occupied arranging his paints and brushes, looked out upon the scene and said, "Good, good. Very realistic. Push him closer to Grandfather." Jin sighed, but complied with the command, shoving the actor's face forward until his lips touched the edge of Supreme Leader's image. It was an awkward position, forcing Jin to twist his arm farther out its socket in order to reach. The youth howled, and tears rolled down his cheeks like rain. Dear Leader chuckled, his smile growing wider. "Excellent," he said, squeezing paints onto his palette and picking up his brush to begin.

*****

That was thirty minutes ago. Over time, the actor had settled into a fairly one-dimensional display of misery as Jin's grip loosened and his fear subsided. Jin, knowing Dear Leader's offhand cruelty, shook the actor repeatedly and hissed warnings, urging him to improve his performance, but to no avail. Now, his lapse had drawn Dear Leader's scrutiny. "More pain please, Jin," he told her, settling on that as the solution to his dissatisfaction with the scene. "I must see the agony to draw it properly."

Jin knew she could break the actor's arm in such a way as to make his pain real and unending, without causing him to faint. It would be easy, just a quick snap, and then her job would be done for the rest of the session. But in truth, he was sweet. He'd done nothing to warrant the break, and his face, so young and freshly scrubbed... it was too much like Chung's. Still, she was in no position to completely disobey Dear Leader's order. Going for the action that would yield the most effect with the least damage, she pointed the actor's pinky finger into an unnatural position and squeezed. The crack reminded her of the crunch of a lobster shell, the actor's shriek like the howl of a dog.

The phone chose that moment to ring. "Ah, the call we have been waiting for," said Dear Leader. He motioned toward the actor and said to Pok, "Clear that away." He wiped his hands on a towel draped near the easel, took a seat at his desk and said to Jin, "Answer it."

Pok closed the door behind him, but Jin could still hear the actor's screams as Pok dragged him away. *You tried to warn him*, she told herself, but knowing that did little to relieve her anger at Dear Leader for forcing her to be cruel. She stepped around the desk and picked up the phone.

"What is it?" she said, her voice harsh and quick.

"Hello, Jin Ae." As expected, it was Geomi, The Spider, one of Dear Leader's Level 1 operatives.

"You didn't answer the question," Jin replied.

Geomi chuckled. "We skip the niceties, then. I have captured the American rat, Dr. Wilkins. He sits frightened before me, as our ruler ordered. He is ready for Dear Leader to speak."

"And where is the device?"

"Not here. But I have seen it in action. It is all that he says it is."

"So stop wasting time. Get the device, and then break his neck."

Geomi laughed outright. "It is not that simple. I think he can still get it. And perhaps we should not be so quick to discard him. We may need him once the device is ours."

Jin grunted, displeased. Geomi was a good operative, but he could be too tricky. *One day, his tricks could kill us all,* she thought. Swallowing her disgust, she said, "I will tell him." She muted the phone and turned to Dear Leader. "Geomi has the American, but does not have the device."

"Pity," said Dear Leader. "Why has he not stolen it and snapped the man's neck?"

"He says we still need him."

"That is doubtful, but I will talk to the doctor. Geomi can show him the picture. Unmute and put on speaker."

Jin did as she was told. Dear Leader spoke in English, directly to the American. She did not listen. It mattered little what he said to the imbecile. Geomi would get the device with or without him. She was more struck by the way Dear Leader spoke to the man, his words full of malice, with an undercurrent of insanity, but on the surface sounding completely friendly.

Her eye caught the result of Dear Leader's painting session. The picture was mostly true to the scene she and the actor had recreated. The actor, as the symbol of South Korea, groveled before a picture of the Supreme Leader, and writhed in extreme agony, as he kissed the image with bloodied lips. Dear Leader's cherubic face appeared where Jin's should have been, grinning ferociously as he beat down on "South Korea", his torso shirtless, muscular, and glistening. His head was bathed in a halo of a sun beam that streamed through a window behind him. The shaft pierced the heart of an apparition of his own father, Great Leader, who stood far off to the side, saluting, intense, and unsmiling. It was all insane, of course, the drawing of a madman, and yet Dear Leader continued speaking reasonably to the American. Jin knew he was anything but reasonable, and she wondered, not for the first time, if she would eventually need to kill him.

"Good! I expect great things from you, Doctor. You have more time, but not forever. Do not disappoint me." The call was wrapping up. Dear Leader motioned to her again and she hung up on the hapless doctor. No sooner had the line gone dead then there was a knock on the door.

"Get that, would you?"

Jin bristled. *This is what I'm reduced to*, she thought, making her way to the door. *Posing with actors, answering phones, opening doors. All the while stopping my hands from throttling the evil little troll. I am a warrior. I should be in battle, commanding a battalion, waging the fight. And yet, I am trapped here, by father's mistake, forced to swallow good sense, protecting a psychopath. Will he ask me for coffee next? Have me wipe his ass?* In her mind's eye she saw herself entering his jewel-encrusted bathroom with a bubbling percolator, flipping the beast off the toilet, and pouring boiling dark roast up his considerably sized butt hole.

It was a pleasing image, but she had scant seconds to enjoy it. She opened the door to see Pok presenting Jek Ru, the scheming wretch from Level 2 Monitoring. Jek was a good inch shorter than Jin. He was a wiry little man, dressed neatly, with slicked-back hair, cruel eyes, and sharp ferret teeth. He snaked his head around Jin, searching for Dear Leader, both hands clasped tightly around his ever present satchel, no doubt containing the latest vital intelligence Dear Leader had not asked for, but which Jek continually volunteered, hoping to curry favor.

Jin could not understand why Dear Leader continued to entertain the toad, who was far too fawning and disingenuous for Jin's taste. Jin suspected that Jek supplied the "intelligence" which had led to her father's disgrace, Chung's conscription, and her current indignity standing guard at Dear Leader's side. Her only consolation was the sure knowledge that Dear Leader would grow weary of Jek, as he did of all informants over time. *That will be a glorious day*, she thought, *when this hateful cur finally gets his.*

She looked at Pok, who'd made no effort to re-enter the room. "What?" she growled.

Pok shrugged. "He says he has—"

"—vital information for the Exalted," interrupted Jek, raising his voice and speaking directly into the room, all the while craning his neck around Jin, wanting to catch Dear Leader's attention before she could send him away.

The plan worked, as Dear Leader called out, "Jek Ru? Is that you I hear?"

"Yes, Exalted!" shouted Jek, speaking completely out of turn. He sniffed at Jin disdainfully, his face beaming at his victory. Jin rolled her eyes.

"Let him in, Jin. He is expected."

Full of self-importance, Jek brushed past Jin and presented himself to Dear Leader.

"Sit down, Jek Ru." Dear Leader motioned to the chair directly in front of his desk. Eyes glittering with anticipation, he asked, "Did you bring it?"

Jek nodded vigorously and said, "The Unity Project, my Leader..." he paused "...and more!" He pulled a padded box, a tablet, and several sheets of paper from his satchel, arranging them along the edge of Dear Leader's desk like fragrant pies on the sill to cool.

With greedy hands, Dear Leader pulled the box to himself and lifted the lid, his face aglow with avaricious desire. "Ah!" he said, his eyebrows lifted high. "It is smaller than before!"

His piggy hand reached in and held aloft a square, charcoal-colored disk, no larger than a notepad and about half as thick. An indentation at the back of the disk could have been a switch, but that was the square's only functional indicator. This *is the special project?* thought Jin. *It looks like a bathroom tile.*

"The science team compacted the formulae, for easier carry, your Eminence," Jek explained. "But it is more potent as well. See!" Jek sifted through his stack of papers until he uncovered a picture. He offered it to Jin, curtly waving it between her and Dear Leader, the command unspoken, the insult obvious. She remained at attention, countering his gesture with a stony glare that forced him to retreat from his foolishness and hand the picture to Dear Leader himself.

At first glance, the image appeared to be an empty field, but then Jin caught glimpses of crumpled girders, rimless tires, and amorphous slag. The empty field had been a town or city, she realized, the gray lumps the remnants of buildings and vehicles, the odd bits of white sticks no doubt the ex-inhabitants' bones. *How could something so small cause so much destruction*, wondered Jin, as a wave of revulsion swept over her. She had a sudden impulse to smack the disk from Dear Leader's fat hand, but she fought it down, watching helplessly as he admired the square once more, like a precious jewel, before putting it back in the box.

"What else?" he asked. Jek shuffled excitedly through more papers until he reached a thick printout crowded with data.

"This, my Leader. A magnificent discovery befitting your Greatness. A new means of travel!"

Jin and Dear Leader exchanged looks.

"Explain," said Dear Leader.

"I can do better. I can show you." Jek switched on the tablet. Data scrolled across the display in a continuous stream.

"It started with this data pack, Superior One. Last week, it passed through the desk of the lazy commander, Hyun Shik, who did not acknowledge it as he should, and so it appeared in my feed. I knew right away it was too big to be ignored, so I fed it into the Wolfram modeler."

Jek, clearly enjoying himself, tapped another button which opened a popup that read, "Retrieving Model," and then, "Model Verified".

"It was stunning what came back, Your Greatness. Not just an analysis, but also this!"

Milking the scene for all it was worth, Jek hit the button a last time with a flourish. The popup disappeared, replaced by a white cursor that blinked out a series of random dots, working from the top of the 3D display, spitting dots from left to right. Slowly, a new image emerged, filling the blank area above the tablet.

"A head," Dear Leader whispered, his eyes wide.

"Yes!" said Jek. "A young man's head. Full size. See the expression. He himself seems surprised."

"Did you track the packet?"

"Immediately. It's from America, a place called Golden, Colorado. It started there, then ended at another place—Colorado Springs. All in a second—maybe less. The boy traveled, it's clear. In an instant!" Dear Leader remained calm, but caught Jin's eye. She knew this could be nothing else but evidence of Dr. Wilkin's promised device.

"And have you told anyone else?" Dear Leader asked. Jin nodded at Pok. They both moved to flank Jek, one on either side.

"Only you, my Leader. It was imperative for me to show you this and warn you about the others."

Dear Leader held up a hand, and Jin motioned to Pok to stop. "Hyun Shik, you mean?" he asked.

"Yes, your Eminence. Even now, he and his lackeys are in the Monitoring sub-basement. They were seen carrying equipment into the elevator, but then disappeared for many days. Finally, today there were more packets, smaller, but still with the biological model. They have built something!"

Jek swiped the boy's head to the side, and it was replaced with 3D renderings of a mouse and then a chicken, both seemingly being squished and stretched, fright imprinted on their faces. Jin felt sick at the sight. "These originate, without question, from the router in the sub-basement."

"Where do they end?"

"They don't. The animal packets disappear, but then do not reappear. Hyun may eventually figure out why. But I doubt it. He is an idiot, as well as a treasonous dog."

"It would be good to have someone trustworthy who could take over this work." Dear Leader smiled thinly, then glanced again at Jin.

Jek saw his opening and leapt in. "Exactly. This is too big a thing for small minds to handle. Only superior intellects like ours can truly understand what needs to be done."

Jin waited, but knew that Jek was on shaky ground from this statement. No way would Dear Leader allow such a comparison of another to himself. Then Jek spoke again and dug himself in deeper.

"That is why I submit myself to you, Great One. I alone see the worth of this device. I alone know how it solves the problem of your Unity Project. It is I who should take command of this device." Jek stopped, his expression smug and expectant. Dear Leader did not disappoint.

"You were wise to bring this directly to me," said Dear Leader.

"Oh, yes, I know. Great minds think alike," Jek beamed.

And that was Jek Ru's next and last mistake. The thin smile remained on Dear Leader's face, yet a coldness descended upon the room, as if Jek had opened a window to let in the arctic wind.

"I appreciate your loyalty," said Dear Leader, getting up from behind his desk. "I will write a song so that none forget you. You will be remembered as a hero. Your family, rewarded with your honor." Dear Leader reached Jek and gave him a paternal pat on the back.

"Thank you, Dear Leader. You are—wait. What?" Jek had heard the words "hero" and "honor" at first. But as Jin took his satchel and Pok trained his rifle, reality began to dawn on Jek.

"Remove him," said Dear Leader, walking to the side door that led to his private quarters. "And then, Jin, return to attend me. We will pay Hyun Shik a visit."

"No!" yelled Jek, only now understanding his mistake, his overstep. "Please! I am sorry! I did not mean—No!"

Jin dragged him to the door. Jek pleaded, "Have mercy on me! Please! Jin, wait, I know your brother. I can get him promoted. Make life easy for him!"

Jin stopped. "If not for you, his life would already be easy. You have done your job, Jek Ru. Now I must do mine." She opened the door and called to the two remaining ante-chamber guards. "Dear Leader has discarded this one," she said when they arrived. "Take him."

"No! Nooo!" cried Jek as he was dragged away. Jin closed the door on his screams and firmly hoped that one of Hyun's lackeys was not her brother Chung.

CHAPTER 18

Stronger String

Chung paused to examine his handiwork. The thing was almost done. Two more screws to secure the dish, then a wire to the switch, and that should do it. He pushed the sweat away from his eyebrows and set to the screws, skeptical that the thing would work at all. They'd done their best to at least make it match the diagram from the American paper, but it still looked ridiculous to Chung. The parts list was a joke—a car battery, magnetic springs, and a mini satellite dish? The more Chung thought about it, the more he was convinced that the Americans had created the thing by accident. Nothing about the parts themselves would make a rational person, upon seeing them clustered together, think, "I could fax myself with these." It must have just been a lucky mistake.

Even so, they couldn't dispute the data which, combined with the paper, made the prospect of the thing actually working more real. Chung's only concern was for the springs the paper called "magna-coils." Unlike all of the other pieces—which Kyung and Hyun acquired by means Chung was sure he did not particularly want to know about—he'd had to make these himself. "Improvise," Kyung had suggested.

Chung did the math and realized they could approximate the same magnetic field if he infused copper wire with magnetic shards from an existing electric motor. He'd found one buried at the back of the maintenance closet of their forgotten room. Fashioning a crank out of even more motor bits, he twisted the coils down as tightly as they would go until they were compact enough to fit on either side of the battery. He'd achieved such a strong magnetic effect that each coil virtually leapt from his hands onto the sides of the battery.

"Good improvising," Kyung had said to him. Chung smiled, remembering the rare compliment, allowing himself to feel real pride for a moment. He attached the final lead to the switch and straightened up. The moment of truth had arrived. It was time to turn it on.

"Guys," he called to Kyung and Hyun, sitting on the other side of the room. They were busy arguing over the black market website they were building to sell "fares" for the travel device. So busy counting their chickens before they hatched, they did not hear Chung call out to them. He cleared his throat and called louder. "Guys! I think it's done."

This got their attention. They trotted to the back of the room. "Turn it on. Turn it on!" Hyun demanded, eyes wide, nearly salivating with anticipation.

"Okay. Stand back." He reached behind the dish and flipped the switch. "Yow!" An electric tongue licked his finger, and he jumped away from the device. The thing made an ugly grinding noise as it shuddered to life, rocking its platform from side to side.

"Is that it?" asked Hyun, frowning and looking disappointed.

"We're supposed to toss this into the dish," said Chung tentatively, showing Hyun the three-quarter inch wrench.

"Well, why do you wait? Do it!"

I'm waiting, thought Chung, *for this thing to not kill me if I try it*. Still, a part of Chung, the part he'd thought long dead since being banished to the army and buried in service to Hyun—the curious engineer this crazy project awoke and engaged— that part spoke over the beaten-down coward. *Try it*, the engineer part said. *See if it works*. The coward part, stronger and more cautious, forced Chung to the device's side while the engineer found just enough courage to toss the wrench at the dish's center.

Sparks enveloped the dish and battery, as if Chung had thrown a firecracker instead of a wrench, but then, miraculously, the expected blue funnel erupted, flickering, shorting, and filling the room with the electric smell of plasma. Each pop and crackle was frightening—mesmerizing!—enhancing Chung's internal war, simultaneously yelling at him to flee, while rooting him, fascinated, firmly in place.

"You did it! It's on! It works!" Hyun shouted. "Let's go!" he yelled. "Manse!" He set off running toward the sputtering, snapping mouth of the Canopy. Chung, appalled, dived after him, managing to tackle him and push him off to the side.

"You don't want to go in there!" he said, pulling Hyun back up to his feet.

"Why not?!" shouted Hyun. "It's on!"

"He has a point," said Kyung, extinguishing one cigarette beneath his heel while lighting up another.

Hyun was apoplectic. "*Both* of you defy me?!"

"Calm down. Be smart. See how it snaps and pops?" Kyung walked to the mouth of the funnel. The smoke from his cigarette curled out like a lazy lash toward the edge of the funnel's blue lip where it transformed into an electric bolt that cracked and exploded before disappearing into the flickering funnel wall. "See?" said Kyung, with a sardonic smile. "That could have been you. Chung did you a favor."

"Well, if we can't go in, how do we test it?" asked Hyun, defiant.

Chung heard the scuttle of tiny claws behind him and turned to see a mouse cowering against the back wall, as far away from the blue funnel as it was able to get. The dish device was perched on the table near the mouse's hole; the mouse most likely was very surprised by the plasma maelstrom blocking his home. Kyung trapped the creature against the wall with a dust pan while Chung found a spool of twine and fashioned the free end into a loop around the mouse's chest. They identified the closest hole.

"On the count of three," instructed Kyung. "1... 2... 3!"

Chung chucked the mouse at the light hole closest to the front of the canopy. Kyung let the twine unravel until it tightened, and he felt the tiny animal tugging against its restraint. "Well, it's still alive," he said. The twine continued to unroll, but suddenly the canopy blinked hard, and they heard a frightened *Squeak!* The twine grew taut and then landed frayed to the ground, falling out of the light hole.

"Fool!" shouted Hyun. "The mouse escaped!"

Chung examined the end of the twine. "It looks like the line broke." He and Kyung exchanged looks. Something bad had happened to the mouse.

"Ridiculous. It chewed through the line," said Hyun. He paused for a moment and then said "Aha!" and ran from the room. A lap of electricity shot out after him, singeing the closed door.

"Anything you can do to make this more stable?" Kyung asked, turning to Chung.

"I'll try," said Chung. He used the dust pan to knock the wrench from the center of the dish and set to work making measurements, tightening the coils, and adjusting the position of screws. He turned it back on. This time it did not shudder or whine on start up, and only seemed to flicker every couple of minutes, instead of every couple of seconds. Not perfect, but a definite improvement.

Hyun returned soon after, carrying a live chicken and a thicker spool of twine. "I paid off the cook in the officer's kitchen," he said, smiling. They attached the new twine around the waist of the chicken and threw it into the same hole as the mouse. As with the mouse, the chicken's twine grew taut immediately after entering the light hole. Chung added more slack to the spool as the chicken seemed to run farther and farther into the light hole.

"We need a camera. To see what the chicken sees," said Chung.

"Good thought," agreed Kyung. "Pull it back in."

But as Chung yanked on the twine to retrieve the chicken, the Canopy began to flicker just as it had with the mouse. Panicking, he pulled faster on the line. The Canopy started whining. Then they heard a frightened *Squawk!* The twine tightened, dropped, and then lay frayed on the floor. No more chicken. Chung examined the tattered end.

"Maybe we need stronger string?"

"No," said Hyun. "I think we need a smarter animal."

"And a camera. Definitely a camera. With a head big enough to hold it." Chung had gone back to examine the magna-coils, seeing if tightening them further would make the Canopy more stable. The room was suddenly quiet. Without even looking,

Chung felt their eyes on him, and without looking he knew what they were thinking.

"Guys... wait..."

Hyun and Kyung pounced on him, pinning his arms to his sides.

"We could use a wire and a flight harness," Hyun was saying to Kyung. Chung struggled between them, attempting to twist out of their grip.

"Guys... no..."

They ignored him. "Wire's good," said Kyung. "Less likely to break."

Chung's eyes widened. "Break?! No, guys... please!"

He struggled harder, but their grip was like a vise.

"Oh, quit your crying. You're bigger than a chicken," said Hyun.

"Much bigger," said Kyung with a smirk.

"You'll be fine," said Hyun. He looked around the room and saw in the corner a large box of coax cable. "We'll use a cable instead of twine. See? That won't break."

"But still—"

"I doubt we will lose you," said Kyung, reassuringly. "We will hold tight to the cable and you will be fine. The camera will tell us where you are and we can come get you."

"But you guys need *me*!"

Kyung nodded, agreeing. "Precisely. Animals can't talk. You can. And if you land in America, you can read the language. We can't. "

"I can't read anything if I am dead!"

Chung continued to struggle, but he knew it was no use. Soon, there was one end of wire attached to the camera and a monitor set up in the rack closest to the funnel.

A second coil of coax crisscrossed Chung's chest, fashioned by Kyung into a makeshift vest. The camera was strapped clumsily to Chung's military hat, its earpiece and microphone duct-taped against his right-ear and cheek, in the hopes that he would talk to his captors as well as let them see into the light hole. Then Kyung and Hyun hoisted Chung to the front of the funnel, the closest light hole just barely within arms' reach.

"The camera's on, so we should see everything that you do," said Kyung.

"Shout out as soon as you get there. If it's New York, bring me back a pizza," said Hyun.

And then with a big heave ho, Kyung and Hyun tossed him through the light hole.

Chung felt himself falling and heard himself screaming. It was terrible, terrifying, but then he "landed". It did not feel like true ground—more like a fuzzy field or the small ball of electricity in a light socket, so warm and seductive, but buzzing enough that you know it's deadly. The walls, if you could call them that, were completely white and shapeless, and just like the blue funnel, they wavered every now and then, a streak of lightning passing through and ending in a pop. This was not what he'd expected at all.

"What happened?" Hyun's voice penetrated the fuzz, all shouty and shrill over the cheap speaker. Chung winced at the too loud sound.

"Don't yell, please. I can hear you."

"Why is it white? Turn the camera back on. We can't see a thing."

"The camera is on. The white is all there is." Chung pulled at the duct-tape, trying to adjust the earpiece to point a little away from his inner ear. Hyun's already annoying voice was even more so, amplified and tinny in the earpiece. Chung's internal engineer wondered if the plasma in the walls had something to do with it.

"All there is? You fool! It's a wall. Look for the door. You must be in a toilet or something."

Chung felt the fuzz on all sides before declaring, "There is no door. This is all there is."

"Do you see any lights? Or people? Can you hear anything?" asked Kyung.

"Nobody is here. It's just me." Chung looked in all directions as proof. "Guys... does it look like the room is shrinking?"

Eeeep! Eeeep! Eeeep! a klaxon wailed suddenly. Then a woman's voice spoke out of the void in clear, distinct English. "Fail safe engaging."

"What?" yelled Hyun. "What did she say? Where is the woman?"

"There's no one. It is a recording, maybe? Something about a 'fail safe'. Guys, it's getting tight in here. Pull me back."

"Find the door first," Hyun commanded. "Run forward. It must be there!"

"No door, guys! Pull me back! Pull me back!" It wasn't Chung's imagination. The walls were indeed collapsing. Chung turned to run, but stopped. There, in front of him, the white wall had transformed into a black, swirling maw. His body was being drawn into it, and his internal engineer thought *Oh no, a black hole!* The gasps in his ear from Hyun and Kyung told him it wasn't in his head and yes, in fact, it was completely horrifying. Chung allowed himself to say what they were all thinking. "Aaaaeeeiii!!!!"

"He's right!" said Kyung finally, a sense of urgency and fear emanating from his voice in a way Chung had never heard before. "We're pulling you back." Chung felt a tug on the coax, but the pull of the maw was stronger. He dug in his heels, hoping to delay the inevitable until, finally, his muscles gave way.

Back in the room, Hyun and Kyung engaged in a tug of war with the coax, bracing themselves against Chung's workstation, pulling with all of their might. But then there was the now familiar, but still terrifying sound of a scream from the other side of the hole, so high and piercing it almost sounded like a woman's voice, but it was all too obviously Chung's. And just as with the mouse and chicken, the coax went taut, then dropped from the hole to the floor, its end frayed, its occupant gone. The camera feed winked out on the screen in the rack.

Without the tension on the cable Hyun and Kyung collapsed to the floor themselves. The cable flicked up past the center of the dish, knocking the wrench out, and closing the blue funnel.

The quiet that followed only amplified the sound coming from the other side of the monitor room door. Someone was entering a key code. A feeling of relief flooded through Kyung. He imagined Chung opening the door to the monitor room, no worse for wear, having found an exit from the fuzzy, white room before he could be eaten by the maelstrom maw.

Then the door opened to an even worse horror. Chunky, mirthless, and flanked by dead-eyed bodyguards, Dear Leader entered the room.

"Gentleman," he said. "I hear you've made a great discovery. Enlighten me."

CHAPTER 19

Out of Time

Hubert ducked into the stairwell across from Bische's lab, carrying a Geiger counter and dragging behind him a large, wheeled storage box. He nestled into the stairwell's darkest corner, focusing his eyes on the lab through a gap in the steps, and waited with growing desperation for Bische to leave.

He checked his watch—almost 5:00 pm. Only one hour left before the benefactor's deadline, sixty short minutes until The Spider found him and demanded payment on their deal—in one way or another. In his mind's eye, unbidden, he saw an image of himself, glassy-eyed and gutted on his office floor. He shook his head. No! That wouldn't happen. His plan would work. It had to.

Damn Bische for resetting the lab's access. His badge was locked out. His! The department head! Some corruption in the database, security said, but he knew that was a lie just to keep him away. If not for the badge, he would have already stolen Campbell's device, been paid for his effort, and be home now, sipping brandy in front of his fireplace. Instead, he was reduced to hiding and skullduggery, just to get the thing that, by rights, should already be his. Damn Gabriel Bische. Damn the man to Hell!

Twenty minutes passed. The flow of students slowed considerably. Other professors closed their rooms for the day, and yet Bische remained. He bobbed in and out of view by the door, tidying the tool chest, clearing the smartboard, sweeping the floor, of all things! *Don't you have a lab tech to do that?* yelled Hubert in his mind. Of course Bische didn't hear it, just continued whistling while he swept. Then he leaned the broom to the right of the smartboard, raised the stylus, and tapped out notes for tomorrow's class, slowly, deliberately, using big block letters. Hubert stifled a groan, pressing fingers to his temples, his eyes boring into the back of Bische's head. Bunching his hair into his chubby fists, the thought exploded in his mind as loud as a shout, *Go home, for God's sake!*

Bische looked toward the door just then, to Hubert's horror. *My God*, he thought, covering his mouth. *Did I say that out loud?* He pressed himself even further into the corner wall, but then relaxed as Bische stared not at him, but at the clock on the wall near the door. Bische saved his place with the stylus, switched off the smartboard and the lights, and promptly left. *At last*, thought Hubert, as he gathered up his props and scurried to the maintenance chief's door. Clearing his throat loudly, he knocked on the door frame. "Ms. Troy?"

Lainie looked up and laughed outright. "Goodness, Dr. Wilkins. What happened to you?"

Hubert glanced toward the door glass and caught his reflection—hair sticking up, face red, eyes bulging. *Get it together, Hubert*, he chastised himself, hastily pasting his hair back down and taking a deep breath. He managed a strained chuckle and said, "Hat hair. Dreadfully cold out."

"I know *that's* right," she said, continuing to smile. "What can I do you for?"

"Yes, well, got a student complaint. Supposedly some kind of radioactive equipment in Dr. Bische's supply room. Threatened to report the school unless we removed it."

"Uh, huh." She frowned. "And what'd Dr. Bische say?"

"He's gone for the day." Hubert hadn't planned on answering questions. Hoping to deflect a full-fledged interrogation he said, "Can't leave it sitting out, though, you know. As the Department Head, it's my responsibility to deal with this as soon as possible."

"Huh. Not like Dr. Bische to be sloppy. Bet it was one of them kids," she said, getting up from her desk, and collecting her key card lanyard from her purse.

"No doubt," said Hubert, relieved they were heading to the lab. "Dr. Bische is far too lax with his classes." He glanced at his watch—twenty-five minutes. Still time, but cutting it close.

"I don't know about all that," said Lainie. They'd reached the lab. "I do know there was one heck of a group over here before break. Kids everywhere. Claimed they was doing research. Humph. Sounded like a party to me. Here we go..." She waved her badge across the panel sensor, and the door unlocked.

"That Campbell boy stayed behind with my crew to help clean up, but it was still a big mess. Seems like we'd notice something radioactive, though."

"Ah, yes, well, she said she saw it in the back room. I've got the detector here," Hubert held up the Geiger counter for emphasis. "Just let me get set up." He went to the bench closest to the back room, turning his back on Lainie to block her view. He reached under the Geiger counter and removed a small vial of cesium-137 he'd taped there just before staking out Bische's lab. He palmed it just far enough from the end of the detector wand to keep it from going crazy, but close enough for it to start making a noticeable tick.

"Sounds like something's in there," said Lainie, unlocking the back room, then standing aside as Hubert walked in. *Good*, he thought. *The ruse is working.*

He started at the most likely place, the shelves off to the side, and was immediately rewarded. There, on a middle shelf, just barely peeking out of the top of a cardboard box, and so nondescript it might have been confused for random trash, Hubert saw a glint of light off metal, highlighting the curve of the mini-dish that could only belong to Campbell's device. Inching the cesium vial closer to the detector as he approached the shelf, the ticks from the Geiger counter increased until they followed in rapid succession as the detector moved right on top of the box.

"And there it is," said Lainie, shaking her head in disgust. "Dr. Bische knows better. It seriously musta been one of them kids."

"Good thing we found it," said Hubert. He couldn't help smiling, knowing that his statement held a double meaning. A quick glance under the flap of the box confirmed the device's presence. *Thank God, all the pieces seemed to be there.* He pulled more props from his suit pocket—safety glasses and disposable gloves—and quickly transferred the pieces from the cardboard box into his large, wheeled container. "That should do it," he said.

"I think we ought to call Dr. Bische to let him know about this," Lainie said.

Hubert thought fast. "I—I've scheduled a meeting with him already for when he's back tomorrow. We'll handle the paperwork. No worries on your part."

"That's good. I'm out tomorrow anyway. As long as you got it, Doc, I'm good."

They left the lab. Hubert headed toward the elevator until Lainie was safely back in her office, then he scurried in the opposite direction, to the building's exit. Pulling out his untraceable phone, he pushed the special button, and when The Spider answered, he said, "I have it. Meet me at the Gordian Knot." *Click.* Hubert checked his watch. *Yes! Five minutes to spare.*

CHAPTER 20

Unity Project

S how me, gentlemen, your great discovery." Dear Leader was not an especially tall man, but his considerable girth and strong personality lent him a massive presence that filled the tiny monitor room, making the fearful quaking of Hyun and Kyung all the more obvious. *They are quivering like cornered rats*, thought Jin. It was one thing for a soldier to have a healthy fear of their easily angered ruler, and another to be almost fainting from fright at the very sight of him. That was her first clue that something was horribly wrong. The second was that Chung was missing. Jek had implicated Chung in the other two's plan. This was his work shift. His uniform jacket hung on the hook by the door. Under no circumstances should Chung be absent from his post in the presence of his superior officer, and yet he was gone, his workstation empty. She glowered at Hyun, who shrank into himself under her scrutiny. *What did you do to my brother, you worm*, she thought.

*****

Hyun looked away, the strength of Jin Ae's anger too much to bear. Once she found out about Chung, he knew he was as good as dead. Only Dear Leader could prevent her retribution, but Dear Leader obviously knew about his scheming, that he had hidden a major discovery, and illicitly, sought financial gain from it. He could order Hyun's death for such a transgression, meaning Jin could kill him still. Hyun imagined her snapping his neck like a chicken bone, or worse, delivering one of Dear Leader's capricious punishments. His knees weakened at the thought of being forced to eat his own entrails or to fight in a pit with hungry, feral dogs. It was too much. This was not his fault. He had to make them see that!

He glanced sideways at Kyung, who stood doleful and shivering, his ever-present cigarette dangling from his lips, his eyes squinting through the smoke, yet fixed on

Jin in a kind of watchful panic. Hyun poked him in the ribs and hissed, "What should we say?"

"Like I should know," Kyung rasped back. "This is your mess. I'm just caught in it."

"Yours too! Yours too!" Hyun shot back under his breath.

"Stop whispering like schoolgirls!" Jin was suddenly in front of them. Her hand snaked out, fast as lightning, and chopped twice. Fire burned through them both from neck to spine, their legs turning to jelly beneath them, leaving Kyung on his knees and Hyun writhing on his side. "Answer Dear Leader!" she shouted over them. "What did you do?" Her eyes bored into them with the intensity of a blow torch.

Hyun struggled back to his knees. "It was him," he said, gasping and pointing at Kyung. "*He* built it, with *her* brother. *They* are to blame. Not me!"

"You lying dog," Kyung spat his disgust. "You say that, but conveniently leave out that the idea was all yours!"

"All mine?! You helped! You saw profit, don't deny!" cried Hyun.

"And what of Chung? You blame him, too?"

"Chung is nothing! He is—!" Hyun stopped, but glanced fearfully at Jin.

"Chung... is... where?" said Jin, her voice measured and cold as ice.

Hyun swallowed over and over, his eyes swinging back and forth between his separate dooms—Dear Leader and Jin.

"He's d—"

"We don't know," said Kyung, shaking his head at Hyun in warning. "He was testing the device and disappeared." He looked Jin in the eye. "I'm sorry."

"Not enough," she said. She lashed out again, her iron-hard palm smashing against his skull. The shock and pain of it blinded him, sent the room spinning. He grabbed the sides of his head to keep from falling over, only barely succeeding. He heard a yelp, then a thump, and saw Hyun crumple beside him, his face scrunched up in pained terror, his hands out to protect himself.

"He's gone! He's gone! Forgive us!" he bleated. Jin raised her fist to punch down on him.

"Enough, Jin Ae." Dear Leader spoke loudly to be heard over Hyun's screeching. He'd moved to examine the sputtering blue cone, walking around it, tracing his fingertips along the protrusion's irregularly pulsating sides. He paused at the entrance, just as a lick of electricity flicked out of the opening and landed like a tap on his shoulder. His eyes widened in surprise, and then he did something Jin did not expect. He laughed.

"You see, people? It has chosen me!" He laughed again. "It knows its destiny as surely as I know mine."

He snapped his fingers at Jin. "Get them up. They have done well. Especially your brother. He is not 'gone.' He has merely traveled. Jek's video showed it. Of this, I am sure."

Jin dragged Kyung and Hyun to their feet and forced them into stiff-backed attention. Dear Leader regarded them, his hands folded on his belly.

"With your help, I and my agents will travel, too. Even now we are in the midst of retrieving the original device from the people who created it. We know it works. You will use what you learned here to improve it."

"See how the hero Chung skirted the outside of his destination? That means your invention is capable of stealth. We can enter a location and not be seen. Our agents will be like ghosts, out of sight, but striking our enemies like a viper. Think of the fear this will inspire!"

"And I... on my grandfather's birthday, I will appear before my people— in an instant!—at the moment of our greatest glory. I will use this device to finally unveil the Unity Project. Behold..."

Dear Leader reached into the side pocket of his tunic and pulled out the disk. He balanced it in the palm of his hand, then pushed a button on its side. The disk began to glow, emitting a bright yellow light. It illuminated Dear Leader's face, intensifying the hard gleam in his eye.

"This. Our path to unity, gentleman. Many scientists worked tirelessly to craft this package as a present for our deluded brothers in the South. It is an invention of beautiful devastation, when delivered to the proper location. It will incinerate their soldiers. Vaporize their leaders. It will send a glorious wave of destruction exposing the lie of the South's superiority. Only then will they see the folly of our people's separation. Only then will they understand my wisdom and see me as the Genuine Leader who can grant them true freedom."

"This is The Great Plan. But as brilliant as those scientists were they could not give me the one thing needed to execute it—a way into the South, undetected. Now," he gestured grandly at the shorting blue cone, "that problem is solved."

Brrrp, brrrp. Jin's phone chirped, a strangely normal sound after all of Dear Leader's talk of devastation. She looked at it and said, "Geomi texted me. He has the device. It will be here in a day."

Dear Leader laughed again. "Excellent! Everything is falling into place." He switched off the glowing disk and returned it to his pocket "A new era begins tomorrow, gentleman. You will combine your device with the American's, and in seven days' time we will reveal The Great Plan!"

He headed toward the door, signaling for Pok to follow. "Jin Ae will remain here, to see to it that you are both properly motivated."

He paused at the door and surveyed the three with his dark, piercing eyes. "Do not disappoint me." And with that, he took his leave, Pok in tow.

The door closed, and they were silent. Dear Leader's words still reverberated, too extreme to believe, too real to ignore. Anger flowed through Jin once more. She reached out, grabbing the front of Hyun's shirt. He squeaked as she lifted him off the floor. "You miserable little man. You've killed my brother and doomed the South!"

"Let me down! Let me down!" Hyun shouted, but struggled feebly in her grip.

"Hurting him changes nothing," said Kyung. He still looked shaken, but had roused himself enough to retrieve his cigarettes from Chung's workstation, and with trembling hands tried to light one.

Jin knew he was right. She dropped Hyun back to the ground, but not before giving him another hard shake. He lay whimpering on the floor, defeated. Kyung squinted at her through the smoke curling up from his cigarette. "You know he is mad, don't you?" It wasn't a question so much as a statement of fact.

Jin just glared at him. "You talk treason."

He inhaled deeply, sucking down half the cigarette, then said, "I speak truth. You must believe it, else you'd have killed me for saying it." He stepped closer. "We all have family in the South. This Unity whatsit won't spare them. They will be incinerated, just like the soldiers and leaders. He will kill our kin. We can't let this happen."

"Quiet!" Jin snapped. "I know my job." *It's to save Chung first, no matter what else is going on.* "You better know yours," she said, getting into his face. "If you do, we can find Chung," she looked away, "...and maybe a way for us all to survive."

CHAPTER 21

A Way Out

O of!" Kyung's back ached. He creaked up slowly, kneading his knuckles into his back muscles, but after three days of constant bending and straightening not much could relieve the rock-like knot near his spine.

This engineering work, combining their crazy-quilt machine with the even crazier American version, was torture. All the bending and lifting, twisting wires and threading breadboards, forcing dull screws into rusty metal racks, was more physical labor than Kyung was used to. It was the kind of work he hated—the kind that he pushed onto Chung, he realized now with shame. At the time, Chung had seemed to accept such tasks gladly, working earnestly, rising to the challenge of doing more than monitoring. He'd only complained when they forced him into the death machine. Now he was—what?

Kyung did not like to think that Chung was dead, but he wasn't sure what else could have happened. The screams and frayed wire should have been enough to erase all doubt, but when his mind was distracted from the death machine, he caught himself mulling over and over the question. Was Chung really dead, or had he simply disappeared?

The longer he rested his back, the more questions bubbled to the surface. If Chung wasn't vaporized by plasma, where was he? What if some "thing" in the fuzzy room—the "fail safe," the voice said—had saved Chung instead of killing him? Weren't fail safes meant to avoid disaster? The more he thought about it, the more he convinced himself it could be true. This "fail safe" had grabbed Chung and deposited him elsewhere. "Yes, that has to be it," he said aloud.

"What has to be it?" Jin's voice startled him. She sat away from him, at the other end of the rack, attaching cameras and headsets to a stack of vests, but was so quiet about it he'd forgotten she was there. Now she stared at him, an unavoidable presence, her eyes intense and accusing. Guilt clinched him and he immediately regretted having spoken.

"Nothing," he mumbled, bending back over the rack.

It's the guilt, he thought, switching on his internal monologue. *My guilt wants me to believe that Chung survived.*

Not just guilt, his rational mind insisted. *There's no evidence that the animals or Chung actually died.*

But the squawks and screams—

They were bad, sure, but where was the blood, the burning, the smell of death?

But the ropes and wire—

They were frayed, yes, but where were the remnants of organic tissue? Where was the ash of carbon char? There should have been some kind of residue, but the ropes and wire were clean! The "fail safe" must have transported them away.

His rational mind was certain about this final conclusion, but he knew the argument would continue until he actually found proof, and he couldn't search for proof until the damn device worked. With Grandfather Leader's birthday celebration nearing—and thus Dear Leader's retribution with it should he fail—the device took priority. It required the rest of Kyung's remaining rational capacity to tweak and adjust what he needed to in the rack to connect their device with the American one.

Not long after, he straightened up painfully once more, ran the controller diagnostic from where he stood at the rack, and sighed with relief as the energy signatures from both devices resonated at the compatible frequencies. He knew that when he turned it on both the fuzzy room and the light holes would be accessible in the canopy. But how to stop the fuzzy room from collapsing? How to keep the "fail safe" at bay? A packet trace on Chung's data session might provide a clue, and with that clue, he would have proof of Chung's survival—or his death.

To run the trace, he needed a workstation. He turned away from the rack for the first time in many hours and saw Hyun hoarding Chung's console. He scowled at his commander. Kyung had never held Hyun in high regard, and the past three days had only confirmed his assessment. In that time, Hyun had offered his help only once, by converting their rudimentary, decade-old headsets into wireless communicators, a feat that had surprised Kyung, who thought Hyun was incompetent, possessing no technical skills. But as with everything Hyun did, his assistance was ultimately self-serving, as he used one of the headsets to connect to the Dark Net. Since then, he'd spent every waking moment typing furtively at potential saviors, flattering them effusively over coms in frantic desperation, hoping for escape.

At the moment, Hyun had several chat windows open, and he seemed to be hissing with increasing anxiety at anyone he could find. The various windows flashed for attention, while Hyun hunted and pecked out replies, talking more than he typed.

Tap, tap, tap. "—must escape." *Tap, tap.* "Yes, now." *Tap, tap, tap.* "Sure, I pay you." *Tap...tap, tap, tap.* "With the army, why? Wait—don't!" *Tap, tap, tap.* "Jen-jang!" *Shit!*

One by one, the flashing windows grayed and winked closed. No doubt, saying "army" had caused any takers to block him immediately and flee.

"Pfft. The idiot," he said, a thought he'd had perhaps ten times today already, but did not say aloud until just now, probably because he was tired. Again, he was startled when Jin replied.

"You are right," she said tightly, watching Hyun from her end of the rack. "The fool endangers us all."

Time to put a stop to it, then, he thought, and in a loud voice called, "Hyun!"

Hyun jumped, knocking his headset off, then looked around, frantic. "What? What?"

"The controller graph to your right. Do you see a spike?"

Hyun turned back to the screen, not sure where to look. "What graph? Where?" He clicked random icons on the screen, opening a cascade of windows, none of which they needed, Kyung realized. The graph he had opened several hours ago before heading to the rack was nowhere to be seen. It got closed, no doubt, by the simpleton while fumbling around on the Dark Net. "Shibal," he cursed, under his breath. *We don't have time for this.*

Groaning, Kyung squeezed out from the space beside the rack and made his way stiffly to the workstation. "Move!" he growled, wresting the mouse out of Hyun's grip, shoving Hyun's roller chair to the side. He reopened the rack controller, fingers flying across the keyboard, re-typing the commands to recreate the graph that would save their heads. In less than five minutes it reappeared in the middle of the screen. At the edge of the expected frequency range, he saw it—the smallest of blips, yet a blip all the same. He made a mental note to enhance the blip by tweaking the extra inductor on the breadboard to increase the height of the spike. But the current size would suffice for now. "Jota," *Good,* he murmured. Their heads were saved.

Kyung turned dagger eyes back to Hyun. "Don't. Touch. This," he said, poking the graph for emphasis.

"Why are you still working on it? You saw what happened to Chung. He disintegrated! It's a death machine!"

"I don't believe that."

"You should! Help me search the Dark Net. The underground knows you. Type to them and tell them to hide us. Get us out of here!"

"To where?" called Jin over her shoulder, the disgust plain in her voice. "You think Dear Leader won't find you? That his agents don't have spies in the Dark Net? Are you stupid as well as a fool?"

"Chung's not dead." It just came out. He did not mean to say it aloud—again— but there it was. Jin dropped the body cam and turned around. Kyung gathered his courage, faced her, and said, "It makes no sense that he would be. He was taken."

"How do you know?" she said.

"I don't, but the trace will tell us. It pains me to admit, but Hyun is right. We must get out. This 'death machine' is our only hope."

Hyun covered his ears. "His screams—I can still hear them. Worse than the chicken's. He can't be alive, he's—aieee!"

Hyun shrieked and pointed in the direction of Chung's workstation. "He's there! He's there! His ghost haunts us!"

Jin looked at the door, just beyond the workstation, eyes alighted, as if expecting to see Chung floating through it, draped in chains and fiery wrath. But it was just the door. Her expression dulled, drifting back to its standard severity, a transition that hit Kyung with a wave of sadness.

"Your guilt makes you imagine things," she said.

"Not there! There!" He pointed more vigorously at the monitor. "Chung, take Kyung! It's his fault, not me! Aieee!"

Hyun dove off the chair and under the workstation, as if the plastic countertop could save him from otherworldly retribution. Kyung turned back to the screen and flinched. Just below the "graph," a new window had appeared. On one side, a flood of data; on the other, a pixelated outline of Chung's screaming head, collapsing in on itself, then shrinking by inches into a hole no wider than a drinking straw.

Good god, thought Kyung through his sleep-deprived haze. *It is Chung, back to get me.* Chung's horrified face pulsated before slowly slipping away. Then the blinking "Complete" beneath the clot of data brought him back to his senses. "Oh, my trace," he said in sudden realization.

Plopping into Hyun's vacated chair—ah, bliss to be finally off his feet—Kyung expanded the window and scrolled through the data until... there, yes! Foreign coordinates, a point outside the sub-basement, most likely outside of the North. To be sure, he first pulled up the American trace that had started it all, then their chicken trace, and finally Chung's, layering all three onto the packet location grid to compare. The origin loci for Chung and the chicken lined up with the Asian continents and the specific coordinates for the Bureau, while the American trace originated from North America, at a location which, he reasoned, aligned with the school that had published the paper. If Chung and the chicken had indeed died within their crazy device, their terminal loci should still be in Asia. All three traces terminated in North America! Not at the school, but some place not far from it. He was right. "Ah, ha! It's proof!"

Jin peered over his shoulder. "What proof? Have you found my brother?"

Hyun peeked out from under the table. "Is Chung gone?" he whispered.

Kyung ignored them both. With renewed determination, he clicked the rack controller app, opening the command shell, his fingers leaping across the keyboard, plotting a custom plan for the controller to pass thru to the Frankenstein's monster that was their amalgamated device. He was back in his element. The command sequence flowed out of his brain into the command editor with a surety he hadn't felt since Chung disappeared. And as he typed, an inspiration hit him—an innovation that could link them not just to the loci of Chung's salvation, but also protect them from the same involuntarily transportation. He'd have to couple the new code with a slight change to the magnetic field alignment, but the chances were good it would work. As line after line spooled out into the command editor, he became more certain. *Yes, this will definitely work. I know it!*

He clicked "Save" and limped back to the rack. He paused first at the breadboard, remembering the final inductor adjustment. Then he grabbed one of Chung's magnetic coils, loosed a wire near the end, and threaded the wire into the back of the battery apparatus, just below the dish. He unwound more of the wire, ensuring enough purchase to reach the top of the dish. He let go, and the coil landed dead center of the top, pulsing slightly on contact, the magnetic field hugging it tight.

"Hyun, get against the wall," he called over his shoulder. Hyun scampered to the side like a frightened rat, leaving the middle of the room clear for whatever came shooting out of the dish. Kyung, safely situated at the back of the rack, hands poised on each machine's power key, counted to three, and then flipped the switches to "On."

The unified device came to life with a gentle hum, a distinct change from the previous incarnation's spastic snaps, crackles, and pops. Then the funnel emerged, deep blue and stable, the arcs of electrical current shimmering along its sides like gold filaments in an incandescent bulb. Inside the funnel, the blue sat beneath a transparent haze that was smoky and stiff as chiffon, each trapped point of light a drop of heavy cream embedded in the blue. And there, near the front, one point of light in particular radiated, its edges highlighted bright orange against the iridium blue.

Hyun stared at the orange light, wide-eyed. "The death hole!"

"The escape hole," Kyung corrected him. "With an orange-flavored filter, to thwart the death."

Hyun threw up his hands. "But where does it go?"

Jin ran back to the rack. Donning a headset and a body cam, she said, "Only one way to find out."

"Nooo!" cried Hyun. "I won't be responsible for your death, too!" He pushed off the wall, arms stretched out to grab her, but Jin needed only two steps to avoid him, two steps to reach the front of the funnel, and then one giant leap!

CHAPTER 22

What a Babe

Mitch, Dean, and Wayne had never been busier, nor happier, than they were now. They'd only put the word out on campus a few days ago that the Jump!Go, the new miniaturized version of the travel Canopy, Big Blue, was ready to go, but they'd already had close to fifty pre-orders. About 75% of those orders came from fellow classmates, the people Mitch had awed way back on Project Day with nachos and beer from the now legendary Sutter's Pub. 20% came from test subjects who'd experienced Big Blue firsthand on that disastrous research day in Bische's lab.

But the biggest surprise came from the remaining 5% of orders which came from people Mitch had not expected to hear from anytime soon—complete strangers. These were people who probably didn't understand what they'd ordered, but who knew someone at Mines that vouched for its awesomeness, or had seen a bootleg video from Project Day uploaded to the interwebs. Regardless how they heard it, Mitch was sure the floodgates of outside interest had somehow snuck open. All he and the guys could do now was keep paddling and ride the tide.

Their current setup was definitely helping. Dean's sister Sam's garage was working out every bit as well as Mitch had hoped. It was free-standing, more like a guest house, recessed far back from the street at the end of the driveway, taking up most of the space in the backyard. It was brand new, just like Sam's house, fully wired, with central air and screaming fast internet. Even better, it was empty, Sam not having had time to move anything into it. Some new project at Tamblyn Tech was keeping her constantly on the road, away from her new house and the multiple boxes in the living room that needed unpacking. Before she left, she'd scored them the 3D-printer, some off-hours time in a Tamblyn clean room, and a few boxes of

Costco snacks. "If you mow the lawn, collect the mail, put out the trash, and save me some snacks, you can build whatever you want in here," she'd told them.

The snacks were what finally convinced Dean. "Guys, you were right," he said, tearing into a pack of chocolate Pop-Tarts. "This is a pretty sweet deal."

They raided a thrift store for shelves and tables, moved in all of their gear— computers, tools, Dean's sound system, Wayne's huge monitors—and immediately set to work. Mitch created the assembly steps, both for the device and the harness accessory. Dean wrote the user app, including the location database and the ordering site. Wayne wrote the mapping algorithm, as well as tracking routines for the light holes and the people using them. They all collaborated on the design for the main board, in particular the singularly important light-trapping circuit.

The first blue plasma cone they created in miniature was cause for celebration at Stinky Keith's. The first fob they successfully tested was cheered with Bische over nachos at Sutter's Pub. They called the new device the Jump!Go, gifting Bische with the one from that first successful test. The light holes were redubbed "jump points", and things took off from there.

They eventually settled into a kind of groove, assembling Jump!Gos, testing the fobs, reviewing their jump sessions, and fixing software bugs. As a result of their efforts, they were a fifth of the way through creating enough devices to fulfill their orders.

Today, it was Wayne's turn to be the session monitor. He sat, wearing headphone pods, at a cramped table pushed against the back center wall of the garage, watching three screens seemingly simultaneously. The left screen was full of mapping data; the center screen was split down the middle between two camera views, currently dark and waiting for the next jump session. The last screen showed a Warrior Ops II battlefield, the first-person display wobbling as Wayne's avatar ran across it, just slightly behind a tall, beefy avatar resembling Dean. Wayne had found a mod for the game that replaced attacking soldiers with alien sea creatures, and ammo with fast food products. He and Dean were trying out the mod while they waited for Mitch to get done with his Jump!Go device before the next jump session.

Dean stood in front of a screen on a table pressed up against the left wall of the garage. Along with his headphone pods, he also wore one of Mitch's monitoring harnesses, a ViewPro camera strapped to its front. His Jump!Go, the ninth they'd made, sat warm and ready, attached to his cell phone, in the harness's right chest pocket. The small Bluetooth headset he'd use to communicate with Wayne during the jump session was clinched between his teeth. On the screen, Dean's blaster sliced through a brigade of crab beings with bazookas strapped to their backs that inexplicably shot out egg rolls and hamburgers.

"Please tell me you're seeing what I'm seeing," said Dean in between blaster shots.

"What? A crab shooting cheese burgers from a Howitzer looks strange to you?"

"Yes, dude! I feel like I'm tripping balls here."

"Nonsense. That was surprisingly common during WWII, especially on the beach in Normandy. The real anachronisms are the land sharks tossing moon pies."

"Why's that?"

"Well, everyone knows that didn't happen till the Korean War. Didn't you ever watch M.A.S.H?"

Dean shot at a flashing wooden crate, unleashing a slew of angry turtles trotting toward them with machine guns, fed by french fry magazines. He collapsed in a paroxysm of laughter.

"Look at their feet," he choked out. "Lookit—stubby little feet. Bwahahahahahaha!"

"Aw, come on," said Wayne, giggling at the sight himself. "It's cute!"

"Hahahaha! Ridiculous, you mean," said Dean, pausing to catch his breath. He put the controller down. "How's it coming, Mitch?"

"Almost done," Mitch called over his shoulder. Tongs in hand, Mitch popped open the 3D-printer to remove the still warm halves of an oblong glass casing from the printer stage. Flicking the safety glasses balanced atop his heavy curls down to cover his eyes, he started the pleasant task of assembly, lining the casing with conductive mesh, stringing wires through the preformed holes, and soldering the CPU, light board, and miniaturized magna-coilss firmly into their respective cavities in each half of the casing. This was the tenth device he'd created in the past week and his hands, already swift and sure, were well practiced with the build. In no time, the major pieces were in place, ready to be topped with his technological cherry, "the linchpin", a scaled-down version of Big Blue's spinning wrench.

Mitch's pulse quickened as he pinched the slither of chromium steel with pronged tweezers. He knew what was coming, counted on it happening as proof that the build indeed was correct and ready to work. Even so, his anticipation and excitement were just as keen as the very first time he, Dean, and Wayne had crowded around the printer, taking turns adding parts to Bische's Jump!Go. Mitch held his breath, then released the prongs. The linchpin didn't drop so much as glide into place at the center of the light board, nestled neatly in the magnetic field of Wayne's smaller, but strangely stronger magna-coils.

He grinned widely as it started its characteristically slow spin. Quickly snapping the two halves together, he watched, mesmerized as the iridescent funnel erupted behind the glass, blue plasma spreading out across the oblong, white streaks of light pulsing through it like lightning filaments, and at the center, deep and dark, a glossy drop of midnight. "Whoohoo," he whispered at his creation. Jump!Go number ten pulsed with a final burst of activity as the light board self-calibrated, then settled down to a final hum, interrupted occasionally by a snake-like ripple.

Mitch trotted over to his workstation, plugged the device into an open port, and fired up the diagnostics. He watched anxiously as, one by one, the progress bar for each test expanded across the screen. So far, only two of the ten fobs they'd made had failed their diagnostics. Although the issues with those devices had been obvious during assembly—no miniature blue funnel, and a non-floating linchpin—fixing the problems had been a challenge. It took them a week of disassembling and then rebuilding each one before they'd figured out exactly what had gone wrong. Now time was of the essence as the final shipping date was drawing near. A screw up now would put them another week behind, all but guaranteeing a bevy of disappointed customers.

Mitch crossed his fingers, willing each progress bar to complete and show green. *Ping!* It passed the first test, finding the "home point", which was their much-loved Sutter's Pub. *Ping!* It passed second test, projecting a 3D grid of known locations on top of corresponding points in the funnel. *Ping, ping ping!* It continued through the list, passing each diagnostic with flying colors. Finally, it reached the last test, a reverse scan of all originating jump points, a safety feature suggested by Bische to ensure that travelers could always return to where they started. The diagnostic hesitated, then seemed to freeze. "No," Mitch groaned.

"Dude, what?" said Dean. He dropped his controller and crossed the room in two strides to look over Mitch's shoulder.

"Aw, it's hiccupping on the reverse scan again."

Wayne glanced at the diagnostic screen and said, "That's not a hiccup! Pause it, pause the scan!" He dropped his controller as well and began typing furiously on his keyboard. Warrior Ops II disappeared, to be replaced with the same frozen scene from Mitch's screen, overlaid with a graph, the lines on it undulating jerkily across the X, Y, and Z axes.

Mitch reached out to pause the test, but the screen chose that moment to unfreeze itself, changing the progress bar from yellow to green, and passing the device. "Sorry, false alarm," he called out to Wayne. "Looks like it's working now."

"Crud puppet!" said Wayne.

"Such language," chuckled Dean.

"It's not a hiccup," Wayne said again, trying to explain. "It's an anomaly. It's something weird with one particular jump point that's intermittent. It's like the light tunnel has a compression surge and freaks, then overloads until it collapses or blinks or something. When I try to focus in on the origin point for the hole, the tracer stops. It's driving me nuts trying to figure it out."

"Don't tell me you think I need to build this again," said Mitch, sounding deflated. He had been really looking forward to spending the rest of the day exploring the jump points, not stuck in the lab reprinting Jump!Go parts.

"No, it's not the device. It's—I don't know—in the 'system' somehow." Wayne typed some more, pulling the overlay up again onto Mitch's screen, but this time no sine waves appeared. All axes on the graph stayed empty.

"Shit cake," Wayne grumbled.

"That's more like it," laughed Dean.

"Well, if it's not the fob, then I'm ready to go," said Mitch. He donned his monitoring harness and attached the device to his phone's power port. Immediately, the Jump!Go controller app opened on the phone's screen. Mitch tapped the app's blue funnel icon, and like magic, a triangular shaft of light leapt out of the iris on the fob's light board, terminating in a blue, person-sized grid, divided into four equal quadrants.

"Where you wanna go, today?" asked Mitch. He rubbed his hands together in anticipation.

Dean powered up his Jump!Go. "Let's start in the new quadrant. I've got a good feeling about it. Babes, beaches, and beer! Send us the coordinates, Wayne."

Wayne flipped open the virtual map they'd been adding to, systematically working through the list of major tech data centers. He pulled up the next one in the list, and ran its location through the mapping program on the left screen. The program thought for a couple seconds, then spit out a series of number couplets— longitudes and latitudes— that enabled the submit button, a flashing smiley face. "K, should be coming at you right about... now." He clicked the smiley face, and the program uploaded the coordinates to the central Jump!Go database. The fob controller apps on Mitch and Dean's phones chirped as the new data got incorporated into the list of newly acquired light points.

Mitch hit the app's blue funnel icon again to refresh the available quadrants, selecting the new one to display all of its jump points. He leaned into the nearest one and breathed deep, having learned from their first experience with Sutter's Pub that you can tell a lot about a place by the way it smells. He was rewarded with the overpowering scent of salt water and sun screen. "Yeah, Dean. This is it. You were right, brah."

"I call dibs, then," said Dean. He hurriedly refreshed his display, and thrust his face into the jump point, confirming with his eyes what Mitch had smelled. Hawaiian boy that he was, he knew immediately that they'd found the beach at Kauai, covered with creamy white sand that edged the volcano on one side, but flowed out to the Pacific on the other. Caramel-colored bodies, either naturally bronzed or baked by the sun, cavorted near the water, dived for volleyballs, and danced in cabanas. "Jackpot!" Dean called over his shoulder. "My turn to hog the fun jump points."

"Too late, pal. Surf's up, hahahaha!" Mitch galloped out of the jump point first, heading off at a dead run toward the group playing volleyball.

"Crap!" Dean fell victim to their unspoken rule—first one to touch the other side of a jump point claimed the right to explore it. They couldn't waste time with two people in the same spot, so whoever came in second had to find another point to hit.

Reluctantly he pulled his head back from Kauai, but began sniffing the other jump points in the quadrant in earnest, determined to find another gem before Mitch could return from paradise to dash his dreams again.

"Dean, just accept it. The beaches are gone for today. Suck it up and choose the next one." Wayne fiddled with the gain on Mitch's camera feed, zeroing in on a particularly handsome hard body lounging on the sand, all wavy locks and oiled biceps.

"Another beach is around here somewhere," Dean said between sniffs. "It has to be. I can feel it. Just have to follow my nose. Hot dog! Salt-water!" He whooped in triumph at a point near the center of the quadrant. "Found it, haha! Diving in, dudes!"

Dean took two giant steps forward and plunged headlong into the heaviest, worst sleet storm he had ever experienced. "Gah!" he exclaimed, big shards of sleet pounding into his t-shirt. Scraping the ice away from his face, he yelled, "Wayne, it's snowing like crazy! Where the heck am I?"

Wayne did a quick check on the coordinates. "Looks like... downtown Milwaukee."

"Milwaukee? Nooo!"

"Um, certainly looks like it from your camera feed." The images playing across Dean's side of the middle screen seemed to place him between a major street and an alleyway.

"Man, it's cold as frig out here. I'm coming back right now."

"You might as well snap a reference pic while you're there," said Wayne, "otherwise, you'll just have to come back."

Dean groaned. "Alright, but just from the curb. Then I'm jumping through another hole to find a proper beach!"

He stepped out of the alleyway and onto the sidewalk, camera raised. A car came speeding up near the curb, and just as it passed Dean, it hydroplaned, kicking up a huge wave of water that slopped all over Dean, his camera, and the sidewalk. Sputtering, he made the mistake of licking his lips, an action that forced some of the icy sludge into his mouth. "Ugh," he said. "Sloppy snow melt. Now I know why it smelled like salt water." He staggered back to the alleyway, shivering. "I'm coming back right now, Wayne." Dean set the reverse on his Jump!Go to return the way he came and climbed into the hole that appeared.

But instead of the garage replacing Milwaukee, Dean found himself in a white space that wasn't so much of a room as it was a fuzzy, spacious, cavity. He looked behind him. There was the small pinhole, through which he could just see the gray, ugly blight of winter in Milwaukee. In front of him, seemingly a long way off, was the pinhole leading back to the garage. To his left and right was just more of the fuzzy white space.

Wayne crackled in his ear. "Dean?! Man, where'd you go?"

Dean checked his hands, felt his body, and inhaled. That he was solid and capable of breathing confirmed for him that he was still alive. *And at least it is kind of warm here, wherever* here *is.* He made the only reply he could under the circumstances. "Uh... limbo?"

"Be serious. My monitoring board is going crazy. There was a huge glitch spike just as you entered the hole, but you didn't come back. Where, dude?"

"Wayne, I don't know. It's all white and staticky. I can see *you*, though. Hello!" He waved at the tiny image of Wayne, far off down the barrel of the space he was in. "If I had to guess, I'd say that I'm in between Sam's garage and Milwaukee. It's like a gap in the network."

Mitch chimed in over coms. "Ah, wow, if that's true, this is fantastic. I bet you're *inside* of a photon. I'm coming back. Sweet!"

"Yeah, I guess that is pretty—whoa! Well, hello, darlin'."

She appeared with a pop out of nowhere, just an arm's length away from him, a beautiful dream of a woman—lithe, athletic, and radiating power. Her deep, almond eyes registered surprise, then anger the moment her feet settled into the white fuzz.

She crouched into a fighting stance and shouted at Dean, "Nae dongsaeng-eun eodiss-eo, saekki ya?"

"Guys... please tell me you see her, too."

"We do, man. What a babe," said Mitch.

"Indeed," said Wayne, bringing up a new scan on the screen, his fingers moving quickly over the keyboard. "But from where? And why's she mad at you? Not that I blame her."

Dean felt himself swooning. "Angry or not, I'll take her. She's gorgeous."

She looked him up and down as he spoke. "American?"

"As apple pie, darlin', body and soul. But my heart belongs to you."

She almost smiled, then seemed to remember to be angry. She set her jaw and said harshly, "Where is my brother, American?"

"Is that the only man in your life?" said Dean. "Got room for one more?"

"Dude, I can't believe you're flirting with her," said Mitch.

"Grab life by the horns, Mitch. She likes me. I can tell."

Her eyes grew wide. The angry, determined expression she'd confronted Dean with clouded over into worry. She put her hand to her ear and let loose a long stream of foreign invective. The longer she spoke, the more she seemed to panic.

Wayne pulled up Tamblyn Translate and turned up the gain on Dean's microphone. "It's Korean!" he said, excitedly pointing at his screen. "They got our tech somehow. She's from Korea. *They* must be the glitches!" Just as he said that, the monitor screen registered another blip. Wayne hurried to click on it, hoping to finally get a good trace on the glitch's point of origin. The longitude and latitude coordinates popped up, and he fed it into the mapping program. The map scrolled, finally coming to a stop over Asia. He and Mitch stared at the map in shock. Wayne shouted into coms, "Dean, get back to the garage. Now!"

"It's fine. *She's* fine," said Dean.

"No, she's not. She's North Korean, dude. The glitch is how they travel. And she's about to have company."

As if on cue, Dean heard another pop. Behind her, a tall, chiseled, dead-eyed man appeared. He was sharply dressed—black shirt in a shiny gray suit—and armed with the biggest handgun Dean had ever seen.

"That guy looks like a psycho," said Mitch in Dean's ear. "Nice suit, though."

"Gun's worse," said Wayne, his tone tense and clipped. "Dean, you gotta go!"

"Not without the Babe," he said, moving protectively to the woman's side.

She shook her head, her eyes warning him away, but Dean, ever chivalrous, ignored her. She stiff armed him, pushing him back behind her, then crouched in front of the dead-eyed man, preparing to fight him herself. The man was faster, sidestepping her with lethal grace. Flashing her an evil, triumphant grin, he raised his gun arm toward Dean. Dean, still gripping his phone, camera-face out, raised his hands up reflexively, then felt a powerful impact in his side that knocked all of the air out of his lungs and sent him sailing backwards through the white fuzz. He heard a loud blast.

Everything seemed to move in slow motion. He saw the woman, his savior, her leg still thrust out in the place where his chest had been. He saw the bullet, slicing through the fuzz, flying back with him, catching up. He angled the phone to what he hoped was a spot just between him and the bullet. Just as the edges of the garage became visible in his peripheral vision, the bullet slammed into the phone. He landed on his back, gasping, just a hair behind Wayne's workstation. It hurt to breathe, but he was alive.

Mitch and Wayne knelt down beside him. "You okay, buddy?" said Mitch, fear and worry clogging his voice.

Dean winced as he pushed himself into a sitting position. "Ow! She really belted me."

Wayne helped him up. "Well, at least you found your Babe."

"Yeah," Dean said, still gasping. But then a grin split his face. "And she just saved my life."

CHAPTER 23

Into the Void

S he was falling. Her arms strained to grab hold of something, anything, whatever solid surface might exist in the white fuzz to stop her or at least slow her down. Vague outlines flew by on either side of her, but whether they were buildings or people or trees, she couldn't tell. The more she strained toward the shapes, the farther they seemed to float out of reach, until finally the white haze closed in and swallowed her. It took all of her training not to scream.

"Jin!" called Kyung. "Jin Ae! Respond!"

"Why did you jump?!" cried Hyun. "Not you too! Jin Ae!!"

Kyung and Hyun's frantic voices blasted her ears, Hyun's bleating in particular reverberating through her earpiece worse than feedback. "Ungh!" she grunted, clasping her hand to her ears. Her body kept falling, spinning, spiraling down, down, down through the blank void.

"It's killing her!" screeched Hyun.

"*You're* killing me with your shouting," she called back. "Calm down the both of you!"

Talking seemed to stop the spinning, and slowly her disorientation faded away. She wasn't falling anymore, she realized. Her feet held firm beneath her, wherever "here" was, yet the floor felt spongy and was virtually indiscernible from the walls and the ceiling. She looked behind her and could just make out the orangish rim of the hole she had jumped through, almost blocked now by Hyun's head, his eyes

146

bulging as he looked in after her. His face leant enough contrast from the unrelenting whiteness to help her eyes adjust.

She noticed more holes dotting the walls, but the openings were too far away to tell where they might lead, nor did they offer a clue as to which one may have engulfed Chung. Plus, there were too many to search through—Dear Leader and The Spider could be back within hours, if not sooner. "Grrr!" she growled again, this time in frustration. *There's no time for this!* But there also wasn't time for her to give in to her anxiety like the fool Hyun and start panicking. She clenched her fists, closed her eyes, and inhaled deeply, willing the return of her control. That made the next words she heard all the more startling.

"Well, hello, darlin'."

Her eyes shot open. Unbelievably, a tall, muscular man-boy, with sandy hair and twinkling eyes set in a young, stubbly face, was standing just an arm's length away from her. He seemed just as surprised as she was to find someone else in this odd space, yet his expression was mixed with humor and, to Jin's embarrassment, unabashed appraisal. She felt her cheeks flush and had a sudden desire to smooth her hair, but for the third time in as many minutes, she squelched the impulses down into control.

"Gah! Who's that?" Hyun yipped, his unrelenting jumpiness enough of an irritant to snap Jin back to herself.

"As if I should know," she hissed back. Who, indeed? Without warning, her brother's pixelated face, frozen and screaming, appeared in her mind's eye, renewing her anger over the whole situation. Whoever this stranger was, he was far too happy to be here in this hellscape. Could that be because he was responsible for whatever had happened to Chung? Dropping into a defensive crouch, she said, "What have you done with my brother?"

He furrowed his brow, adding confusion to his expression, on top of the open ogling and amusement. She'd spoken Korean, she realized. He didn't understand her.

"Guys... please tell me you see her, too," he said. *Who's he talking to*, she thought.

"He has friends," said Kyung in her ear. "Plus he's American. Not good."

Just over his shoulder, Jin spied what must have been his entry hole, as wide as the one behind her. She deepened her defensive crouch and set her body ready to spring at his throat should his friends suddenly appear and attack. He continued to grin at her goofily, so open and good natured. So much like Chung. He seemed unlikely to be her brother's captor or to have done Chung harm, but smiling faces could hide lies. Best to make him talk. In English, keeping her voice as harsh as possible, she said, "American?"

"As apple pie, darlin', body and soul. But my heart belongs to you."

She bit the inside of her cheek to keep from smiling. "Where is my brother, American?"

"Is that the only man in your life?" he said. "Got room for one more?"

I can't believe he's flirting with me. Kyung snorted in her ear. "Smooth talking bast—"

A loud banging drowned out Kyung, followed by a faint "Open up!" from what must have been the other side of the sub-basement door. Some commotion followed, then in her ear she heard a cold, familiar, drawl. "Kill him."

Her eyes grew wide. It was The Spider. She checked her watch. *Shit!* She'd missed her check in time with Dear Leader.

"Geomi," she said. "Playing fetch for Dear Leader?"

The Spider made a sound that might have been a chuckle. Warped by coms, it sounded more sinister. "I'm no man's dog. But the Great One missed you. I offered to look. Kill the American and return here to report."

She did not want to. She did not know why. She understood the logic, but it seemed so—

"It's wasteful," she said, speaking quickly. *Have to buy time.* "I could bring him back. Make him talk. We can learn his secrets first."

"Not wasteful. Prudent," Geomi reasoned back. "We can't be exposed. These are academics. Kill him, and any others will be too scared to follow."

"Listen—" she started

Geomi sighed loudly. "I'm joining you."

"No!" Too late. The coms went dead. Seconds later she heard a pop, and The Spider appeared, wearing a headset, unruffled in his silk shirt and shiny gray suit, seemingly unbothered by the transition from the sub-basement into the haze. In one fluid movement, he uncoiled out his landing crouch, unholstered his gun—equipped with a silencer—and pointed it at the American's friendly, clueless face.

Jin's leg whipped out reflexively, just as Geomi squeezed the trigger, striking the American squarely in the gut with a kick so powerful, it lifted him off his feet. He flew backward toward his entry hole, as if sucked by a vacuum. The hole widened the closer he got to it until finally he fell backwards through the opening like a marble through the top of an inverted bubble.

Geomi lowered the gun. "That was... unwise," he said.

Jin swung toward him and said, "...and you are rash. He could have told us how to use this place. You jeopardize the mission."

"You *forget* the mission. Things have changed since you've been babysitting in the basement. Now, more than you, Dear Leader trusts me."

Geomi reached into his pocket and pulled from it the very thing she, Kyung, and Hyun had hoped to escape—the Unity Project disk.

"When we deposit this and use it, we will rule all of Korea. More disks, combined with this," he gestured at the whiteness all around him, "and we will soon rule the world."

"You are as mad as—" Jin stopped herself.

"As who? As he is? That is what you were going to say, isn't it? Your treason is as plain and obvious as your dead brother's face. Good thing Dear Leader has already decided he no longer needs your services." Geomi made the rasping sound again, that horrible attempt at a light-hearted laugh. Suddenly, Jin knew she had to move fast.

She feinted toward his gun hand, then grabbed at the hand holding the Unity disk. Geomi dodged, raising the gun once more, and pointing it at Jin's head. She was quicker. Stepping to the outside of his arm, she thrust her palm into the soft spot between his wrist and elbow, hitting a nerve that made his hand spasm and drop the gun. Shifting her weight forward, she followed through with a hard strike into his ribcage, punching two more times until she heard the familiar crunch of bone splintering within muscle.

Geomi grunted and dropped to his knees, the Unity disk plopping into the spongy surface beside him. Jin picked it up, and with one giant leap, dove forward and through the closest hole to her, the one with the street lights. Jumping out into an actual place was not nearly as disorienting as leaping into the white haze had been. She could see she was in an alleyway. *And whatever I see*, she reminded herself, *they can see back in the sub-basement.* She turned off her body cam and slid into the shadows behind a dumpster, just a step to the right of the light hole, and waited.

Geomi limped through the hole soon after, wincing as he looked in all directions in the street. "Jeng-jang!" he cursed, then said into the headset, "I am returning. The traitor Jin is not found. Put a trace on her immediately." At that, he leapt back into the light hole.

Jin debated walking off into whatever city this was, never to return to the sub-basement, hopeful that one day she and Chung would be reunited, if not in this life then the next. But then a quiet voice said in her ear, "Jin?"

It was Kyung. "He's gone to the hospital. Come back."

"You heard him. I am a traitor. I cannot come back."

"We will talk to Dear Leader. We will say he attacked you."

The lights outside of the alley beckoned to her. She could easily blend in with the throng of strangers walking past it, disappearing into anonymity, away from Dear Leader and his madness. But she knew that the thrill of freedom would be temporary, quickly replaced by self-loathing for abandoning Chung to foreign prison or death, and for shaming her family by taking the coward's way out.

Kyung spoke again. "What will you do?"

She looked down at the Unity disk and said with a sigh, "What I must." She leapt back into the hole.

CHAPTER 24

Back to the Fuzz

I gotta go back. Uhng..." Dean managed to roll over onto his knees. *If I can just get back on my feet*, he thought, *I can save her.* He accepted Mitch's outstretched hand and pulled himself up off the garage floor. Pain flared across his rib cage, and a wave of vertigo hit him. "Don't drop me, man," he mumbled. *Wow, I hope I don't pass out.*

Mitch lifted his shirt. "Geez, your whole left side is purple! You're not going anywhere."

"Mitch, she's in trouble! That shiny suit psychopath is gonna kill her! Grrrn!" His eyes watered. He was doing his best to straighten up, but damn if it didn't hurt like hell.

"And what are you gonna do about it? Moan at him? You just said 'Grrrn', for Pete's sake."

"Not to mention Mr. Psycho Suit's packin'," said Wayne, holding up Dean's destroyed cell phone, bullet lodged squarely in its center. "You got lucky with the first shot, pal. Even if you weren't hurt, I'd bet Asian Babe's better at dodging bullets."

"But what if she isn't?" said Dean. He was feeling better. He let go of Mitch's hand and fingered his side gingerly, hazarding to take a deep breath. "Man... still hurts, but... don't think anything's broken. Just loan me your phone and give me my fob."

"Will you slow down?" said Wayne. He'd plugged Dean's Jump!Go into the diagnostic computer and was scrolling through the logs. "You can't go back if we don't know how you got there in the first place."

Mitch leaned over Wayne's shoulder, watching the data scroll by. "We kinda do, though, right? I mean the glitch burst out plain as day when Psycho Suit showed up."

"You're not helping, dude," Wayne said quietly.

"Yes, he is," said Dean, loud enough to let Wayne know he'd heard him. "I'm sore, not deaf. What's your theory, Mitch?"

Mitch took over the scrolling, backtracking to a particularly dense clump of data. "See, right there at the beginning? That's how our data always looks, right when a jump point appears. It stayed that way right after Dean jumped to Milwaukee. Nothing new. But then the 'glitch' happened..." Mitch scrolled forward until he reached the timestamp for Dean's return jump, "...right here, at this orangish margin. See how the data stream gets even more dense and drawn out? It's like something..." He paused and shrugged. "...I don't know. 'Unfolded' the jump point? Stretched it out after it got trapped."

Wayne squinted at the screen, then snapped his fingers. "That's it!"

"Ha, ha!" Dean whooped and slapped Wayne on the back. "I knew you'd get it. What do you see?"

"The margin. It's orange!"

Dean stopped smiling, less jubilant. "K, maybe I don't get it."

"It's okay. No way you could know. See, it's output from the optical detector," Wayne explained, opening the log's detection settings and pulling up the sensor list to show him. "The damned glitch was driving me insane, so I threw every kind of sensor parser at the log, trying to find a pattern, and there it is."

"Ooooh!" said Mitch, bouncing up and down. "You're a genius."

"I still don't get it," said Dean.

Mitch pointed at the orange margin. "Optical detector, dude. It's a wavelength change."

"Exactly!" said Wayne. He and Mitch high fived.

It took Dean only a few more seconds to comprehend. He smacked his forehead. "Now I get it. The wavelength got longer."

"Right," said Mitch, his finger tracing the thick clump of data at the center of the screen. "But it's trapped, no place to go. Short wavelengths get compressed. Long wavelengths—"

"—decompress!" said Dean. Mitch nodded rapidly, his curls bouncing up and down. "So, all we have to do is figure out how to change the wavelength of a jump point and we'll be all set."

"We could use a timer chip," said Mitch.

"Yeah, but then the change would only be temporary," said Wayne. "The wavelength could snap back before we want it to."

"We're not camping in there," said Dean. "We're just gonna jump, grab the Babe, and skedat. What's that? Like five minutes?"

Wayne did some calculations. "With a 555 chip, we could get about... nine minutes and forty-eight seconds before the modulator pulse's back. That might be enough time."

Mitch rummaged around in the chip drawer. "Bingo!" His hand emerged, the tiny black component resting in his palm, prongs up, like a capsized insect. For the third time today, he removed the casing of his Jump!Go and set about the task of soldering the chip in place.

Dean sat down at the diagnostic computer. "I can update the firmware, but somebody's got to set up the modulation and pulse cycle."

"I'm on it," said Wayne, pulling up his chair to the main monitoring computer. The three worked in companionable silence, each moving quickly through their respective tasks, exchanging data, the program, and the device until finally Mitch snapped the casing in place, and handed it to Wayne to run the diagnostics. *Ping...*

ping... It cycled through the tests, the end of each punctuated by the reassuring switch of the progress bar from yellow to green. The last diagnostic looped through the appware user interface, pausing only to review Dean's latest additions—a neon orange button labeled "Jump Space" and next to it a timer counting down from nine minutes, forty-eight seconds. They crossed their fingers as the progress bar slowly creeped forward until, at last, it reached "100%" and turned green.

"Do the honors, brah," said Wayne, making way for Dean to click the button. The blue goo grid displayed immediately, each quadrant pulsing with trapped lights as before. The only difference now was that each light was surrounded by a bright, dreamsicle orange halo.

"Plug 'er in," said Dean. "I'm ready to go." He donned a headset, then gingerly slid his arms into a body cam vest.

"Dean, no," said Mitch. "You're putting on a good show, but not good enough. You barely got into the vest."

Dean was ready to argue about it, but the open concern on Mitch's face stopped him.

"Further," Wayne continued, "you've got no phone. No phone, no jump. Besides, I've been stuck inside watching you yahoos all day, so it's my turn. I'm shorter, too. Mr. Psycho Suit might miss me if he shoots."

"You trying to edge in on my girl?" Dean blurted out, immediately regretting as the others started laughing.

"You're mental," chuckled Wayne.

"And Asian Babe's an independent kung fu goddess," said Mitch. "I doubt she's anybody's 'girl.'"

Dean chewed his lip while he thought, then said, "We'll draw straws." More laughter.

"You can't be serious," said Wayne.

"It's only fair, guys." They laughed some more. "I know you're trying to protect me. I'll be fine."

Mitch and Wayne exchanged looks, some of the amusement dropping away. *That's right, guys, I see right through you,* Dean thought.

Finally, Mitch said, "Ok. We'll draw straws."

"Hot dog!" Dean grabbed four coffee stirrers from the snack shelf, cut one short, then rolled them around in his hands to mix them up, being sure to keep the short one closest to him to ensure he'd grab it. Foolproof plan!

They each held up their straws.

"Looks like I'm the winner," said Dean, broad smile on his face.

"Look again, pal," said Mitch, thrusting his straw under Dean's nose.

"What?!" He couldn't believe it. Mitch had the short straw. "No!"

"Hey, man, it's only fair," said Mitch with a smile. "It's also safer."

"Oh, alright," said Dean. "But if you see her, you better save her."

Mitch sobered, clasped Dean's arm, and looked him in the eye. "I'll try, buddy." Dean transferred the headset from his buzz cut to Mitch's curls. Mitch helped him out of the body cam vest, then attached the modified Jump!Go to his phone. He navigated through the app to the friendly "Jump Space" button and gave it a push. The blue goo grid displayed, embedded with orange-rimmed dots.

"One sec," said Wayne. He strapped a spare body cam to the end of a dowel and poked it into the Milwaukee jump point. White fuzz filled the monitor screen, but that was all. "I don't see Psycho Suit or the Babe." Turning back to Mitch he said, "If you're lucky, all you'll have to save is data."

Dean watched wistfully as Mitch slid into his own vest and waved his hand in front of the body cam to make sure it was on. His wiggling fingers appeared on the main monitor. Wayne flashed the thumbs up. Dean leaned over Wayne's shoulder to switch on the speaker. "Ready, Mitch?" he said into the mic.

"Ready." Mitch's wiggling fingers reformed into the "okay" sign. The image on the monitor shifted ever so slightly to the right as Mitch positioned himself in front of the Milwaukee jump point. Then Mitch took two great steps and leaped. The orange-rimmed hole filled the screen, expanding enough to let Mitch through, then dissolved slowly into the fuzz of the white room, at the end of which should have been the dim outline of the exit hole, leading to downtown Milwaukee. Instead, directly in front of Mitch, hurtling toward him much too quickly, was a small dark shape.

The dark thing grew the closer Mitch got to it, shifting from an amorphous blob into something that looked surprisingly human. "Mitch, look out!" Dean called into the mic. "It's— " He almost said "Psycho Suit," thinking the worst, but as the blob grew nearer on the screen, he could see the dark almond eyes, the lithe physique, the flowing jet-black hair. The Asian Babe!

Mitch's momentum was carrying him straight to her on a collision course and there was no way for him to avoid it. Dean didn't want him to. Her face was almost close enough to the screen for him to kiss it. He felt himself leaning in the closer she got. Then Mitch threw his arms up, blocking her face. The image on the screen shook violently, stopping only when Mitch fell down into the fuzz, his groans emanating from the speaker. *Musta hurt*, thought Dean. *But what I wouldn't give to feel that pain.*

CHAPTER 25

Skullduggery

Beep-beeeep! The lab timer in the corner of Room 103 went off, signaling the end of Bische's last class for the day. He stood near the door while students filed out, waiting to remove the doorstop, the first chore in locking up the lab for the night. Lainie Troy arrived at the tail end of the throng, dragging a trolley of recycling tubs for the maintenance crew to distribute overnight. He smiled at her, playfully miming exhaustion behind the lone remaining group that stood laughing and talking and moving much too slowly out the door.

"Ha, ha, there he is," she said, rewarding his silliness with her throaty laugh. She plucked a tub from the stack on the trolley and handed it to him as the very last student ambled away.

"Haven't seen you in a while," he said, dropping the tub against the wall just opposite the door. "Hope you were off having fun."

"Hmph, wish I had been," she said, dragging the trolley to the alcove just outside her office. "Messed with my car instead. Some idiot called himself stealing it, but was too stupid to do it right and wound up breaking the steering column so's it couldn't drive. Been gone arguing with the insurance company and the dealership tryna get it fixed for days. Finally got it back so's I can come to work. Don't hardly steer right, but whatever, it drives."

He nodded sympathetically and was heading back toward the lab when she called over her shoulder, "You clear up that student complaint?"

158

Bische stopped, not sure he'd heard her right. "Come again?"

Lainie dropped a tub outside the maintenance door and walked back over. "That girl or whoever," she said. "Before I left work, the night my car got broke, Dr. Wilkins shows up, waving a Geiger counter, talking about some student or other lodged a complaint, saying your back room was 'radioactive' and you were 'neglectful,' which I know you aren't, but he was all sweaty and worryin' about a lawsuit and being himself, pulling rank on me and carrying on, so I let him into your lab to look. Surprised he found something. Geiger counter clicked like crazy."

"The back room, you say?" Bische furrowed his brow and headed into the lab toward the storage room.

"Yeah, some kind of isotope, he said." Lainie followed him in. "It's alright now, he boxed up whatever and carted it off. Probably the student's fault anyway, but I betcha she got scared and was all like, 'Uh, oh, I screwed up' and was tryna pawn it off on you as if you'd ever be 'neglectful,' and ol' Hubert heard the 'L' word which you just know musta freaked him out, so he comes rushing down here to 'handle it,'" she rambled on, punctuating her disdain with an eye roll.

Bische waved his key card at the sensor panel to unlock the back room door. He spotted Mitch's box immediately, still where they'd left it, on the middle shelf of the storage rack off to the right. As he walked up to it, though, he noticed the flaps of the box sagging in on themselves, rather than propped up at attention by the mini-dish, whose steel rim he could not see. One look inside the flaps at the emptiness within told him everything he needed to know about the so-called radioactive spill. "Hubert," he muttered disgustedly under his breath.

"Hmph, I know that's right," said Lainie, another throaty laugh bubbling up from her chest. "But don't worry, he didn't report it. I woulda seen it at the top of the report list this morning when I logged into the network. I betcha he dealt with it himself, probably dropped it down a mine shaft or whatever, tryna hide it and avoid embarrassing the school. You know how he is."

"Yes," said Bische with a sigh. "I know very well." *The rat bastard.*

Lainie breezed back to her office, leaving Bische to ponder just how much of a rat bastard Hubert might be. Did he steal Campbell's canopy to make a point, or did he aim, as President Hayman had suspected weeks ago, to sell it to the highest bidder? *I bet if I shake him hard enough he'll tell me*, Bische thought, and got halfway to the door before good sense took over. As satisfying as pummeling Hubert would feel, it wouldn't be anything but counterproductive. *The stubborn weasel might not fess up, would more likely call the cops and toss me in jail. Where would that leave Campbell?*

He took a calming breath and set to pacing along the benches, unconsciously traversing his standard lecture path, pondering what to do. He paused in front of his junk drawer, reminded of the business card he had so recently tucked into it, and wondered if the watchful woman might be the better solution to the problem. It meant dealing with the Agency again and possible exposure. But she didn't seem to know him. Maybe enough time had passed that no one there did. To protect Campbell, it might be worth the risk.

He opened the junk drawer and rummaged around until his fingers brushed against an eagle-shaped embossment on stiff, expensive, paper stock. He withdrew the blue business card heralding "Travers and Lake" and dialed the number. No turning back now. She answered after the first ring.

"Not as fast as I expected," she said, right off the bat. "I take it Campbell is ready to deal?"

He chuckled at her directness. Agency training on display. "Actually I was calling to say that I've been—"

"Burgled?"

Huh. He hadn't expected that. Keeping his voice even, he asked, "You know this how?"

"A little birdy... surveillance, maybe. Wanna meet?"

He laughed outright. She wasted no time. "Where do you suggest?"

"Downtown. The Lonesome Rose."

"Fifteen minutes?"

"I'm not far," she said. "Let's make it ten."

He hung up and tossed the card back in the drawer. No going back, indeed.

CHAPTER 26

Burgers and Pool

B ische and Marion arrived at the Lonesome Rose, a dark and boozy music bar nestled in the heart of downtown Golden, popular with tourists for its burgers and craft brews, but equally loved by the locals as a colorful relic from the city's Gold Rush past.

They ordered at the bar—Parmesan bacon burgers, plantain fries, and a couple of Dale's Pale Ales—then carted their food to a high-backed booth in the game room, right beside the pool table. The speakers in the ceiling blared out the music of a local band scheduled to play the back room later that night. Along the walls, vintage game machines vied for attention, jingling, whistling, and barking their names every few seconds. Beyond the pool table and near the back, a largish group in School of Mines gear stood jawing and cheering around the dartboard. Overall, the atmosphere in the room was raucous, crowded and loud—the perfect environment for Bische and Marion to blend into for an anonymous conversation, one not easily overheard.

They slid into the wooden booth, its thick walnut seats absorbing some of the cacophony of drunken banter mingled with an aggressive guitar solo pounding from the speakers. Marion took an experimental nibble of her fries, murmured "Mmmm," then set to work putting a serious dent into the pile. Bische relaxed into his burger, sighing deeply as the cheese, beef, and bacon flavors mingled on his tongue. He hadn't eaten all day, so his hunger made the burger taste all the more delicious. He washed it down with a long, deep pull from his cold, cold pint, punctuating his satisfaction with a low, grateful burp, drawing a chuckle from Marion.

He walked over to the pool table and racked up the balls. Grabbing a cue, he offered it to her and said, "Break 'em?"

"My specialty," she replied with a sly grin. She set the cue ball on the head spot and thwacked it mightily, dispersing the balls to all corners of the table, one solid ball landing in the right side pocket. "Guess I'm solid," she said.

"You are indeed," he purred, slipping into his charm mode quite unconsciously. Marion rolled her eyes, but couldn't hide the slight blush that colored her cheeks. A pang of shame pinched him. *Dial it back*, he told himself. *Whoever you were with the Agency, you can't be that guy now and help Mitch.* He took another sip of beer and switched tactics.

"Not sure I'm happy about being surveilled."

"As interesting as you are, we weren't watching you."

"Good to know. The Agency and I had a deal, you see."

"And we've kept it—mostly." She banked the 6-ball off the left side of the table, the angle shooting it behind a clot of stripes. It landed neatly in the right corner pocket, so hard it rattled the plastic casing. *She's good*, he thought.

"Besides," she said, squinting as she sized up the 5-ball. "You'd have seen us coming a mile away."

"So, Hubert, then."

"Yes, Hubert. The Angry Troll. He didn't disappoint, either. He hid under the stairwell—"

"—a troll's natural habitat—"

"—until you left for the day, then scuttled over to maintenance —"

"—to lie his way into my back room."

"You've heard this already?"

"Lainie Troy gave me an earful. Seems Hubert was the first in a string of inconveniences for her that night."

"Ah, yes. That may not have been a coincidence. Do you know his lab assistant?"

"Christian?"

"Correct. We had an agent tracking him as well. He may have had something to do with Lainie's 'inconveniences.'"

"Interesting. So Hubert tells Christian to steal Lainie's car to keep her out of work so that she can't talk to me. Kind of clever, actually. I'm surprised Hubert had the imagination for that."

"Betcha two to one it was Christian's idea. Hubert probably suggested some artless attack, like 'Break her legs.'"

Bische laughed. "Christian would be hard pressed to break one of Lainie's nails, much less her leg."

"Exactly. He's a twig. She'd snap him in two like a Wheat Thin." The 5-ball sank into the side pocket.

"Fun to imagine, but not the real question."

"Which is?"

"Why let Hubert burgle me?"

"That was my call. We knew he was up to something. As sloppy as he is, we still couldn't find out what. That meant a bigger fish was running the game. I wanted to see where Dr. Troll would take it—maybe get a lead on the big fish."

"Did you?"

"We have a clue. He delivered Campbell's device to a foreign national." Marion pulled her phone from her pants pocket. After a couple of taps and swipes she gave it to Bische. The picture on screen showed Hubert handing an oversized suitcase to a tall, thin, Asian gentleman sharply dressed in reflective sunglasses and a gray, tailored suit.

Bische waited for Marion to continue. "...and?" he said when she didn't.

Marion stayed quiet, pretending to study trajectories for the 4-ball, but Bische wasn't fooled. She had a straight shot with #4, right at the left-side pocket. Her mimed angle measurements and sight lines were obviously stalls for time. Bische waited for her to line the cue up to take her shot, then said, "So you lost him?"

The cue slipped and overshot as she struck. Both the 4-ball and the cue ball landed in the pocket for a scratch. Marion looked at Bische accusingly, then handed him the cue.

"Not me, per se," she answered. "Our tracker did. He tailed Hubert for a week, thought the job was easy. He got sloppy and failed to take precautions."

Bische chalked the cue, then knocked two striped balls off the table in quick succession. "So the sharp-dressed fish bit through the line," he said.

"Mm hmm. Iced the tracker. Gone without a trace. We suspect he left the country."

"And Hubert's a free man why?" *Bing. Bing.* Two more balls rocketed off the table. "Up to me, he'd be in Supermax counting floor tiles."

"Believe it or not, he's got his uses," said Marion.

"Enough to keep him out of stir?" All the striped balls were gone, cleared from the table in under three seconds. He set to work on what was left of Marion's solids.

"As long as he's bait for the real catch. So we kept monitoring him. Sure enough, a couple days later a sizable deposit lands in his offshore bank account from what looked like a South Korean company, based on the name... but with a Pyongyang address."

Bische had aligned his cue with the one remaining solid, set close to the front-left pocket, but almost blocked by the 8-ball. This statement pulled him up short. He straightened as the truth of it sank in, and for the second time today, he rubbed his eyes and muttered "Hubert" under his breath. "Hubert probably thinks it's all corporate espionage. Lucrative trade secrets."

"To be sure. If it was, he'd be in iron bracelets and you and I wouldn't need to have this chat. As it stands, Hubert got tricked into treason, but if we cluck too loud about it, it'll become an international incident."

"That's only if they can get the Canopy to work. The device is in pieces. Even when it was still assembled, Campbell admitted that it was a fluke it had even worked at all."

"They've had some practice." Marion beckoned him to the relative quiet of the booth. She tapped her phone again, pulling up a set of files. "Another group in the agency was monitoring the North Korean network, back when Campbell published his paper. They didn't know what they were looking at, but after Hubert committed the big 'T,' we got all of their data and saw this."

Marion pointed to a series of charts, all with the telltale markers of jump points, but with wild fluctuations in stability.

"Looks like a series of failures," he said as he swiped from file to file, the data growing bigger and uglier in each.

"You're right. They kept tossing things at their version of the canopy, but nothing ever came back."

"Some of this data is huge. What kind of things?"

"Random animals, mostly, and one poor human. Kind of a mess. Up until here." Marion opened the most recent file. "This is after Hubert's dance with the tailored suit. The data is stable, a success, and almost looks like an improvement over Campbell's original design."

"Right, but..." He studied the data some more. There were spikes tangled up with the human and jump point signatures, nothing like he'd ever seen with Campbell's data, nor even the failure data from the previous files. They appeared muffled at first, like an underlying carrier wave or a secret message, but then the spikes rose dramatically, energetically, almost as if there were tied to —

"An explosive," he said—not a question, a certainty. "Powerful one, too, if that spike there can be believed."

Marion nodded agreement. "We did the math. It's enough to level a large city."

"Which one?"

"From the communication intercepts, our guess is Seoul. The day after their man got Campbell's device, Dear Leader announced a major reveal, supposedly happening at his dead grandpa's birthday celebration. It would 'unify the masses under one country,' if I'm remembering the grandiose megalomania correctly."

"When's grampy's party?"

"Three days. Two, if you factor in the time zone. We're guessing about Seoul, though. The real target could be any place. Pike's Peak is just as likely."

"Where's the rest of the file?"

"What rest of the file?"

"There's no exit point here for the person carrying the explosive. There must be another part of the file," Bische said, scrolling back through the folder on Marion's phone. "I want to see where they went."

"You've got the whole thing," said Marion, her voice grave, her eyes intense and unflinching, focused on Bische's own. "We think they've found a way to hide inside of Campbell's light holes. The explosive and the carrier are there until Grampy Day, as far as we can tell."

"This is where I say 'Oh, shit.' "

"Be my guest. 'Fucking hell.' and 'We're screwed.' also work, at least for me."

Bische thought for a moment. "Campbell's device works via the network. Shut it down."

Marion scoffed. "Flip the switch on the whole internet? Oh, no one's gonna notice that."

Bische shrugged away her sarcasm. "Outages happen."

"Explainable ones do. What if shutting off the network collapses the light hole and triggers a boom? The internet blinks *and* Pyongyang disappears, simultaneously? No amount of explaining will make that sequence of events look like a coincidence."

"The agency shouldn't care. Take the hit."

"It's too loud. No squawking, remember? Our directive is to clean this up quietly."

"Disinform. It's the agency's specialty."

"Campbell spoiled that idea once he published his paper, then held a public party— widely advertised—to test it. If he hadn't, we could have painted the device and its usage as a purely academic curiosity, like another Earth-like planet we'll never travel to or artificial meat. But with so many witnesses, in town and out, the genie's out of the bottle. It would be louder trying to shove it back in."

"Why are you talking to me, Marion?"

She seemed startled by the question. "Well, obviously, your lab—"

"No," said Bische, harsher than he'd meant to, but only because he'd had the sudden feeling he was being played. "It's not obvious, Marion. You could drive to Samantha Chamber's house right now, take all of Mitch's devices, and lead a commando team right here," he pointed to the explosives file, "to take out the poor sucker carrying Dear Leader's big boom before the corpse of his grandpa gets propped up next to a cake. Instead, you sit here with me, eating burgers and drinking beer. Me, specifically. It's not obvious. Why?"

Marion munched on a fry and sighed before answering. "Campbell's a loose cannon. We take his toys, he won't be quiet. That goes for Chambers and Hirano, too. It's loud. If word got out, the Agency might want to... cut its losses. There's a lot I'll do, but deleting kids—that's not in my list. Campbell trusts you. You talk, he'll comply. It's that simple. We only have three days." She glanced over at the pool table. "I'm behind the 8-ball, here. Help me."

Bische followed Marion's eyes to the solid yellow 1-ball trapped imperfectly between the 8-ball and its hole. His beer sat sweating on the edge of the pool table. He got up, drained it, and with a quick flick of his cue banked the 1-ball away from the 8-ball into the far-right pocket.

Marion raised an eyebrow and said, "That's not what I meant."

"I know," Bische replied with a wink. "But it's a start. Let's go."

CHAPTER 27

Fail Safe

M itch, look out!" He'd seen the blob hurtling toward him before Dean shouted his warning, but there was no way to avoid it. Or her, rather. He could tell from the diamond-shaped face, straight flowing hair, and form-fitting suit, that it was the Asian Babe.

They could have been mirror images, both with arms pumping, chests thrust out, and legs tucked under from their enormous leaps. *It'll look symmetrically hilarious when we crash*, he thought. He crossed his arms in front of him at the last minute, hoping to absorb at least some of the collision. *Bang!* It happened. She hit into him so hard his head swam, as if he'd slammed into a bag full of pudding and bricks.

Something flew out of her hand, landing about a foot away. Effortlessly, she curled into a ball mid-air, then flipped down to the "ground" into a shoulder roll that pushed her to her feet. *Whoa*, thought Mitch as he dropped artlessly into the fuzz, expecting the impact to hurt about as bad as the crash. It surprised him that the jump point's floor felt spongy, almost like landing on a gym mat. He attempted his own athletic roll, but only managed to flop onto his face.

"Looking good, brah," said Wayne in his ear.

"Ouch," mumbled Mitch. "She looked softer from far away."

"Introduce yourself," Dean urged. "Tell her I sent you to save her."

Mitch scrambled to his feet to face her. She dropped into a defensive crouch. He held his hands up, palms forward, and grinned in what he hoped was a friendly, ingratiating way.

"Hi, Asia—um— you. I'm Mitch. Dean—um— that other guy... he sent me to save you. From Psycho Suit." Mitch winced. This was worse than the crash.

"Dude, you're wrecking it," said Dean. "Turn the volume up and I'll talk to her."

"You'll hit on her, you mean." Mitch saw her eyeing something to his left. It was the blocky thing she'd dropped when they collided, closer to him than it was to her. "Hold on, I got this," he said into his headset, then reaching for the blocky thing, he said, "Hey, you dropped something. Ooof!"

He'd been focusing on picking up the blocky thing and did not see her hard-booted foot lashing out. It hit him in the upper thigh, dropping him immediately to his knee. She snatched the thing away, then stepped back, scowling and watchful.

"Will you stop with the kicking, for Pete's sake? We're trying to help you!"

"Release my brother."

Mitch struggled back to his feet. "From where? Who's got him? I don't know where he is."

She continued to stare at him suspiciously, but after a few seconds seemed to deflate. "Then stop helping. Leave. I cannot protect you." She took off running, the fuzz splintering into spokes in front of her, orange-tinged jump points appearing at the end of each. She sprinted down the closest spoke, bending it into the shape of a corner as if by the force of her will.

"Gods, she's amazing," said Dean.

"Time's ticking, Mitch," said Wayne. "Either catch her or come home."

Mitch skidded to the corner's edge and paused to look. She was moving away swiftly, *but to what?* he thought. He checked his phone. Wayne was right—just four minutes left. He tested the fuzz with his toes, bouncing up and down. "This stuff is springy, guys. I bet I can catch her if I jump and fly."

"Do it!" said Dean.

Mitch ran, then leapt. Ran and leapt, stretching his legs out to cover the distance like a champion hurdler on the track. Within seconds, he'd covered the distance between them, until he was close enough to be bombarded by her bobbing hair.

"Hey!" he yelled into the back of her head. "Turn around. We'll be crushed. This place is about to collapse."

"You lie," she snapped over her shoulder. Speeding up, she and pulled away from him, clearly headed for the jump point at the end of the spoke.

Mitch increased his leaps until he was at her head again. "No lie. We timed it." He held his phone up near her face, so that she could see the timer; only three minutes left. "We have to leave before zero. Else *splat*! We'll be squished."

She ignored him. He reached for the wrist that held the blocky thing, hoping to grab onto it and slow her down. *Wham!* He got a face full of elbow. His eyes welled up with tears.

"What the hell!" Mitch stumbled backward, covering his face with his hands.

"Why do you want this?" she demanded from somewhere to his left. He couldn't see her anymore, didn't care. His face ached so bad, he thought he would vomit.

Swallowing, he said, "Want *what*? Geez, we... we've got to get out of here." He wiped his eyes and checked the phone. Down to two minutes. "Like, right now." He staggered forward and tried to grab her again.

She twisted into the punch, driving it squarely into his gut, forcing a gurgling sound out of him that was so unexpected he wasn't sure that he'd even made it. He didn't remember falling down, but somehow there he was on his knees again, his mouth tasting salty, full of something he hoped was spit. He coughed, and the fullness escaped as a great clot of blood, landing onto the back of his hand. "Gah, you busted my lip," he said. His head felt thick and sluggish.

"Dammit, Campbell, she's getting away. Get up!" A woman's voice, sharp and commanding, filled his headset.

"Wha—?" He shook his head, confused. *Not Wayne*, he thought. Or was it? He coughed again and felt sick to his stomach. *Maybe I've got a concussion. I'm hearing things. How hard did she hit me?*

His phone began buzzing. He looked at it dully. Less than a minute. Shit! Fear cleared his head. From his knees he could see just barely around the bend in the fuzz to the jump point for the garage.

"Shake it off. Go after her," the woman spoke again.

"No," he said, his voice sounded feeble and far away.

"To your left. High tail it, Mitch. Outta time, buddy," said Wayne.

"Ignore him, Campbell. Chase the girl. Get the box," said the mystery woman.

"Don't listen, Mitch! Go now!" said Dean.

Mitch staggered to his feet and stumbled toward the outline of the jump point, but he was too late. 00:00 blinked red on his phone. And from somewhere in or beyond the ether, a mechanical voice said, "Fail safe engaging."

Something felt like it latched onto his shirt, stopping his forward progress. Around him, the white fuzz took on a distinctly grayish hue, the sharp corners of the room dissolving into something rounder. The outline of the jump point faded completely, almost in concert with the tightness of the grip on his shirt. Whatever haze the Asian Babe had slapped Mitch into lifted as the clamp on his shirt became a pull, the feeling of being yanked backwards growing ever stronger. "Wayne? Exit's gone. Something's grabbed me. Help!"

"Hold on, buddy. Working on it," said Wayne, his voice calm, but strained. Dean seemed to be saying something, but Mitch couldn't make it out. A wave of static filled the comms. Whatever had grabbed his shirt had worked its way down his back to his ankles, pulling him off his feet.

"Aaaaeeeiii!" The sound again was ripped from him unbidden. He didn't care. He scrabbled, clawing the now dark gray, ungraspable fuzz with useless hands, desperately groping for a solid anything to keep from being dragged away. The Asian Babe appeared unscathed out of nowhere, it seemed, a horrified look on her face. She rushed at him, reaching out her hand toward him, but stopped short, as if realizing that she could get sucked in, too. "No! Help me! Please! Aaaaeeeiii!" He couldn't reach her. He was falling. The gray blackened. And then nothing.

CHAPTER 28

Along for the Ride

Marion pulled her car through to the backyard, as far as Samantha's driveway allowed. Bische parked on the street. They walked around back to the free-standing garage. The door was closed and it was quiet—not what Bische had expected. Usually, the door stood open, gracing the neighbors with music, loud banter, and the rhythmic thrum of the 3D printer. He tried the knob, and it was unlocked, but as they stepped in he knew something was wrong.

Hirano sat at the main computer typing furiously, while Chambers leaned over him, speaking into a microphone, which was plugged into comms. The blue plasma grid suspended off to the side told him where Campbell likely was. A young Asian woman's face, beautiful, yet severe appeared on the main monitor. He heard Campbell's voice over the speakers. Marion cursed under her breath and leaned toward Bische. "There's the carrier," she whispered. Bische's stomach knotted.

He closed the door, the sound of the latch catching Hirano's attention. "Kinda busy right now, Doc," he called over his shoulder.

On the monitor, the Asian woman turned away. Campbell's body cam followed, the focus shifting from her back down to her hand. She was carrying a blocky case, the size and thickness of a sandwich. "And there's the payload" said Marion, moving across the room until she was directly behind Hirano. Campbell's hand appeared on the monitor, reaching for the woman's wrist. She whirled around and lashed her hand across the camera's eye like a whip.

Campbell grunted. The woman's face wobbled and was immediately replaced by white fuzz. "What the hell!" said Campbell, his voice sounding small over the speaker.

"That's it," said Bische. He grabbed a harness off the closest bench, secured it's bungee to an eye-loop embedded in the wall, and then stood by the grid, looking for Mitch's light hole.

Out the corner of his eye, he saw Marion poke Chambers in the back. "Tell him to get up. We need that box."

"Who the hell are you?" came Chamber's angry reply.

The grid looked strange. Orange halos encircled each jump point, and some lights burned brighter than others. He followed the trail of dimming lights until he saw one in particular, flickering off and on. *Must be Mitch*, he thought. He stepped back to leap in.

"Wait!" "Not yet!" Marion and Hirano's voices overlapped. Bische wanted to slap the both of them, but fighting the urge, he turned to Hirano and demanded, "Explain."

Without looking away from the main monitor, Hirano pointed to a timer on the diagnostic computer—two minutes remaining and counting down. "Hole's unstable. Gonna collapse. Too far. No time. Finding closer hole." He continued typing furiously.

Marion pushed in front of Chambers and said into the mic. "Shake it off. Go after her."

Campbell's voice came back weakly, "No..."

"Found one," said Hirano. He slid his chair between Marion and the mic and said, "To your left. High tail it, Mitch. Outta time, buddy."

Marion forced her way back to the mic. "Ignore him, Campbell. Chase the girl. Get the box."

Chambers dove in front of her. "Don't listen, Mitch! Go now!"

"Back off, Beefcake. I'll flatten you like a squirrel."

"Go for it, Giganta!"

"Trying to concentrate, people," said Hirano. "Losing signal—no!"

The countdown on the diagnostic computer hit all zeros. A mechanical voice intoned over the speakers, "Fail Safe engaging." This was followed by a blast of static. The image on the monitor faded from fuzzy white to gray.

"Something's grabbed me! Help!" Campbell shouted.

Marion leaned into the mic. "Don't panic, Campbell. You'll be fine. Chase the girl."

Chambers snapped. "You unfeeling bitch!" He tried to wrangle the mic away from her, but Marion grabbed his thumb and twisted backwards, hard. Chambers fell to his knees. Putting her face directly up against his, she said "Shove me again, Thundarr, and you'll lose this arm."

"Stand down, Marion," said Bische, and with a flick of his wrist broke Marion's grip on Chamber's thumb. Chamber's rolled away to his feet, rubbing his hand, and glared at her.

On the monitor, the Asian woman appeared again against the gray. She ran over to Campbell, a look of fierce determination on her face. "That's my girl!" Chambers called out to the screen. "Save him, Babe!"

Campbell's arm appeared, stretching out to her. She reached out to him, but his hand kept receding from hers. Then she stopped, frozen, her fear at what appeared to be dragging Campbell away palpable through the screen. Over the static, they heard Mitch shout, "Help me! Please! Aaaaeeeiii!"

The blue grid collapsed. The image on the monitor winked out.

"Mitch? Mitch!" Chambers yelled into the mic. One last blast of static spilled out of the speaker and then—silence.

"Calm down, Conan," said Marion, her nonchalant tone a crime. Chambers lunged for her, wild-eyed. Bische didn't blame him, almost let him succeed, but stepped between them at the last minute, stiff-arming Chambers. He turned cold eyes toward Marion. She didn't flinch. "He's not dead," she said.

"Maybe," Hirano gulped. "...maybe, I can... pull up the grid again... maybe..." His fingers raced over the keyboard, his eyes never leaving the screen. A choked sob escaped from him. He stopped typing and dropped his face into his hands. "He's gone."

Chambers watched the monitor, his hands on his head, curled into fists around his hair. Tears streamed down his face. "No..." he groaned, the word emerging as an ache.

Marion snorted. "For the tenth time, Campbell is fine. The Fail Safe will have kicked in."

"You keep saying that! *What* Fail Safe? How do you know he's fine?" shouted Chambers.

"You'd do well to lower your voice, Bobo."

"Or what, Brünhilde? I dare you to make me."

"Oh, please. A first grader could 'make' you."

"Guys!" Hirano was on his feet. "Mitch is vaporized, or phased, or something else awful has happened! Insulting each other isn't helping." Wayne wiped his eyes, took a deep breath, and faced Marion. She was much taller than him, but he squared up to her, stiff-backed, and said, "If he's fine, and for your sake, he better be, tell us where he is. Now." Bische nodded assent. *Good play, Hirano.*

Marion thought for a moment."...I'm not sure."

"See?!" yelled Chambers. "She doesn't know!"

"Yo, Tarzan, pipe down. I can find out." Marion pulled out her phone and poked in a number. After a short wait, she said, "It's me. You got him? Good. I'll be there. In a bit." She put her phone away and said, "He's fine," then turned to Bische. "I'll be in touch." She headed for the door.

Bische moved deftly to intercept, sliding effortlessly between her and the door, almost in the same second that she moved. She rocked back, surprised. Bische locked eyes with her, pleased in spite of himself to see her expression morph from mild shock to admiration, but then the moment passed. She relaxed in that way fighters do, just before they strike, and said quietly, "The game's changed, Doctor, sorry. I'll handle it from here."

She took a step to his left, but he moved right with her, continuing to block the exit. "This isn't a game, Marion. Mitch isn't your pawn. And if you think you're leaving here without us, you are mistaken."

She rolled her eyes. "You know I can't do that."

"Why not?"

"*Classified*," she said impatiently, as if it was obvious. "Keeping it quiet, remember? The smart one, Hirano, maybe could come, but Lothar here's way too loud."

"Hey!" yelled Dean. "I'll show you lou—"

Bische raised a placating hand and silenced him with a stern look. Turning back to Marion, he said, "Then you'll spend the night here."

"I have people I can call to prevent that,"

"And you think Chambers is too loud? You think the neighbors will ignore your 'people' storming the garage?"

Marion glared at him, clearly not happy to be trapped by her own logic. She sighed, then pointed at Chambers and Hirano. "Your responsibility. Whatever they see or do, it's on you."

Bische acknowledged with a nod, then stepping away from the door, he said, "Lead on, Brünhilde."

CHAPTER 29

Underground

F ail safe retrieval—completed."

Cold. Dark. Falling? No. Mitch's mind came back to him slowly. He could tell he was laying on something—a cold, hard, unyielding something. He wasn't falling anymore, and whatever had grabbed him had let him go. His whole body felt numb, and he realized with a shock that he wasn't breathing. *Oh no, I'm dead!* This thought made him flail. He opened his mouth to inhale, expecting it not to work. When it did, he spent the next sixty seconds gulping in big draughts of air. *Okay, I'm not dead,* he thought, *but geez, where am I? And why's it so dark?*

More seconds passed. As his breathing slowed, he felt the area around him and determined that he was on his back. He rolled onto his knees, then waved a hand in front of his face, which made him aware that his eyes were closed. He laughed at himself. *Now I know why it's dark.* He opened his eyes and saw he was in a room. Tall, black, rectangular closets covered in blinking lights lined the faded yellow walls in front of him. Metal nameplates with the initials "NEC" were hammered into the top of each closet. Two workstations sat on his left, occupied by old-style, boxy computer monitors, each with a single white cursor blinking forlornly on an otherwise dark, empty screen. It all looked vaguely familiar.

He considered standing up, but noticed a stickiness all over his clothes and a wetness in his hands. It was the tell-tale blue ooze, the plasma residue that had covered him the very first time he'd used the travel device so many months ago. "Ick," he said out loud, his voice swallowed by the whir of late '80s technology.

A voice somewhere in the vicinity of his neck said, "Thought you were dead, didn't you."

"Gah!" Mitch yelped and flopped onto his stomach. A balding man wearing a white lab coat and a mischievous smile peered down at him, thin wisps of gray hair poking out in patches across his dry, peeling scalp. His brown polyester pants, white socks, black shoes, and tan polo shirt looked as outdated and unkempt as the contents of the room. Mitch was inclined to dismiss him as simply the doddering caretaker of the room's relics, but that thought died the longer the old man stared. His piercing eyes gleamed with intelligence and authority, and regarded Mitch with a strange mixture of bemusement and mistrust.

It was creepy. Mitch could have sworn he'd been alone in the room when he'd landed. He hadn't heard anyone enter. *Did this guy appear out of thin air?* The man's intense stare, advanced age, and ironic clothing gave him an unreal, otherworldly quality. Mitch fought the urge to ask him if he was God.

"A lot harder to break into here than you thought, eh?" Mitch's face wrinkled into a question. "C'mon," the old man continued. "Don't play your hand that way. It's obvious what you're after. If you fess up now, I'll make sure they go easy on you." Still Mitch stared blankly.

The old man furrowed his brow. "You've got no idea what I'm talking about, do you?"

Relieved, Mitch shook his head. "No, sir."

"Ha!" The old man threw back his head as he laughed, and when his eyes met Mitch's again an amused twinkle had replaced the thinly veiled distrust. He regarded Mitch more closely. "Ah, I got it now. Mitchell Campbell, I bet. Right?"

"Yes, sir." Mitch gulped. *Uh, oh. He knows me. That* can't *be good.*

The man helped Mitch to his feet. "Son, there's some people who want to talk to you. I'll—" *Brrrp, brrrp.* A phone chirped in the old guy's lab coat. He rummaged around in an oversized pocket before finding it and answering. "Travers," he said, just sharply enough to let the caller know that he was annoyed by the interruption. "Yeah, he's fine. When? K, we'll be here." He returned the phone to his pocket and said, "Let's go," ushering Mitch out the door.

They walked through a twisting, brightly lit corridor. People milled passed them, some in military dress, others not, but all of them wearing name tags and moving with efficient purpose. Mitch stared dully at the steady stream of workers passing them by, wiping his hands absently on his pants—not fully aware of the blue goo anymore, but registering subconsciously that his hands were wet. Finally, he asked, "Where am I?"

The old man looked at Mitch and chuckled. "Wonderland."

"No, seriously. Where are you taking me?"

"To see my boss. She's over at the SMOR. It's not far from here."

"What does she need more of?"

"Whaddaya mean?"

"You said 'some more.' Some more of what?"

Scott laughed again. "You're killin' me, kid. It's an acronym—S.M.O.R.—but we pronounce it 'SMOR' for short. You'll see."

They walked along in silence. Mitch looked at the guy's badge again—"Scott Travers," it read. He committed it to memory in case he would ever need to refer to the man as something other than "old, dry-scalped, poorly dressed dude."

They rounded a corner at the end of the hall and were met by a large set of blast doors. Travers waved his badge in front of the key panel, and they passed through into yet another corridor filled with casually dressed, lanyard-toting techie types, all in various states of anxious haste. Once in a while, someone knowingly glanced their way or acknowledged the old man, but for the most part they all seemed preoccupied. *Something must be going on*, Mitch thought, *and it must not all be related to me.*

"You know, kid, you're really surprising me," the old man said suddenly. "I mean, you're the only thing folks around here have been yakking about for the last month. 'Kid Genius' and all that. You went and took something that was little more than a thought experiment back in my day and turned it into a reality—better than I could do, and *I'm* the one who built it. But now you say you have no idea where you are?"

179

"How could I know?" Mitch said, unsure why he felt so defensive. "It's not like your badge says anything besides your name. I've never been here before, I honestly swear. I'm clueless."

Travers veered into a stairwell and they descended it into a long, cold tunnel that led to another set of blast doors. Travers pace quickened as they crossed through the tunnel. Mitch almost had to trot to keep up.

"We got proof you were here already. You and one of your friends, exactly four weeks ago. You tripped the alarm and scrammed."

"That was here?" Mitch couldn't believe it, but as soon as he'd asked the question, he realized it was possible. When he and Wayne had landed in the room that night, it was dark and only one console had been on. In his mind's eye, he thought back to the cabinet he'd peered into curiously that night, one giant rack of black knobs and red switches beneath rows of dead bulbs. He'd seen that same cabinet briefly today, just before Travers had hustled him away from his landing spot. He realized that the cabinet had been awash in lights. *Oh, man*, he thought. *I must have triggered something. Maybe all this bustle* is *about me.*

They had reached the blast doors. Travers raised his hand, signaling Mitch to stop.

"Look, if you got anything to say, say it now to me before I take you in there, and maybe we can work something out. Otherwise, kid, you might have to wait to go home, if you get what I'm saying."

Mitch didn't know what to tell him. In all the weeks since the Canopy had first erupted, he'd felt smart—brilliant, even. He'd convinced himself that he knew what he had done, wrote the paper with Wayne and Dean, and acted like the super star. Now, this old dude was treating him like a criminal or spy and implying he was about to go to jail. It was a bit much.

"Okay, I admit it. I didn't know this was here and barely understand why what I did worked," he snapped. "It's like the chicken before the egg. I made this thing and it worked bizarrely, but then I had to figure out *how* after the fact. You're acting like I did some deliberate thing and that I have some treasure trove of secret knowledge, but you know what? I don't. We just have this fluke that makes holes in space people can jump in and out of. We shrunk it and wrote some apps to support it. Beyond that, you know way more than me."

Travers stared at him long enough to make him feel even more uncomfortable. Then he said, "Tell me, kid, what you think you did. Right now." He said it with such intensity Mitch was taken aback.

Why is he asking me this? I just said I can't explain it. I just feel how it works. All of his pride in creating Big Blue and the Jump!Gos flowed away in the cold light of deep analysis. He wished Wayne was there, to provide the technical details. He wished Dean was there, to make a distracting joke. They weren't. The old man wasn't backing off. *Gotta rely on myself*, he thought. *Explain or go to jail.*

He closed his eyes, conjuring in his mind the image of the plasma grid and Wayne's network map and, suddenly, an answer came to him. "I created a quantum cage that, when projected, attracts and traps photons. We don't know how, but the photons we trap are amplified by nearby internet data centers. The data centers, plus the cage, keep the photons open all the way back to the source, so we can jump in and out of the photon holes, essentially traveling at the speed of light."

"And you know nothing else, aside from that?"

"Right."

"It's just you and your friends? No one working with you?"

"Right."

Travers studied Mitch for another long, uncomfortable minute. "Alright," he said finally. "I believe you, kid. Tell it the same way when we get in there. Hopefully, my boss'll believe you, too."

The sign above the blast doors read "Satellite Monitoring Operations Room." *Ah*, Mitch realized, *the SMOR*. Travers waved his badge at the SMOR's keycard panel, opening the door to reveal a high-tech control center. Large screens lined the walls, showing data of various sorts, some graphed, others raw, all on a continuous scroll. The middle screen looked milky white and a lot like the "other space" Mitch had just been saved from. A couple of blobs popped out in the white, one large, one small, both blurry. The people in the room gasped in surprise. Then the blobs vanished almost as quickly as they had appeared, followed by more milkiness and more data scrolling on the large side terminals.

Travers guided Mitch across the room by the elbow until they both stood behind a tall woman who barked a rapid-fire series of orders at the technicians and military-types scurrying between workstations beneath the middle screen. "Get it back, Wilson. Hurry up! Dammit, doesn't anyone know how to lock onto this phantom?"

Travers tapped the tall woman on the shoulder. "Kid's here, Francine. Where you want him?"

Francine glanced back and, upon seeing Mitch, grimaced. "For God's sake, Travers. Why did you bring him down here? Does restricted area mean nothing to you? The boy's already stolen one of your inventions."

Scott guffawed, then turned to Mitch and said, "You recognize anything in here?"

On reflex, Mitch shook his head. "No."

"See," said Travers. "He's clueless. It's not what we thought. Kid's got no idea what he's messing around with. 'Boy genius?' Pfft, like hell." He winked at Mitch.

Mitch smiled in what he hoped was a stupid way. *Anything to get me out of here.* He dropped his mouth open and squinted as he looked around at the various workstations, pretending to be puzzled by all of the "fancy" equipment. But then his gaze fell upon a large, silver cylinder under the data screen on the back wall, encased in plastic and pulsing blue. His eyes opened wide in a genuine expression of wonder and surprise. Before he could stop himself, he blurted out, "Hey, is that a quantum entanglement processor? Those things are real?"

The boss lady stared at him, stunned. Mitch realized his mistake and tried to cover. "My, uh, professor, showed us a picture—once. In class." Travers covered his face. Mitch tried again, recalling his speech to the old guy prior to entering the room. "I've got no idea where I am, how I got here, and I am only vaguely aware of what we are doing with the jump points. If this is some kind of top-secret spy facility, I'm really sorry. Just blindfold me and take me home. I don't care what you're doing. I just want to go back to my life."

Boss lady turned to Travers. "I'd say 'boy genius' is confirmed. Now we gotta lock him up. I'll have the MPs meet you on S-level."

"What?!" Mitch yelped. "Why? I just told you, I don't care what you're doing."

Francine had already walked away, back to dealing with the "phantom." Travers, looking sad, said, "Sorry, kid. You should have kept playing dumb." He hustled Mitch out of the room.

"But I *am* dumb. I know nothing. It's like you said."

"Yeah, I know. But you're smart enough to pick out an entanglement processor without batting an eye. There's other stuff back there that you might know; we can't take the chance." They were upstairs again. A security team met them on the other side of the first set of blast doors. "Don't worry, we just have to background check you, and then we can let you go. Sit tight."

They'd reached the door to a new room, requiring both badge and keycode access. Travers waved his badge, and one of the security detail entered the keycode. The door creaked open slowly like the entrance to a crypt. *Definitely not good*, Mitch thought. The guard shoved him into the room. "Wait! You can't leave me here!"

"Again, sorry. It's gotta be done." Travers pulled the door shut, and the guard re-entered the keycode to lock it.

Mitch thumped futilely on the door. The old man's voice was muffled, but still loud enough for him to hear. "Poor kid," he said, presumably to the guard. "Shoulda just shut his mouth."

CHAPTER 30

Through the Wall

C ome back! Let me out!" Mitch listened, his ear to the door, as Travers' footsteps faded away down the hall. He banged on the door more out of frustration than expectation that anyone would open it. He listened again. The hallway was completely silent. "Dammit!" He kicked a chair away from the conference table. It made a satisfying thud against the wall.

Thump, thump. Mitch froze. The sound had come from the wall. A muffled voice called out, "Annyeong?"

Someone had heard him! Mitch rushed to the wall and flattened his cheek against it, listening. He put his lips against the wall and shouted, "Hey! Help! You there?"

"Annyeong! Nugu issnayo?"

It was a male voice, very excited, calling him "Anton", probably Anton's friend. *Okay, I can be Anton,* Mitch thought to himself. *Anything to get this guy to open the door.* He pressed his lips back against the wall.

"Yeah! It's Anton, buddy! The door's locked over here! Can you hear me?"

The man called back, sounding less animated. "Yes. I can hear you." *Was that a sigh? Gotta play it up.*

"Yeah, uh, heeey... Can you, like, come over and open the door? I, uh, forgot the code. I'm locked in." He took his lips away and pressed his ear against the wall. *Please let him believe me. Please think I am a very stupid coworker and come let me out.*

"No, I cannot open the door," the voice called back, sounding defeated.

Anger flooded back into Mitch. "Oh, come on!" he shouted. *Old Travers must have spread the word about him.* "I am *not* a threat, okay? I won't tell anybody. I just want to go home!" Mitch punched the wall with his fists.

"Oh, please, no anger me," the voice said.

"What's that supposed to mean?" Mitch was so angry, he barely understood the guy. Then it dawned on him, that the occupant in the next room might not be a native English speaker.

"I mean that my door does not open," the man continued. "I cannot get out. Like you. We are... you know..." he hesitated, as if searching for the word. "Ah yes... prisoner."

"Crap! Just perfect." Mitch paced along the wall, swatting rolling chairs out of his way.

"No," the voice said through the wall. "No 'crap,' either. Just table and chair. Maybe you use trash can?"

"What?!" It took Mitch a minute before he realized what the man was talking about.

"Oh, dude, no. I meant like 'Shit!' "

"Right. No place to go 'shit'."

Mitch paused in his pacing, and laughed out loud. "Good one, man. I gotta save that one for Dean—" Out of habit he reached into his pants pocket for his phone and flipped on the messaging app. He froze looking down at the handset. "Wait a minute. I've still got my phone!" He reached into his other pocket and felt the now familiar oval lump of the Jump!Go. "*And* I've still got the fob!" He couldn't believe the old man hadn't taken either away from him as he lay incapacitated on the floor of the Fail Safe room.

"Dude, I think I can get us out of here," he said, pressing his mouth against the wall.

"Yes, please!" the man called back, suddenly excited again.

Mitch opened the map app on his phone. "If the map tracked my last location, I can plug the coordinates into the Jump!Go app and go back to the room where Old Guy found me." Conceivably, they could jump there and he could open a hole back to the garage. "It's as simple as 1, 2, 3!" he said and laughed.

The voice on the other side of the wall said, "Okay?"

"Sorry. I know that sounded crazy. You've got no idea what I just said."

"No," The voice said it so forlornly. *This guy sounds like a teddy bear*, Mitch thought. *I wonder what he did to get locked up?*

His connection to the network was fairly weak. The map app crawled, chewing on the request to display his previous location, but after several minutes, it opened. A red dot blinked, showing his current position, then a blue line snaked from it to another dot about fifty meters away. Both dots sat solidly within the outline of a large brown mass. "Cheyenne Mountain Air Force Station?" *Geez, I thought it was a lab, not the government.* But as Mitch thought about it, the location did make a kind of sense. Cheyenne Mountain was well known for housing an extensive, subterranean, surveillance and research complex. The facility was created around the same time as the ARPANET, the parent of the internet. It wasn't too farfetched to assume that parts of the original ARPANET infrastructure lay buried somewhere within the complex, nor was it much of a reach to imagine the architecture having a light-based segment. *It was probably a failure*, Mitch thought, *a one-off experiment that didn't quite work.* It would have stayed broken, too, if he hadn't created the Canopy. Obviously, something within the device woke up the dormant, light-based network protocols. *But why would that make Old Guy and Francine freak out? And what did the North Koreans want with it?*

The last question reminded Mitch of the guy in the next room, and made him consider whether it was smart to help release him. The man didn't sound American, and might even be one of the reasons why Travers and Boss Lady were so upset. *Maybe he's a bad guy?* Mitch wondered.

Unbidden, Bische's voice sounded in his head, "Critical reasoning, Campbell. Apply it." Whenever Bische had said this to him the past, it caused Mitch to slow down and examine the facts. Taking a deep breath now, he counted to ten and forced himself to step through the reasoning. If Foreign Guy was truly heinous, why hadn't they carted him off to prison or, at least, to Peterson Air Force Base? It seemed unlikely they'd just lock a major spy in a conference room like, "He can't cause trouble here." That could only mean that Boss Lady didn't consider him to be a major threat. Plus, the whole "crap" misunderstanding was killer. No hardened criminal would say something so simple and innocently funny. Yeah, he'd have to release him. But how?

"Think, Campbell. Do the work," he said aloud, imitating Bische's stern tone.

The Foreign Guy giggled. "Who is that?" he asked.

"My physics professor."

"Oh. Sounds like my father." The guy cleared his throat and said harshly, "'Put down cake. Pick up wrench. Study math.'" He giggled again. "Very strict."

"Ha, ha," Mitch laughed along with him. *This guy's a sweetheart. He's definitely coming with me.* Suddenly, he had an idea. *Maybe I can jump to him?*

He pulled up Dean's Jump!Go app and configured it for manual data entry. Then typing in the coordinates for both the conference room and the Fail Safe room, he invoked the plasma grid and hoped for a strong GPS lock. The Fail Safe jump point shone brightly, no doubt because it existed at the epicenter of the light-based network protocol. The conference room, much further away, warranted barely a blip. How could he augment the weaker jump point?

You don't have to, he told himself. *Ignore that point and make a stronger one.* Mitch's eyes roamed around the room. *If I could find a way to maybe focus one of the lights in the ceiling onto the wall and then pass the plasma grid in front of the light beam, it might capture a particle on its way into the next room.* The trick was to choose the right particle in the beam, one energetic enough to make it all the way through the wall. He didn't want to think about what would happen if he chose the wrong photon and got stuck half-way through. He'd have to do some tests first to find the right one.

Mitch put his mouth against the wall and said "Look, I think I've got a way to get over to you."

"Manse!" the guy called through the wall.

I guess that means 'Hooray' for him, thought Mitch. "Thing is," he continued," we're gonna have to do a test."

"Oh?"

"Yeah, I've got this device attached to my phone. It's kind of like a transporter—
"

"Nooo! No! No!" the man yelled back at him suddenly.

Mitch was taken aback. "What? Dude, it's totally safe. I do it all the time."

"You know about human fax?" the man said. He still sounded pretty scared, but Mitch caught a note of curiosity creeping in.

"I know lots of human facts," Mitch replied. "What's that got to do with anything?"

"No, I mean, fax. As like a... fax machine. As when you send paper using phone line. But with people."

"Oh! Right, yes, that is what I mean. I can send us out of here using my phone."

"That is what scare me. That's what put me here, in prison with crazy, shouting people. It almost kill me. I did not enjoy it. Good research paper, but you are mad man! Why did you make it?"

"You actually read my paper?" Mitch is truly surprised. He'd submitted it like it was a term paper, never expecting any real person outside of the university world would notice, much less read it.

"Yes. We downloaded from the network... lots of maths."

Mitch chuckled. "Cool! But seriously, it's okay, we worked out all of the bugs. It will be fine. I can get you."

"I do not know."

"I can prove it to you. We'll do some tests. It'll work. Trust me?"

"You are mad man. I cannot trust you."

"We'll do it together. You can trust yourself more than me, right?"

The voice was quiet for a time. "Perhaps. But I am not that smart."

"Dude, are you kidding me? You read my paper. In English, not your language, obviously. Sounds like you understood the paper, too. Even the 'maths.' You're plenty smart."

"You are kind. Still crazy."

Mitch laughed. "My buddy Wayne says that. He wrote the paper with me, him and Dean. My friends. You have friends, right?"

"I don't know. Maybe. Yes."

"If we get out of here, we can both see our friends again."

The voice was quiet, then said, "Maybe. My family, too."

"This test will be easier than reading my paper. We'll do trial and error. Piece of cake, okay?"

The man chuckled wanly. Adopting his father's gruff tone again, he replied "'No. Put down cake.'" They both laughed, and the man said finally, "Alright. I am ready to try."

"Let's do this, then!"

Mitch grabbed one of the rolling chairs. "First we have to calibrate the machine. Stand away from the wall." He turned over the chair and stomped on the plastic casing at the base of one of its legs until it cracked, freeing the shiny, metal wheel within. Then he jammed the back of a second chair against the side of the conference table to hold it place while he stood on it to reach a light in the ceiling.

He tapped the Jump!Go app on his phone, pulling up the plasma grid, and with one hand used the wheel to focus the light onto the wall. With his other hand, he slowly moved the plasma grid in front of the beam. Immediately, white dots appeared on the projection like tiny supernovae as photons from the beam became ensnared. "Bingo! We've got some gateways here." Mitch jumped down from the chair. Now that the grid was engaged, he could drop the wheel and let the program take over.

"Can you see light beams streaming into your side of the room?"

The voice, clearly in awe, replied, "Yes. I see points. On our wall, on the table, on wall behind me."

"Wonderful. I'm going to pass in this..." he searched for something small to send "...broken plastic chair leg, and you tell me where it ends up, okay? Here goes." Mitch tossed the leg into the closest light hole.

"Gah!"

"What?! You okay?" *Did I poke his eye out with the leg?* Mitch worried.

"The chair leg is stuck in the wall! That could be me! Gah!!"

"K, calm down. It's alright. That just means we don't use that hole. I'll—" he spotted a marker for the whiteboard. "—mark it off on this side so we know that one won't work. Trying another one now. Here comes a notepad."

"Gah!" the man cried out again.

Mitch sighed, willing himself to be patient. "What's the matter now?"

"The paper is stuck in the back wall. Always the wall. There is no escape from wall!"

"Alright, that's marked, too. How about this one?" He pushed through a stapler.

"That worked. It fell from air to the floor."

"Great! I'm coming through."

"Be careful!"

Tentatively, Mitch leaned into the light hole, and finding no impediments, jumped all the way through. "Huzzah!" he said with a flourish.

The room's occupant, a slightly beefy Asian man who looked no older than Mitch himself, raised his arms above his head in triumph. "Manse! Happy meeting!"

"Hello, stranger!" Mitch mirrored the man, throwing up his arms, laughing, and pumping his fists. *Yes! I figured it out. We're getting out of here.* He clapped his new friend on the shoulder and shook his hand. "Where should we go? Home? The zoo? Ha, ha!"

The man's eyes sparkled, and, grinning widely, he said "The zoo! But not the lion's cage."

Mitch had been kidding, but seeing the man's enthusiasm, he searched the Jump!Go app for any points near Cheyenne Mountain Zoo. Two loci pulsed on the display. He picked the closest one, then brandishing his fob like a sword, stabbed the space between the door and the conference room table, and invoked the plasma grid.

"Oooh!" said the man, taking several steps back as the large, blue rectangle sprang to life, seemingly out of thin air.

"Yeah, great isn't it?" laughed Mitch. He loved watching the grid appear, the cobalt and midnight gradient swirling like water, then settling into the familiar quadrants pocked with milky opals, each one, an invitation to adventure and parts unknown. Eagerly, he approached the point for the zoo, expanding it with his hand so that they both could see it. The sun had set, but the facility was still open. Huge floodlights illuminated the wrought iron gate, people milled about, and a steady stream of cars flowed by. "It's the main entrance. We're totally golden. Let's go."

Mitch beckoned him forward, but the young man remained near the wall, swallowing nervously. His face, so flushed and animated moments before, was now blank and pale. It was a stark reminder to Mitch that not everyone shared his daring spirit. *Why should he trust me? The guy barely knows me. Better fix that.* "Hey, what's your name?" he asked.

"Chung," the guy replied, his eyes transfixed by the grid.

"Glad to meet you. I'm Mitch," he said, stepping in front of the grid, blocking it from Chung's view.

It had the desired effect. Chung shook his head and looked up at him wanly. "Hello."

Mitch took his hand. "Just hold on to me. We'll jump together. It'll be fine. Friend?"

Chung smiled. "Friend."

They leaped into the hole, but instead of landing at the entrance to the zoo, they stepped back into the white.

"Chung!"

Mitch whirled around. It was the Asian Babe. Suddenly, her anger and anxiety made perfect sense.

"Sister!" Chung called after her. He took a step toward the Babe, but got no further.

The mechanical voice intoned, "Fail Safe engaging."

Mitch groaned, "Not again."

The space that he and Chung were in collapsed around them, the floor dropping beneath their feet, their bodies pulled by invisible hands. Just as before, Jin reached out to grab them, but the robotic voice said, "Fail Safe engaged," and before Jin could gain a hold, they were gone.

Mitch surveyed their location—in the Fail Safe room again. Laying on his back on the platform—again.

"Crap!"

"The trash can is there," Chung mumbled weakly, pushing himself up into a sitting position.

Mitch couldn't help but smile. Looking up at the ceiling, he wondered if maybe he'd tweaked his fob a little too much getting into the conference room. *I just probably need to reset it. Then we can get out of here.* He sat up on the platform and waited for the wave of vertigo that washed over him to fade. Then he pulled the power pack from the fob to reset it. The green light blinked, showing it was ready.

"I think I just needed to reset the Jump!Go. Ready to try again?"

Chung groaned, but said. "Okay. But I hope it works this time. I may need the trash can to vomit before you use it to crap."

"Seriously, this time it really should work."

Mitch opened the grid, found their hole, and grabbed on to Chung's shirt once again "1, 2, 3... Go!"

CHAPTER 31

The Last Full Measure

Jin couldn't believe it. Chung had just suddenly appeared. Alive! "He's here!" she yelled into the headset at Kyung. "I see him! He's with the American."

"You see who?" Kyung growled.

"Chung, he's close, in front of me, he's alive!" she said, all in a rush. She took off running, leaping through the fuzz, desperate to reach him.

Hyun said in her ear, "You are hallucinating. The inner space has made you insane."

She ignored him, focusing instead on her brother and the American. Chung turned around, his pudgy face breaking into his familiar grin. Oh, how she had missed him!

"Sister!" he called out and began his own sprint in her direction, but as he shifted, the mechanical, female voice spoke again, everywhere and nowhere.

"Fail Safe engaging."

Immediately, Chung toppled down as if pushed there by an invisible hand. "Not again," he groaned. His pleading eyes locked with hers. He strained an arm toward her, but the unseen force had already started dragging both him and the American away.

As they receded, the American called out to her "I'm sorry!"

Determined not to lose them again, Jin pushed hard against the "ground," then lunged forward, propelling herself to the spot where they'd fallen. She grabbed both of their hands and pulled backward with all of her might, but the invisible force was stronger, and she could not hold on. "Chung!" she cried, but it was no use. The yawning vortex appeared again, and they were gone.

She knelt, panting in the white fuzz, at war between despair and joy. Chung was gone again, slipped from her grasp. But, he was alive! She tapped her headset. "You heard him, didn't you?"

"Yes," Kyung said. "We both did. We believe you." He sounded as relieved as she felt.

"Where is The Spider?" she asked.

"He's gone," said Kyung. "He left a guard outside the door. You can return, but we cannot leave."

He guided her to the closest light hole until she materialized somewhere near the back of the canopy and crept cautiously forward, to the funnel's edge, back into the sub-basement. Kyung and Hyun gathered near the lip to greet her. "How long will Geomi be gone?" she asked, keeping her voice low in case the guard could hear.

"Who knows," said Kyung, just as quietly. "Take this." He handed her a different headset, connected to a multi-channel switch. "Push 'A' to talk, 'B' to mute. You can't speak on 'B,' but you will hear Geomi when he talks to me."

She still clutched the Unity disk in her hand. Cautiously, she propped it against the inside wall of the canopy while she swapped the old headset for the new one. Kyung pointed to disk and said, "What do you want to do about that?"

"We must destroy it," she said.

Kyung watched her gravely. "You say that as if it can be done."

"Geomi intends to use it for his own purposes," she said. "He is as mad as Dear Leader. Maybe more."

Hyun pushed past Kyung, stopping short of the canopy, but eyeing the disk greedily. He dove for it, but Jin was faster, scooping it out of the fuzz and securing it within a velcroed pocket of her cargo pants. Hyun pressed his fists to either side of his head, eyes fixed on the space where the disk had been, and keened like a despondent child. He spun toward Jin and, whispering desperately, said, "You've been to an American city. I heard you. We can sell the disk to the Americans. We can flee!"

"Aren't you listening?" Jin hissed back at him. Flattening her hand against her pocket, she said, "We cannot keep this. Not us, not Dear Leader—not Geomi, especially. It is madness in a box. It must be destroyed."

"No!" said Hyun, wide-eyed. "We have the advantage. Don't you see?" His voice rose, becoming more anguished as he spoke. "We can bargain. Escape to the South. Trade the disk for sanctuary. We must go!"

Jin stared at him. "You still think there is an easy way out of this," she said, incredulous. "You honestly believe we should trade mass destruction just to save our miserable lives." She shook her head, unable to make sense of the proposal. "Do you think the South would hide having such a weapon?" she continued. "When they speak of it openly to their allies, Dear Leader and Geomi will both know who betrayed them. Then, who do they punish? Who suffers while we 'live'? Our kin will not survive a day. Their heads on spikes will adorn the walkway to Dear Leader's palace. Your cowardice disgusts me."

Hyun took one last dive toward Jin's pocket, clawing at the Velcro flap. She wrenched free and swatted him across the face. "Soldier, control yourself! Remember what you are!"

"I do!" Hyun wailed. "Doomed is what I am!" Defeated, he sank down into Chung's workstation, sobbing into his hands.

"Listen," said Kyung to Jin. "I agree with your analysis, but your plan is no better than Hyun's. Destroying the disk will kill us and everyone else in the building. You may want to be a martyr, but I am not ready to die."

"Then find me a light hole to an unpopulated space. I will detonate it. You tell Dear Leader that it was an accident. Tell him I misjudged the location. Blame me, and he will spare your lives—and my kin."

Hyun brightened in his corner and said, "That could work."

Kyung regarded him bitterly. "You have no shame."

"She is a soldier. She can choose to die," Hyun said, defiant.

"He sickens me, but he is right. It is my choice." Jin said it with finality, but Kyung rolled his eyes.

"Your choice is stupid, but also not possible."

"Why not?"

"All light holes end near data centers. The American's paper was very clear. No mountains. No deserts. No forests. Always cities. Your plan simply will not work."

Jin thought a moment, then said, "If we cannot destroy the disk, then we must disable it. Let the munitions division take the blame."

"Better," said Kyung, scratching his chin. "But how do we disable it without looking like we did?"

There were voices at the door, one of them the guard and the other very clearly Geomi. Jin hissed at Kyung, "You are the scientist. Figure it out."

They tensed, listening, as Geomi typed in the keycode and the door lock buzzed. He entered in a cloud of cigarette smoke. Jin ducked into the closest light hole, back into the glaring white, hoping Kyung would have the sense to lead Geomi toward some other hole to continue his search for her. She activated 'B' channel.

"...still nothing?" Geomi was saying. "I am finding it hard believing you."

"Then have someone else read the data," Kyung said, affecting his old petulance, tinged with boredom.

Geomi chuckled. "That day will be here soon enough. For now, we need you. Where do you suggest?"

Kyung growled under his breath, then said, "There's a blip in the west quadrant. Perhaps she's there."

Jin's heart raced. She'd jumped through a western hole. She flattened herself as much as possible against the fuzzy white wall, hoping at least to conceal herself enough to take The Spider by surprise. He grunted as he leapt through, then appeared in the white space some distance in front of her. He pulled a gun from the inside pocket of his suit, and moved cautiously ahead into the white space, looking left and right, but never back. As his long legs led him farther away from her hiding place, she sighed in relief. She was safe for now, but for how long?

CHAPTER 32

Signal Loss

*B*abump... babump... Wayne absently noted the muffled sound of the highway under the woman's car as she drove them to wherever Mitch was supposed to be. They'd taken her over-sized SUV, which should have been about as maneuverable as a bus, yet the woman steered it skillfully through traffic like a race car, barreling at top speed down I-25. She hadn't said a word since they'd left Sam's garage, but to Wayne, it was obvious from the aggressive lane-jockeying that their presence on this excursion was hacking her off.

Bische sat up front. Wayne and Dean sat in the back, isolated from the front seat by a glass, privacy partition. If the lady had been feeling friendly, she could have slid open the glass, and explained to Wayne and Dean exactly where they were going, but she wasn't, and so she didn't. Instead, she smoldered, staring straight ahead mostly, but occasionally glancing angrily at Bische, and getting angrier by the minute, it seemed, as Bische ignored her completely.

Wayne stared out the window, watching the scenery, hoping to distract himself from the memory of Mitch's panicked screams and his own feelings of guilt at stopping Bische from jumping in to save him. By now it was too dark to see much aside from the headlights of cars that Marion fiercely cut off, frustrating any attempt by other drivers to pass or remain alongside her. It registered at the back of his mind that the windows were tinted, probably bulletproof or sound proof or both. Under normal circumstances, this fact would be intriguing. He'd wonder more about Marion's job, might even search on his phone for glass thicknesses, and read about the bullet speed or sound level required to shatter the SUV's windows. He'd do that if he cared, if they were touring around in this car for fun. But Mitch was likely hurt or dead, despite the woman's assurances, so he didn't give a rat's ass about anything else right now.

As soon as they'd left the garage, Wayne had opened a chat window on his phone and pinged Mitch, setting the window to continuously refresh. If Marion was right and Mitch was indeed okay, he should've been able to reply. Mitch was a fast chatter. He'd usually answer a ping in seconds, but twenty minutes had passed. No response.

Now he opened the Jump!Go app and clicked the Friend!Go tab, a feature Dean had added to help them track each other's fobs. A 2-D version of the plasma grid displayed, overlaid on top of a map of their current location. A red dot labeled "Wayne" appeared at the center of the grid, and his fob buzzed in his pocket, responding to the app's ping. Another dot labeled "Dean" appeared, almost on top of his. Dean's fob lay on the seat beside Wayne, and it, too, buzzed in reply.

Dean slid from his window to look over Wayne's shoulder, saw Friend!Go running, and said, "Good idea." The label for Mitch's fob remained grayed-out. Wayne tapped the "Locate" icon next to it, and they both waited anxiously for the progress bar to expand.

25%... 50%... 75%... 100%. It held steady at 100% for several seconds. "Hurry up," Wayne urged through gritted teeth. As if answering him, the progress bar disappeared and was replaced by the message "Not Found". Dean slid back to his seat, his hands clenched into fists, his eyes staring daggers into the back of Marion's head.

Maybe Mitch's phone is off, thought Wayne. Maybe the power cell in his fob had died. He scanned the apps on his phone, not quite believing that technology was failing him. "There's gotta be... something. I can try to... grrr!" He shook the phone, a silly and pointless gesture, but testament to his growing frustration and anxiety. He closed and re-opened Friend!Go, hoping to reset it, as if clearing cache and flushing the garbage collector would miraculously make Mitch appear. It didn't, and a lump formed in Wayne's throat as the evidence persisted that their friend was completely gone. His eyes felt hot. Gone. *Babump...* Mitch, gone. *Babump...*

"Help me! Please!" Mitch screamed in Wayne's mind, his panicked voice drowning out the sounds of the road. Wayne closed his eyes to trap the hot tears, only to see the replay of Mitch's outstretched hand, straining toward the Asian Babe, her face a mask of horror as Mitch was no doubt crushed by the collapsing fuzz. All they and the Asian Babe had been able to do was watch helplessly while—wait. The Asian Babe had watched. Just like them. That made no sense. If she wasn't crushed, if he and Mitch were wrong about the "glitch" causing a bubble that could easily collapse, then—

Wayne grabbed Dean's arm. "He's not dead," he said, relief flooding through him.

Without taking his eyes off the back of Marion's head, Dean said "I know. But not because *she* said so."

Wayne jerked back in surprise. Sliding closer to Dean he asked, "How did you know?"

"The Asian Babe. Nothing touched her. She's Teflon. And you heard Giganta. She wanted Mitch to capture the Babe—bad. I bet whatever ate him was meant for the Babe. When we get wherever we're going, Giganta better belch him out or she's dead."

The tick-tock of the turn signal told them they were exiting the highway. Marion sped onto the off-ramp and took a right at the green sign pointing toward Cheyenne Mountain. They drove another ten minutes, passed hotels, restaurants, and several ritzy mansions, until the streetlights all but disappeared. She veered off suddenly onto an even darker, two-lane road that seemed to spiral down and down until stopping in front of a heavy, steel-plated gate. Marion waved a badge in front of a security pad, opening the gate into a tunnel that dipped even further underground, eventually popping out into a cold, cavernous garage. She parked, slid back the privacy partition, and said, "Don't look or talk to anybody, you hear? You people are ghosts."

She steered them into a side entrance, past the one guard at the desk, and waved her badge at the security pad to open the door into the main facility. Instead of releasing the lock, the pad beeped. "On lock-down, ma'am," said the guard. "Guest badges revoked. Only facility personnel."

Marion seethed. "You *know* I've got clearance, Mandy. Open up."

"Can't do it, ma'am. Director's orders. You'll need to talk to her or Dr. T."

Wayne could all but hear Marion grinding her teeth. "Alright. Ping him."

Mandy pushed a button on the desk comm. A craggy voice answered over the speaker, "Scott here."

"One sec, Dr. T. You've got visitors." Mandy handed the comm mic to Marion.

"It's me," she said. "We're top-level. Come open the door, please."

"'We're'? What's this 'we're'?" said Scott, his cragginess intensifying.

"Professor Doctor and his baby geniuses. Long story."

Dean leaned in next to Marion and said loudly, "Where's Mitch?!"

After a pause, Scott said, "Who's the moron?"

Marion stepped away from Dean and sighed into the mic. "Like I said, long story. Top-level, please. Now."

"Cripes. I'll be right there."

CHAPTER 33

Leap of Faith

The security door buzzed. Out stepped a balding old man wearing rumpled clothes and a sour expression. *This had to be the craggy-voiced "Scott,"* thought Wayne, *the guy the desk guard referred to as "Dr. T."* Scott's badge bounced up and down on his chest as he marched over toward them, the miniature of his face scowling in 2-D as well as in real life. *The guy must live in a perpetual state of anger and frustration*, he thought, half expecting him to announce, "I'm getting too old for this shit" once he arrived.

"Five bucks he says 'Cripes,' then has a stroke right here," Dean whispered. Wayne snorted, stifling a laugh. Scott glanced in their direction, then immediately looked away, disgusted, like he'd just seen a pile of sawdust and vomit. "Cripes," he muttered under his breath. They waited for the subsequent stroke. It didn't happen.

Instead, he planted himself in front of Marion and said "Whynt'cha bring the whole film crew? Take some pictures? Do a radio remote?"

"Will you calm down," she said. "If I hadn't agreed to bring them that might actually have happened."

"Containment, Marion," he said, as if speaking to an obstinate child. Scott's tone reminded Wayne of his own father, laboring to make some obvious point he thought Wayne had missed. Not *a* child. *His* child, perhaps? Wayne looked more closely at the old man's badge. Beneath the frowning face it read "Dr. Scott Travers" in bold, black letters. Could be a coincidence, but as he compared the two—Marion tall and thin, Scott short and squat, both standing hands-on-hips, glaring at each other— something in their stubborn face-off drew a kind of resemblance.

"This is as contained as I could keep it," said Marion, waving her hand to encompass their little group. "So gather Campbell, please, and we'll be out before they're caught."

"Kid fell out of the ether, *Marion*," Scott said, emphasizing her name in that impatient way only parents know how to do. "Kinda late for worrying about folks 'getting caught'."

"And whose fault is that, *Dad*?" said Marion, confirming Wayne's suspicion with her mocking retort.

"Dad?" said Dean. Marion blushed—at her slip, Wayne surmised.

Scott jerked a thumb in Dean's direction. "That the moron?"

"Yes, but don't change the subject," said Marion. "Remand Campbell to my custody and we'll be on our way."

"Can't."

"Why not?" Both Dean and Marion spoke.

Scott ignored Dean. Focusing on Marion he said, "The kid's too smart by half is why. Saw a piece of classified equipment and described its function to a T. Now Francine's in a tizzy and the kid's locked up. It's a mess, I tell ya'."

"Locked up?!" said Dean belligerently.

"You part myna bird?" said Scott, finally looking at him. "Just repeat things? Butt in while the grownups arc talking?"

Dean elbowed Marion out of the way and poked Scott in the chest. "Take us to Mitch. Now!"

Dean towered over Scott, his muscular frame imposing under the best of circumstances, but Scott didn't seem to care. He swatted Dean's finger away and said, "Back off, Polly. Unless you want a cracker." He balled his swatting hand into a fist and shook it under Dean's chin.

Suddenly Bische was there. Stepping in front of Dean and looking down on Scott, he said, "Still practicing knuckle diplomacy, I see."

"Listen, pal, don't start up with me cuz I'll—" Scott stopped, rocking back on his heels as if Bische had pushed him. A look of astonishment spread across his face. "You!" he rasped. Then a genuine, joyous laugh erupted out of him. He grabbed Bische's arms, squeezing him as he laughed. "My, god, it's you!" He pumped Bische's arm up and down vigorously, grinning and exclaiming, "You dog! You old dog!" all the while.

Marion frowned at them both. "You two know each other?"

"You kiddin'?" said Scott. "This guy is—" Bische kept smiling, but something in the professor's eyes stopped Scott for the second time in as many minutes. Recovering, he said, with only a hint of irony "—one of my 'oldest' friends."

Wayne wondered what that meant, but got distracted by Dean stepping into the background of the group and edging his way behind Scott to the security door. Wayne caught his eye. Dean jerked his head toward the door, signaling him to follow. Verifying that Scott and Marion were completely focused on Bische, Wayne snuck over to him.

"Whatcha got?" he whispered once he reached Dean's side.

"The old fart's badge." Wayne looked down at Dean's hand and just barely stopped himself from whooping out loud.

"Oldest trick in the book," Dean whispered. "Distract 'em, then go for the steal."

"Brilliant! But what do we do once we're in."

"We'll think of something. Let's get Mitch."

Dean waved Scott's badge in front of the reader. The door buzzed loudly, and they both cringed. They should have expected it, been ready to dash through the door as soon as it opened, but the split second of cringing was just enough time to allow Scott to whirl around and see his badge in Dean's hand. "Hey! Stop!" he yelled.

Wayne unfroze and yanked at the door, but the desk guard Mandy was quicker.

Her arm easily reached across the counter and slapped the door shut. Their opportunity was lost.

"Where do you think you're going?" said Scott, the cragginess returned, the momentary happiness at seeing Bische again gone.

"To get our friend," said Wayne.

"Bad choice, kid. And here I thought you were the smart one."

He ripped his badge from Dean's hand and was clipping it irately back to this shirt pocket when an alarm went off. "Now look what you did," said Scott.

"It's not them, Dr. T," said Mandy.

"Really?" He walked around the guard desk to peer over her shoulder.

To Wayne, the klaxon seemed familiar, but he couldn't quite remember why it would be.

"I think it's coming from one of the old mainframe rooms," said Mandy.

Wayne's phone buzzed in his pocket. His heart beat faster as he pulled it out and saw the Friend!Go icon blinking in the notifications bar. Mitch! Wayne tapped the icon and the app opened to show Mitch's yellow dot pulsing inside the blue grid, his location no more than a hundred feet away. Whatever had blocked Mitch's signal outside of the facility didn't block it down here within it. Now that they were inside with him Mitch's signal came in strong and clear.

And what had Mandy said? An old mainframe room? That was it! The alarm going off right now was the same one he and Mitch had heard the night they jumped into a computer room that looked like an electronics museum.

"Aw, cripes," said Scott.

"What is it?" asked Bische

"The kid. He did it again."

"Did what?" asked Marion

"Hit a homer. What do you *think*, Marion? He triggered the gateway!"

"Wait a minute. You locked him up, but didn't take the magic travel device? You let him keep it?"

Scott looked sheepish. "Reception's shit down here. I figured it wouldn't work. My mistake."

"Clearly." She bit her lip, thinking for a moment, then said, "Maybe we can use this."

"No!" said Dean. "You can't use Mitch!"

"He-Man's right," said Scott. "Kid's got the trace on him. You can't use him. The Fail Safe'll grab him just like before."

"Well, can you turn it off?"

"It ain't a light switch, Marion!"

"And, more importantly," said Bische, "Mitch is neither a soldier, nor an agent. This isn't his fight."

"Once he stole our tech he lost the right to choose," said Marion.

"*We* haven't," said Wayne. "Mitch is coming with us." He tapped Mitch's yellow Friend!Go dot. His Jump!Go came alive, manifesting the blue plasma grid directly in front of him and Dean, with Mitch's jump point pulsing brightly at its center. As he and Dean leapt into the hole, he heard Scott say to Marion, "You let *them* keep it?!"

CHAPTER 34

Déjà vu

Mitch looked around the Fail Safe room, with its dim fluorescent lights, wood paneling, and outdated computers, and seriously considered having a good cry. For the third time, he and Chung had jumped out of the room, only to wind up right back in it, sucked like dust mites through the Fail Safe vortex, lumped like laundry onto the cold Fail Safe platform, the flat Fail Safe voice telling them "retrieval—completed" yet again. He laughed at the "retrieval" part, which held the connotation of "rescue" or "recovery." It wasn't like they had been airlifted from the fuzzy white room or lassoed with a life preserver and gently tugged back to shore. After four times through the process, it honestly felt like being inhaled into a giant toilet and flushed.

He was nauseous, his head hurt, the room was spinning, and his nerves were fried. If they'd made even an inch of progress toward escaping from this place, the sense of hopelessness enveloping him might have a chance at being pushed away. But the multiple failures, getting them nowhere, opened the door for despair. *You can't blame me for a few tears*, he thought. No sooner had he allowed that idea into his head did his inner voice mock him. '*Giving up, Campbell? That's the easy way out.*' Chung groaned beside him. '*Way to disappoint your new friend,*' the voice continued. It sounded a lot like Bische. Dammit. *Can't my subconscious just let me cop out without creating a fake Bische to shame me?*

Chung sat up and cradled his head in his hands. "I do not think I can do that again," he said, then let out a gurgling belch that left him looking shaky and wan.

Mitch didn't feel much better. He rolled over onto his knees, choking back a cough that felt too close to a spew. Gritting his teeth against the nausea, he said,

"You're right. This isn't working. Need a new plan." But what? He looked down at his Jump!Go. What was wrong with it? Maybe it had gotten tied to the facility somehow? He couldn't think of what would make that happen. He sighed. *I wonder if it would be easier to look for a backdoor to sneak out of.*

As if reading his mind, Chung said, "Maybe we can just walk out?"

Okay, if Chung had thought of it, too, it might not be that bad of an idea. Why not just ease into the hallway like they belonged there, like they were some scientist's kids heading for the exit after hanging out with their dad or mom. No alarms had gone off. Chances were, no one was aware that they were missing. Mitch wondered if anyone besides the old guy and the crabby boss lady even knew that they existed. It was likely no one did. He and Chung could play it off, make up a plausible name for their fictitious parent—Dr. Hayes?—should someone ask, then just waltz away from the facility, with no one else the wiser.

Mulling that idea took much less effort than figuring out what was wrong with his Jump!Go, or how to fiddle with the Fail Safe program to turn it completely off. *'Too easy, Campbell,'* Fake Bische murmured in his head. Ignoring the voice, he said aloud, "Works for me." The room had stopped spinning, so he swung his legs over the side of the platform, planted his feet on the floor, and stood up.

"Wait!" Chung lunged for him suddenly, grabbing his arm to pull him down. Mitch dodged instinctively, taking a step toward the door. *Whoop! Whoop! Whoop!* An alarm blared from a speaker on the ceiling. Mitch remembered the sound, remembered the look of shock on Wayne's face and the faint jingle of keys outside the door.

"Nooo!" he howled.

"I tried to warn you," said Chung. "There's an electric eye in the wall." He pointed at a white plastic casing embedded in the wall board, close to the floor, near the base of the Fail Safe platform. "Do you think the bald man will hear this?"

The keys jangled louder in Mitch's memory. "I can guarantee it. Geez!" He grabbed his curls in both fists. *Gotta think.* "Let's jam the door. Buy some time." He grabbed a chair to shove under the door knob.

"That might work," said Chung. "I may be able to short the card scanner." He took a multi-tool from his pocket.

"And I'll look for a manual or something for this thing," said Mitch, gesturing toward the PDP terminal. "Maybe there's a command or switch we can flip to turn the friggin' Fail Safe off."

Mitch rummaged around in the drawers of the desk holding the PDP, the hopelessness and fear he'd pushed off minutes ago returning and making his heart pound against his chest and his hands shake. For a second, he smelled and tasted metal, felt a burning at the edges of his eyes like from acrid smoke. *Is that Dean's cologne? Am I having a stroke?!* Before he could freak completely out, a diamond-blue ring appeared in the middle of the room, a familiar gleam of white at its center.

"Mitch!"

They just appeared, Dean and Wayne, bursting from the jump point, looking by turns both worried and elated. To Mitch, they looked like the cavalry.

"Guys! Guys!" Mitch didn't care about his tears, didn't try to hide them or stop them flowing.

Wayne slapped his back and shook his hand so hard he felt as if he'd lift off the ground. Dean, grinning ear to ear, crushed him in a bear hug. "We thought you were dead, buddy."

"So did I, man. So did I. My Jump!Go's busted. It won't let me out of here. You guys just saved us."

"Us?"

"Hello," Chung called over his shoulder.

"Hi," Dean called back, looking puzzled.

Wayne stabbed his thumb toward Chung. "And he is?"

"Chung. We met in stir. I'll tell you back at the garage. Open the grid, we gotta go."

The door panel shot sparks and went *Zap!* "Manse!" Chung exclaimed, smiling.

"They cannot get in now."

"Wonderful," said Mitch, high-fiving Chung as he joined them. "What are you waiting for, Wayne?"

"Thinking, not waiting. This might not work."

"Why not? The garage hole was there in the grid. I saw it just now before you shut your fob down."

"Right, my Jump!Go can access the home point, but you, and I betcha, the new guy can't use it."

Dean slapped a palm to his forehead, "Oooh, right."

"What?" asked Mitch, not sure he wanted to hear the answer.

"The old guy, Dr. Travers—" Dean began.

"You met him?"

"Yeah," said Wayne. "No time for the whole story, but we jumped here to you to get away from him. Before that, he said they put a tracer on you, probably Chung, too. Something that keeps you in the facility. Me and Dean can jump, but not you."

"And we'll be damned if we're leaving here without you," said Dean.

Then there it was, the jingle of keys at the door and the irate, though muffled, voice of Dr. Travers crabbing at whoever was with him, probably a guard. The scanner clicked unhappily, making a *ziiiit* sound as he tried unsuccessfully to open the door with his card key. The crabbing got louder. Dean turned to Chung. "Good job, new guy."

"Thanks," said Chung, beaming.

"It's good, but it might not hold them long," said Mitch. As if on cue, a power tool vibrated to life on the opposite side of the door. The doorknob screeched as the tool made contact, and the acrid smell of metal on metal filled the room.

"We are officially out of time," said Mitch.

Chung ran to the wall behind the Fail Safe platform and knocked on it. "Sounds hollow. Maybe hide in there?"

"How?" said Dean, giving Wayne an incredulous look.

Mitch's eyes went wide. "The same way I got us out of the conference room. Chung, you're a genius! Dean, shine your penlight on the wall!"

Dean pulled his key ring from his pocket and aimed the small, but powerful flashlight at the wall. Mitch invoked his Jump!Go's plasma grid and moved it slowly between the flashlight and the wall until the telltale, diamond-blue, nickel-sized jump point appeared.

Wayne expanded the hole by stepping closer to it. They could see lights, a floor, and some kind of wire mesh just beyond. He put his hand through the hole and waved it around. "There might be enough space for us to get through." The screeching from the door got louder, the doorknob wiggling more against the door frame the nearer it got to being completely shaved off.

"Now or never. Better than jail," said Mitch. The doorknob dropped, and the door cracked open. They leapt through the jump point into the cavity encased in wire mesh. He watched as the old man burst into the room, the few wisps of hair atop his head flapping wildly after shoving open the door. Chung was the last one through the hole.

"Cripes, they're gone!" the old man bellowed. With a swipe across the grid, the jump point closed.

CHAPTER 35

Inside Men

They were crammed into a smallish, dark, oddly shaped space, recessed into the back wall of a larger room and closed off from it by a simple, wire cage door. Most of the space was taken up with boxes of office supplies, many of which lined the front of the cage, affording them some measure of protection from being discovered by anyone working in the room.

Mitch surveyed the area, trying to understand why the space looked like a trapezoid. As if reading his mind, Wayne whispered, "We're under a flight of stairs," and pointed up. Lifting his eyes, Mitch detected the outline of corrugated steps leading to a security door, and supporting the enclosure that surrounded him, his friends, and the boxes.

"Well, that explains the weird shape of this place," Dean whispered back. "The real question is, can we get out of here."

Mitch squeezed past Dean and crouched down behind the box closest to the cage door. Cautiously, he peered around the box and through the wire mesh, noticing that they were in the back of the monitoring room—the SMOR—that Dr. Travers had taken him to earlier. It was quieter now, with fewer people milling about, but those that had remained in the room seemed no less anxious.

Grim faces stared intently at data flowing by on their workstation monitors. A threesome, gathered at one workstation in the front row, took turns gesturing at a colorful graph displayed directly above them on the enormous flatscreen that covered the wall. Periodically, a pointer moved across the graph as, one by one, members of the group explained the data. Just behind them stood a beefy guard with a gun, arms folded across his chest, ham-thick neck craned up at the screen. His stance was so tense, the muscles in his back looked ready to pop out of his shirt.

"Wish I knew why everybody's freaking out," said Mitch.

"Us, maybe?" said Wayne. He slid a stack of notepad boxes to Mitch's left to give himself cover, then crouched down behind them.

"No, can't be. No jump points on the big screens. No digital maps of Golden. Something else is going on."

"Whatever it is, no one's looking back here," said Dean, just behind Mitch's head. "Maybe we can sneak out."

"To where?" asked Chung over Mitch's right shoulder.

"I've been here before," said Mitch. "With the old guy, Travers. There's an exit to a garage not too far from here. I saw people walking in like they were starting a shift. We could get out that way."

"Or maybe we'll be trapped like rats with nowhere to hide if someone notices us," said Wayne.

"Is being squished in here any better?"

No one spoke. Taking their silence for assent, Mitch slowly pressed down on the door handle. *Please don't be locked*, he thought to himself. The door unlatched. Just as he cracked it open wide enough for them to sneak through, they heard the familiar buzz of a key card above them, followed by the pang of hard-soled shoes descending the metal stairs. He re-latched the door, and the four of them crouched down again behind the coffee filters and pens. A tall, brown, slender woman in a cream-colored blouse, sheer black jacket, and straight-cut slacks over leather boots whipped around the staircase, striding with purpose toward the row of workstations as her boot heels echoed through the room.

"Crud, that's the boss lady," whispered Mitch, crouching even lower behind his box of paper.

"She looks like a spitfire," says Dean, appraisingly.

"And then some. Met her already. She's Travers' boss."

Chung peeked at her from around a box. "Oh, I met her also. She's quite nice."

Mitch looked at Chung as if he was out of his mind. "Are you serious? She about tore the old man's head off, and then locked me up without a thought."

"She was very angry first. Said, 'You're a spy.' Asked lots of questions I could not answer. Then she called me 'cream puff' and gave me a sandwich. Nice."

"Dude, she threatened me with federal prison." Mitch said, still incredulous.

Chung looked down, thoughtful for a moment, then said, "She gave me a sandwich."

Boss Lady stopped in the back row near a young, bearded man with a boxy haircut, who was murmuring into a headset and tapping a pencil absently against the side of his keyboard. He looked up at the shadow looming over his monitor. "Ma'am."

"Charlie." She leaned closer to the monitor. Her voice rang out, clear and strong. "Any change in the readings?"

"Nope," Charlie answered, more softly. Mitch strained forward to listen. "More of the same. Been quiet going on," he pulled up a timer, "thirty minutes now."

"If only it would stay that way. For a while, it looked like Grand Central Station in there."

"Not anymore. Once we sucked out the Campbell kid, it's been a ghost town."

"What, she left?" Boss Lady managed to sound both hopeful and fearful.

"Don't think so. More like she's holed up somewhere. We keep getting audio spikes in the receiver, so I figure she's communicating with somebody. But without the Campbell kid's video to home in on, we can't see jack."

"Did we at least find out who she is?"

"Yeah, we got lucky there. Ran recognition on the picture Agent Travers sent over and found this in the long-range satellite archives." Charlie tapped in a command and pulled up another window on the monitor.

"North Korea seemed the most likely place to start, given the other guy who showed up. Sure enough, ran through surveillance images from that side of the world and bingo. There she is."

"Guarding the Happy Dictator himself. Lord," she said, shaking her head. "Send it up front." Donning a headset, Boss Lady signaled the group in the first row to look at the far-right quadrant of the big screen. Charlie tapped and clicked some more, and—then to Mitch's amazement—there she was.

The Asian Babe's face appeared on the big screen, just one of a group of people walking through what looked like a factory. She wore dark glasses and had her hair pulled back into a bun, but Mitch had seen her enough times now to recognize the determined clench of her jaw and the lithe strength of her frame, despite the image's static pose. Beside her was a taller man, also in dark glasses, bulky and lumbering and completely bored. Behind them both, sandwiched between them and two other guards walked the cherubic leader of North Korea, waving and smiling.

"Whoa," said Dean.

"Didn't see that coming," said Wayne.

"What? What is it?" asked Chung. He tried to push forward to get a better look over Mitch's shoulder.

Mitch twisted around to answer, pressing his mouth to Chung's ear, and said quietly, "They found your sister."

Chung tried to crane his neck over Mitch's curls. "Where? I cannot see. What do you mean?"

Just then, the security door above them buzzed again. Three pairs of feet descended the stairs. Mitch signaled the others to be quiet, pushing them away from the cage door to press farther into the enclosure's back wall. The new arrivals rounded the stairwell railing—the old guy, Travers, Bische, and a woman Mitch didn't recognize. Travers paused, scanning the room, then, spotting the boss lady, made a beeline toward her with Bische and the other woman trailing behind.

"Terrific," said Dean. "Now we're never getting out of here."

"Who's the amazon?" asked Mitch.

"The old guy's daughter, Marion. Bische tricked her into bringing us here. If she talks, you'll recognize her," said Wayne.

"Yeah, she gave you that 'pep talk' while the Fail Safe ate you alive," added Dean.

"Oh. What's she got to do with all of this?"

"No idea," said Dean. "Bische showed up at the garage with her. When you got snatched, she knew where you went and tried to leave us behind, but Bische conned her into taking us along. So we got here and the old guy met us, but he was too busy being a jerk to takes us to you. Then you set off the alarm, Wayne locked on your signal, and we ditched Giganta, her dad, and Doc to get to you. It's been a whirlwind, frankly. Not much opportunity to figure it all out."

Travers, with Bische and Marion, arrived at the row behind the Boss Lady. "Francine," he began, his craggy voice carrying even better than hers had in the cavernous space.

Without turning around, Francine said, "Good, you're here. We're about ready." She tapped a button on her headset and said, "Bill, send Briggs back. Scott just walked in."

The intense, beefy guy behind the threesome spun on his heel and marched toward the back row, his sidearm bouncing against his thigh with each step. The hairs on the back of Mitch's neck stood up.

The old man didn't like it any better. Grimacing at Francine's back, he said, "Listen, we gotta talk."

"No, we don't," she said, her irritation evident. "Briggs has been briefed. Just hand over the device and we can end this." She still hadn't turned around.

"Yeah, about that," said Scott, blanching.

"Hang on, Bill." She sighed, then turned around. The sight of Bische and Marion killed whatever else she was about to say. "What in hell are these two doing here? Especially him?" she said, pointing her long arm at Bische. She faced him directly. "Didn't you die, quit, retire, or something?"

"Hello, Francine," said Bische, a sly half-smile on his face, his voice low and sounding, to Mitch's amazement, practically playful.

She put a hand up, seeming to blot out his face. "Oh, god, don't you start," she said.

Marion waved her badge at Francine and said, "He's with me. You can attach him to my clearance, since this is my operation."

"*Was* your operation. Not anymore." Francine shifted her glare to Marion. "Look at the screen. That's the bogey we've been tracking. Do you see who she's with? This isn't some accident. She's not some hapless goofball who stumbled into Campbell's magic travel bubble unawares."

"You're panicking," said Marion.

"You're damn right I am! This is the top bodyguard for the world's number one maniac, running around Campbell's instant transport tunnel with an annihilation-level weapon."

"Exactly why we need to stay calm and do a qu—"

"Don't say it," Francine cut Marion off with a wave of her hand. "The time for 'quiet intervention' has passed. It's too big and too late by my watch." Briggs moved to her side and crossed his massive arms, as if to emphasize the point. Nodding her approval, Francine said, "It's time to take her out."

"No!" Chung's shout was so unexpected that Mitch jumped, banging his head on a metal stair. Chung pushed past him to the storage room gate and tumbled through it out onto the slick linoleum floor. Dean and Wayne belly-flopped immediately and scrambled to hide behind the stacked office supplies. Mitch thought to pull the gate shut, but couldn't figure how to do that and not be seen. He slid on his back behind the boxes then, staying low, peeked out again.

Chung ran toward Francine. "Don't hurt her! Ooof!" He'd gotten within a step of Boss Lady, but Briggs plowed into him, finally finding an outlet for his pent-up tension. The two tumbled to the floor, but Chung did not give up. "She's not bad! She's my sister! Please! Don't 'take her out'!"

Francine, Marion, Bische, and Scott stared, stunned, as Briggs untangled himself from Chung and dragged him up to a standing position, arms pinned to his sides. Francine turned to Scott, her voice level, but her eyes blazing.

"Is *this* why 'we gotta talk'?"

"...Mostly," Scott said. He scratched his bald spot, the red in his face deepening.

Her attention moved back to Chung. "Sorry, Cream Puff, but she keeps bad company. If she wasn't dangerous, your Dear Leader wouldn't need her."

"You're wrong!" said Chung.

"Am I? Her boss makes me think otherwise."

Marion gestured toward Briggs. "You can't seriously be considering sending this Neanderthal after her?"

"Why not?"

"He's got 'commando' written all over him. If I was stuck in Campbell's whirligig and all of a sudden saw this guy leaping out of the white at *me*, I'd shoot him before he landed."

Briggs smirked and said, "I'll get her first."

"Oh, really," said Marion, folding her arms across her chest and perfectly mimicking his earlier stance. "She's pretty quick—I've seen it. Can you 'get her' before she sets off the exploding disk she's carrying? What if you aim your big gun at her, but miss and shoot that disk instead? Did you think of that?" Briggs glared at her, but Mitch saw doubt in his eyes.

"This whole mountain could come crashing down," Marion continued, "and when it does, Colorado Springs will be wiped out with it." She swung back toward Francine. "We're trying to prevent a war, Director, not jump into one. He can't go."

"No one else is as qualified or available," said Francine.

"I'll go!" This time, it was Dean yelling in Mitch's ear. Mitch found himself squished against the stack of boxes as Dean struggled to squeeze past him out the gate into the control room. Dean winced as he straightened up, but still managed to cross the room quickly, taking a protective stance next to Chung. "I'll do it," he said, panting and holding his bruised side.

Francine looked ready to pop a blood vessel. "And who in hell is this?"

"Another Neanderthal," said Marion. "Except this one's broken."

Dean thrust out his chin defiantly. "I said I can do it, Giganta."

"Hey, cool it, Conan!" snapped Scott.

Bische held up his hands placatingly at Scott, then to Dean said, "Chambers, you can barely stand."

"I hate it, but Giganta's right, doc. the Babe'll clock this bozo on sight."

"And what makes you think you'd do better?" asked Francine.

"She knows me. She saved my life!" said Dean, twisting toward Francine. "Grrrn!" Dean doubled over from the sudden movement.

Mitch couldn't take it anymore. "Doc's right, Dean," he said, crawling out of the space, pulling Wayne with him.

Scott jerked his thumb at the now empty storage area. "It's like a friggin' clown car."

Francine raised her voice and said to the room at large, "Is there anyone else hiding in here?"

Bische said, "Unlikely. They're like the Three Musketeers," and with a nod toward Chung, "plus D'Artagnan."

"More like the Three Stooges plus Shemp, if you ask me," said Scott.

"I can do it," Mitch continued, "But only if Chung comes with me. She knows me, too, and Chung can vouch for me. Between us, we can convince her. I swear it."

"Yes, I will go with Mitch. Please!" said Chung. He tried to shrug out of Briggs' grip, but Briggs held tight.

Francine shook her head and said firmly, "You're untrained and your chances of success are low to none. I won't send kids to their possible deaths. That's what Briggs is for."

"Right!" said Briggs emphatically, but then he frowned as Francine's words caught up with his fervor. "Wait, what?"

Wayne said, "I know how to increase their chances." Stepping away from the group, he pulled out his Jump!Go, dialed up a plasma grid, and leapt through.

"Hey!" yelled Briggs, bracing to leap in after him. Bische appeared in front of Briggs, stopping him short. Mitch could have sworn Bische had been across the room, closer to Francine, but somehow he'd managed to place himself right by the plasma grid. Before Mitch could ponder that fact more deeply, Wayne returned, loaded down with gear from the garage: monitoring harnesses, min-cams, and headsets.

He flicked off the plasma grid and said to Francine, "We've got these and this." He held the gear in one hand and a data drive in the other. "All of our monitoring apps are on this drive and connect to these harnesses. Suit them up, put me on a workstation with the apps, and you can see and hear everything they do, talk to them about it, and yank them back when you need." He handed two sets of gear to Mitch and Chung, along with his Jump!Go.

"And you." Wayne handed a harness set to Briggs. "You gear up, too, but stay in reserve. At the first sign of trouble, I'll find the closest hole and you can run to the rescue."

"I thought Dear Leader's bodyguard would freak and take me out on sight," said Briggs, sounding less confident than he had been earlier.

"Not if Mitch warns her first," said Dean.

"Yeah, as soon as we find her, I can let her know about 'Commando,' " said Mitch.

Bische was beside Wayne. "Good thinking, Hirano. Looks like you just saved this operation."

Wayne smiled ruefully. "She's got to agree first," he said, looking at Francine.

Mitch strapped into his harness and donned his headset. "So, Boss Lady, are we a go?"

All eyes turned to Francine. She met each one with her own severe gaze. "This isn't amateur hour. These are real stakes. No one can fail."

They were quiet. Then Wayne said, "Sounds like a go to me." He walked over to Charlie and asked, "Mind if I share your workstation?"

Charlie swiveled in his chair toward Francine. She gave him a curt nod. "Alrighty, then," he said, taking the data drive from Wayne. "The station next to me is free. Think we can link the two?" Soon he and Wayne were engrossed with the setup, jargoning back and forth as if they worked together every day.

"Well, they're a natural fit," said Marion.

Scott walked over to Mitch as he helped Chung into a harness and said, "Unless you want CC to yank the both of ya' back here again, you'll need this." He pulled a jet injector from his coat pocket.

"Who's CC?" asked Mitch.

"You know, the Fail Safe lady. That's my name for her. Gimme your arm." He inoculated Mitch, then Chung. "That'll take away the trace."

"Thank you so much," said Chung. "I could not take another sucking into the Fail Safe."

Soon after, Wayne and Charlie called ready. They did voice and camera checks, extrapolated the Asian Babe's current position, and found the closest jump point to that. Finally, there was nothing left to do but jump.

Dean wrapped Mitch and Chung in big bear hugs. Wayne shook their hands, and then to Mitch said, "Look out for flying babes."

Mitch opened a plasma grid to the coordinates of Asian Babe's last known location. "On the count of three," he said to Chung. "1... 2... 3."

They leapt, the blue plasma enveloping them before gradually dissolving into the milkiness of interstitial space. They didn't see the black hair or the slick gray suit—in sharp relief against the white fuzz—until it was too late. Chung landed and immediately froze beside Mitch. "Oh, no," he said, voice hushed, his face blanching. Then he hissed a word that Mitch did not understand.

"'Gummy?' Wha—?" Before he could finish asking, Chung clamped his hand across Mitch's mouth and dragged him down into the fuzz, forcing him to lay flat. The flash of gray and Chung's reaction immediately told Mitch who they were hiding from—Psycho Suit. Suddenly, he wished they had not talked Francine out of sending Briggs.

CHAPTER 36

Ultimatum

Does he have the disk?" Chung heard Marion's voice in his ear.

"I do not know," he whispered, cupping his hand over the mouthpiece of his headset. "Busy hiding."

"I'll look," murmured Mitch. He popped his head up and down then, following Chung's lead, shielded his mouthpiece and whispered, "No disk, just a gun. Definitely a gun." He peeked again. "And it's huge. Big gun. We are screwed."

"Only if he sees you," said Marion. "But I'll bet he cares more about finding Mr. Ae's sister than either of you."

"Let's find out, shall we?" Mitch's friend Wayne broke in. "Charlie found the 'listen' frequency for their channel. Patching it in." The comm unit clicked and whined, then Geomi's thin voice rose up from the background, quiet, menacing, and clearly angry.

"–ing liar. She is not here. *Nothing* is here."

"We can only guess where she might be." It was Kyung, sounding as raspy and bored as ever. A small beat of happiness pulsed through Chung. At last a familiar voice, after so long!

"Or," Geomi continued, biting every word, "you are purposely sending me to where she isn't." Kyung was quiet. Chung imagined him taking a long drag on his ever-present cigarette and shrugging. Geomi spat a curse into the too-long silence. Voice thick with malice, he said, "I am returning."

"Suit yourself," said Kyung, laconic, deliberate in not caring. Chung covered his mouth again, this time to stifle a chuckle. It was heartening to hear his friend unfazed by the assassin's wrath.

Geomi strode to his left until a break in the white revealed the subbasement. Kyung stood just steps away from the jump point's edge, disinterested and resentful, flicking the ash from his cigarette and squinting at Geomi through his smoky haze.

"Why does she not answer your calls?" Geomi barked.

"Maybe her headset is broken. Why blame me?" Kyung growled back.

"I am sure Dear Leader can answer that question," said Geomi coolly. "But only after ordering me to slit your throat." Kyung scoffed, a mistake, as the next sound Chung heard was a loud *smack*, no doubt Geomi's reward to Kyung for such open scorn.

"You think you are alive because you are important?" spat Geomi, his derision echoing over the comms nearly as loudly as the slap across Kyung's face had. "You live for expedience and secrecy only. Once Dear Leader walks out of this device and into the stadium for Supreme Leader's celebration, you... and you... and all your kin... will die." Hyun yelped in the background. Geomi chuckled without humor or warmth.

"Unless, of course, you find Jin Ae, kill her, and give me the disk. Anything less? Erased, all of you. I will see to it personally. You have until morning." Chung heard footsteps and then the buzz of the door.

Some seconds passed, with Kyung exhaling deeply, deflating. "He's gone," he said finally. "You can come back."

A lithe figure leapt through a ripple in the white and leaned into the subbasement jump point to expand it. "Jin!" called Chung, overjoyed at the sight of his sister. He jumped up from their hiding place, loping through the white to meet her.

"Sister!" he shouted when he reached her. "It's me! I'm—ooof!"

She did not let him finish. Her arms wrapped around him, tight as iron bands, squeezing him so hard he thought his ribs might break. "I've got you, Brother!" she said and, with a massive tug, dragged him with her through the jump point, back into the subbasement. Shaking and breathless, Jin continued to hold him, her face buried deep against his chest. "You're safe," she said. Her voice cracked, yet her vice-like grip around Chung's waist did not relent.

"Sister," he gasped. "Please. I cannot breathe." Jin released him, pushing away and hurriedly erasing the trail of tears from her face with her thumb.

"I'm sorry," she said, her voice still quiet, but stronger. "I thought you were dead. It... distressed me." She smoothed her hair and stood up straighter. "I am not myself."

It was a familiar gesture, Jin sheepishly sweeping aside her hair, but one she'd rarely used since they'd grown. Seeing it now warmed him, bringing back, if only for a moment, the Jin of his youth: the joking friend, the thoughtful playmate, his fiercest protector always. This was the real Jin. He locked eyes with her and said, "Not true."

The hint of a smile touched her lips, but before she could reply, Hyun squeezed between them and flung himself at Chung's feet. "Forgive me!" he blurted out, eyes frantic, tears spilling out the sides. "It was my fault, I admit it! I'm sorry! Don't let your sister kill me! Please!"

Kyung reached in and dragged him back. "You have no shame," he rasped.

"I do not want to die! She will kill us all!"

Chung was flabbergasted. What was *this* all about? "Sir, no. I do not think she would do that," he said, not quite sure what to make of the commander's blubbering.

"She said it! She will destroy the disk to keep it from Dear Leader, but we will die when she does. Or The Spider will kill us if we don't get the disk from her. Talk to her, Chung! It is us or her!"

"Quiet, coward," said Kyung, squinting down at Hyun with disgust.

"This is not good." To Chung's surprise, Mitch had spoken. His curly, disembodied head had suddenly appeared out of the light hole. Chung had forgotten about him in his rush to reunite with Jin. As all eyes in the room turned toward

Mitch, his friend shuddered under their scrutiny. "Whoa."

Chung beckoned him in to the room, but before Mitch could move, Jin crossed the distance to the Canopy, shot her arm out fast as a snake, and yanked Mitch through the light hole. "We've been followed!" she shouted, pushing Mitch up against the wall.

"Ow!" he cried out. "*Why* do you keep hitting me?"

"Why do you keep following me?" Jin retorted. "Are you after my brother? Or do you want this?" She pulled the Unity disk from her pocket and held it up close enough for Mitch to see, but just out of his reach.

"I think the real question, Ms. Ae, is not what *he* is doing, but what *you* intend to do?" Jin froze. Chung had heard Marion perfectly in his earpiece, but Jin's startled expression told him that Jin had heard her as well. Wayne or Charlie must have also found the subbasement's "talk" frequency and patched Marion in.

"What the hell?" said Kyung. He punched his headset off and on, as if resetting the comm unit would get rid of the mystery woman's voice. "How did she—"

Jin raised her hand sharply to cut him off. Not taking her eyes off of Mitch, she spoke into her headset. "Who is this?"

"You can call me Marion, Ms. Ae," the woman replied. "And if you're ready to listen, I might have an answer for your problem."

CHAPTER 37

Bait and Switch

You cannot have the disk." Jin spoke slowly, over-enunciating the words. Her English was good, but she wanted no doubts from the Americans about where she stood.

"To be fair, Ms. Ae, I haven't asked for it yet," the woman—Marion—replied.

"But you will, correct? It is why you send this child to follow me. Why you kidnap my brother."

"I've been trying to save you!" said the inept spy, still pinned to the wall by her fist. "Which you'd know if you bothered to talk to me instead of hit me."

Jin eyed him with disdain. "You are feeble and unskilled. I do not need a baby to save me."

"Funny," said Marion. "From what I hear you don't have a lot of options. It's either give your leader the disk or be betrayed by your friends. Makes handing it to the hapless urchin look a lot more appealing, don't you think?"

"You ignore my original solution. Destroy the disk and all of us that know about it."

"Nooo!" cried Hyun.

"I agree with the coward," said Marion. "Blowing yourself to kingdom come won't stop your leader from ordering another doomsday disk. He'll wipe your remains from the walls and just start over."

"Then I'll have Kyung find a light hole to the palace and I will detonate the disk in Dear Leader's presence. We will end the cancer where it began."

"Are you sure of that? The 'cancer' could have already spread to someone else in your leader's inner circle. That Spider psycho, for instance. He seems okay with mass destruction. Will he be at the palace too?" Jin didn't have an answer for that. Marion pushed it further. "And what about the scientists that created the disk? Would they just stop making them once Dear Leader is gone? Have you ever met a scientist that didn't want someone—anyone—to use their work?"

"I could convince them otherwise," said Jin, the threat easily heard in her voice.

"Jeez, lady, is beating people to hell your answer to every problem?" said the spy, his face red and glistening as he struggled to free himself from her grip.

"I've found it to be quite effective."

"So's thinking, if you ever gave it a try." The spy was panting now.

"[Jin, please, let him go,]" said Chung in Korean. "[Mitch is my friend.]"

"[He is a lying spy.]"

"[No, he saved me. He freed me from the room they locked me in. Please, Jin.]"

She could not resist Chung's kind face. "Hmph," she said, then unclenched her fist. Mitch, mid-struggle, staggered forward and into Kyung.

"The boy has a point," growled Kyung in English, pushing Mitch off of him. "You fight more than you think. Even so, boy," he continued to Mitch, "thinking takes time. We only have until morning."

"We don't need all night." said Mitch, rubbing his chest where Jin's fist had been. "Just two hours should do it."

"What do you mean?" said Jin, a bit too intensely, she realized, as Mitch flinched away.

"We've got a 3D printer. We can make a replica of the disk—one that doesn't explode."

"That is not possible." Jin waved the disk at him. "The Unity technology is very specialized. Dear Leader will be able to tell if it is fake."

"Our printer is Tamblyn Tech, top of the line. It can make a darn close duplicate, if not exact."

Jin shook her head. "A visual copy is not good enough. The *detonation* must also be real. If it isn't, Dear Leader will know he's been tricked. He will publicly execute me, Chung, and the rest of our family to deter further betrayals. I cannot allow that to happen. I will watch the palace carefully and ensure both Dear Leader and The Spider are there before I detonate. It is the only way."

A sudden burst of background noise erupted over comms.

"Let me talk to her," said a young, male voice. It sounded vaguely familiar.

"This is serious, Chambers. We're handling it," said Marion.

"By letting her choose to die?!"

"If need be, yes," said a different woman's voice. "She's a soldier, she knows the odds. One for thousands."

"Wrong answer!" the familiar male voice said again.

More scuffling, then another man's voice, profoundly commanding, cut through all of the others. "Stand down, Briggs. Now."

At once, the familiar male voice spoke loudly in her earpiece, "Thanks, Doc. Hey, babe? It's me, Dean. You saved me by kicking me in the ribs, remember?"

Jin's cheeks felt suddenly hot. Of course, it was obvious now. The voice belonged to the beefy flirter. "Yes," she said, scowling, fighting to keep her tone neutral. "I remember."

"Listen to Mitch, darlin'. He's right. We can do this. Don't kill yourself!"

Why do you care? It was disconcerting to hear this stranger plead so passionately with her to find another way out of Dear Leader's madness. All she could think to say in reply was, "I am not your 'darling'."

"Well, not yet, anyway," Dean said. She felt her cheeks get hotter.

"[Sister,]" Chung whispered at her, "[are you blushing?]"

"[Of course not,]" she whispered back.

"I agree with Ms. Ae." The other woman spoke again.

"One second, Francine—" the commanding male voice began.

"We don't have one second! Didn't you hear the assassin, that spider person? He gave them until their morning to turn over Ae and the mass-murder disk. If we waste time on Chambers' and Campbell's scheme, it's a lost opportunity. If the Ae girl thinks she can stop all of this by blowing them all up when the assassin and the leader return, then I'm sorry for their loss, but they are all soldiers. Better them than thousands. We should let her do it."

"Then what does that makes us?" asked Dean.

"One up on the enemy," said Francine.

"I'd think we want allies and not enemies," Dean retorted. "Jin and her friends can hear you, you know, and I just bet they think you're the enemy, not them."

"Chambers, listen—"

"And if you asked me, I'd agree with them. You act like you represent all that's good and right, but if you hang Jin and Chung out to dry, you're no better than this 'dear leader.' You might as well be Psycho Suit. If their families survive and decide to come after us, whose fault will it be then? Yours!"

"Also," the woman Marion spoke again, "blowing the hell out of Pyongyang and its leader is bound to be noticed. Campbell's plan is much quieter."

The comms were silent. Jin knew that Francine, undoubtedly a soldier herself, was just being sensible. Dean, though sweet, was not a soldier and couldn't understand all that was at stake. Still, she looked at Chung, imagined his kind, cheerful face changing after her sacrifice, replaced with the same heavy sadness that had debilitated their father. It might be worth it to try Mitch's plan if only to keep Chung from their father's fate.

"I will agree to the weakling's plan on one condition," she said. "The Unity disk must be disarmed. No one can have it. If you just hide it, it might be stolen. We must completely destroy it. If you cannot guarantee that, then," she took a deep breath and stood up straighter, "my original path is clear, no matter how 'loud' it might be."

Kyung snorted. "Any way you do it is loud. No way to keep an explosion that size from being noticed. Dear Leader will see it and know what it is, and then he will just ask the science ministry for another."

"Perhaps," said Jin, "but it will take the ministry several months to do it. Anything can happen in that time to delay the Unity disk scientists. I can make sure of that."

"You will not survive a week once the Americans destroy the real disk. Yours," he waved his cigarette hand across the room, encircling Jin, Chung, Hyun, and himself with a ring of smoke, "and our heads will be on spikes outside of the palace within two hours of the blast. The Americans will have to send the real disk into space to destroy it."

"Hmmm." The sound had come from the hapless spy, Mitch. Jin heard it over the comms, but when she turned toward him, he obviously hadn't directed the "hmmm" at anyone in particular. He just stared up, eyes unfocused and hooded, seemingly lost in thought. Then he said, "That actually could work." He muttered the words to himself, but they rang out clearly over the comms.

"What would work, Mitch?" Chung asked.

Mitch's gaze shot back into focus, and he looked around the room, startled. "Did I say that out loud?"

"We all heard you. I have seen this look on your face before," Chung said, becoming excited. "Right before we got out of the conference room."

"Chung!" Dean called over the comms, sounding equally animated. "Was he biting his lip and staring at the ceiling?"

"Yes, that is it!"

"Hot dog, that's his 'flash' face! What did you come up with, Mitch?"

Mitch swallowed several times before speaking, then stammered, "It—well—I might be wrong."

"Take a breath, Campbell," the commanding voice said. Jin suspected it was the person Dean had called 'doc.'

For a second, the distracted look returned, but Mitch shook himself, inhaled, and said, "I think we could deflect it up, then detonate it. Not as far as space, but pretty high up into the sky."

"Wow," said Marion. "Where did *that* come from?"

"Just wait for it," said Dean.

Mitch closed his eyes and continued, "My lame-o-doohickey. It passively absorbed energy, then released it in a controlled fashion. I still have most of the pieces and can rebuild it. We could stick the disk inside of it along with a remote detonator, and shoot it at Wayne's dual field emitter with Dean's Corn Capper. We just have to crank the emitter's force field and calibrate it to deflect straight up. When the detonator triggers the disk, the doohickey will *absorb* the explosion's energy, then release it in controlled bursts. It'll look like... a roman candle, maybe lightning. No one will think it was anything else."

"Brilliant!" said Dean.

"Interesting idea, Campbell." said the 'doc.'

To Jin, it sounded like gibberish. She turned to Chung, who had always been better about technology. He frowned slightly, but didn't look completely confused. "[Brother, what is he talking about?]"

"[I am not sure. I think he is saying that he has other devices that will help him push the disk into the sky and detonate it remotely.]"

She studied Mitch, who'd lapsed back into silence, his eyes unfocused as he stared off into space. "[He seems so stupid. Do you think he can do what he says?]"

Chung opened his mouth to speak, but Kyung cut him off, exasperated, "[Jin, the boy created a body faxing machine out of a satellite dish and mattress springs. Trust him!]"

Chung smiled at Jin and said, "[And if you cannot trust Mitch, then trust me. I will stay with him and see to it that he does what he says.]"

"Ms. Ae, the clock's ticking," said Marion. "What's your verdict?"

With one final nod from Chung, Jin decided. "Alright. We will do it."

CHAPTER 38

Best Laid Plans

Two jump points opened simultaneously, one from the subbasement and the other from the SMOR.

Mitch closed the subbasement's jump point as soon as he, Chung, and Jin landed. "Wait here. I'll be right back," he told them, then immediately opened the point to Bische's lab.

Briggs hopped out from the SMOR and blocked Mitch's path. "Hold on. Nobody's going anywhere else but here."

"Who says?" Mitch sniped back.

"I do," Francine spoke from the edge of the SMOR's jump point.

Jin turned sharply toward the hole. "I know your voice," she said.

"Hello, Ms. Ae. I'm Francine Drake. I run this facility." She gestured at the control room behind her, then shifting back to Mitch, she continued, "Something you'd do well to remember, Campbell. Until we put a lid on this situation, anything you do, any place you go, is at *my* discretion. We need to contain this issue, but can't if you keep opening portals, popping out of nowhere, drawing attention to yourself—"

"I get that," Mitch interrupted, "but I need some things from Doc's lab. The plan won't work without them. It's a twenty-minute walk, both ways. The Jump!Go's faster."

Francine relented. "Alright, but make sure you get it all in one trip. Anything you need after that, ask us. As you saw, we've got a cage full of supplies."

"Will do," he said, and with a quick leap, was gone.

"Cover the exit, Briggs. No one else enters or leaves."

Briggs took up residence by the garage's front door, feet planted wide, arms folded across his chest, and eyes darting between Jin and Chung, daring them to try and get past him. Jin had known soldiers like Briggs her whole life, all of them full of bluster and belligerence and an inflated sense of their own competence. Yet their actions betrayed their lack of skill, and Briggs' wide stance was a prime example. She could drop him with a swift kick between his legs, and she and Chung would be gone before he groaned. She dismissed him from her notice with contempt.

"[He is very masculine,]" Chung whispered to her in Korean, dropping his voice an octave and flexing a bicep.

Jin snorted and bit the inside of her lip to keep from laughing aloud. "[He is also very exposed,]" she replied quietly. "[Even *you* could punch his groin from here, his legs are split so wide.]"

"['But I'm covering the door!']" Chung said in the same fake-deep voice, shifting his stance into an exaggerated match for Briggs.

Jin couldn't stop the chuckle from escaping. Briggs scowled at Chung, his face reddening, no doubt aware that he was being mocked. Still, he dropped his arms to his sides and affected a more natural pose.

"Well, hello again, darlin'." Jin recognized that voice. It belonged to the flirtatious boy she'd saved from The Spider's bullet. He climbed gingerly through the SMOR hole, holding his side, then headed across the room straight toward her.

Chung intercepted him. "Hi, Dean," he said cheerily. "I am most happy to see you also." He stood in front of Dean, their eyes about level, seemingly oblivious to blocking the boy's path, but sporting a mischievous grin nonetheless.

"I think he meant your sister, brah," said another young man who hopped gracefully into the garage after Dean. He was shorter than the beefy one and about the same height as Mitch, but with spiky hair and Japanese features.

"He cannot mean that," she said to the new boy. "I am *not* his 'darling.' "

"You could have fooled me," said Dean, clapping Chung playfully on the shoulder before sidestepping him to talk to her. "Cuz you sure left your mark." With difficulty, he lifted the right side of his shirt to reveal an ugly purple bruise, vaguely shaped like a boot.

Jin winced. "You should ice that."

"And erase my one memento from you?" he said, sporting a big, goofy grin. "Never."

She felt a reciprocating smile tickle her lips, but managed to control herself enough to look away.

"[I must admit,]" said Chung, beside her suddenly, stroking his chin as he stared at Dean's bruise, "[that does look a lot like your shoe.]"

"[Hush, you.]" She flicked her fist out fast and punched his shoulder, an unconscious move stolen from their childhood, elicited now by Chung's teasing. Jin did not know which was more embarrassing: Chung's unrepentant giggles as she glared at him or the realization that she actually liked Dean. The spiky-haired American saved her.

"I'm Wayne, by the way." He nudged Dean aside and extended his hand. She shook it gratefully and gave him her full focus. "If we want to be done in time for your boss' party, we need to scan the disk into the modeler," he said, gesturing toward her left hand.

It took Jin a moment to realize he meant the Unity Disk. She'd been holding it for so long, it almost felt like a part of her hand. Looking down at it now, a wave of revulsion flowed over her, washing away any lingering embarrassment or playful amusement at Chung's antics. She held the disk out to Wayne, relieved to be rid of it—at least for the moment. "My apologies for delaying you. Please proceed."

Wayne didn't look any happier to take the disk. He carried it over to the printer and gingerly secured it to the modeler's stage. "Whoo," he sighed, then plopped into a chair in front of the printer's workstation and pulled up the modeling software. Probes above and on each side of the disk glowed as the stage gimballed about in all directions. Soon, a bare outline of the disk appeared on the monitor.

Chung hurried over, wide-eyed, and stood at Wayne's shoulder. "Oh, may I watch you?" he asked, gawking at the screen as more details were added to the image.

"Sure thing," said Wayne. He pushed a rolling chair toward Chung and immediately launched into a detailed description of what the modeler was doing and why. *A natural teacher, this one,* Jin thought. Chung engaged with him eagerly, asking questions, making suggestions and listening with rapt attention to everything Wayne patiently explained.

"Wayne's pretty happy right now," Dean said, walking over to stand beside her. "Nothing he likes more than playing professor. Chung looks happy, too."

Relieved to discuss someone other than herself with the boy, she said, "Yes. He was forced to be a soldier, but he was born to be an engineer. He is doing what he loves."

"I know the feeling," he said. She did not look at him, but could see his wide smile from the corner of her eye. Minutes ago, she would have been happy to carry on the banter, but Wayne had reminded her of her duty. The weight of it pressed down on her, so she remained sober and silent; the time for playing had passed.

Dean must have sensed her shifting mood, because he changed the subject. "Not much to do until the scan is over. How about a snack? We've got tons of food."

"There is food?" Chung's head swiveled around and he pushed away from the monitor. "I am very hungry. Food would taste good, please." His words came out in a tumble.

"K, we can cook instead. I'll make burgers. Be done in a jiffy." Dean headed for the connecting door between the garage and the house.

"Stop!" shouted Briggs, still rooted in front of the external door. "Director Drake said no one else leaves." Dean paused and put his hands on his hips. He was as tall as Briggs, maybe taller, and had about the same muscle mass and level of fitness. Comparing the two, it surprised Jin to realize that they both seemed to be about the same age as well. That would explain Briggs' zealousness and general lack of maturity. If not for his bruise, Dean and Briggs would be evenly matched, but injured, Dean would likely lose. Jin balanced on the balls of her feet, ready to kick crotch should Briggs make a move.

Dean was unfazed. "Oh, come off it, brass ass," he said. "I'm just headed to the kitchen. Here, have a Snickers and chill." Dean retrieved a candy bar from a shelf near the door and tossed it at the fuming soldier. Briggs caught the chocolate easily, but made a big show of crushing it in his fist as he glared at the boy. Dean ignored him and propped the door open, gesturing toward the kitchen.

"See? Clearly visible. You can track my every move. You like cheese on your burger? Want some veggies on top?"

Briggs pressed his lips together so hard the line between them almost disappeared. But Dean just grinned at him, unintimidated, completely at ease. Jin could see the soldier deflating with each passing second. Eventually, he said, "Cheddar. No tomatoes."

"You got it." Turning to Jin, he said with a wink, "See you soon, darlin'. And Chung, I'm giving you extra cheese!"

"Thank you!" her brother called back enthusiastically.

The buzz of electricity filled the room and the now-familiar white oval of a jump hole appeared near its center.

"I'm back!" Mitch popped out, his curls bouncing as he landed, his arms awkwardly balancing a large cardboard box filled to the brim with assorted equipment. He hurried to the closest open workbench, and up-ended the box's contents on top of it. Aside from a breadboard and a few spools of wire, the only other thing Jin could identify was a kind of rifle-shaped object with a silver barrel that was much too wide.

"Mitch!" Chung sprang up from the 3D printer and trotted excitedly over to Mitch's side. "Did you find what you needed?" He poked through the pile of components, obviously recognizing more than Jin, 'oohing' and 'aahing' as he examined each one.

"Just about. The most important parts, anyway." Mitch gathered up two identical pieces, then placed them on the floor opposite each other in the empty space beside the workbench.

To Jin, they resembled intercom speakers, but Chung caught a glimpse and declared, "Mobile field emitters! I have never seen these up close." He crouched down to pick one up, but Mitch stopped him with an impatient gesture.

"Wait'll you see what they do," he said. Jin sympathized. She was starting to wish her brother would calm down.

Mitch picked up a tablet and typed in a command. The area between the speakers sparkled, and soon a reddish, gray wall of energy appeared. *Is there no end to these people's energy fields?* Jin wondered. He typed some more and the wall tilted backward until it almost faced up.

Chung was beside himself with amazement. "Uwa!" *Wow!* he exclaimed, wide-eyed. "Will that destroy the disk?"

"No," Mitch answered, "but it's a good start." He picked up the toy rifle and pulled the trigger. A round, sweet-smelling wad of goo flew out of the barrel, bounced off the energy field, and slammed into the ceiling. "Bullseye, ha hah!" He pounded Chung on the back, clearly elated by the result.

"This is good, yes?" asked Chung, looking back and forth between the energy wall and the goo it had splattered onto the ceiling.

"Darn near perfect, I'd say," Mitch laughed in reply. "Now all we need is an absorber for the blast."

Chung's face fell. "Sounds hard."

"Piece of cake. I've made one before." Mitch turned back to the bench. "All of the pieces are here. Just gotta put 'em together. You game?" Chung brightened and practically danced with delight, infecting Mitch with his glee. Suddenly, the two of them were bobbing up and down, laughing and high-fiving each other. A flash of anger sliced through Jin.

"No games!" her voice reverberated through the garage. Mitch and Chung froze, shocked into silence. She'd shouted without meaning to—had only intended a gentle rebuke—but they were celebrating victory for a war they had not won. To her eyes, there was still much to do, and their cluelessness to that fact grated on her. She let them have it. "*He* is the only one taking this seriously." She pointed toward Wayne, grimly studying the 3D printer as an image of the disk slowly materialized on his workstation monitor. "Dear Leader will *kill us all* if the fake disk does not work. The *real* disk will kill everyone else if *you* do not build this 'absorber' correctly. No more games!"

The both of them sobered. "[You are right, Sister,]" said Chung solemnly. Mitch could not have understood Chung's words, yet the sentiment was clear, and he nodded assent.

Digging out two sets of goggles from the pile, he handed one to Chung, and said, "Let's go."

CHAPTER 39

Sky High

They made good time. With Chung's help, Mitch reassembled the lame-o-doohickey back to its former glory. All three energy collectors—one each for light, heat, and sound—filled the power reserves without a hitch. A couple of lines added to the managing software allowed the doohickey to release its energy in discreet bursts. They'd even managed to reapply the quick charge, which lead them to re-christen the doohickey as the PEAPOD—Passive Energy-Absorbing Power on Demand.

Every one of their successes sent a thrill through Mitch. It felt just like the old days in Bische's shop—a pile of parts, a great idea, and good friends to work on both. Chung was an excellent substitute for Wayne and Dean, who were still busy finalizing the fake version of the disk. Mitch found that he and Chung worked easily together, each knowing something the other didn't, both of them equally skilled at assembly. When Chung had a question, he'd instantly grasp Mitch's answer, barely interrupting their flow. Mitch understood the Babe's criticism—this wasn't a party, the stakes were real—but he liked Chung and they were hitting on all cylinders. He couldn't help but do a little dance inside.

With the PEAPOD functional, they started in on the retrofit, which involved attaching the Corn Capper's barrel and triggering mechanism around the PEAPOD's energy release port. This, too, proceeded smoothly. Bische had patented many modular parts, so all of their builds that were made using his kits shared a certain measure of connectivity. The base container for one project could accept components from another, thus the barrel for the Corn Capper snapped easily into latches on the PEAPOD. Likewise with the trigger board, sliding snugly into an open slot within the PEAPOD's encasement. After a bit of soldering to secure the trigger mechanisms wires, they were ready to do a test. Mitch calibrated the PEAPOD to release energy in discreet bursts. Then Chung placed the combined device in front of Wayne's dual field emitter, the barrel aimed at the gray wall's center. Mitch retrieved a small power pack from the garage's supply shelf and set it to overload.

"Fire in the hole!" he called to alert everyone else in the garage, then dropped the power pack down the Corn Capper barrel. As the pack reached critical mass, the PEAPOD activated and siphoned all of the energy out of the blast. The power reserve indicator blinked green as it filled, then the release valve opened. *Phoomp!* A small blob of energy shot out of the barrel, hit the field emitter dead on, and then fizzled out, its energy spreading across the emitter like fine gold filament before it disappeared.

"Manse!" exclaimed Chung. "It appears to work!"

Mitch frowned. "That shouldn't have happened." He hadn't expected the fizzling. The energy burst should have deflected upward, just like when he'd first tested the emitter, and just like he'd imagined when the idea to build the device had popped into his head. His imagination was usually right in projecting the results of his builds. It puzzled him why this particular build was different. "Let's try it again. Maybe the fizzle was a fluke."

He grabbed another power pack from the shelf and set it to overload. "Fire in the hole!" he called again. *Phoomp!* Another burst of energy shot out of the barrel and hit the field emitter, but the result was the same—the emitter dissipated the power rather than deflecting it. Much worse, the floor behind the emitter was singed. There was a leak!

'Better?" Chung asked. *No, not better. It's not doing what I want.* Mitch knelt down to examine the device, checking for loose wires or missing parts. Something nagged at the back of his mind about the setup, but he couldn't quite put his finger on it. All appeared to be in order, and yet they weren't achieving the desired effect. His euphoria drained away, and suddenly their "successes" over the past couple of hours seemed minor and petty. Cold doubt mixed with burgeoning panic conspired to unravel his confidence. Something was wrong, but what?

"What's your progress, gentlemen?" Bische stepped across the threshold of the SMOR hole. Mitch felt a moment of relief. *Perhaps Doc can help me figure this out.* But before Mitch could snag him, Dean and Wayne called him over and started regaling him with their status on the fake disk. Mitch felt ashamed. There his friends went again, showing off their perfect, no doubt brilliant work. The question he wanted to ask died on his lips. Chung swung around to listen, but Mitch couldn't bear it. And though he turned away to ponder his own problem, Wayne's voice, confident and professorial, still bled through.

"As you can see, the replication is nearly flawless. They've got the same weight, same texture, the activating switch is consistent. If it weren't for the tiger tape on the fake, you'd be hard pressed to distinguish the two."

"And Jin gave us great info about the disk's functionality," Dean added. "The real disk whines and glows before it detonates, and the full detonation takes about three minutes. Making it whine that long wasn't hard, but getting it to glow brighter and brighter over time took some figuring."

"On top of that," Wayne continued, "we have to make it look like a failed explosion when it 'blows.' Since it's supposed to be a dud, I don't know how authentic the explosion part has to be. But to sell it, we combined flash paper with the innards of a few firecrackers. That should give it some kick and be kind of convincing. We hope. Ready to see it in action?"

Mitch had moved on to checking the emitters themselves, but his curiosity was piqued. He joined Chung at the back of the group, just out of Bische's line of sight, and watched Wayne prepare the disk for a test.

"How long does it take to reset the disk after you 'detonate' it?" Bische asked.

"No more than 10 minutes. We've done it a few times now." He pressed the switch on the fake, Dean started the timer, and they all waited. The fake disk emitted a low whine and after a few seconds began to glow. The whine and the light emission increased as more time passed, until at the two minutes and fifty-eight seconds mark, the whine was pretty loud and the center of the disk glowed bright. When it finally blew, there was a quick, bright flash, followed by the smell of charcoal and sulfur.

"Well done, boys," said Bische. "Now let's reset it and demo for Francine." They and Jin gathered back around the printer workstation. Mitch sighed. Bische would be tied up with the fake disk for a while. It was back to solving his problem on his own.

"Have you found the problem, Mitch?" Chung asked him quietly.

"Maybe. I was thinking about boosting the gain to stop the energy bleed out the back of the dual-field wall. "

"Yes, that might do it. But it is strange that the energy is no longer deflecting. The discharge should go up, yes?"

"Right."

"But if the field diffuses the energy, that should be just as good, yes?"

"If it was diffusing all of the energy, sure. But some of it is bleeding through. It shouldn't allow that."

"Allow what, kid?"

Mitch groaned inwardly. The old guy had snuck up on them. From what he'd learned in the short time he'd spent interacting with Dr. Travers, the man was light on helpful suggestions, but heavy on the criticism. The last thing he needed was have him around making snarky comments, and grousing about the device not being done. He let his irritation with the old man get the better of him though. "Why are you here? Checking up on me?"

"Yeah. I drew the short straw. Since you don't look happy to see me, I assume you've got a problem."

Mitch decided to ignore the old man and went back to looking for a resistor he could use to boost the gain on the emitter field, but Chung, ever guileless, let the cat out of the bag. "The mobile field emitters no longer work as they should."

Travers surveyed the area, taking in the devices and wrinkling his nose at the PEAPOD and the pile of loose parts. "That's surprising. Of all your toys, the field emitters look the most legit. You make 'em?"

"No, Wayne did," Mitch replied sullenly.

"Explains *that*. You aren't too shabby, but that kid's got some brains. So what didja do to mess 'em up?"

"I didn't *do* anything. They just stopped working. Or at least... they aren't working the way I need them to."

"Show me."

Mitch demonstrated the energy burst and the fizzle, and pointed out the singed spot on the floor. Scott took a gauge from his pocket, held it up to the emitter, and scanned the area around the emitter.

"Looks rock solid to me, kid. No radiation or excess heat. What's the problem?" Travers looked over at Chung, who just shrugged and pointed to Mitch.

"It fizzles when it should be deflecting."

"But that's how it's supposed to work, kid."

"No it's not! Not the way Wayne built it. We shoot popcorn balls at it all the time, and each time, it always deflects up." Mitch felt childish saying this. It even sounded kind of crazy coming out of his mouth.

"You sure about that, kid?" The way Travers looked at him confirmed that what he'd said sounded insane. Scott didn't wait for him to answer, so continued, "I'll tell you what it is. It's a dual-field emitter— field emitters do one of three things. They can block, they can rotate, and they can oscillate, but they don't deflect. Now step away. Let me take a look."

"You don't know anything about it!" said Mitch.

"*I* don't know what I'm doing? Tell me this, you ever throw anything at it besides candy?"

"It wasn't candy. It was candy-*coated* popcorn balls," Mitch sniped in reply.

"Ah, that makes it better. Anything else, Einstein? Ever?"

Mitch blanched. They had never really needed to shoot anything at it other than popcorn balls. Wayne must have tested it with something else, but Mitch had been too distracted with his own builds to take much notice. He had to admit it. "No."

"Pfft. No wonder you can't make it work. Step away."

"No! You don't understand—"

"Get back, kid, before I pull you back and embarrass you even more." Mitch looked up and noticed the curious glances from the group surrounding the 3D printer and realized that he was making a scene. Fuming, he stepped away from the emitter and let the old guy through.

Travers started by shutting down the field. He picked up an emitter unit and pulled out its controller board. Speaking to Chung, he said, "Hand me that boost wheel, would ya?" Chung stared blankly at the parts pile. It was clear he had no idea what the old guy meant. "That fat, puke-green piece near your hand," the scientist clarified. Chung's eyes lit up with recognition. He picked two boost wheels from the pile and plopped them into the old guy's hand.

He made room on the board for the component, snapped it into place, and reassembled the unit. He did the same for the other unit and switched the device back on. Instead of a wall built slowly from a gradual sparkle, the twin fields reignited in a flash, looking stronger, brighter, and cleaner than before.

"That's better," said Travers. He yelled over his shoulder at Briggs, "Hey, Oliver, got any charges on ya'? Need to see if this thing can stand something stronger than a popcorn ball."

"Never leave home without 'em," said Briggs. He fished a thick cylinder from one of the many Velcro pockets on his cargo pants and tossed it at the old guy.

Travers caught it like a pop-fly. He turned off the energy wall, then gathered up the emitters and their controller tablet and headed for the external door. "Time for a real test, you two," he said, motioning for Mitch and Chung to follow. "Oliver, hold the door open, please. We're stepping out for a sec."

"Sure thing, Dr. T."

Mitch stooped to pick up the modified PEAPOD, but Travers shook his head. "Nuh, uh. Not bothering with that."

Mitch steamed. "You still don't get it," he said, throwing up his hands in frustration. Pointing at his device, he said slowly, "We need the PEAPOD to *control* the flow of energy, else the emitter's field lattice will get overwhelmed. Why can't you understand that?"

"'Cuz it's garbage," said Travers, perfectly mimicking Mitch's condescension. Briggs held the door open, and Chung and the old guy walked out into the night.

With the field emitter gone, the singe marks on the floor were even easier to see. Mitch's insides twisted with anxiety. They were missing something important, he knew it, and if they didn't figure it out, lots of people were going to get hurt. *Gotta make him see reason.* He picked up the PEAPOD and rushed to the door.

Travers and Chung had already invoked the field emitter. Before Mitch could stop him, the old guy popped the top on Briggs' charge, dropped it on the energy wall, and hustled away. Mitch saw it explode just as it touched the field, a bright flash that he was sure would envelope the emitter units, the grass, the old guy, and Chung, who was just inches away. Instead, the flash was sucked straight down, as if the energy lattice were a giant magnet and Briggs' charge just a hunk of steel. The light from the blast rolled across the surface of the energy wall, dissipating in all directions, losing its brightness, until finally—with barely a pop of an aftershock— all traces of the explosion drifted away.

While Chung collected the field emitters, Travers walked back to the door and he and Briggs traded smirks. "That's how it's done in the professional world, kid," he said as he brushed by.

Mitch was stunned. The old guy's tweak had actually worked. He'd been so convinced that he was right, that his solution was the best and only option. But in less than fifteen minutes, he'd been proven wrong and made to look like a fool. Still, the feeling that something was off about Travers' plan nagged at him. He couldn't just leave it alone. He walked over to the spot on the lawn where the emitters had been placed. Seeing in his mind's eye the center of the emitters' wall, he dropped to the ground and let his fingers probe. It didn't take long to find the warm spot and the ashen remains of Sam's perfect grass. He ran back inside the garage and skidded to a stop in front of Travers.

"Please, stop," he said.

"Oh, brother," the old guy muttered under his breath. "Look, kid, it's a done deal. You gave it a good shot, but it's time to move on."

"You burned the grass." He held up his blackened palm, but the old guy wouldn't look at him. "There's something we're missing."

"Yeah, a check on your ego."

"It's not about that. Listen."

Travers chuckled and finally turned around. "To what? You moanin' cuz we ditched your plan? This isn't playtime, boy. We're talkin' life and death here and at least I know what I'm doing, unlike you."

"Says the man who couldn't figure out how to make his own invention work right," Mitch said, regretting his retort immediately as the old man's cheeks burned red. But he couldn't apologize—could barely breathe. He just gulped repeatedly, desperate to tamp down a rising sense of dread.

Travers eyes compressed into hard slits and he got right up into Mitch's face. "You shut your mouth, you little shit. I knew enough to not try to sell it. To put in controls to yank people out of it when something went wrong. From what your prof tells me, you barely even know how *your* thing works. You got lucky and you've been riding that ever since. So don't high horse me, you prick."

He signaled for Chung to follow him and they headed toward the SMOR hole. "It's go time, people," he growled at the group, who were still fussing over the fake disk. "Now or never." As he passed by Bische, he said, "See you up top at the blast zone."

Wayne and Dean shut down their workstations, then they and Jin followed Chung through the SMOR hole. Wayne looked up at Bische expectantly, waiting for him to join them. Bische glanced toward Mitch and shook his head. With one last look back at his friend, Wayne tapped his Jump!Go and the jump point closed.

Mitch grabbed the sides of his head, wanted to call out "Don't go!" Hot tears streamed down his face and he felt like an idiot. He couldn't make the old guy listen, and now everyone was going to die. He collapsed back against the workbench and slid down to sit on the floor.

"Campbell," said Bische.

"Go ahead. Lay into me. I deserve it." Mitch braced himself, ready for Bische to chastise him for unjustly berating the old man. To his surprise, Bische joined him and sat cross-legged on the floor.

"Hit you where you live, didn't he?" he said, quietly.

"He's right. The Babe's right. Boss Lady's right. All I do is make guesses and get lucky. I've got no idea *why* I'm right when things work. They just work. I thought that was enough."

Bische pursed his lips and said, "But there's more to it than that, isn't there? Why do you think Scott's plan won't work?"

"I don't know!" wailed Mitch. "I just told you! It's—I can *feel* when things will work and when they won't. What the old guy did... *looked* right, but there's soot on the floor and ashes outside. Something about it is wrong. He can't see it and we're all gonna die!" The tears flowed again.

"Calm down," said Bische. "No one will die if you think it through. Close your eyes. Take a breath. Was it something you saw?"

Mitch covered his eyes with the palms of his hands, but all he saw was his PEAPOD with the Corn Capper strapped on top. He removed his palms and searched the room for the ridiculous thing, and wanted to wail anew once he found it, abandoned by the door, useless and completely stupid. "Why couldn't it have been Wayne or Dean's idea? Why'd it have to be mine? They always do things right. Hell, Wayne even does things twice! Two magna coils, two field emitters, two countermeasures—" And that's when he knew.

He scrambled to his feet and rushed over to the PEAPOD, running his hands along the Corn Capper's barrel. "It's not here! How could I have been so stupid?!"

Bische followed after him. "Campbell, what is it?"

Mitch rushed back to the workbench and rummaged through the pile of parts, while explaining. "Countermeasures. Wayne does things in twos. He made the dual field emitter to disintegrate Dean's balls. When Dean added a disruptor, Wayne countered with two oscillators. But the oscillators won't trigger until the dual fields are disrupted. The disruptor fell off the Corn Capper. That's why it didn't look right!"

He lifted a breadboard and saw it: a thin, silver tube, the same length of the barrel, with a single connector dangling off the end. With trembling fingers he picked it up and reattached it to the underside of the Corn Capper barrel. "Where's

Dr. Travers?" he asked Bische after verifying for the third time that the disruptor was fully powered.

"In the blast zone bunker by now. It's directly above the SMOR. But we need to ride an elevator to get there. "

"Let's ride a beam of light instead."

Mitch pulled up the coordinates for the SMOR, extrapolated up by ninety degrees and dialed the point in. A dirt field, illuminated by a flood light, appeared, allowing them to see Travers' white lab coat flapping as he trotted down the dugout bunker's stairs. Mitch didn't wait for Bische and hit the jump point hard.

Travers looked up, startled by the jump point's sudden appearance, but his expression soured immediately upon seeing Mitch come through it. Bische followed a second behind and said, mid-leap, "Scott, stop what you are doing. This attempt will fail."

"What? Why? You saw at the garage. It worked perfectly."

"Energy bleeds through. We have to force it to deflect. Mitch knows how to do it. He showed me."

"Please, this piss ant. You're gonna take his word over mine?"

Mitch cut Bische off before he could continue. "I'm sorry, Dr. Travers. I was wrong for what I said and you were right. I'm just lucky. But this isn't luck now. The energy will bleed through and it will crack the ground wide open. We've got to deflect it up. I've got the right part to do it. The emitters have smart oscillators, they just need a disruptor to trigger."

"Break the ground open?"

"Yes," said Bische. "If the disk is as powerful as Chung's sister says, Hirano's emitters will be overwhelmed in seconds. The force will bleed straight through and burn everything in its path. Including the SMOR."

Travers had turned completely white. "I hit the remote detonator just before you showed up. There's less than 3 minutes left."

"I can run," said Mitch.

Bische shook his head. "No time."

Travers collapsed into the bunkers console "Marion... my god, what have I done?"

"Mitch, use your mini light hole," said Chung.

"Right, the Jump!Go. Um, coordinates..."

Bische thought fast. "Bunker coordinates plus twenty degrees."

The plasma grid flowed from Mitch's Jump!Go and a single point appeared. Mitch prepared to jump. "I will help you, Mitch," said Chung.

"Go!" yelled Bische.

Without looking, Mitch leapt, Chung close on his heels. They had made it to just north of the dual field emitter, surrounded by blast shields. The Unity disk lay humming in the center of the energy wall. Its center glowed dully, a signal that the detonation reaction had begun. Mitch handed the PEAPOD/Corn Capper to Chung and reached for the disk. It wouldn't budge. The emitters' energy well held it tight in the latticed field.

"Mitch, use your phone. It will redirect the lattice," suggested Chung.

"Got it. Put the Corn Capper barrel close to the wall," yelled Mitch.

The hum was growing louder. Mitch touched the edge of his phone to a corner of the disk. A shock ran from the phone up his arm. The disk fell into the barrel, but his phone dropped to the ground, releasing the Jump!Go fob. The PEAPOD's collectors sprang to life. The humming was muffled now, being syphoned by the sound collector, but Mitch looked down the barrel at the disk. The light at its center was burning bright.

"We have to leave now!"

They turned back toward where the jump point had been, but saw to their horror that it had closed. There would be no quick getaway. *So this is it*, thought Mitch. *This is how I die.* He didn't want this ending. He wanted to live, to make it up to Chung, and his sister, to see his friends again, and share nachos and dark beers and bad pizza together. *I won't go without a fight.* "Fire in the hole!" he shouted and, dragging Chung beside him, set out for the bunker at a dead run.

The bunker was straight ahead. He could see Doc Travers beckoning him and just barely hear him yelling, "Run, both of ya'! Run!"

He looked behind him and saw that they hadn't made much progress. It was no use. The disk would go critical any second now. Chung lagged behind, unable to keep up with Mitch, so Mitch slowed and grabbed his arm. "I won't let you die alone!" he yelled in Chung's ear.

"You are a good friend, Mitch!" Chung yelled back in reply.

But suddenly Bische was between them both, dragging them still faster, and in what felt like barely a second they were back at the bunker, gasping, doubled over, but very much alive. *Phoomp!* He heard the familiar sound of the Corn Capper firing. Staggering to the viewing slit in the bunker, he looked out upon the dirt field in awe.

Phoomp! Phoomp! Phoomp! ...

Thick gouts of energy shot out of the PEAPOD/Corn Capper, one after another, every ten seconds, just as he had programmed it back at the garage, just as he had seen it in his head at the subbasement. Over and over, the blasts rose into the sky, like shells from a roman candle, until after several minutes, it was done. As the last of the blasts fizzled away in the sky, Mitch sagged against the back of the bunker wall, completely relieved, but spent.

Travers pulled his phone from his pocket and with shaking hands dialed a number. He bit his thumb waiting for the person on the other end to answer. Finally, Mitch heard Marion's brash voice over the old guy's too-loud speakers. "Agent Travers, here."

"Marion, baby, you alright?"

"Yeah, Dad," came her tinny, bemused reply. "Everything good up there?" Scott didn't answer. He covered his face with his trembling hands. Mitch thought he heard a muffled sob. "Dad?" Marion asked again. "Are you okay?"

Eventually the old guy found his voice. "Just fine, dear. The disk is destroyed. We're on our way down."

"Good. Dear Leader will be back soon. Let's coordinate when you return." And with that, the call ended.

"Thank god," Travers breathed, returning the phone to his pocket. He wobbled, but Bische was there to steady him. He looked up at Bische with anguished eyes, and said, "CC woulda killed me."

Bische smiled, but locked the old guy in his own piercing gaze. "You might also thank Mitch. His quick thinking saved the day."

Travers nodded and, grabbing Mitch by his shoulders, said, "Thanks, kid. I owe you one."

"I'll remember that," said Mitch, with a wan smile.

They left the bunker and gathered up the various devices, as well as Mitch's phone, then headed back into the facility. Bische stood beside Mitch on the way down in the elevator. Speaking only so that Mitch could hear, he said, "Now that, Campbell, is what is called thinking it through. Good job." They were traveling down, but Mitch felt like he was floating on air.

*****

They arrived back at the SMOR just as Jin was preparing to leave. She secured the fake disk in one Velcro pocket and the tiny remote detonator Wayne had specially made for it in another.

"Once Geomi sees me," said Jin "he will no doubt tell Dear Leader to send me off with the disk, hoping I will die in the process. I will volunteer, but fumble it like a fool, and set it off. We must shut down the Canopy when that happens, and then destroy it, to make Dear Leader think that I have destroyed the subbasement instead of Seoul."

"That's where I come in," said Briggs. "I'll lay down charges, and then blow their subbasement to hell."

Jin fixed him with a steely gaze. "You will remove Kyung and Hyun before you do anything."

"You don't tell me what to do," he said back at her defiantly.

Marion stepped in. "But yes, Ms. Ae, we will remove your friends before Briggs sets off the C4 to destroy the room."

"Good."

The old guy approached Jin. "Take this," he said, dropping a jet injector into her hand.

"What is this?" she asked.

"Insurance. In case things go sideways and you wind up needing to scoot before the big boom. Just inject yourself with this. The Fail Safe'll detect the trace and send you back here tout suite. Your leader and that spider guy will just think you got disintegrated in the explosion. I'll be there waiting for you."

"I will be there, too," said Chung, stepping up to his sister. "Be sure to hold on to your stomach when you feel the Fail Safe. It is very nauseating. You may lose your food." He squeezed her hand and said to her quietly, "[Be careful.]"

The subbasement's jump point opened, and Kyung's gruff voice called through, "They're coming back." With a grim nod toward Chung, Jin leapt into the light hole, its orange-rim pulsing, until finally it winked out.

CHAPTER 40

End Game

Q uickly, Spider," Dear Leader breathed impatiently behind Geomi. They exited the elevator at the sub-basement, stepping into the dim corridor that led to the monitor room, and walking in a diamond formation with Geomi at the head, Dear Leader in the middle, two guards at either side, and the camera crew at the back. Geomi lengthened his stride, but only a little. He saw no need to rush things. Kyung and Hyun were going nowhere, regardless of whether or not they had found Jin, taken the disk, and disposed of her. Dear Leader's "glory" would come soon enough.

Either way, his own ascension had already been sealed. Jin was gone, no longer Dear Leader's protector. Of the two guards remaining, Pok had already pledged his loyalty to Geomi, as had the guard posted at the sub-basement door. They both knew that Dear Leader's focus was misplaced on the Unity Disk, which was simply a one-time tool of destruction. Geomi had convinced them that the real power existed in the means of transport, the ability to move unimpeded from place to place. The true power, then, lay in the Canopy. Controlling it was all that mattered.

Once the device was secured, he'd give the signal and they would make their move. With the cameras on, he would grab Dear Leader, snap his neck like a chicken bone, and walk through to Victory Stadium. A guard would still be sent to destroy Seoul, again on camera, as a warning to all other nations of the instant death his agents could deploy to any location in mere seconds. His men would guard every light hole, demanding a fee for all travel, immediately dispatching any traveler too stupid or stubborn to pay. And no one would refuse, once they saw the convenience of this technology. Then he alone would control the Canopy and all travel to every location on this world. His scientists might even find a way to extend it to other worlds. He would be the true power, leaving to memory and eventually to dust the false power of Dear Leader's corrupt and fetid dynasty.

The group arrived at the monitor room door. The guard saluted Dear Leader, but smiled slyly at The Spider. Geomi drew near him to type the key code into the lock. "Only enter on my command," he whispered. The door guard nodded slightly in acknowledgement. There was shuffling on the other side of the door as the keypad buzzed and unlocked to let them through. *That's right*, he thought. *Scatter like the rats you are. You will soon bow to your new ruler.*

His prediction seemed to have come true when he saw both Kyung and Hyun first stand at attention, then bow deeply, as he entered the room. Neither held the Unity Disk. No matter. The scientists in the Unity division were on track to build another. Seoul's destruction could happen just as easily next month instead of today. Today was Dear Leader's deadline, after all, not his—a deadline that would be meaningless once Dear Leader's neck dangled like a rag from his spine.

He smiled imagining it, a smile that froze on his face when he pushed the door open farther and saw Jin at attention, beside Kyung, bowing just as deeply, the Unity Disk clasped firmly in her hand. A bolt of heavy red fabric extended from her feet into the canopy, stopping at one light hole in particular, a hole Geomi presumed to be the entry to Victory Stadium. The red carpet was a nice reverential touch, damn her. Damn Kyung and Hyun as well. She should be dead and the disk given to him as insurance on their lives. Now they would all die with Dear Leader this day. He cocked his head at the guard beside Dear Leader. "Arrest Jin Ae! A traitor to our leader!"

The guard lunged forward, but she dodged him, quick as a cat, and knelt at Dear Leader's feet. Geomi swung around, furious. *What are you playing at, girl?*

Still with head bowed, Jin said, "Excellency, it is not true. I serve you only, in all that I do."

Dear Leader looked to Geomi. "Spider, what is this? In what way has Jin Ae betrayed me?"

Geomi told the truth, as far as he knew it, saying, "She disappeared, Superior Ruler. She took the disk, abandoned her duty. She—"

"I hid, Dear Leader," Jin interrupted him. "You entrusted me with the disk. To keep it from others," she looked meaningfully to Geomi, "that pay lip service to loyalty, wanting the disk for their own means only. I hid myself and it away. It may be that I over-reacted in protecting it and you. But both have been safe until now, your greatest hour."

"As I would expect," said Dear Leader, gesturing for Jin to rise. "Spider, surely you would have done no less."

Geomi bowed his head, feigning the basic respect. *One last time*, he thought. *A final kowtow before he's dead.* "Of course, Dear Leader. I must have misunderstood Jin Ae's true intentions."

"Excellent," said Dear Leader, his voice expansive, his arms outstretched. "Today is not for baseless accusations. Today we celebrate my grandfather's victory with another—my victorious unification of our people."

"Sir, Pok is prepared," said Geomi, gesturing for Pok to take the Unity Disk from Jin.

Dear Leader stopped him with a magnanimous wave of his hand. "Ah, Pok will accompany me. You and Jin will contribute to my victory as the camera shows you both depositing the disk." He beamed at them, his round face red with anticipation.

Geomi clinched his jaw against his anger and said, "But, sir, I thought I was to be by your side as you addressed the crowd, as a sign of strength, as a means of protection." *Damn Dear Leader and his theatrical improvisations!*

"The proof of loyalty is more important, Spider. The North and South must see my inner circle united, a reflection of our country's returning unity. This is no small part."

Geomi chewed the inside of his cheek to keep from cursing the man. *You dare thwart me, you pig-faced dolt?*

"Dear Leader, you do us honor," said Jin, bowing as well, but no more sincere in her deference than Geomi. With a quick motion, she secured the Unity Disk to her weapon's belt with a Velcro loop.

"Then let us proceed. Destiny awaits!" Dear Leader walked cautiously to the Canopy.

Noting the still furled red carpet, Kyung said, "Allow me, sir," and kicked the roll at the jump point. Immediately, the point expanded, and as the bolt unfolded, the band on the Victory Stadium dais struck up the theme to Dear Leader's most popular musical. Loud gasps mingled with dutiful clapping, emanated from the light hole.

The first camera man ran out ahead of Dear Leader—to more surprised gasps—and trained the camera just above the red carpet at a spot that looked like normal sky. When Pok followed, breaking through a white cloud and striding confidently to his spot behind the podium, the assembled responded with thunderous applause. Dear Leader stood frozen in front of the light hole, gape-mouthed and wide-eyed. Then, giggling, he walked across the red carpet and out onto the dais, causing a new paroxysm of whistles, clapping, and cheers.

Geomi waited until Dear Leader began speaking then, turning around, he nodded at the remaining guard, who promptly shot the second camera man right between the eyes. The guard turned his gun toward Hyun, but Jin fell on him in an instant. She slammed her fist into his trachea, shoving it so far through his neck Geomi thought it would come out the other side. Then she broke his shooting arm across her knee, bending it almost perfectly in half. Hyun vomited as he caught sight of pieces of the guard's tibia poking through the muscle and sinew in his arm. Barely five seconds had passed. With a look of surprise, the guard gurgled once, dropped his gun, and then fell to the floor dead.

Jin dove for the gun, but Geomi was closer and faster, grasping the barrel before she could reach it. Jin, pulled by her momentum, could not stop her fall. Geomi smashed the gun across her face, and she fell to the ground. He kicked her until she flopped onto her stomach, then stomped his foot into the small of her back, pinning her to the ground. Pointing the gun at Hyun, he said, "Pick up the camcorder. Leave it off until I tell you otherwise."

Whimpering, Hyun pried the video equipment from the dead camera man's hands. Then gesturing to Kyung, Geomi commanded, "Take the disk." Kyung undid Jin's Velcro loop and handed him the Unity Disk. He tucked it into a front pocket of his suit. Grabbing a headset, he yanked off the wire between it and its channel guard, and holding it out to Kyung said, "Bind her hands." When Kyung was finished, Geomi stepped off of Jin's back and dragged her to her feet. "Which is the Seoul hole?" he asked, staring at the Canopy.

"There," said Kyung, pointing to the left of the stadium's jump point. "The one with the orange ring. I have extended inner space there, to protect you from the explosion."

"Sungyeol!" Geomi called. The second external guard entered the room, his jaw dropping as he took in his partner's and the camera man's stiffening bodies as well as Jin Ae's bleeding cheek and bound hands. "Cover him!" Geomi snapped, pointing at Kyung. Sungyeol shouldered his rifle and skidded in the blood and bone shards to Kyung's side. Geomi grabbed the barrel of Sungyeol's rifle and positioned it at Kyung's head. Leaning in to Kyung's ear, he said, "Know that you failed me. Move against me while I'm in the Canopy, and Sungyeol will ventilate your head." Then turning to Hyun, he ordered, "Follow us."

Geomi pushed Jin ahead of him into the Canopy. "Time to die, Jin Ae."

"What do you mean to do?" Jin's words fell thickly from her swollen lips.

"What Dear Leader commanded—deliver the Unity Disk to Seoul and blow the South to Hell. The only change is you will be strapped to the disk. A fitting end for you and your meddling."

"And once the South is gone, what will you do?"

"Magnificent device, this travel canopy. I will keep it, of course. Control who uses it. Deposit more Unity disks. That's right, Dr. Sang-Yeob is loyal to me. With the Canopy and more disks, I will take my place among the world leaders—until only I am the leader."

"Dear Leader will know of your treachery."

"Ha!" Geomi chortled. "Not before I snap his neck."

"Then Pok will stop you."

"I own Pok. He will taste lead before he turns on me!" Geomi shouted. He squeezed Jin's arm tighter as they bounced along the spongy white toward the end point of the Seoul hole, his anger and fervor rising higher within him.

"Unlike the rest of you, this Canopy will not fail me," he continued. "Its power will elevate me. It will bring me to Victory Stadium a second after the explosion. And I will pluck out Dear Leader's eyes like grapes from his dead, pig head. All will thank me for ridding our country of Dear Leader's scourge. And my armies will ride the beams of light throughout the world. No one who sees this power will oppose me. Everyone who sees it will say *I* am Supreme!"

Geomi paused, breathless. They were almost at the Seoul jump point. Jin struggled against his grip. "You are a traitor and you are insane," she said through gritted teeth. "Hyun!" she called out, "Will you not do your duty?!"

"Expect no help from that mealworm," scoffed Geomi, casting a quick glance over his shoulder back at Hyun. "He is spineless and weak. See how the camcorder shakes? He..." Geomi stopped. *Oh, no... the camcorder.* His mouth dropped open, but whatever insult he'd intended to hurl at Hyun died on his lips. The "Live Feed" indicator blinked red near the base of the unit, leaving no doubt that the camcorder was on. Everything he'd said until that moment had been broadcast—to Victory Stadium and throughout all of Pyongyang. Surely Dear Leader had heard every word. Enraged, Geomi pointed his gun at Hyun and said, "I told you to turn it *off.*"

Hyun yelped. "You are mad, Spider. Dear Leader will stop you!" He dropped the camera and ran back toward the subbasement's light hole.

"Your duty is to me! *I* am Supreme!" Geomi yelled after him, then he aimed at the center of Hyun's back and shot. Hyun dropped immediately and did not move.

Seizing the opportunity, Jin shook loose from Geomi's grip. With a mighty pull, she broke free of her binding, knocked the gun out of Geomi's hand, and punched him in the face. He staggered back, but recovered quickly, and though Jin continued punching, he matched her, blow for blow. Forming his open hand into a knife-like blade, he jabbed two fingers at her jugular—a killing move. She dodged to her right, but leaned in toward his chest, and crashed her fist into his side. He grunted as his ribs cracked. Rolling into the pain, he hammered down on Jin's arm with a swift chop. Her hand spasmed, and as the disk fell from her grasp, Geomi leapt forward to catch it before it could disappear into the fuzz. His hand closed too tightly around the disk. He heard a loud *snap* and suddenly the disk began to glow. "No!" he shouted.

"You fool!" Jin cried out. "You've killed us all!"

The disk burned brighter and the buzzing from it grew louder. "Only you will die!" he said, and immediately he scrambled to attach it to her weapon's belt, pushing her all the while toward the Seoul hole.

Jin, though laboring and dripping with blood and sweat, blocked Geomi, blow for blow. "You are a traitorous dog," she sneered at him, "but I will teach you the meaning of duty."

Then she grabbed him around the waist, her arms like iron bands. She stumbled back under his weight and her boot landed hard on the video camera, scattering the broken pieces of the lens against Hyun's motionless body. A searing-hot pain shot through Geomi's right buttock. He howled. The whine from the disk was unbearable. He covered his ears. The explosion burned bright, then a great maw opened, its black jaws clamping around his legs and dragging him down, down, down. "Argh! Aaaargh!! Aaaarrrrgghhhh!" he screamed.

As his brain and stomach twisted into the spiraling void, a soft female voice intoned, "Fail Safe engaging."

CHAPTER 41

Traitors Revealed

*T*his is *true glory*, Dear Leader thought to himself as the crowd cheered loudly, hanging on his every word. He had just told them of the Great Plan, the path to Unity and the means by which they would make it. Big screens on either side of the stadium showed the crowd shaking their fists in excitement and chanting his name. The largest screen, directly facing him, showed his face beaming at his people. They loved him, and he loved them, and all was right with the world.

But then his face disappeared from the screen, only to be replaced by the shaking image of the back of a man's head. The man spoke, and Dear Leader knew immediately that it was The Spider, Geomi. Jin was with him, and they appeared to be walking through a Canopy tunnel. At first, Dear Leader thought that Geomi simply started the feed early, too eager perhaps to share the Unity Disk's victory— *my victory*—with their countrymen. The crowd cheered at the sight of his champion, Jin, who was known to all, unlike the shadow assassin, but as her battered form limped beside The Spider, both the crowd and Dear Leader fell silent.

"What do you mean to do?" Jin's words fell thickly from her swollen lips.

"What Dear Leader commanded—deliver the Unity Disk to Seoul and blow the South to Hell. The only change is you will be strapped to the disk. A fitting end for you and your meddling."

"And once the South is gone, what will you do?"

"Magnificent device, this travel canopy. I will keep it, of course. Control who uses it. Deposit more Unity disks. That's right, Dr. Sang-Yeob is loyal to me. With the

Canopy and more disks, I will take my place among the world leaders—until only I am the leader."

"Dear Leader will know of your treachery."

"Ha!" Geomi chortled. "Not before I snap his neck."

"Then Pok will stop you."

"I own Pok. He would sooner taste lead than turn on me!"

Treachery! Dear Leader's senses—expertly honed over the years for moments such as these—flared into overdrive. Behind him, he heard the slight rustle of Pok's uniform, the subtle click of the machine gun safety being disengaged. He smiled to himself, knowing without looking that Pok thought he was unaware. So stupid. They were all fools, thinking he was soft, unprepared.

With a nimbleness that belied his mass, Dear Leader spun around, pivoted to Pok's side, and chopped down on the guard's shooting arm. Pok howled and dropped the machine gun, but Dear Leader caught it mid-air, aimed, and fired, holding down the trigger until Pok's torso was severed from his trunk and slid with a mushy plop down to the dais. *Now you know—I am* always *prepared.*

He trained the machine gun at the stands, then squeezed off exactly four shots, one for each section of the stadium. Four bodies fell. He did not know who they were. It did not matter. What *did* matter was the skill he exhibited in shooting them. His view through the machine gun's sights told him that the assembled got the message. Many looked upon their dead comrades in horror. The smart ones ducked and cowered.

Striding back to the podium, he thundered into the microphone, "Thus is the payment for treachery. Betray me and *die.*" He raised the machine gun above his head and brandished it at the four corners of the stadium. "Remember this and be assured—The Spider and his followers' fates are sealed."

"No!" Geomi's scream echoed through the stadium.

Deceitful cur. You dare contradict me? Dear Leader's eyes shifted to the big screen, expecting to see the backstabber's over-confident sneer, but all traces of Geomi's earlier defiance had gone. Instead, the assassin stood ashen-faced and horrified, staring down at the Unity Disk as it whined and glowed in his outstretched hand. *Damn the idiot. He activated it too soon.*

"You fool!" Jin shouted. "You've killed us all!"

Her cry unfroze The Spider. "Only you will die!" he said, and then he pounced on Jin, thrusting the disk at every pocket of her uniform, desperate to be rid of both it and her.

Jin Ae, grimacing and breathing in ragged gasps, still managed to dodge Geomi, matching him attack for attack until finally her fist connected with his jaw and he crumpled against her.

"You are a traitorous dog," she said, "but I will teach you the meaning of duty." She forced his hand, still clutching the disk, into the jacket of his shiny, gray suit and dragged him toward an orange rimmed jump point suspended in the white fuzz. The light hole expanded, revealing the glittering spires of Seoul's Yongsan district. *Yes,* Dear Leader exalted. *Push him through. Fulfill the plan!* The whine from the disk had become so piercing that Dear Leader covered his ears. Geomi, struggled, wild-eyed, but could not free himself from Jin's grasp. A blinding light obscured them both. Geomi let loose a terrified howl and then—the feed cut out.

Silence fell over the stadium. A bright flash to the west of the stadium followed by an aftershock should confirm Seoul's destruction, yet neither appeared. Then a man close to the dais shouted, "The Champion is dead!" His exhortation started a wave of murmuring from the crowd. All of North Korea knew Jin Ae to be Dear Leader's defender. With her gone, his top assassin turned traitor, and only one guard remaining to protect him, it wasn't much of a reach for Dear Leader to hear within the murmuring a threat. Shouldering the machine gun once more, he aimed at the shouter and picked him off. Silence returned.

Leaning into the microphone, he said, "All who oppose me suffer the same fate. Did you see the fear in the traitor Geomi's eyes? He opposed me and failed. Do not delude yourselves. I cannot be beaten. Model the character and bravery of Jin Ae. Remember her brother, the hero Chung Ae, who gave his life in the pursuit of our country's unity. They died, but their loyalty lives on. Follow their example, and you, too, will live!"

As if to punctuate his speech, there was a loud *Boom!* in the distance and the whole stadium shook, drawing gasps from the crowd. Dear Leader smiled.

Confirmation at last. The South is mine. Now to deal with the rest of the traitors.

Crouching low, machine gun at the ready, he advanced toward the red carpet, but after two steps, the blue sky camouflaging the subbasement's light hole puckered inward and transformed into a maelstrom. On instinct, Dear Leader flung the weapon and ran back to the podium. Hard suction threatened to drag him into the maelstrom, but he wrapped his arms around the podium and clung to it with all his strength. The crowd panicked and scattered toward the exits, while the vicious whirlpool lapped at Dear Leader's heels. After five minutes, he felt his grip on the podium slipping away, but then the maelstrom dissipated until all that was left was a tiny pinhole, and after that, nothing but blue sky.

He breathed deeply to steady himself and pondered the situation. *Had the* boom *come from the South? Had there been a bright flash?* Black smoke rose into the sky, but it came from the wrong direction and was too close to be from Seoul.

The one remaining guard cowered at the base of the dais steps. As Dear Leader approached, the man threw aside his weapon and fell to his knees before the dictator. Dear Leader motioned for him to rise. "Get me a car."

The guard retrieved his machine gun, and ran to the street. Within seconds, he'd commandeered a vehicle and dragged the driver out of it and to the curb. Dear Leader nodded his approval and sat in the back seat. "Drive me to The Bureau. Quickly." The guard sped off. Dear Leader looked out the back window, toward the South. It was over 120 miles away, but still there should be some sign, some evidence of destruction. Nothing of the sort showed itself. Something had gone dreadfully wrong.

CHAPTER 42

Evacuation

Argh! Aaaargh!! Aaaarrrrgghhhh!" Geomi screamed as the vortex of the Fail Safe opened and dragged him away. Jin gripped his waist until she was sure he could not escape the Fail Safe's pull, then she let go, watching with satisfaction as he flailed in terror and confusion down the vortex's spiral. Finally, the vortex collapsed, and he was gone. *Good riddance*, she thought. *You're the Americans' problem now.*

With a groan, she reached down and dragged Hyun's body back to the subbasement, dropping him at Kyung's feet. She doubled over, light-headed from the effort and the effects of Geomi's beating. Kyung examined Hyun's body, but it was clear to Jin that Hyun was dead. She panted, waiting for Kyung to make some cutting remark about his foolish commander. He remained silent, and when she could finally raise her head to look at him, she saw tears in his eyes.

"He was a coward," she said between gasps for breath. "He was greedy and self-serving." Somehow, she thought that would make him feel better.

Instead, Kyung swung toward her, angrily crumpling his cigarette. She thought he would throw it at her, but he stopped himself. Taking a deep breath, he said, "In the end, he did his duty. He broadcast the feed to Victory Stadium. Dear Leader—everyone—saw Geomi's treason." He gestured at the body of his friend. "He made you a hero."

There was nothing she could say.

In the space between them, a rift opened, and Chung jumped out, wild eyed. "Jin!" he called to her, skidding to a stop at her side. "You're bleeding! Are you hurt!?"

Exasperated, she said to her brother, "Chung, go back. This isn't over."

Briggs popped out of the jump point behind Chung, a bulging messenger bag slung across his shoulder. "She's right. We gotta blow this place pronto and scoot, else Dear Asshole's gonna know something ain't right." He set about retrieving charges from his bag and affixing them to key areas of the room—the Canopy rack, Chung's workstation, and structural joints along the walls.

"How much time do we have?" Jin asked.

Briggs paused at the one workstation monitor showing the feed from Victory Stadium. On the Stadium's big screen, Dear Leader, moving gracefully as a cat, disarmed Pok and shot him. The shooting continued even after Jin looked away. She knew Pok would be mush before Dear Leader was through.

"I'd say zero minutes minus ten," Briggs answered drily. He finished connecting the charges and headed back toward the jump point.

"We need charges for these bodies," said Jin. "The real Unity Disk would vaporize them if the explosion was this close."

"No time," said Briggs, grabbing her and Kyung's arms. "Let's go."

Jin disengaged easily, ripping the charge bag from his shoulder and the trigger from his hand.

"Hey!" yelled Briggs as she pushed him back into the jump point. He lost his grip on Kyung's arm as he fell.

"Chung, Kyung, go after him. I will stay behind," Jin yelled at them as she dropped charges onto Hyun and the guard's bodies.

"I'm not going anywhere!" Chung yelled back at her. "Not without you!"

"Someone has to trigger all of this. I will stay and end it."

On the monitor, Pok lay in pieces in front of Dear Leader while he ranted at the crowd. Then he eyed the red carpet, as if he contemplated returning to the subbasement through the stadium jump point.

"We need to blow this now!" yelled Jin. She leapt over the dead guard to Mitch's modified machine. The beefy one, Dean, called out to her, his eyes frantic with worry and alarm. "I am sorry," she said, and with a sweep of her hand, she swiped the spinning wrench out of the center, shutting the canopy down.

Grabbing Kyung and Chung's arms, she pushed them out of the subbasement door and toward the main stairway, the pressed the trigger as she ran after them. The force of the explosion flung them against the wall near the stairway door. Kyung regained his feet first, flinging the door open as more explosions cascaded out into the hallway, rocking the building to its foundations. An enormous fireball erupted out of a hole blown in the ruined monitor room wall. It rolled greedily toward them, feeding off of the oxygen pouring into the hall from the stairway.

Chung rushed past her, pure fear propelling him ahead. She felt herself slowing. The fight, the beating, the tension from hiding, it was all too much. As Chung pulled away, she felt herself fading. But then Chung was beside her, pulling her back up, pushing her in front of him. "Get in here!" Kyung yelled at them from behind the heavy stairway door. Chung pushed her through, the heat of the fire licking their backs. Kyung closed it seconds before the fire ball reached them. They ran up to the ground level.

In the lobby, Kyung located the emergency alarm button and hit it, setting off red-lights and a loud siren, both of which could be seen and heard on all floors throughout the building. He pushed the entrance guard away from reception monitor and, opening a channel on the general PA, called out "Evacuate! This is not a drill! There's been an accident, we must all get out!" Even as he spoke, cracks formed in the wall behind the reception area.

Jin watched the cracks, feeling weary, detached. They were steps away from the exit. The evacuation procedure was efficient and well-practiced. It wouldn't be long before the building was empty and everyone in it had been moved to safety. Victory Stadium was over twenty miles away, but that was still close enough for Dear Leader to have heard the explosion and seen the smoke. No doubt he would put two and two together and find his way back to The Bureau, but for the moment at least, she could rest.

Kyung repeated the evacuation order over the PA, per protocol. Jin leaned heavily against the reception desk, her eye following the longest crack as it wound its way up the wall to the mezzanine, stopping at the security door leading back into the labs. And then Geomi's words returned to her: "Deposit more Unity Disks. That's right, Dr. Sang-Yeob is loyal to me. With the canopy and more disks, I will take my place among the world leaders." The memory revived her like a shot of adrenaline.

Jin pulled on Kyung's arm. "Make sure everyone gets out," she said, then, grabbing the gun from the holster of the stunned entrance guard, ran toward the mezzanine stairs.

"*Now* where are you going?!" Kyung growled after her.

Without breaking stride she called over her shoulder, "To clean up Geomi's last mess!"

Chung followed close behind, catching up easily, and managed to stay parallel to her as they ran up the mezzanine stairs.

"Stop following me!" she yelled at him.

"You'd be vaporized in the subbasement with Hyun if not for me!" he shouted back. "I'm coming with you!"

There was little time to argue. She needed to reach the Unity lab before the scientists could protect the work. And if Geomi had been telling the truth, she also needed to stop Dr. Sang-Yeob. Anyone foolish or psychopathic enough to follow The Spider could not be trusted.

They got through the security door, and found the lab in a controlled panic. Support techs rushed between workstations, detaching data drives and gathering readouts into boxes. Dr. Sang-Yeob stood in an enclosed glass room at the back, frantically shoving padding into a strong box. One half of a Unity Disk was suspended upright on the workbench, its insides a tangle of disconnected wires. The other half lay on the benchtop, waiting, Jin supposed, for Sang-Yeob to wrap it in the padding and add it to the strong box.

Waving her gun at the techs, she said, "Stop packing. Get out."

Gratefully, they dropped their tasks and ran for the door. One tech reached for a box to take with him. She shot as he leaned over to get it, the bullet passing just over his hand. "Take nothing. All of you, empty your hands and pockets."

Wallets, keys, disks, and papers all hit the floor. Soon, only Jin, Chung, and Sang-Yeob remained. Jin undid the safety on her gun and crept into the glass room behind the doctor. "Who owns you?"

Sang-Yeob spun around and yelped at the sight of her. "The Spider will kill you if you kill me," he squeaked.

"The Spider is already dead." She aimed at the spot between the scientist's eyes. He darted toward the door, but his brains got there before he did.

Jin holstered the gun and examined the halves of the incomplete Unity Disk. Separated as they were, she did not think they posed a risk of detonation. The climbing crack in the wall meant that the building would be crumbling soon enough anyway, but there was no guarantee that the two halves of the Unity Disk would not survive. She applied charges to the two disk halves while Chung gathered the remaining data drives, papers, and print outs into a box. She laid a charge on that as well, and after wiring it all together, ran before triggering the second blast.

The fireball didn't hit until they reached the mezzanine stairs. They got down the first flight before the stairway crumbled beneath them altogether. It wasn't that far to the lobby floor, but once they landed, even that began giving way. Pulling, tripping, running, pushing each other, eventually they made it to what was left of the lobby entrance and the great plaza. Kyung was waiting for them. Together, they reached the curb just beyond the plaza. A great roar arose from the building, and in a final spray of debris, it tumbled, blocks of concrete and steel, crumbling down into dust.

Jin wearily surveyed the people crowded in the plaza, staring stunned at the remains of their workplace. "Did everyone get out?" she asked Kyung.

"Enough did," he rasped in reply.

A car pulled up to the curb at that moment. Dear Leader emerged, followed by a frightened guard. "Bow to your leader!" the guard shouted at the evacuees, training his machine gun on them.

Everyone bowed low. Jin wanted to stay where she was, between Kyung and Chung, dust-covered and unnoticed, but she knew he would see her eventually. *Best to get it over with.* She limped to the front of the group to stand before Dear Leader. Kyung and Chung joined her. She wished they hadn't, for their sakes, but after all they had been through today, she was not surprised.

Dear Leader stared at them sternly before saying, "Jin Ae. You survived."

"At a cost, Dear Leader," she said, coughing. "Geomi betrayed you."

"I saw it all. It is... unfortunate," he answered gravely.

"When the disk blew, I pushed him toward the jump point for the South, but it was not enough. Kyung grabbed me just as the canopy imploded. Before it disappeared completely, it spit out Chung." She glanced sideways at her brother, hoping he'd take the hint and explain.

"I was in a small space and could not get out," Chung continued, picking up the thread from Jin. "I had no sense of time. Then I heard shouting and an explosion and I popped back into the subbasement." He trailed off, not knowing what else to say about it.

Then Kyung picked up the story. "It started a chain reaction. Once the subbasement was compromised, we knew we had to get everyone out."

Dear Leader nodded his head. "I see. I see. And what of Dr. Sang-Yeob?"

Jin, looking at Dear Leader intently, said, "He has been dealt with."

"Good," said Dear Leader. "A great waste, but one he brought on himself." Gesturing to them, he said, "Get up. You three have done well."

Jin, Chung, and Kyung slowly raised their heads. Looking at the rubble which had been The Bureau, Dear Leader clapped Jin on the shoulder and said with certainty, "We will rebuild. We will start again. Grandfather's spirit demands it."

Then beckoning the guard, he ordered, "Take me back to the palace."

Chung whispered to Jin, "Sister, we cannot allow a rebuild."

Kyung grumbled back, "What choice do we have?"

"The choice we give ourselves," said Jin. She turned to face the rubble, the destruction that she and the Americans had caused. The Bureau wasn't their only development facility, but it was the best equipped. Rebuilding all its capabilities would take months. "At least we have some time before we choose."

CHAPTER 43

Aftermath

...Thirty minutes earlier...

The crew at Cheyenne Mountain listened intently to Jin and Geomi's battle. Chung's kind face grew more anxious as their fight raged on, his fists clinching with every grunt drawn from Jin. But then The Spider unfurled his world-dominating scheme, and Chung could take no more. He flung off his headset and said to Mitch, "Open a jump point. I need to help her."

"No you don't," Francine shot back. "She's holding her own. You interfere now, this whole plan goes up in smoke."

"But he's killing her," cried Dean, grabbing Francine's shoulder. Briggs smacked his hand away, but the boy ignored the soldier. "We can save her," he said, "Open it, Mitch!"

Francine squeezed between Briggs and Dean. "Stand down, all of you! Only Briggs is going through. That's the plan."

"Might be time for that now," said Charlie. "I found the stadium feed."

The image on his monitor shifted from an external shot of The Bureau to a packed stadium. Dear Leader stood at a dais, gape-mouthed, watching Jin fight The Spider on the JumboTron above. Geomi cried out and a white flash filled the screen.

"Briggs, that's your cue," said Francine. "Campbell, open the jump point, on the double." She switched her headset channel to speak to Kyung. "Mr. Ru?"

"Yes," Kyung growled.

"Get ready on your end. Time to close up the Canopy."

"Agreed," Kyung replied.

Mitch opened the plasma grid and homed in on subbasement's orange-tinged point.

"Ready, ma'am," declared Briggs, an ammo bag slung across his shoulder.

"Go, now!" Francine ordered.

Chung sprinted from Mitch's side to reach the jump point first. "My sister needs me. Jin!"

In a flash, he jumped through.

"Shit!" cursed Briggs. "I'll get him, Ma'am." He jumped after him.

"The entanglement processor!" Mitch called, pointing to the pulsating tube across the room. It had suddenly sprung to life. "The Fail Safe's been activated!"

"It's the Babe!" exclaimed Dean.

Francine poked the intercom. "Scott, come in. We saw the Fail Safe ignite. Do you have Ms. Ae?"

"Nope, she pulled a switch. It's the psycho."

"That explains the screams," said Marion.

Francine shook her head in disbelief. "Do you need MPs?"

"Already here, ma'am," said a new voice.

"Who's this, soldier?" Francine asked.

"Sergeant Randall, ma'am. It's me, Brady, and three more."

"He's too busy puking his guts out to cause a ruckus, Francine," said Scott, taking over. "One good thing about the Fail Safe."

Francine turned to Marion. "I don't want that man in my facility."

Marion nodded her assent. "The lockup at Fort Carson can hold him," she replied.

Francine returned to the intercom. "Did you hear that, Sergeant?"

"Five by five, ma'am."

"Blindfold him first."

"Copy, we're on it."

Charlie signaled to Francine, then pointed at his monitor. "Our team needs to move it. Dear Nut Job's taking heat."

At the stadium, one of the honor guard had advanced on the ruler, his machine gun raised. Uncoiling like a snake, Dear Leader struck the guard, disarmed him, and proceeded to shoot his body into mincemeat.

Wayne stared at the screen and deadpanned, "He didn't take that well."

"Briggs, Kyung, how's it coming?" Francine called over the comms.

Briggs poked his head through the jump point and said, "All set, ma'am. We're about to—hey!"

Jin appeared behind Briggs, grabbed his charge bag, and pushed him through the light hole. She grabbed Chung and Kyung by the arm and tried to do the same with them.

"Chung, Kyung, go after him. I will stay behind!" Jin yelled at them as she pulled more charges from Briggs' bag. She dropped them onto two bodies Mitch couldn't identify.

"I'm not going anywhere!" Chung yelled back at her. "Not without you!"

"Someone has to trigger all of this. I will stay and end it."

"Somebody decide soon," Charlie called over his shoulder. "Dear Leader's on the move."

On the big screen, Dear Leader shook his fist at the crowd, and then turned toward the red carpet to make his way back to the subbasement.

"Darlin'," called Dean. "He's coming back. Jump through, jump through!"

"Out of time, Ms. Ae!" Francine yelled.

Jin dove to the floor and rolled to the rack that contained Mitch's machine. She stared out of the jump point first at Francine and then at Dean. "I am sorry," she said, sadly. Then the jump point winked out.

Dean tore off his headset and headed for the plasma grid. "Jin!"

The orange-tinged hole for the subbasement fluttered and emitted a high-pitched whine. "It's too late, Chambers," said Bische. He caught Dean around the waist and held him back. "Campbell, shut down the grid!"

"But, Doc—" Mitch began.

"Just do it! Now!" The whine grew louder, then *Boom!* A powerful gust of hot air and white light shot out of the subbasement's hole. Bische covered Dean with his body and pushed him down until they both were flat on the ground. Mitch disengaged the fob from his phone. The hole closed and the grid fizzled away.

"Where'd it go? Mitch, get it back." Grimacing, Dean scrambled to his feet and hobbled toward Mitch, clutching his side. Mitch just stared blankly at the empty space in front of the storage cage where the plasma grid had been.

Dean shifted to Wayne. "What about your Jump!Go?"

Wayne scrolled through the point list on his Jump!Go app. He opened a grid and zeroed in on the subbasement's quadrant. No orange-tinged jump points appeared in the square, and the area where the subbasement's point had been was dark and smooth. "Dean, it's not here. I don't think we can get it back."

"Good," said Francine. "Ms. Ae's plan worked."

"What do you mean? You gotta find it! It was right there!" Dean insisted.

"What I mean is there's no electromagnetic trace on the map. Either the circuit overloaded or what we saw was an explosion and everybody on their end is—" he stopped before stating the obvious.

"It can't be. They're not dead. She's strong. She got them out." He ran back to his headset. "Jin! Chung!" The comms were silent. Dean squeezed his eyes shut, but the tears still rolled down his face. Whirling on Bische, he said, anguished, "Why did you stop me?!"

"That's why, son." Bische pointed at the big screen.

Charlie had shifted back to the satellite feed for The Bureau and projected it from his monitor onto the room's main screen. "The building's not looking too good," he said.

The whole lower level of the building was smoking. People poured out of the exits into the surrounding street. An explosion occurred on a middle floor, and the whole center section spewed fire, glass, and debris. Then the middle floor collapsed, falling in upon itself. The rest of the building soon followed, toppling over into ash.

"Jin!!!" Dean yelled at the screen.

"People ran from the building, Chambers," said Bische. "They may have gotten out."

Francine watched the screen and tapped her lips. "Run a scan, Charlie. Prioritize it for Dear Leader, but let's see who else turns up."

Scott picked that moment to return. "Francine, The Spider's on his way to lockup." He came to a stop near Bische and looked up at the big screen. "Cripes! What happened? Did we do that?"

"Indirectly," said Marion. "Ms. Ae gets full credit."

"Good for her. Got to play hero, after all." He looked around the room. "Where is she? And her brother?"

No one answered right away, then Charlie said, "I've got a lock. Only 85% probability. All the dust might be throwing it off, but I'm pretty sure we got 'em."

"Show it," Francine ordered.

The image on the screen shifted as Charlie rotated the view and increased magnification near a car parked in front of the rubble. Dear Leader was easy to spot, distinguished by his tremendous girth and boxy haircut. A row of people stood before him and bowed. The recognition software drew red squares over two heads in particular.

"It's them! It's them!" Dean whooped, then sank down into a chair, visibly relieved. "You can't keep the Babe down. Right, Mitch?"

Mitch wiped tears from his eyes, and said, "They got lucky, Dean," then returned to watching the screen intently.

Marion said to Francine, "Now that everyone's accounted for, we need to talk about next steps. This wasn't quiet, but it wasn't an international incident, either. The jump point's gone, but what about the Canopy and Unity Disks?"

"Ma'am, no way the Canopy survived the blasts," Briggs reported. "Ms. Ae and I dropped enough charges to blow Campbell's device and the rest of the equipment sky high."

"And as for the Unity Disks," Charlie added, "our intelligence says the main lab was inside of the Bureau. With the building gone, that's bound to stop production. Plus, that spider guy said the main scientist was in on the double-cross with him and the guard. The way Dear Leader shot the guard to pieces, I'd bet that scientist won't survive the night."

"Okay," said Marion. "So they're crippled without the lab, and they lost the power to instantly travel. But Dear Leader is still alive, so chances are he'll regroup and try again."

Bische glanced at Scott, and some silent communication happened between them. He didn't look happy about it, but inclined his head, so Bische continued, "I know how we can stop Dear Leader from regrouping altogether."

"How's that?" asked Francine.

"I've been thinking about it," Wayne interjected. "Just like the tracer Dr. Travers used to tie people to the Fail Safe, we could attach a blocker to the network to prevent jumps from certain places."

"Not a bad idea, Hirano, but I was thinking of something more fundamental."

"Like have a jump point police force?" offered Briggs.

Bische chuckled. "I can see how that would appeal to *you*, but really I think our best option is to—"

"Shut it down," Mitch said. Aside from his comment to Dean about Jin and crew being lucky, Mitch had been quiet since the subbasement jump point had imploded. He glanced at both Bische and Scott. They nodded their approval, and waited for him to again speak.

Wayne didn't give him the chance. "Mitch, with the proper controls in place, the jump points can still work. We just have to establish some rules and stop free-wheeling it," he said emphatically.

"Wayne's right, Mitch," added Dean. "Granted, today was pretty rough, but we'll learn from it. We just tighten up the ship and keep on sailing. It's our dream, dude."

Mitch took several deep breaths, then pointed a shaking finger at the screen. "Is *that* even registering with you guys?"

By turns, Dean and Wayne each started to answer, but their eyes drifted to the smoke filled screen and, soon, they both lapsed into silence.

Mitch went on. "The old guy, Boss Lady, Marion—they all nailed it. They said I made something without understanding it and they're right. Someone tried to use it to blow up a *country*. To prevent that, we had to knock down *a whole building*. People may have *died* when we knocked it down. And that was the *best* thing that could have happened. If we hadn't found a way to destroy the Unity Disk, it could have taken out Seoul. That's not 'free-wheeling.' That's a *country*, guys. Not just buildings, but people, families, *kids*."

He paused. Dean and Wayne looked stunned as the truth of what he said began to sink in. "We tried to remake the airplane. In reality, we remade an ICBM. When you make something... sure, you can't predict how people will use it. But you also can't just leave it out there once you learn that it is dangerous. We got lucky. We won't again. Shut it down. Just... shut it down. I don't want to worry that I've killed my friends or someone's family or even dogs and chickens. I don't want anyone else's pain. It's too much."

Bische crossed the room and puts his arm around Mitch's shoulder. Mitch sagged into his mentor and tried hard to keep from crying again.

Marion broke the silence. "Couldn't have said it better myself."

*****

Bische pulled Scott away from the others and with a wry smile said, "Let me and the boys jump back to Golden. I don't think we can take another ride with Marion."

"Now hold on," whispered Scott. "You owe me some answers. Like where've you been all this time? And what's with the kid?" He jerked a thumb toward Mitch. "Don't tell me he's the—"

"Yes, he is."

"Cripes. I said don't tell me."

"Too late," Bische chuckled. "Besides, you already guessed. But now's not the time for details."

Scott shook his head. "That'll be some story. Promise me you'll tell it over lunch or dinner or whatever passes for a meal these days."

Bische smiled at his old friend. "Only if I drive. You're no better than Marion."

"Geez, you're as bad as CC," Scott growled. "But forget it. Whoever drives, pays."

"Deal."

They shook hands, then Scott walked over to the quantum entanglement processor, opened a side panel, and indicated a particular circuit board. "Give me the word when you're ready."

Mitch fired up his Jump!Go and dialed in the garage. First Wayne, then Dean, then Mitch jumped through. Bische started to leap, then paused and asked Marion, "What about Hubert?"

She grinned. "Oh, yes, the troll. We got an anonymous tip—from someone who sounded a lot like his assistant Christian—that Hubert was on the verge of another illicit sale. We'll be dealing with that in the next day or two. Tell Hayman I'll be in touch."

"Will do."

There was nothing more to say, no more goodbyes to make, so with a final nod to Scott, Bische jumped through. The jump point and the surrounding plasma grid shimmered for a minute, then Scott pulled a fuse and it all fizzled out.

*****

The garage door opened and Sam breezed in. "Thought I heard you guys out here. Just got back. How's the biz going? Hey, Doc." She punched Dean in the shoulder, then said, "Man, you look like hell."

Dean sighed and said glumly, "We hit a snag. Have to shut the biz down."

Sam raised an eyebrow, and scanned Mitch and Wayne, taking in their rumpled clothes and hang-dog expressions. She cast a questioning eye toward Bische, but he just shrugged. "Well, too bad, sport," she replied, softening her tone. "It's better to find out now before you get too far into market. With new tech, there's always a risk that someone could get hurt." Mitch snorted, and the boys all exchanged dejected looks.

"Cecilia mentioned to me she's opening up some intern slots. You guys interested? You could work on cool stuff and learn about the business at the same time. As long as Doc here vouches for you, you're in. What do you think?"

Wayne perked up. "That sounds great, Sam. We'd do it. Right, guys?"

Mitch and Dean both nodded. "Yeah, thanks, Sam," Mitch mumbled.

"You guys look like you could use a good meal. How about I make dinner? We could have brats and my famous home fries. Sound good?"

Dean brightened. "Sure, I'm hungry," he said.

"I'm game," chimed in Wayne. "Mitch?"

Mitch felt empty. He hadn't eaten for the better part of two days. The prospect of food was enticing, but he didn't think he'd made great company. And Sam's home fries, though legendary, wouldn't cure the pain he felt in his gut when he remembered The Bureau imploding, the guard shot to pieces, the panic in Scott's eyes when he'd thought Marion would die from an earthquake he'd caused.

He realized that Sam was still waiting for him to reply. "Guys, I'm pretty beat. I think I'll call it a night and go back to the dorm."

"You could sleep here," Sam offered. "There's plenty of room. Kind of cold for your skateboard today."

For a moment, Mitch was confused. *What was she talking about? I'll just jump back to the dorm*—then he remembered there would be no more jumping. He sighed. The old way would take some getting used to again. He picked up his skateboard and headed for the door.

"What about you, Doc?" Sam asked Bische.

"Thanks, but actually I need to check something on campus. Hang on, Campbell. I'll give you a ride."

They said their goodbyes. Mitch leaned his cheek against the passenger-side window. The dorm was just ten minutes away, but he still felt a strong urge to close his eyes while Bische drove and just let himself sleep.

"I'm going to take your paper down from the internal site," Bische said once he'd pulled out of Sam's driveway onto the side road toward school.

"That's fine," said Mitch. He sighed deeply and wished that Bische would just let him be.

"When you're ready, the three of you can submit an update to the paper explaining that the gateway was unstable, so you needed to shut it down. This is accurate. Do you understand?"

"Yeah, I got it. Whatever. I'll tell the guys." His eyes felt hot again. He closed them and pressed his fingertips against his eyelids. They felt cool and comforting, but still, his eyes burned. *Will I ever stop feeling such loss?*

Quietly, Bische said, "I know you think you did a bad thing, but I want you to know that you didn't. Your device made it possible to stop the escalation of something far worse."

Mitch inhaled and the sob he'd been holding in ever since he'd thought Chung and Jin had died, flowed out of him in great wracking spurts. It took a few minutes before he could speak without his voice breaking. "I wanted to be Richard Branson," he said. "Instead I'm Robert Oppenheimer."

Bische scoffed. "Don't get ahead of yourself. 'I have become Death' was pretty pretentious even for him."

"It was exciting. I felt smart. Now it's over and I don't know what else I'd ever want to do."

"The gateway is shut down, and it should be. But that doesn't mean that there's no other uses for the tech."

Mitch hadn't considered that. They'd been so wrapped up in becoming the new gods of travel that he hadn't thought that the concepts could be applied in a different way.

"Interning at Tamblyn Tech could help you work out new applications. This door has closed, Mitch, but you're not completely locked out of the house."

They'd arrived at the dorm, but Mitch's stomach rumbled loudly, and Bische let out a hearty laugh. "Let me get you something to eat."

"Can it be nachos?"

"You bet. With extra jalapenos, just like you like them. If you come back to the lab, I'll tell you everything I know about CC Tamblyn. Might come in handy when you interview as an intern."

Bische wheeled out of the dorm's parking lot, and soon they were headed to the Moose Hill Cantina to pick up two orders of double nachos, slathered in avocados, pulled pork, and jalapenos. Mitch wondered if any Tamblyn Tech interns had posted videos about the program on PicsterGram. He opened the app and started a search. The sun was setting, but a stray beam of light threw a flare across his screen, obscuring the search results from view, but it was over in an instant. A dark cloud returned. Mitch scooped up two corn chips— dripping with cheese—crammed them both into his mouth, then opened a link to read.

EPILOGUE

Feelin' Good

They came for Hubert abruptly. An unmarked Agency vehicle parked on the service road behind the CASE building, led there by an anonymous tip received the night before. The tipster said they'd find Hubert in his lab selling proprietary American tech to a group of Chechen separatists masquerading as Finnish executives. At the appointed time, Christian Meadows excused himself from that meeting, under the pretense of fetching coffee for everyone and, adopting an appropriately wounded, contrite demeanor, met the Agency agents as they exited the van.

Brandishing his cast, he plead coercion, psychological duress, and the very real threat to his life and livelihood as reasons for his complicity. He played a recording of Hubert's last interaction with the North Korean spy, the same spy who had broken his arm, then dangled a data disk at the agents—his trump card. He claimed it contained all the evidence they needed to nail Hubert's head to the wall for illicit foreign tech sales and economic treason. All he wanted in return was his life back— and, of course, freedom from prosecution.

It surprised him how easily the agents agreed, once they verified the contents of the disk. He accepted their terms, filming an affidavit in the back seat of the car that explicitly affirmed Hubert's guilt, then signed a promise that he would not flee prior to the trial. The agents left and Christian secreted himself by the frosted door in the lobby of the Green Center, directly across the service road from CASE. They reappeared shortly after, marching the Chechens and Hubert—in handcuffs—out the side door.

Hubert protested loudly, "This is an outrage! There's been a mistake! It's

Hayman you want, not me!" but to no avail. The agents shoved him head-first into the back of the van. The Chechens followed, red-faced and glaring. "No! Wait! Don't leave me alone with them!" Hubert pleaded. The van doors closed. Christian waved at the vehicle as it pulled away. Just like that, he was free!

He didn't bother going back to Hubert's lab. There was no point. The agents told him it would be sealed until after the full investigation. So, instead, he drove to Thai Bistro, bought a large bowl of Tom Kha Gai with a side of brown rice to go, and then headed across town to a small industrial park at the corner of Violet Street and Corporate Drive.

Hubert had finalized the lease on a unit in the facility the previous week—or at least he thought he had. Christian, who'd been given the task of delivering both the payment and the signed paperwork to the realtor, had given Hubert a copy to sign, then thrown that copy in the trash on his way over to close the deal. The rental agreement that Christian had given to the realtor named him as the lessee, not Hubert. And the payment that he had provided came from his own account, one that he'd padded slowly these many months with funds siphoned from Hubert's illicit deals. For all intents and purposes, warehouse unit 411 belonged to him.

That didn't stop him from approaching the facility cautiously, circling the streets around it first to verify the lack of Agency vehicles, marked or otherwise, before actually parking. It was late evening by this time, and only a couple of cars remained in the lot, none of them anywhere near unit 411. Satisfied that the little facility was nowhere on the Agency's radar, he parked and went in.

The unit had few amenities, but the previous tenant had left behind a microwave, so Christian used it to heat his soup and rice. Then he sat at the long table he'd dropped off the night before and set about the task of eating. The sweet, spicy soup mingled perfectly with the nutty rice, its fragrant, peppery heat warming him to the point of sweating as he slurped large spoonfuls and read through Mitch Campbell's fascinating paper for the seventh time.

For that was what the rest of the equipment in the room would be used for once he'd finished his supper. Ever since he'd seen the unbelievable travel canopy in action, having snuck into the back of Dr. Bische's lab on that crazy, chaotic research day weeks ago, he'd been obsessed by it. He saw a possibility in it that Campbell and his cronies no doubt had missed—the deeper, long-term game of not just trapping the light particle for the duration of the canopy, but encapsulating it, like a hard candy in a wrapper, a sugar-coated plum from the time-space tree.

Draining the last of his soup, he set to work following Campbell's instructions, one meticulous step at a time. His cast slowed him down, so it took until midnight before he was done. He flipped the switch and was dazzled to see the telltale eruption of the plasma cone, just as Campbell had described it—just as he'd seen in Bische's lab. He verified that each of the "home holes" worked: the Embarcadero, Times Square, the Navy Pier, and, of course, Sutter's Pub. Then he turned off the device and began work on part two—turning the trapped lights into packaged pearls.

This part required more circuits, more detailed, intricate, delicate work that strained his attention as well as the mangled muscles of his broken arm. When he finished some three hours later, he had a headache and his clothes were soaked through with sweat from anxiety and exertion, but it was done. The moment of truth had come. He flipped the switch and stepped back in awe as his concept, born in idle theory, actually sprang to life. He'd done it!

The canopy itself had not changed, just its contents. Instead of light holes pocking the surface, its roof and sides appeared to drip with condensation as each light hole was encapsulated in a blueish-white, translucent skin. He stepped into the cone, eyes wide in wonder, the fingertips on his good hand caressing each dew-colored bauble.

Rather than expanding like a light hole, the dew drops wiggled in reaction to his body's electrical field. *Intriguing. I wonder if*—but he never finished the thought. A man laughed behind him and he froze. *It couldn't be*, he thought, recognizing the voice as it continued, sounding every bit as malicious in Korean as it had in English the first day he'd heard it, just as its owner snapped his arm.

He whipped around, but saw no one there, yet still the voice assaulted him. He followed it to a dew drop at the back of the canopy. Other voices, shouting, leaped out from the light, but The Spider's rose above them, his flat drawl drowning them out. Every instinct in Christian told him to run, but he couldn't, and without thinking he cupped the dew drop in his good hand, drawing it to him, to see how on earth The Spider had been trapped within it. Suddenly, he heard a loud pop. The dew drop changed from light blue to white hot. The Spider screamed, and the world fractured around him. Like brittle glass, the blue plasma cracked and large chunks of the canopy drifted away like burnt flash paper. The dew drop expanded until it burst, sending Christian flying backward from the force of the concussive wave. He lay on his back in the blue goo, dew drops raining down around him, bouncing on the warehouse floor and as bright as glistening pearls.

And then there was nothing. He was nothing. He felt as weightless as a light beam, everywhere and nowhere, his body freezing, his brain on fire. The Spider's hole had exploded, he realized. *Its light fell on me. It's somehow* in *me.* He touched what should have been his chest with things that should have been his hands, but all he felt was an electrified tingle. All he saw were a million suns. Then his brain shut down.

He woke up to the first rays of dawn filtering through the blinds of the single window near the unit's door. He looked at his hands. The suns were gone. All around him lay the dew drops like ripe fruit. He staggered to his feet and into the bathroom, careful not to step on any of the freed drops of light. His reflection in the mirror seemed unchanged from the night before, yet he *felt* a difference. Stronger, maybe? Smarter? For a moment, he flashed back to the instant that he could only think of as his immolation—the brief glimpse of the universe and the far-away suns. He looked at himself in the mirror a final time and said, "I'm hardly the same."

Christian walked back into the warehouse, found the box of liter-sized beakers, and carefully began collecting the dew drops. Outside the window, the sun rose higher in the sky. It was a new dawn, he thought, a new day. Christian knew it would be a new life. That was when he noticed that his cast was gone. He flexed his left hand, then closed it into a fist. The tendril of light that leapt off of his palm was so brief his conscious mind didn't register it. Still he smiled. For the first time in a long time, he felt good.

ACKNOWLEDGEMENTS

No one succeeds without the help of others. Although writing is a solitary activity, the resulting book is a collaborative effort. My thanks to Josiah Davis for editing the manuscript (twice!); Lae Twina for crafting the cover; Rick Magyar for fantastic logo design; Daniel Dociu for creative inspiration; my beta readers, the Portal Guild—long may you glassy humans reign! But the most thanks go to my family, Michael and Arthur. I would not have fulfilled this dream without your non-stop support, encouragement, and constructive criticism.

And last, but not least, thank *you*, Dear Reader, for leaping into the first Jump Light adventure. If you enjoyed the book and have a moment to spare, I would really appreciate a short review. Your help in spreading the word is gratefully received.

Be lights for each other.

AJ Kilgore
September, 2018

THE STORY CONTINUES

JUMP TECH

Welcome to Humanity 2.0

Mitch and crew battle for control of the Jump Point technology. An old enemy tweaks the underlying framework, changing the fundamental nature of light holes and the people that use them. As their foe grows in power and prestige, the boys must find a way to reconnect him to humanity before the technology overtakes them all—and learns to fight back for itself.

For more information, visit Penny Candi Press: https://www.penycandi.com.

COPYRIGHT

Copyright © 2018 by Anita J. Kilgore
Cover by Lae Twina.
Ebook ISBN: 978-1-7327829-0-7
Print ISBN: 978-1-7327829-1-4

All rights reserved. This book or any portion thereof may not be reproduced or used in any manner whatsoever without the express written permission of the publisher except as permitted by U.S. copyright law. For permissions contact: info@pennycandi.com.

www.ingramcontent.com/pod-product-compliance
Lightning Source LLC
Chambersburg PA
CBHW071543110726
47908CB00007B/1979